EX LIBRIS

HINC IN ALTIORA

THE HALL
HAMPSTEAD

PRIVATE ANGELO

PRIVATE
ANGELO

A Novel by

ERIC LINKLATER

THE REPRINT SOCIETY
LONDON

FIRST PUBLISHED MARCH 1946
THIS EDITION PUBLISHED BY THE REPRINT SOCIETY LTD.
BY ARRANGEMENT WITH JONATHAN CAPE, 1948

PRINTED IN GREAT BRITAIN IN THE CITY OF OXFORD
AT THE ALDEN PRESS

To

The Eighth Army in its new clothes:
an entertainment for virtue

CHAPTER I

'THE trouble with you, Angelo,' said the Count severely, 'is that you lack the *dono di coraggio*.'

'That is perfectly true,' said Angelo, 'but am I to blame? Courage is a gift indeed, a great and splendid gift, and it is idle to pretend that any ordinary person can insist on receiving it; or go and buy it in the Black Market. We who have not been given the *dono di coraggio* suffer deeply, I assure you. We suffer so much, every day of our lives, that if there were any justice in the world we should receive sympathy, not reproof.'

With the back of his hand he rubbed a tear from his cheek, and turned away to look through the tall window at the splendid view of Rome on which it opened. In the westering sun the walls of the buildings were the colour of ripe peaches; the domes of several churches rose serenely, firmly round and steeply nippled like the un-impaired and several breasts of a Great Mother whose innumerable offspring, too weak to drain them, had even lacked sufficient appetite to use them much; while in half a dozen places, within easy reach of sight, Victory in a four-horsed chariot drove superbly through the golden air. Soft green foliage clothed the river-bank, and some-where a military band was playing a gallant march. How beautiful was Rome, how beautiful all the land of Italy!

Sitting behind his handsome large table — inlaid with intricately patterned brass about its flanks and furnished with a brass inkstand as big as a couple of flower-pots, with a statuette in bronze of the Wolf and the Twins, and a signed photograph of the Duce — seated in state though he was, the Count felt a softening of his heart, and his hands which had lain flat and severe upon the table half-rose, half-turned their palms, in a little gesture of under-standing and sympathy; a gesture like the prelude to a softly acquiescent shrug. Angelo was a good-looking boy.

7

True, he was very dirty, his ill-made uniform was sweat-stained and caked with dust, his left knee showed through a long rent in his breeches, his right boot was tied with string to keep a loose sole in position, and he stank a little; but his black hair curled and the bones of his face were as comely as if Donatello in his prime had carved them; he had eyes like his mother's, and in his voice the echoes rose and fell of hers.

With the fingers of his left hand the Count played a small tune upon the table and thought of Angelo's mother when she was seventeen. His estate of Pontefiore, in the Tuscan hills between Siena and Florence, had always been renowned for the prettiness of its peasant-girls and the excellence of its wine, but in a year when the vintage was better than anyone could remember, and the girls — or so it had seemed to him, in the flush of his own youth — were more enticing than ever before, Angelo's mother had stolen all the light of the sky and left in shadow every other prospect of pleasure. Her lips and her long fingers and the suppleness of her waist! The round of her hips and the white of her knees when she stooped with a lifting skirt over the washing-trough with the women and the other girls; and then, when she turned to speak to him, the darkness and the laughter in her eyes! And how short, how tragically brief, had been their time together.

Desolation like a sudden storm enclosed him in its hail and darkness when he thought of those vanished years. He, like Angelo, was now in need of sympathy, and for a moment his impulse was to rise, embrace him, and let their tears flow in a common stream of sorrow.

But as he moved, restless in his chair, his glance encountered the Duce's portrait: the autograph, the massive jaw, and the unyielding mouth. Though the Duce had lately been dismissed from his high office, and his Grand Council dissolved, the Count still kept the portrait on his table, for it was signed *Your friend Mussolini*, and he prided himself on loyalty. How often had those piercing eye, inspired him! They inspired him still, and with an effort with reluctance, he dismissed his tender thoughts.

Stiffening his muscles and sitting bolt upright, he cast out sadness like a recognized traitor, and instead of tears forced into his eyes the atrabilious gleam of the eyes in the photograph. Not only was he Count of Pontefiore, Angelo's patron and once the lover of his dead mother; he was also Commanding Officer of the 914th Regiment of Tuscan Infantry, the Sucklings of the Wolf. He was Angelo's Colonel, and when he spoke it was in a colonel's voice.

'You are a soldier and it is your duty to be courageous,' he said loudly. 'The illustrious regiment in which you have had the honour to serve, and I the honour to command, is even now fighting with the most glorious courage in Calabria. By this time, perhaps, your comrades have slaughtered the last of the English invaders or driven them into the sea. And you, you alone deserting and disgracing them, have run away! You have run all the way from Reggio to Rome!'

'The last time I saw my comrades,' said Angelo, 'they were all running away. I looked over my shoulder once or twice, and they were running as hard as they could. But none of them was so swift and determined as I, and therefore I am the first to arrive. But if you will have a little patience, I am sure that you will presently see your whole regiment here.'

'Silence!' cried the Count. 'No one in my presence shall ever deny, or even dispute, the indomitable valour of my gallant men!'

He struck with an ivory ruler the gleaming surface of the table, and then, frowning a little, leaned forward and asked, 'Is it really as bad as that?'

'Quite as bad,' said Angelo. 'It has taken us a long time to lose the war, but thank heaven we have lost it at last, and there is no use in denying it.'

'It is treason to say that.'

'It is common sense.'

'You are still a soldier,' said the Count, 'and you have no right to talk about common sense. You are subject to military law, and since by your own confession you are

9

guilty of cowardice and desertion — well, my friend, you know the penalty for that?'

'Death,' said Angelo in a gloomy voice.

'If I do my duty, you will certainly be shot.'

'The English have been trying to shoot me for the last three years. In Cyrenaica I had the greatest difficulty in avoiding their bombs and bullets and shells. I had to run hundreds of miles to escape being killed. And now, after three years of that sort of thing, I come to see you, my patron and Commanding Officer, and almost the first thing you say is that you too want to murder me. Is there no difference at all between friend and foe?'

'There is a great deal of difference,' said the Count, 'but a soldier's duty is the same wherever you go.'

'It is, however, only a very good soldier who always does his duty.'

'That is worth bearing in mind,' said the Count thoughtfully. 'I am not eager, you must realize, to have you shot, for it would create an awkward precedent if, as you say, my whole regiment is now on its way to Rome. And yet, if I were openly to condone your cowardice, and wholly ignore the fact of your desertion, I should bring myself down to your level. I should stand shoulder to shoulder with you in dishonour.'

'It would be a new experience for you,' said Angelo. 'During three years of war you have never stood shoulder to shoulder with me or with any of your men.'

The Count replied a trifle haughtily: 'It is perfectly true that while you served with the regiment in Africa, I commanded it from Rome. But it is quite absurd for you to refer to the fact in so unpleasant a tone of voice. For you cannot deny that I set you a splendid example, since I have never abandoned my post, nor ever, in three years of war, run a single yard. And who else in the regiment can make such a boast?'

'I give you my word,' said Angelo, 'that I was speaking with perfect respect. I made a short and simple statement of fact, and I can't see why that should be regarded as unfriendly criticism.'

'You are old enough to realize,' said the Count, 'that a statement of fact is nearly always damaging to someone. And furthermore,' he continued in an animated voice, 'you should ask yourself what would have happened if, as you appear to think proper, I had indeed commanded you in the field. I myself can perceive three possibilities. I might have been killed; I might have been seriously wounded or taken prisoner, and in either case debarred from further service; or I might have been dismissed the Army for incompetence. And a pretty pickle you would be in to-day, if any of those things had occurred! You wouldn't be standing before an old friend who is devoted to your welfare, but confronting a total stranger who didn't care what happened to you!'

'I confess,' said Angelo, 'that I hadn't thought of that. I am only a private, and common soldiers often fail to appreciate the plans and the methods of senior officers. Your very habit of thought, indeed, sometimes appears strange and foreign to us.'

'Lack of understanding is the greatest evil in the world,' said the Count. 'My God! if understanding came to our minds as readily as condemnation to our lips, how happy we should be! — Or should we?'

While the Count was pondering this question Angelo discreetly turned his back, and tearing the wristband from a ragged sleeve of his shirt, blew his nose on it. The sweat was cold on his body, and he had begun to shiver. He was very tired.

He had folded the damp wristband, and was putting it into his trouser-pocket, when the inner door of the room was thrown noisily open, and a fat white-faced captain with very short legs and a nearly bald head came clumsily in and stammered, 'The radio! the radio! They are going to make a special announcement!'

'Who is going to make an announcement?' asked the Count. 'The Duce?'

'No, no! It is the Allies, it is the Americans, it is General Eisenhower himself who is going to speak!'

'Nonsense!' said the Count.

'But I have just heard them saying it, and the voice had an American accent. Stand by, it said. Stand by for one minute and you will hear General Eisenhower make an important announcement.'

'Who gave you permission to listen to foreign broadcasting?' ask the Count. 'It is a grave and serious offence, as you well know.'

The Captain wiped his forehead with a yellow silk handkerchief, and stammering again, muttered, 'But if I had not been listening I could not have told you about General Eisenhower's announcement.'

'That is so,' said the Count. 'It is a tolerable excuse, and I must admit that to show a strict regard for every trifling piece of legislation would lead us, eventually, into the deplorable ways of our good friends the Germans; which God forbid. — I shall come and listen to your illegal instrument.'

He rose, and with dignity led the way into the inner room, an office with maps upon the wall, where two smart young subalterns stood expectantly before a small wireless set. It was emitting the angry sounds of a far-off electric storm, but these suddenly gave way to what might have been the voice of a man with a hurricane in his lungs and a throat like the dome of St. Peter's.

One of the subalterns hurriedly made an adjustment, the voice was reduced to human volume, and its accent became recognizably American. The tone was flat, the voice was soberly inflected. A plain man was speaking plainly, but every word he uttered was momentous, every sentence affected millions of lives, and he spoke with authority. Here was one of the decisive utterances of history. They were listening, thought the Count with enthusiasm, not merely to an American general, but to Clio herself. — And then the voice grew smaller, it receded to an infinite distance, and the electric storm was heard again, angrier than before, and now, as it seemed, filling all space.

'However,' said the Count, 'we have had the gist of it. We have been offered peace on honourable terms, we have accepted the offer, and an armistice has been signed. The war is over!'

Angelo threw himself on to his knees, and grasping the Count's left hand, covered it with kisses. 'Peace!' he exclaimed. 'Peace has been restored to us, and now you will not require to have me shot!'

'No, of course not,' said the Count. 'Of course not!'

'And I shall no longer be miserable because I have not the *dono di coraggio*. In time of peace one can live well enough without courage, like everybody else.'

'It is the eighth of September in the year nineteen forty three,' said the Count. 'It is five-and-twenty minutes to seven. We must forever remember the hour and the day, for they are part of our history. At this moment we and all Italy are stepping, like joyous pilgrims, into a new and happier age!'

The fat Captain was again wiping his forehead with his yellow handkerchief. 'Do you suppose, sir,' he asked, 'that we shall be compelled to resign our commissions?'

'Immediately,' said the Count. 'Now that the war is over, what need have we of commissions?'

'I need mine to keep a roof over my head,' said the Captain.

'Farewell, my mistress,' murmured one of the subalterns.

'*Our* mistress,' corrected the other. 'You see, sir,' he explained, 'on a subaltern's pay it is impossible to maintain a mistress who is both agreeable to the senses and presentable to one's friends; but by using every economy Luigi and I have, for some time past, been able to share such a one. Now, of course, we shall have to relinquish her, and because she has spoiled my taste for any coarser fare, I can see for myself no prospect but emotional famine.'

'Come, come,' said the Count, 'you are unduly pessimistic. We shall all have to make certain minor adjustments to accommodate ourselves to new conditions, and some of us, during the brief period of transition, may even suffer small inconveniences. But we must not fret about them, we must ignore them, because at last, after three

13

long years of fighting, we have won that for which we have always striven: Peace! Whatever trials you may have to endure, gentlemen, never forget that on the eighth of September, at five-and-twenty minutes to seven, you entered, after an eternity of suffering, the promised haven of peace.'

At that moment the windows rattled in their frames, and the fat Captain said, 'A thunderstorm is a bad augury for peace.'

'It is not thunder,' said Angelo in a trembling voice. 'It is gunfire.'

'Guns!' exclaimed the Count. 'Whose guns, and why should they be firing?'

'They may be firing a *feu de joie*,' said the younger subaltern with a cynical smile.

'That is undoubtedly the explanation,' said the Count. 'They are shouting their welcome to peace!'

'Perhaps they are firing against the English,' said Angelo.

'Impossible,' declared the Count. 'The English are hundreds of miles away.'

'They were coming very fast when I last saw them.'

'But it's unthinkable! And even if they have achieved the impossible, and arrived at the gates of Rome, why should they continue to fight against us when Clio herself, borrowing the lips of General Eisenhower, has declared an armistice?'

'They may not have heard about it,' said Angelo. 'The English are frequently unaware of what goes on in Europe.'

'Then we shall go and inform them,' declared the Count. 'You and I, my dear Angelo, shall be the first to give them the good news that henceforth we and they must live together in perfect amity and mutual assistance. Come, Angelo, let us waste no time.'

The windows rattled more violently as the gunfire grew louder, and Angelo tried to evade his errand with one excuse after another. But the Count would listen to none of them, and presently they were driving out of Rome towards the aerodrome that lies along the Appian Way. For that was the direction from which the firing came.

The evening was now darkening, and against the first veils of twilight the flashing of the guns was faintly hued with orange. Every shell that was fired made Angelo wince as though he were equipped, like the field-pieces, with a recoil-mechanism; but the Count was deeply interested in what he saw.

'Why, bless my soul,' he declared, 'they are Germans. It's a German battery! The poor Tedeschi, they have not heard the news. No one ever tells them anything!'

Briskly leaving his motor-car he approached the German officer in command, saluted him smilingly, clapped him on the shoulder with his other hand, and with a great deal of geniality started to explain that an armistice had been signed, and the war was over.

The German, already in a vile temper, listened for five seconds only, and then interrupted to abuse the Count in a loud voice and with vulgar detail.

'So you also are a traitor!' he shouted. 'You too are a rebel, are you, like the mutinous swine over there whom we are now liquidating?'

'Mutinous? Surely the English have not mutinied?' asked the Count.

'Not the English, you blockhead, but those garlic-eating Judases, your fellow-countrymen!'

'It is impossible!'

'They told us the war was over — and this is our answer.'

'You cannot be serious. You are not firing against Italian soldiers?'

'They may have been soldiers once,' said the German. 'Most of them are corpses now.'

'But we are your allies,' exclaimed the Count. 'You cannot fire against us! Good heavens, even a German should realize that this is no way to behave.' And turning toward the nearest gun-crew he shouted, 'Cease fire immediately!'

The German officer at once drew his revolver, and pressing the muzzle against the Count's stomach, declared in a voice so hoarse that it drew a little blood —

which he swallowed noisily — 'You are under arrest. Move one inch or utter a single word, and I shall kill you!'

The Count was hard put to it to comply, for there were twenty things he wanted to say, but fortunately, before the strain became intolerable, there was a compelling sound in the air, a sibilance that swiftly grew louder and came nearer, and with a common impulse he and the German threw themselves flat on the ground.

Within half a minute the Count had recovered consciousness, and sitting up he perceived that the shell, which seemingly had landed within a yard of the nearby gun, had instantly killed all its crew, while the German officer had been mortally wounded by a heavy splinter. Towed by their tractors, the remaining guns of the battery were moving to a new position.

Though beyond human aid the German officer was still conscious, and the Count was able to deliver, without interruption, a brief lecture on the evils of intolerance.

'You Tedeschi,' he concluded, 'have persistently underrated us, and made light of our military qualities. The excellence of our artillery, for example, is quite generally admitted by impartial observers, and our gunners have frequently used it to great advantage. But have you ever praised them? Never! It may be, of course, that until now you have never seen for yourself what they can do — '

A barely human sound came from the German's lips, and his booted heels twitched on the ground. The Count, after stooping to examine him, shrugged his shoulders and murmured, 'They will never learn.'

He returned to his car and was about to drive away when, from somewhere on the ground, a voice in agitation cried, 'A moment, please! Wait a moment, do!'

'My dear Angelo,' said the Count, 'I had quite forgotten you. Where have you been? Underneath the car?'

'Of course I have,' said Angelo. 'It was the obvious place to choose.'

'And while you were lying there, safe and snug, I came near to losing my life,' said the Count. 'Several Germans, less fortunate than I, were killed outright.'

'By the English?' asked Angelo.

'No, no!' cried the Count. 'Really, my dear boy, your appreciation of the situation is woefully at fault. They are Italian gunners, our own splendid soldiers, who are now engaged in battle with the Germans. Look there! Oh, bravo, bravo! They have found the range again. I have always maintained that our artillery is first-class — and who will deny that now?'

'Do you mean to tell me,' asked Angelo, 'that now, when we have stopped fighting against our enemies, we must go to war against our allies?'

'Surely there is some better way of expressing the situation,' said the Count, and driving slowly while he considered the problem, turned the car towards Rome. Behind them the night was loud and the sky lurid with gunfire. 'From what we have just seen,' he continued, 'we may reasonably infer that the Germans are no longer, in fact, or strictly speaking, our allies; and if that is indeed the case, we must, before we can discuss the situation clearly, find some new and more accurate title for them.'

'They will become our gaolers,' said Angelo bitterly. 'If they have turned against us they will hold the mountains to the north like a great door between us and the rest of the world, and all Italy will become a prison. We shall be the starving convicts and they will be the gaolers with whips in their hands.'

'But you must remember,' said the Count, 'that now we have powerful friends who will come to rescue us. The English and the Americans will not allow the Germans to ill-treat us. The English are already in Calabria, and we expect the Americans to land somewhere near Salerno either to-morrow or the day after. — That is in confidence, of course. — We may indeed be in the toils of Germany at this moment, but soon, very soon, the Americans and the English will come and liberate us. *Pazienza!* It will not be long.'

'*Speriamo,*' said Angelo.

17

CHAPTER II

SHORTLY after noon on the following day the Count was driving home to lunch. He was displeased to observe an unusual number of German soldiers on the streets, and the occasional sound of distant gunfire brought a little frown to his forehead. But when he entered the Piazza di Spagna his attention was taken by the exceptional colour of the flower-sellers' stalls, and ordering his driver to stop, he got out and bought, in wilful defiance of the hour, a bunch of every variety displayed. These he sent, by a convenient boy whom he found waiting beside the stall, to his dear friend the Marchesa Dolce, who lived in a small house high above the Piazza. The boy with his many-coloured, scented burden slowly climbed the steps, and the Count returned to his car.

Having lunched alone he sent for Angelo, and at once complimented him on his improved appearance. Cleanly shaved and diligently washed, smartly attired in a new uniform, Angelo now looked a credit to his regiment. Embracing him, the Count lightly stroked his hair and said with a sigh, 'Mine still grows as thick as yours, but it's turning grey. The first of the winter snow has fallen on it.'

'In the most attractive manner,' said Angelo.

'It is not uncomely, I have been assured of that,' the Count agreed, 'but white hairs are a warning of the coldness that comes with age, and I do not like them. — That, however, is a topic we can discuss at some more convenient time. There is an affair of the moment that we must talk about now. The fact of the matter is that we are living in difficult and dangerous days.'

'Have the English and the Americans changed their minds? Are they not coming to liberate us?'

'Of course they are, but the process may take some weeks, and in the meanwhile the Tedeschi are in power. The King and Marshal Badoglio have fled from Rome, and General von Kluggenschaft, whose troops control the

18

city, has made it perfectly clear that he no longer regards us as his loyal friends and indispensable allies.'

'How many of our soldiers have the Tedeschi killed?' asked Angelo.

'Several score, I believe — but we must not let emotion obscure intelligence. We must remember, my dear Angelo, that the soldier's anticipation of a violent end is part of his contract. The shadow of the recruiting sergeant is very like the shadow of death, and a soldier's life, even in our army, is a flimsy structure. We must be practical — and to come to the point, I want you to take some of my pictures to Pontefiore, where, I think, they will be safer for the next few weeks than they might be in Rome.'

'That is prudent indeed. You are sending the Piero della Francesca?'

'That, and my little Raphael, the two small Bronzinos, and Simone Martini's portrait of Petrarch. I have several others packed up; the Filippino Lippi, and the Lorenzo di Credi with the light blue sky. Indeed, the best of my small collection is going, and though I do not for a moment suppose that the Germans would take them from me, I shall feel happier when they are in Pontefiore, where the Countess will be able to find secure hiding-places for them.'

'But how am I to take them there?'

An arrangement had been made, the Count assured him. Several weeks before, in preparation for an emergency, he had had the pictures packed in wooden cases, and that very morning he had called on General von Kluggenschaft to ask for the loan of two German army lorries.

'So you and the General are friends, are you?' asked Angelo.

'Far from it,' said the Count. 'He has a revolting personality, and whenever I see him I have to be extraordinarily polite in order to prevent an open quarrel. But as I needed his lorries I offered to sell him some wine if he would provide me with the necessary transport to bring it here. I mentioned an absurdly low price, his greed was instantly aroused, and when he had further diminished my figure we closed the bargain. Come, now, and let me show you the vehicles in which you will travel.'

In a small courtyard the lorries were already loaded, and their drivers, in German uniform, stood beside them. With wooden precision they came to attention and saluted.

'You need not be very frightened of them,' said the Count. 'Like so many people in the army of our late ally, they are not real Germans, but wretched prisoners forced into service. This one is a Czech, and that, I believe, some sort of a Russian who was taken captive in the Caucasus.'

'They don't look very happy,' said Angelo.

'They have very little reason to,' replied the Count, and unlacing the canvas cover of the nearer lorry he revealed how well it had been loaded. The pictures in their wooden cases were only a small part of the cargo. The bulk of it was softly filled sacks among which the cases stood, gently held and firmly guarded.

Angelo fingered one of the sacks and exclaimed, 'But this is flour.'

'That is so,' said the Count.

'And is the other lorry loaded in the same way?'

'In precisely the same way. I had been wondering how to protect these old and immensely valuable pictures against the jolting and tremors of a long journey, when I happened to remember that I had a certain stock of flour available.'

'How very fortunate,' said Angelo.

'A lucky chance,' agreed the Count, and having told the drivers to be ready to move within half an hour, he invited Angelo to have a glass of wine before he set off.

They drank a glass or two in the small library where Angelo had already been received. Neither spoke for a few minutes, and then the Count asked, 'Were you ever hungry when you were in Africa?'

'We came near to starvation once or twice,' said Angelo.

'Those English submarines sank hundreds of our ships,' said the Count. 'At certain times they were sinking so many that it really seemed useless to send you any stores at all. Ship after ship we loaded, and what happened to them? They went to the bottom of the sea. Our labour and our goods were wasted. Utterly wasted. And now and again I felt that I could no longer be a partner in such destruction. My whole being rebelled against the idea of sending, to no other destination than the engulfing waves, great shiploads of boots and shirts and guns and ammunition and oil — '

'And flour,' said Angelo.

'And flour,' the Count agreed.

'The lorries, then, are loaded with what should have been sent to your regiment in Africa?'

'And if the regiment had been commanded by a man less prudent than I, it might indeed have been dispatched,' declared the Count. 'And what would have happened to it?' he demanded. 'It would have gone, like so many other cargoes, to the bottom of the sea. What horrible and wicked waste, when all over Italy our peasants are in just as great a need of flour as ever our poor soldiers were!'

'So you are sending it to Pontefiore to be given away to anyone who is hungry?'

'Not *given*,' said the Count. 'Our Tuscan peasants are proud people who would not ask to live on charity. I am too much devoted to their welfare to wish to pauperize them. No, no! But my steward has orders to sell the flour at a fair and just price, and it will, I am sure, be very welcome to all my people. — And now, Angelo, it is time for you to leave. Here is your pass, and the permission signed by von Kluggenschaft for two motor lorries to go to Pontefiore for some urgently needed military equipment. I do not think you will have any difficulty on the road, but if you are stopped, by some officious Tedesco, you will find in each lorry a dozen bottles of wine, and that will certainly dissolve the obstruction. God bless you, my boy, and give this letter to the Countess. Tell her that I am well, in spite of my grey hairs.'

Angelo was appreciably moved by the kindness with which the Count had treated him, and he was forced to admit that there was something to be said for the prudence which had saved so much flour from the British Navy, and now, with an equal regard for the appetite and dignity of a Tuscan peasant, was sending it where it would certainly be useful. Stammering a sentence or two of gratitude, he took his leave, and, descending to the courtyard, elected to travel in the lorry driven by the Czech soldier. The Czech was a smaller man than the Russian.

Suddenly a vision filled his mind, an enchanted view of the home that he had not seen for three long years, the landscape lighted with the dark green candle-flames of the cypress-trees, and his boyhood's sweetheart. Ah, the black eyes and the milk-white throat of dear Lucrezia! He was going home, and as he spoke the words.aloud, to give them reality, his eyes filled with tears and he failed to notice the German staff-car that stopped before the Count's front door at the very moment when the flour-laden lorries drove past.

The Count was composing himself for his seista when he was informed that two German officers desired to see him. He returned the answer that at three o'clock in the afternoon he could receive no one, but his reply was ignored and a moment or two later the library door was thrown rudely open, and two heavy-footed steel-helmeted Germans marched in.

What louts they are, thought the Count, and in his most courteous voice inquired, 'To what am I indebted for this honour, gentlemen?'

'You are Lieutenant-Colonel the Count Agesilas Piccolo-grando of Pontefiore?' asked the senior and more repellent of his visitors.

'I am.'

'Then you are under arrest.'

'Really,' said the Count. 'May I offer you a glass of wine?'

Unhappy Angelo, he thought, I suppose they were waiting for him when he went down. But I cannot believe that this is going to be a serious matter. The flour is not theirs, and never was, and I fail to see that they have any legal claim to it now. Nor did von Kluggenschaft specify for what purpose the lorries were to be used on the outward journey . . .

These musings were interrupted by the German who had already spoken, and now, having swallowed his wine, said harshly, 'Last night you treacherously endeavoured to interfere with certain gunners of a German battery then in action against a regiment of Italian rebels and traitors.'

'Last night?' said the Count, who was much surprised. 'Last night? Why, yes, I remember now. Of course I did. So that is what has brought you here. Well, well!'

'Your attempt to obstruct the gun-crew in the execution of its duty was observed by Major Fluchs, commanding the battery, who promptly put you under open arrest.'

'Poor Fluchs. And now he is dead.'

'Before he died, however, he regained consciousness long enough to inform Captain Bluther of his action.'

Captain Bluther, the other officer, looked proudly over the Count's head and spoke in a loud voice: 'With his last breath Major Fluchs did his duty as a German should, and expressed the wish that the Count Piccologrando should be punished for his swinish behaviour with appropriate severity.'

'I am amazed,' said the Count. 'I thought he was dead when I left him. Had you asked me, I should have said that he died in my arms. But there is, of course, no truth in those last rambling words of his. Poor fellow, his mind was wandering. You cannot be so foolish as to arrest me on no surer evidence than a fragment of delirious conversation which I shall totally deny, and which you cannot substantiate by witnesses; for none of them survives.'

'The word of a German officer does not require witnesses to prove it nor evidence to substantiate it, and is utterly indifferent to events which contradict it or enemies who deny it.'

'In that case,' said the Count, 'I think I had better telephone to General von Kluggenschaft, who is my very good friend. You will excuse me?'

'You will be wasting your time. The General is no longer in command.'

'He was in command this morning. I know that, because I saw him.'

'He is now on his way to the Führer's Headquarters. He was replaced an hour ago by General Hammerfurter.'

'But why? I cannot understand it. He was an excellent soldier. He did his work with admirable efficiency, and he was universally popular.'

The senior of the German officers smiled sourly, but Captain Bluther indignantly explained: 'General von Kluggenschaft had formed a most undesirable friendship in Rome. He was on intimate terms with a woman of vicious character whose other associates were known to engage in subversive conversation.'

'That is slanderous!' declared the Count fiercely. 'Your statement contains a monstrous and abominable slander!'

'What are your grounds for saying that?'

'General von Kluggenschaft was on intimate terms with one lady only in Rome, and of all her sex she is the most lovely, prudent, and desirable. He was entirely faithful to her — and had he ever been unfaithful, he would have had to deal with me!'

'You refer to the Marchesa Dolce?'

'As the name is known to you — I do.'

'So you know her also, do you?'

The Count's brief anger subsided. For a moment he stood, very straight and still, and then, his slim figure losing its rigidity like a tall reed when the morning wind blows up the river-bed, he slightly bowed and very quietly answered, 'For seven years she has been my dearest friend.'

Captain Bluther shuffled his feet, coughed behind his hand, and was clearly embarrassed; but his senior and more repellent companion lost his temper, raised his voice, and began to abuse his prisoner in violent language. The Marchesa Dolce was widely known to be a beautiful, witty, and cultivated woman, and this poor German, who had been on close terms only with some ungainly girls in

24

Wuppertal and Bochum, and with overworked foreign prostitutes, was wildly jealous of the Count — whose nation he despised — and therefore became furiously angry with him, because of his good fortune and superior happiness in knowing such a charming person as the Marchesa.

The Count did not know how to reply. He was in no degree frightened of the German, but so deeply shocked by the display of violent rage that he could not protect himself against it. And in this state of helplessness, urged on by a pair of automatic pistols, he was presently marched out of his house, into the waiting car, and removed to a large villa on the outskirts of Rome which was maintained by the Schutzstaffel for their own peculiar purposes.

CHAPTER III

Angelo's journey was uneventful. He was halted several times by German soldiers, but the gift of a bottle or two of wine quickly persuaded them that he was fully entitled to travel where he liked; and the two drivers, of whom he had been somewhat afraid, showed clearly their desire to be friendly, and before very long were telling him their troubles.

To avoid driving in the dark they spent the night in a villa — one of the Count's smaller properties — on the eastern shore of Lake Bolsena, and there, after they had all drunk a good deal, the Czech and the Russian very earnestly sought his advice. They were both anxious to desert, and they wanted the help of someone who could guide them through the mountains to the southernmost parts of Italy, which, as they knew, had now been liberated by the English. Did Angelo know of such a person? Or would he himself show them the way?

For a long time they discussed the technique of desertion, as they had learnt it from the legendary exploits of those who had succeeded and the sad tales of their friends who had failed in the attempt; and Angelo promised, with much repetition, that when they returned to Rome he would introduce them to the most reliable accomplices that could be found. Then, having embraced each other warmly, they retired to sleep. They dreamt of happiness, and early in the morning resumed their journey.

It was an hour or so short of noon when they turned the last corner on the steeply climbing road to Pontefiore, and saw, like a crown of coloured stone on the hill-top, the old castle and the tightly gathered village. A narrow ravine divided the southern slope of the hill, and this, in one noble arch, was spanned by an ancient bridge whose abutments, at the proper season of the year, were overhung by blossoming trees. Even in Tuscany, where a handsome view is the merest commonplace, Pontefiore was notable for its dignified yet gentle beauty, and there was little wonder that Angelo, prone as he was to weeping, poured from his eyes a flood of delighted tears to see again its yellow roofs, the cobbled streets, and the castle tower rising among cypresses against a clear blue sky.

He called excited greetings to some eighteen or twenty people whom he recognized in the doorways of their houses, but dutifully did not stop until he had reached the castle, and there, with a sudden dignity, he requested an indoor servant to inform the Countess of his arrival.

She came out at once, for she did not believe in wasting time. She was small and trim, and though the prettiness of her girlhood had long since gone, much of its charm and some of its vivacity remained. Her hair was faded but her eyes were bright, and she still spoke Italian with an English accent. Had she spoken English, indeed, her accent would have been that of Yorkshire. She had formerly been a school-teacher in Bradford, and she had first met the Count in the railway-station at Florence, during a holiday-fortnight that should have been devoted to the art of the Renaissance. She had won immediately — while waiting for a train to Pisa — the Count's most passionate interest, and though their early friendship had been greatly troubled, and scarred by tragedy, she now, after twenty years of marriage, enjoyed his profound respect and the assurance, generally from a distance, of his enduring affection.

'So you've come back safe and sound after all?' she said to Angelo. 'Well, I'm glad to see you. How long have you been away?'

'Three years, madam.'

'And now, I hope, you're ready to do some honest work for a change?'

'No, madam, I can't do anything of that sort. I am still in the army, you see.'

'Haven't you had enough of it yet?'

'Oh, more than enough!'

'Has it done you any good?'

'None at all, so far as I am aware. It has taught me,

indeed, that I shall never be a good soldier, but I was pretty sure of that before they called me up. Because, of course, I have not the *dono di coraggio*.'

'Don't you think you should keep that to yourself?'

'How can I, when all my actions reveal it? — But I am forgetting my duty. Here is a letter from Don Agesilas, who asked me to tell you that he is very well, though his hair is turning a little grey.'

The Countess read the letter quickly, for she had no interest in the art of correspondence, but was merely impatient to learn the news. Then she remarked, 'He's behaving quite sensibly, for a change. But where could he have got two lorry-loads of flour at a time like this?'

'How should I know, madam?'

'He says that you can explain everything.'

Angelo thought for a moment, and then said with a certain hesitation. 'Since all our soldiers in Africa have been taken prisoner, they are being fed by the English, and so our Government has no use for the food that was ready to be sent to them. And I remember, now, hearing that it was to be sold quickly, before it went bad, and that Don Agesilas had bought some flour for a small price. A very small price, I think.'

'Well, it will come in handy, there's no doubt of that. And you brought the pictures too?'

'Yes, madam.'

'Then we'll get them unpacked at once.'

But Angelo, blushing a little and speaking very rapidly, asked leave to go now on business of his own, and being pressed to explain it, admitted that he was burning with desire to see Lucrezia, his boyhood's sweetheart.

'You mean Lucrezia Donati, whose father sells charcoal?' asked the Countess. 'But she was only a chit of a girl when you left here.'

'I was not very old myself.'

'Has she been writing to you?'

'Yes, three or four times.'

The Countess was about to ask another question, but checked herself and looked at Angelo in doubt, then

28

tightened her lips to a line of thin severity and thought again, and finally said, 'Be kind to her, Angelo.'

'Be sure of that,' cried Angelo, laughing loudly and happily. 'I'll be as kind to her as she will let me, and all I hope is that she will be one half as kind to me.'

He turned to go, but saw at that moment a young man who had newly come in to the hall and stood now, as if uncertain where to go, at the far end of it. He had a fair complexion and light brown hair, a lively look, and small neat features. He was about the same height and figure as Angelo himself. He stood a moment longer, then swiftly turned and went out again.

'Who is that?' asked Angelo. 'I have not seen him here before.'

'Italy nowadays is full of people whom no one has ever seen before,' said the Countess, 'and sometimes your best course will be to look the other way when you meet them, and then forget about them.'

'That does not seem very courteous.'

'Not to see a man who doesn't want to be seen is the very height of courtesy,' said the Countess.

'But you are quite right! I had not thought of it in that way,' said Angelo. 'And you can be sure of this: that as soon as I clap eyes on Lucrezia I shall forget everything else in the world — except your kindness to me, which I shall always remember.'

Nearly everybody in the village wanted him to stop and talk. The women sitting in their doorways hailed him and asked for news of their sons and husbands who had gone with him to Africa, and men crossed the road to greet him and ask him to drink wine with them. But Angelo put them off, one and all, saying there would be plenty of time for gossip, but now he wanted to see Lucrezia. Where was Lucrezia Donati? he demanded. At the washing-place, they told him, at the end of the village.

He started to run, and though the way was downhill he was out of breath when he arrived and saw the girls and the women bending over the great stone trough in which they were soaping and wringing and beating their linen.

It was a charming and familiar scene, and even while his eyes were searching for Lucrezia, and his lungs labouring for breath, he took the greatest pleasure in it nor wholly denied an errant wish to embrace, not his sweetheart only, but all these brisk and buxom creatures. How gaily they chattered, and how lovely was their laughter and the sound of the splashing of water! And there, in the middle of the row, was one with the prettiest pair of legs he had ever seen, so properly plump, as smooth as a chestnut and almost as brown, then paler behind the knee where the soft skin dimpled, and pale above — for now she was stooping forward and rubbing the linen so vigorously that her prim little bottom looked like a pair of apples when a boy is shaking the branch they grow on; and the back of her short skirt lifted higher still. White above her dimpling knees rose two entrancing columns into the modesty of occluding shadows, and really, thought Angelo, though legs and arms are the commonest things in the world, there are certain pairs of them with so remarkable a texture and shape that their effect upon the sensitive observer may be almost overwhelming.

His heart beat so hard that he lost his breath again, and while he stood there panting, the girl with the long brown legs, conscious of someone staring at her, suddenly straightened herself and turned to see who it might be.

Angelo's voice was no louder than a whisper when he spoke her name. That was the first time. Then a little strength came to it, and he said 'Lucrezia!' as a man in a dark room might say it. But the third time his voice was so loud he might have been hailing a ship at sea.

'Lucrezia!' he cried, 'I have come home again, and you are more beautiful than ever! I thought it was impossible for you to be more beautiful, but you have wrought a miracle and made perfection lovelier than it was, and that is why, in the first moment that I saw you, I did not' recognize you. O Lucrezia, let us be married immediately!

As if by the pulling of a blind on a summer morning, joy had flushed Lucrezia's cheeks and lighted her eyes when she first saw Angelo, and she had made a swift movement as though she meant to run straight into his arms. But then she halted, still as a statue, and her eyes grew round with fear, and she lifted a hand to her mouth like a child restraining a cry of pain. Her fingers were wrinkled, her wrists pink from the washing-trough, and drops of water, running down her arm, fell hesitantly from her elbow.

Then Angelo, seeing her like that, laughed and embraced her, kissing her wet hands, and her startled eyes, and her warm neck. The women and the other girls, gathering in a close circle round them, laughed loudly and applauded. Some of them, impatient to hear of their own menfolk or eager for recognition, pulled Angelo by the sleeve and clapped him on the shoulder. But Angelo paid no attention, for by now Lucrezia's arms were tightly round his neck. She was whispering endearments and a practical suggestion to go and look for some more private place where they could talk in peace.

'*Pazienza*' he cried to the women, all of whom were now clamouring for news. 'I shall be here for two or three days, and before I go I shall tell you everything I know about the regiment. But first of all I must talk with Lucrezia.'

They spent the rest of the day together, and Angelo had supper in the house of Lucrezia's parents, a sturdy and honest pair who in twenty years of married life had produced eleven children without loss of interest in each other or diminution of affection for them. The youngest, a fair-haired boy of about twelve months, was remarkably vivacious, and Angelo was about to congratulate Signor Donati on such a testimony to his vigour when it occurred to him that the child might be the son of Lucrezia's elder sister, who certainly had one or two of her own, and whose husband had recently been arrested on a false charge and sent to a labour battalion in Germany. Before he could make up his mind on this point, Signor Donati had refilled his glass, and the matter no longer seemed important. They drank a great deal of wine, and ate black figs and the well-cured ham of a black pig.

In the morning Angelo had another conversation with

the Countess, and the day was spent in selecting safe hiding-places for the pictures. Two were stored in a wine-cellar among gigantic tuns whose perfume made the mere air intoxicating, and others were laid in the dry lofts of nearby farmhouses. But the Adoration of the Shepherds, which Piero della Francesca had painted, was hung in a little-used bedroom in the castle, and this was done because Angelo argued, with a great deal of feeling and considerable eloquence, that a work of such divine perfection should not, even for its own safety, be imprisoned in darkness or humiliated by confinement in a farmhouse attic.

'Let it remain where it can give happiness and consolation to at least a few,' he said. 'There is more life and truth and beauty in this picture than you will find in forty living villages — and you would not bury what is alive? It is very seldom that a man has shown so greatly and so triumphantly his power to create, which he inherits from the Creator himself, and we should not conceal what proves quite clearly that some of us are certainly the children of God, and therefore all of us may be; for evidence of that kind is extremely rare. You can buy security at too high a price, and I say that a world which buried and forgot its Piero della Francescas would not be a world in which we could take any pride. I do not ask you to put it in some very public place, for that would be indiscreet, but hang it where those who know of its existence can go from time to time and breathe the air which it ennobles. We have a lot of bad company now in Italy, and therefore the greater need to associate with what is good.'

The Countess was not uninterested in painting, but her appreciation of it was more detached than Angelo's. She could not share his emotion, but she was moved, none the less, by his argument. For she had her own enthusiasm.

She was devoted to the novels of Ouida, and in every one of the several houses belonging to the Count there was a complete set of her works. Here, in Pontefiore, was the finest of them all. Bound in a soft white leather adorned with golden blossoms, it had been Ouida's own property — the title-pages bore her signature — and poor Ouida had sold it in the sad years before her death when she was selling nearly all her treasures to feed her dogs. Now all this commotion about pictures had set the Countess to wondering if it would not be wise to put her own favourite masterpieces in hiding, and she had been cogitating what would be a good place. But when Angelo spoke so bravely about Piero's Adoration, she decided to be equally courageous with her Ouidas; for what he said about the painter applied, in her opinion, with equal force to the novelist.

'Very well, then,' she said. 'We'll hang the picture in the small bedroom under the tower, and lock the door of the corridor that leads to it, and trust in Providence to do whatever else is necessary. Does that satisfy you?'

But Angelo made no answer. All his mind — and this had happened a hundred times before — was full of wonder at the skill with which Piero had painted the Blessed Virgin's coif, for the pallor of her unlined forehead showed clearly through the whiteness of the lawn, and its transparent folds were as firmly shaped as the forehead itself. And what mild dignity lay in the curve of the temples, what calm assurance in the wisdom of the eyes, and though the chin, perhaps, was a little heavy, the lips were drawn with grace ineffable. — They were the very shape of Lucrezia's, though hers were more brightly red.

Suddenly he returned to the mortal moving world about him, and with a little cry of distress exclaimed, 'But I am late, and she is waiting for me! Oh, madam, may I leave you, for I promised to meet Lucrezia, and it is long past the time we set? Oh, please, may I go at once?'

'Was she glad to see you?' asked the Countess.

'Of course! She has been waiting three years for my return, and she has been very lonely. But now I am here to comfort her, and presently we shall be married, and neither of us will ever be lonely again.'

'Hurry up,' said the Countess. 'If she is still waiting for you she may be feeling lonely now, and there are limits to what a girl can bear.'

So for the second day in succession Angelo left the castle at a run. In the short avenue of cypresses that led to the main gate he encountered the strange young man with light brown hair who had roused his curiosity on the day before; but now he paid no attention to him, except from the corner of his eye, and ran past as though the stranger were invisible. This is true courtesy, he thought. The stranger, indeed, paused and made a little gesture as if he were willing to talk. But it was too late. Angelo had gone.

A pair of tall white oxen with widely sweeping horns stood on the bridge, while their driver, with Lucrezia beside him, leaned upon the parapet in contemplation of the depths below. They had their backs to Angelo, their elbows were touching, they were talking in soft voices. Roberto Carpaccio, the driver of the oxen, was a clever young man who had evaded conscription by feigning epilepsy, and taken to the hills whenever German press-gangs appeared in the neighbourhood. He was about Angelo's age, and not ill-looking.

Angelo spoke to them sadly. 'Here I am,' he said. 'I am sorry that I am late.'

'But are you late? I hadn't noticed it,' said Lucrezia.

'I am very late,' said Angelo, and looked so extremely sad that Roberto laughed aloud, and laughing still bade Lucrezia a gay good-bye, called to his team, and went off in high good-humour.

'What is the matter with you?' asked Lucrezia.

'You did not realize I was late. You were so interested in what Roberto had to say that you forgot me altogether.'

'Am I not allowed to talk to anyone but you? Dear Angelo, how silly you are! I never have forgotten you, and never shall.'

'You are not in love with Roberto?'

'Not a bit.'

'Nor with anyone but me?'

'Nor with anyone but you!'

'Darling Lucrezia! And you never have been in love with anyone but me?'

Lucrezia put her arms round his neck, kissed him several times with the most agreeable warmth, and said, 'What a lot of foolish questions you ask! Tell me what you have been doing all day, and why you were so dreadfully late that I remembered, all over again, how unhappy I used to be while you were in Africa.'

'Were you very unhappy?'

'Oh, terribly so!'

'All the time, and every day?'

'You would like me to tell you so, wouldn't you?'

'Well yes, in a way I should.'

'Would it really please you to know that I had been miserable for more than three years? With never a moment of pleasure in all that time?'

'I should be very sorry for you. It would make me promise to do everything possible to give you happiness in the future, and help you to forget the past.'

'But why do you make conditions? Promise now that you will!'

'Lucrezia, I promise.'

'Truly and faithfully?'

'Truly and faithfully! Dear Lucrezia, let us be married very soon!'

But Lucrezia pushed him away, and leaning over the parapet again, looked down into the ravine. 'No, not yet,' she said.

'But why not? Don Agesilas will give me leave of absence — '

'I will not marry you while you are in the army, and while Italy is still at war.'

'But we are no longer at war with the English. They are coming to liberate us, not to fight against us.'

'You said last night that some of our soldiers are fighting against the Tedeschi, and the English certainly are fighting, and the Americans also, and they are all fighting here in Italy.'

'But I shall not fight again, if I can help it. And I am so bad a soldier that Don Agesilas, I think, will let me leave the army, and then I shall come home and stay here.'

35

'Then someone else will take you away. No, Angelo, I will not marry you until the war is truly finished, for I do not want to be a wife for two or three weeks, or only for two or three days, perhaps, and then be left alone. It is not good for a girl who is newly married to be left alone.'

'You mean,' said Angelo, 'that it would be like starting to read a new book —'

'Or sitting down to dinner —'

'Then someone borrows the book —'

'The plate is snatched away —'

'You want to know what happens in the next chapter —'

'You are hungrier than you were before you began —'

'But if you have strength of mind,' said Angelo —

'You can carry a great burden,' said Lucrezia. 'But there are limits.'

'On every road in Italy you see women carrying enormous burdens.'

'And their backs are bent, their faces tired, and they are old before their time. So also if you put too grievous a load upon their minds — no, Angelo. I will not do it.'

Nothing he said would change her opinion or undo her decision, and Angelo, in spite of his disappointment, became aware of a new respect for her. He even felt a little draught of fear that was somehow quite delicious. Sooner or later he would marry Lucrezia, and then he would be at the mercy of this strength she had developed in the years of absence, he would surrender himself to an unknown power. Though the prospect was alarming it was also alluring, and with some curiosity he perceived that fear is not always a deterrent to action. It may be, he thought, that I am a poltroon in war not merely because I am afraid of being hurt, but also because I do not enjoy fighting, neither the act of it nor the idea. For I now perceive that I am a little bit afraid of Lucrezia, yet I have no intention of running away from her. I should say not! So I am not altogether a coward, it seems.

Comforted by this reflexion he accepted her refusal, and walked home with her in the darkness in a cheerful mood. It was Lucrezia, some little while later, who was reluctant

36

to part, but now Angelo was quite firm, and with no regard for what lay upon her mind, bade her good-night.

He spent the following day talking to everyone in the village, the evening was passed in tender conversation with Lucrezia, and early the next morning he set off for Rome. The lorries were now laden with wine in great vessels of green glass jacketed in straw; and they arrived without misadventure.

Pleased and self-important about the safe conclusion of his mission, Angelo demanded to see the Count.

'He is not here,' replied a middle-aged butler. 'Very soon after you left us, two German officers arrived, and a little while later he went away with them in a motor-car. I have not heard of him since.'

'*Dio mio!* He has not been arrested?'

'It happened several days ago. I do not think that any-one would stay so long with the Tedeschi of his own accord,' said the butler.

CHAPTER IV

LORENZO the butler, a timid man who went in great dread of the Germans, had done nothing to ascertain the Count's fate or his whereabouts, and for safety's sake had even concealed what he knew from the several people who had inquired for his master.

'If anyone has heard of him it will be the Marchesa Dolce,' said Angelo.

'She knows nothing,' answered Lorenzo. 'She has telephoned every day to ask for him.'

'And what did you tell her?'

'What could I tell her? The Tedeschi listen to all our conversations, and if you so much as mention them your name is noted as that of a person interested in politics; and that is the end of you.'

'I had better go and see the Marchesa,' said Angelo thoughtfully. 'She is a person of great accomplishment, she will know what to do about this.'

He went immediately to the house that overlooked the Piazza di Spagna, and after only a short delay was admitted to the Marchesa's presence. She was a very beautiful woman with a long nose and long slender hands. Her habitual expression was sedate and serious, a permanent reproof, as it were, to those who were first attracted by the voluptuous quality of her admirable figure.

'I remember you quite well,' she exclaimed. 'Where is Don Agesilas?'

'That is what I hope to find out,' said Angelo, and repeated the alarming tale he had heard from the butler.

'What a fool that man is! I telephone every day, and he replies that his master has gone out. Nothing more than that. If I had known a little earlier . . .'

She was silent for a while, and then, with sadness in her voice, said, 'It is going to be difficult. I do not think I can secure his release without help of some kind. I need advice, I must borrow a little wisdom. What have you learnt, Angelo, while you have been away all these years?'

'That before the war I was better off than I realized: there is one thing. That soldiers can suffer much and still survive, but are not always improved by their suffering: there is another. That if men are as cruel at home as they are abroad, then their wives have much to complain of —'

'Your time has not been wholly wasted,' said the Marchesa.

'And finally,' said Angelo, 'that if living at peace were as simple as going to war, we might have more of it.'

'That is probably true,' said the Marchesa, 'but the discovery, if it is one, is not helpful. Listen to me, Angelo. The Count, your master, has certainly been arrested by the Germans, and is therefore in grave danger. Until recently the senior German general in Rome was von Kluggenschaft, a person of unpleasant character but normal temperament, over whom I had some influence. He, unfortunately, has now been replaced by a man called Hammerfurter, who is different. That is to say, his nature is different. With him I can do nothing. He is greedy and could be bribed, of course, but I am not a wealthy woman.'

'I have just brought two lorry-loads of wine from Pontefiore,' said Angelo. 'Don Agesilas was going to sell it to General von Kluggenschaft, but it might serve for a bribe instead.'

'Not for a general,' said the Marchesa. 'Generals put a high price on their integrity. — But is it good wine?'

'No, not very good, but there is a large quantity of it.'

'There is an unpleasant little man called Colonel Schwigge who might be influenced,' said the Marchesa. 'One could offer such a bribe to a colonel without much fear of giving offence, I think. He could not, I am afraid, secure the release of Don Agesilas, but he might tell us where he is.'

'What, then, shall I do with the wine?'

'Have it unloaded and I shall let you know.'

The Marchesa had no difficulty at all with Colonel Schwigge, who, as it happened, was being blackmailed by a brother officer and stood in urgent need of money. He knew where he could sell the wine for a good price, and in return for it he quickly discovered that the Count was a prisoner of the Schutzstaffel. He gave the Marchesa his address, and informed her that the person in immediate charge of the prisoners there was a Corporal Hisser.

'I have two other favours to ask you,' said the Marchesa. 'Here is a gold watch belonging to Don Agesilas: perhaps it might be sent to him. And I should very much like to meet this Corporal Hisser.'

The watch was a valuable one, and Colonel Schwigge, quickly appraising it, was grateful for the tactful way in which it had been offered to him; for the Marchesa quite understood that he would keep it. He readily undertook to arrange the meeting she desired, and telephoned that evening to say that the Corporal would be waiting, at noon the next day, in the gardener's lodge of the Schutz-staffel villa.

The Marchesa arrived at five minutes before the hour, and found the Corporal expecting her. In his smart black uniform he made a handsome figure, and though the Marchesa had little cause, at that moment, to feel much liking for the Germans, she had to admit that Hisser was an excellent example of Teutonic youth. He had flaxen hair, the ruddy skin of perfect health, and candid blue eyes. Here indeed was an advertisement for the Nordic myth. His manner, moreover, was engagingly correct, and he accepted the present she offered without loss of dignity.

Yes, he would do what he could to make Count Piccolo-grando as comfortable as possible. Not that the Count had anything to complain of, except loss of liberty, for all the prisoners were well treated and accommodated in excellent rooms. He agreed, however, that prison-diet was apt to be monotonous, and that private addition to it would be welcome. — The Marchesa would like to have special meals for the Count sent in? But certainly! Nothing was easier than that to arrange, and he himself would see to it that the Count received them punctually and decently served.

The Marchesa was delighted, and said to herself: We must not be too hasty in our judgment. If we knew the Germans better we should discover, I am sure, that many of them are like Corporal Hisser. — She had a basket that contained a pot of anchovies, a cold roast chicken, a small cheese, and a bottle of wine. This she gave to the Corporal with a little note for the Count — he had no objection to that — and having thanked him again, returned to her car with a lighter heart than she had known for several days.

As soon as she had gone the Corporal took the basket to his own quarters, and setting out its contents on a clean white cloth, made an excellent lunch. Then he went to inspect the prisoners.

There were only ten of them at that time, including the Count, and they all lived in a cellar. When the Corporal opened the door the smell was unpleasant, but he had long since grown accustomed to the disabilities of human-kind, and he uttered no complaint. He carried a large electric torch, and most of the prisoners, blinking in the white glare, rose hastily to their feet and stood at attention as he entered. Two of them, however — elderly men and therefore clumsy — were slow to move, and to induce a proper alertness the Corporal had to knock them down two or three times.

'Discipline,' he said, 'is the basis of all decent living. You must learn discipline. I had ordered a very good lunch for you to-day — anchovies and white bread and butter, roast chicken, some fine cheese and excellent wine — but now, because of the lax behaviour of those two ridiculous old men, I shall be compelled to countermand the order, and you will get nothing. Take this lesson to heart, and improve your discipline.'

Carefully locking the door, he returned to his own room, and having taken off his tunic and his boots stood for a moment yawning on the balcony. His blue eyes were as clear as the pellucid sky, and in their candour there was no deceit. It was quite a simple pleasure that he took in beating his prisoners, and he enjoyed the smarting pain of his own torn knuckles. When he lay down he slept like a dog on a rug, twitching and yelping in his dreams.

Every day for several days Angelo took a basket of food for the Count and delivered it to Corporal Hisser, who never failed to enjoy it. Angelo and the Marchesa were greatly comforted to think that Don Agesilas was not only well-treated but now, by their effort, well fed. They could not, however, discover why he had been arrested, nor could the Marchesa find anyone to offer hope of his release. It was worrying, but '*Pazienza!*' said Angelo.

Then one day, returning from his usual errand, he avoided by a handsbreadth a motor-cycle in the Via Quattro Novembre. It was one of a pair, ridden by German soldiers, that preceded a large open car. All three vehicles came fast round the corner. The motor-cyclists in a sudden blare sounded their sirens, Angelo nimbly jumped aside, and a cab-horse took fright and swerved into the middle of the street. Braking hard, the driver of the motor-car swerved the other way but could not avoid the cab. He struck it hard, knocked it over, and came to a halt with his bonnet between its spinning wheels. The elderly horse lay sprawling and kicking till Angelo, with great presence of mind, sat upon its head and held it still.

The motor-cyclists, quickly returning, dispelled with threatening gestures the small crowd that was gathering, and General Hammerfurter, rising in his car, condemned everyone within hearing of his harsh voice for their unexampled ineptitude, their bestial appearance, and malignant intentions. The cabman, dazed by his fall, lay bleeding on the ground. One of the German soldiers kicked him in the ribs, and the other, taking Angelo by the collar, was about to drag him from his seat on the horse's head when the General shouted 'Stop!' and at this command, which sounded like the splitting of a sail, they all became intently still, and the scene took on the likeness of a complicated group of statuary.

The General was immensely tall, and his long narrow body was elegantly uniformed. His hairless face was the colour of a turkey's egg, pale and mottled, and round the jaw were the scars of an old skin-disease. He stared at Angelo with a concentrated interest.

To avoid interference from the military, Angelo had put away his uniform and was wearing a pale grey suit belonging to the Count. It fitted well, and excellently became him. He was hatless, and his face a little flushed by exertion. A breeze played lightly in his curling hair.

The General spoke angrily to the soldiers and said, 'That young man is the only person here who has not behaved like a fool. — Come here, young man.'

The nearest soldier took his place on the horse's head, and Angelo approached the General's car.

'Who are you?'

Angelo, who spoke German fairly well, explained that he was private secretary to a gentleman in Tuscany, and had but recently arrived in Rome. He mentioned the Count's name. General Hammerfurter had apparently not heard it before.

'Where are his estates?'

'The principal one is between Siena and Florence.'

The General continued to study Angelo so intently that Angelo felt himself blushing. Then the General asked, 'Is it true that a very good sort of Italian is spoken in those parts?'

'In Siena, where I went to school,' said Angelo, 'they speak with a great correctness and a purer accent than anywhere else in Italy.'

This information evidently pleased the General. 'Good, very good!' he exclaimed. 'Now come into my car. You will have lunch with me. There is something of much importance that you and I must talk about.'

Then he spoke sharply to his driver and the other soldiers. Leaving the cabman and his struggling horse to look after themselves, the soldiers remounted their bicycles, the driver steered clear of the overturned cab, and they resumed their journey to the accompaniment of shrieking sirens. Angelo, concealing as best he could his fear and confusion, sat straight and prim beside the General.

Their conversation at lunch was hardly more than a monologue in which the General described his affection for the Italian people, his admiration for their works of art, and his enthusiasm for natural scenery of every sort. Primarily, he said, he had come to Italy as a soldier, and his immediate purpose was to defeat and destroy the barbarous English and Americans who were desecrating its classic soil. But secondarily, he explained, he was a lover; a lover of Italy and all its life, and nothing would make him happier than to serve its charming people and promote their welfare. But how could he serve them, wisely and efficiently, without knowing their language? He must learn Italian, and quite certainly his teacher must be one who spoke the very best sort of Italian.

'And so I consider it a great stroke of fortune, my dear fellow,' he said, 'to have met you, who were educated in Siena. For now that I have explained myself to you, laid bare my heart and confessed my love, you will not, I am sure, refuse my proposal. You will not grudge me your time, but will become my teacher and help me to know my Italy as I desire. Yes? I think so. Have some more brandy.'

'But I am quite inexperienced,' said Angelo unhappily.

'Good, good!' exclaimed the General. 'It is better so, for so we shall both make our blunders, very laughable blunders no doubt, and have sympathy one for another. We Germans are famous for our sympathy because we have so good an understanding of people. — Let me show you how to make what is one of my favourite drinks: a glass of benedictine and a glass of cognac: mix them together. It is quite simple and very good. You try it. — Now tell me, my dear fellow, what is the Italian for "a true friend"?'

'What is the German for "a helpless captive"?' asked Angelo in Italian; and when he had translated his question the General laughed immoderately, complimented Angelo on his wit, and with honest affection pinched the lobe of his left ear so tightly that Angelo's eyes filled with tears.

Not until four o'clock was he permitted to leave, and

44

then, after walking in the gardens of the Pincio for half an hour to collect his thoughts, he went to call on the Marchesa Dolce.

'Have you any news?' she asked.

'I have just been giving an Italian lesson to General Hammerfurter. I have become his tutor.'

'But what an achievement! How did you manage it?'

'The appointment was not really one I sought for,' said Angelo, and described the street accident which had caused them to meet. 'Though he speaks in the friendliest way the General is very fierce and masterful,' he said. 'I am extremely frightened of him.'

'What does that matter?' asked the Marchesa warmly. 'It would be too paltry — selfish and paltry and mean — if in such a time as this you were to attach the smallest weight to your own feelings. It is not of ourselves we must think, but of Don Agesilas. By the greatest good fortune in the world you have made the acquaintance of General Hammerfurter, and now you must take every possible advantage of it. Play your cards properly, and we may look forward to the very early release of an unhappy prisoner. But if you are petty and small-minded, if you run away, why, then he may lie for ever, without hope or mercy, in his German prison.'

'That is what I have been thinking,' said Angelo sadly.

'Tell me what the General spoke about,' said the Marchesa.

'Chiefly about himself. About his love for Italy, the sympathy and good understanding which characterize all Germans, and so forth.'

'Good,' said the Marchesa. 'Now when you return to give him his next lesson, you must impress upon him the belief that those are the things of which Italy is most in need, and in return for his sympathy and understanding we should quite certainly, and almost immediately, offer him our passionate allegiance. — Do not hesitate to credit him with great ambition, it can do you no possible harm.— Then in the third lesson you must introduce the name of Don Agesilas. Mention, in a light and conversational

45

way, his admiration for some aspect of German life —'

'He has none.'

'Then your invention will be untrammelled. Proceed more lightly still, with a careless laugh and a flutter of the hands, to the revelation that he is now in gaol. "Mistakes will occur," you must observe, "but how ironical that such a great lover of Germany should by error now lie in a German prison!" Add to that, as quickly as possible, the information that Don Agesilas is a very wealthy man . . .'

Angelo paid close attention to the Marchesa's advice, but found some difficulty in putting it into practice. With his native regard for order and authority, the General preferred the smoothness of monologue to the ragged give-and-take of ordinary conversation, and rarely would he consider any topic not of his own choosing. 'I wish to explain myself to you,' he would say. 'I have a remarkable character, and you will be deeply interested to hear about it. I am, for instance, equally capable of tragic perception and Homeric laughter. Intrinsically I am a nobleman, very simple and honest and kind-hearted, a true aristocrat of the old sort. But also I have a modern understanding so subtle that often I am amazed at myself. — But how German! you will say. For you, being intelligent yourself, know how typical of the German soul is its universality. How do you say, in Italian, "the universality of the German soul"?'

Talk of this kind, which Angelo found very tedious, prohibited any reference to the Count and his affairs for several days. And then one afternoon, when the General in a mood of languor toyed with a melancholy silence, Angelo found opportunity and a sufficient courage to broach the subject. How greatly his master the Count would enjoy their conversation, he said. Few Italians, he ventured to think, were more deeply interested in the complexity of the German mentality or more truly impressed by its grandeur, than Count Piccologrando.

'Where is he living?' asked the General.

'He is now in prison,' said Angelo.

'What a scoundrel he must be.'

'No, no! It is entirely by mistake that he is in prison. Two officers arrested him — '

'A German officer never makes a mistake.'

'Of course not! It must have been the Count, my master, who made a mistake. Like many rich men — I mean exceedingly rich men — he is sometimes very careless.'

'So? He is rich?'

Angelo named, in succession of value, the Count's several estates.

'But what is wealth compared with happiness?' exclaimed the General. 'It is my peculiarity that I despise mere riches. I have seen more true contentment in a humble cottage on the Baltic than in all your Roman palaces. Ach, when I think of the cabbages in the garden, and old men smoking their pipes, and everywhere our little swine running to-and-fro! How beautiful a scene, is it not? — Ring the bell, my dear fellow. Let us drink a bottle or two of champagne, and I shall tell you about my Prussian home.'

Angelo was sadly convinced, when he went home that evening, that the General had utterly forgotten the Count's existence. — I have been wasting my time, he thought. I detest my employment, and I have submitted to it only in the belief that somehow it might help me to secure the release of Don Agesilas. If that is not so, then *basta!* Enough! I shall never return to the house of that hateful and boring old man.

In the morning, however, he decided to make one more trial of his persuasive power, and was infinitely surprised to find the General not merely in a brisk and businesslike frame of mind, but waiting to discuss the very subject which Angelo had so often found impossible to introduce.

'I have had inquiries made,' he said, 'and found it to be true that this man whom you call the Count Piccologrando is in a German prison. Therefore, of course, he is a criminal. But I found also that he is not charged with any specific offence, for the two officers by whom he was arrested were too busy to make a detailed statement, and are now in some other part of Italy. And so it was quite

47

easy to deal with him. I decided to fine him an appropriate sum, and release him.

'How noble of you!' cried Angelo. 'How truly wise and clement you are! What an administrator you would make for all Italy!'

Unmoved by these compliments, the General continued in a cold and formal voice: 'I have ascertained that his bank is the Banco di Santo Spirito, and I have informed the manager that the Count Piccologrando is about to draw a large cheque in your favour.'

'Why in my favour?' asked Angelo; but the General ignored him and went on with his story.

'From his residence I obtained his cheque-book, which I had conveyed to him in his prison, with the information that he had been found guilty and fined the sum of so many lire. I also gave him my own word that he would be released as soon as his cheque had been honoured. After some discussion he perceived the justice of my sentence and the mercy of my intervention. Here, then, is the cheque. You will go to the bank, cash it, and return immediately. The signature is a trifle shaky, but it will serve. If you have any trouble, let me know.'

'But good god!' cried Angelo. 'This is a cheque for five million lire!'

'The Count is a very wealthy man.'

'Not so wealthy as he was.'

'Had he not valued his freedom he would not have purchased it. — No, I have no time at present for discussion. My car will take you to the bank, wait for you, and bring you back. The quicker you go, the sooner will the Count be free.'

The General had made excellent arrangements, and Angelo had no difficulty in cashing the cheque. One of the soldiers who accompanied him had brought a leather bag into which they packed the notes, and within ten minutes of their return the General had counted them with a methodical and yet not ostentatious care, and signed an order for the Count's release. He counted the money again before locking it into a safe, and then, after a moment of solemn thought, his mood quite suddenly altered. He unbuttoned his tunic, became boisterously genial, and from a silver bucket pulled a slender green bottle and poured brim-full two enormous glasses of primrose-coloured wine.

'Let us drink!' he exclaimed. 'Now that we have settled all that dull work let us enjoy ourselves for a change, and drink! And to-day, my Angelo, we shall drink German wine, which is the best in the world.'

The General smacked his lips and refilled his glass. With interest and some foreboding Angelo saw that the silver bucket held half a dozen bottles.

'Ach, how I hate the sordid claims of business! It is only the inferior breeds of people who take pleasure in money-making,' said the General. 'We are poets, we Germans, and our natural communion is with the eternal thoughts of nature. And mark how nature has blessed our understanding by giving us vineyards that grow a poet's wine. Already I feel my spirit soaring! I am so sensitive, I respond as quickly as a woman — but with a truer perception, of course, of the eternal values. Yes, we are poets! Let me tell you about our German soul...'

It was late before Angelo was allowed to leave and the sky was darkening when, with the utmost impatience, he hurried home to greet the Count. It was almost a lover's eagerness, or the tyrannical hunger of a child, that he felt, now, for the sight and the sound and the touch of that handsome trim figure, the musical and witty voice, those delicate and accomplished hands. Dear master! he thought. My wise, graceful, kindest master, how I long to welcome you!

He was sadly taken aback when the butler told him that the Count was in bed, and the doctor who had been called in had given orders that he was on no account to be disturbed. — But the butler was a dull creature, with no faculty but for misunderstanding. He was always making mistakes. Angelo decided to go and see for himself.

With feather-soft fingertips he tapped upon the bed-room door, tapped again, and waited. In a little while it

49

was opened, and Angelo was surprised to see, against a shaded light, the Marchesa Dolce. She came out, closing the door behind her, and spoke in a whisper. Angelo listened with bewildered sorrow.

Then she said: 'You must not stay very long, and do not let him see that you are surprised by his appearance. The bandage, after all, makes a lot of difference.'

Angelo promised to behave with composure, and went gently in. Bending low to the pillow, so that the Count might recognize him, he uttered the hope that his master was already feeling better.

'To meet old friends again cannot fail to make me better,' said the Count with a courteous gesture of the hand which had not been hurt. 'But the truth is, my dear boy, that I am not so well as I used to be. Neither so well nor so well-off. My physical health is depreciated, and my account at the Banco di Santo Spirito is overdrawn. The poet Shelley, now happily buried in this city, once compared life to a many-coloured dome. And how right he was! For my poor body is black and blue, and to the Holy Ghost I am altogether in the red.'

CHAPTER V

ANGELO gave no more Italian lessons to General Hammerfurter. He had a generous nature and the springs of gratitude flowed freely in his heart — having been educated in
an old-fashioned way he had never learnt that gratitude
is a sign of inferiority and should therefore be suppressed —
but after carefully weighing the evidence, for and against
the General, he had come to the conclusion that he owed
him nothing. True, the Count was at liberty, and that
was through the General's influence; but the Count had
paid five million lire for his freedom, and would need
several weeks of careful nursing before he could enjoy it.
'I abhor a mean or grudging temperament,' said Angelo
to the Marchesa, 'but facts are facts and should be
recognized. We owe that man nothing!'

The Marchesa, though she disliked the General for
more reasons than one, would have preferred a continu-
ance of his friendship with Angelo, for the sake of peace
and the possibility of further benefit; but when she perceived the strength of Angelo's feelings she made no more
attempt to persuade him. She merely said, 'You must try
to avoid an open quarrel. Tell him that you have to return
to Pontefiore.'

'I shall tell him nothing,' said Angelo.

He trembled, even as he spoke, to think of the consequences of such heroic stubbornness, but escaped them,
as it turned out, with the help of the butler's timely
stupidity. The General sent his orderlies, and finally his
aide-de-camp, to ask what had happened to Angelo; and
always the butler answered with disarming frankness,
'He has gone out. No, I do not know where, and I do
not know when he will come back. To tell you the truth,
I know nothing about him.'

Angelo, in the meantime, had more than once met the
two soldiers, the Czech and the Russian, with whom he
had driven to Pontefiore. They had reminded him of his
promise to help them escape, and because he now felt a

certain prejudice against the German authorities, he had bestirred himself to find someone who could give them practical assistance. He met one evening an old comrade of his own regiment, who had deserted by feigning death in battle, and succeeded in returning to Italy from Cyrenaica. This man now earned a precarious living by reproducing, where they were needed, the purple die-stamps on official documents, which he did in a very simple but ingenious way; and after some discussion with Angelo he promised to introduce him to a person called Fest.

Within a limited circle, it appeared, Fest was well known, though no one could tell much about him except that, for reasons of his own, he was hostile to the Germans. He spoke Italian fluently, but with a clumsy guttural accent, and his appearance was remarkable. His thick growth of pale brown hair was streaked with grey, and he wore a monocle of clouded tortoiseshell to conceal the loss of his left eye and the burnt lids that betrayed the manner of its destruction. A deep scar, breaking the bridge of his nose, extended to his left cheek-bone, and half a dozen parallel scars, bone-white and thin as a knitting needle, ran from his forehead into the thickness of his hair. He dressed with distinction, his manner was cold, his carriage upright.

Angelo met him in a trattoria near the little Piazza dei Satiri that was commonly used by cabmen, flower-sellers, and petty agents of the Black Market; and there he spoke diffidently of his friends' desire to escape from German service. Fest appeared to be sympathetic and said he would make some necessary inquiries.

Two days later Angelo met him again, and Fest invited him to bring the Czech and the Russian to the trattoria on the following evening. The four of them spent nearly an hour together, and the two soldiers spoke at great length on the injustice they had suffered, the hardships they had endured, and their hatred of the Germans. Fest listened attentively, without saying much in reply, and made another appointment. He would then be able, he said, to let them know what arrangements had been made for their escape, and give them their instructions.

To Angelo's surprise the soldiers brought a stranger to this meeting. He was a short broad-shouldered man in the uniform of a German private. His expression was amiable, and according to the others he was a Lett from Dvinsk. He also, it appeared, was eager to desert, and having overheard the Czech and the Russian discussing their plans, he had asked as a great favour to be allowed to join their party. Angelo thought they had been indiscreet, but there was nothing he could do to redress the situation. They sat down together, ordered wine, and waited for Fest.

The trattoria was unusually empty, and Fest was late. The Lett paid for another flask and asked Angelo how many soldiers he had smuggled out of the country. Angelo answered with a knowing look and a shrug of the shoulders. They finished the flask, and still Fest did not come. The Czech and the Russian had begun to look worried, and the Lett was turning sullen. 'I think you have been deceiving us,' he said. 'I do not think your friend means to come.'

'Perhaps he has been prevented.'

'By whom?'

'How should I know?'

'Who else should know? It was you who introduced these men to him, and asked him to arrange their escape. You are responsible for the whole plan.'

'I offered to help them if I could — '

'That is enough,' said the Lett, and knocked the flask off the table. This was evidently a signal, for a few seconds later the door was thrown open and a sergeant of the Schutzstaffel came in, followed by four troopers, all carrying revolvers.

'Where's the other one?' demanded the sergeant.

'He hasn't come,' said the Lett.

'Why not?'

'This one tipped him off, I think,' and the Lett pointed to Angelo.

'We'll hammer your liver into paste for that,' said the sergeant.

53

Angelo and the would-be deserters were in a white trance of fear, and when the troopers dragged them from the table, to which they feebly clung, their loosened knees could scarcely bear their weight. They were hustled to the door while the other drinkers, the few who had come to the trattoria that night, shrank into dark corners or huddled against a wall, and watched them in a silence broken only by a flower-vendor's nervous hiccup.

They were driven to the prison called Regina Coeli, where for an hour or two they were questioned, not about their intentions — which had already been revealed by the Lett, who was an agent of the police — but about Fest. As none of them knew anything, however, they could tell very little; and because their interrogators had had a busy day, and were tired, they escaped with little worse than a formal beating for their incompetence.

Angelo, the Russian, and the Czech spent fourteen miserable days in the Regina Coeli gaol among some thirty or forty nondescript prisoners, none of whom dared speak freely to anyone else for fear he was talking to a German agent. Angelo and his two companions were so disconcerted by the Lett's betrayal of them that they regarded each other with mutual dread, avoided conversation almost entirely, and were reticent about the torture they suffered. They were all beaten every second or third day, but Angelo's interrogators were either bored by their duty or physically exhausted by it, and his injuries were superficial. The Czech and the Russian were less fortunate and they regarded Angelo with ever-increasing suspicion.

He was rescued from this unpleasant atmosphere by a sudden order, one night, to parade in the prison yard. A group of about two hundred men stood there under a fine rain, while guards moved about them, shouting. Presently they were marched to the railway station, where two smaller companies were waiting, and after a tedious delay during which the most alarming rumours were discussed, they were hustled with a sudden feverish haste into the open trucks of a waiting train. There they remained, cold and shivering, till dawn, when the train started.

All day the rain fell from low clouds. From time to time the train stopped, and the prisoners were ordered from their trucks to repair the line, which had been bombed in several places. Night was falling when they entered a mountain gorge, and quickly the sombre hills disappeared in a general gloom. It became very cold, and some of the prisoners were much distressed. Fortunately for Angelo the truck in which he was travelling was grossly over-crowded, and his companions engendered a natural heat which greatly comforted him. Towards morning, however, he was annoyed by an oldish man who, held against him by the crowd, fell sound asleep in his arms. Angelo supported him, partly because he was good-natured, partly because it was very difficult to get rid of the fellow; but it was unfair, he thought, that a stranger should use him so. Not until morning did he perceive that the oldish man was dead.

They were now in a very wild and rugged part of the country, but the weather was fair again, and as they descended from the mountains into the coastal plain the sun warmed them, and the steam of drying clothes rose above the jolting train. Several of Angelo's companions now felt sure that they were going to Ancona, though for what purpose none could guess.

But when the train reached the coast it went northward away from Ancona. Angelo squeezed and pushed his way to the right-hand side of the truck, and looked with pleasure at the pale blue sea that stretched so far, in silky calm, beneath a milk-white sky. It was the first time he had ever seen the Adriatic, and though he disliked the means by which he had come there, he was glad to increase his knowledge of the world.

They arrived at the little port of Pesaro, where they left the train and were marched to the outskirts of the town, from which the native inhabitants had been removed. They slept in some empty houses, and in the morning began to knock them down.

Most of the houses were quite new, and well-built. The furniture remained in some of them, and when the Germans had taken all they needed for themselves, such as beds and cooking-pots and blankets, they sold what was left to the people who had been evicted. These unhappy creatures used to come every day to watch their houses being demolished, and some of the women cried aloud when they saw the walls tumble. The German officer who was in charge of the work was a pale young man, with the eager but careworn look of a student, who believed there was no virtue like efficiency. Angelo and his fellow-prisoners were compelled to break the houses down to single bricks, and spread the debris flat. Then the officer would smile and say, 'Good, very good! That is beautifully done!'

He appeared to be a kindly young man, and one day Angelo plucked up courage to ask him what was the purpose of this destruction.

'I suppose it is hard for you to understand,' said the officer. 'You feel guilty, you poor Italians, because you have betrayed us and broken our alliance. And because you feel guilty you fear that we shall desert you, and leave you to your fate. But no! A German promise is a sacred thing, and cannot be broken. You do not understand that, but nevertheless it is so. And therefore we are still fighting for you, and here in Pesaro we are making the most careful preparation to defend your country to the last. Have no fear! We shall never allow the English and the Americans to destroy your beautiful Italy.'

'Would they destroy it as carefully as we are doing?' asked Angelo.

'No, no! They are a lot of bungling amateurs,' said the officer. 'It is only we Germans who are truly efficient.'

'In that case,' said Angelo respectfully, 'I think Italy would be better-off if you did desert us.'

'Shut up, swinehound!' shouted a sergeant who had been listening to their conversation, and with the back of his hand struck Angelo across the face so heavily that he fell upon a pile of bricks, and the Sergeant kicked him in the ribs.

'Do not be too severe,' said the officer. 'He comes of an

56

inferior race, they lack understanding.' And he went busily to inspect the destruction of another house.

The demolitions were intended to open fields of fire for certain guns which the Germans were mounting, and when their work in Pesaro was done the prisoners were marched along the high road that runs inland from there, and whenever they came to a village they stayed in it until they had knocked it flat. Then they were ordered to fell all the trees on the flat river-fields south of the road, and Angelo grew sadder every day to see how thoroughly a country had to be ruined in order to be saved.

He was too unhappy to make friends with the other prisoners; many of whom, indeed, were in the same mood as he. Though never for a moment alone, he and those of his temper lived solitary lives and nursed their grief like a young widow suckling her orphan babe.

The Germans, about this time, were much alarmed by the success of the Allied landings, and contemplated a long retreat to the mountains north of Florence. Hurriedly they had chosen defensive sites, and were fortifying them to create from coast to coast what was later known as the Gothic Line. But then their Führer perceived the moral impossibility of abandoning Rome to the barbarians, and with the approach of winter — a potent ally — resolved to fight for it in the southern passes. So work on the Gothic Line came to a stop, no more houses were demolished, and for a week or two Angelo and his companions, with nothing to do, were lodged in a large school on the sea-shore south of Pesaro. The ejected pupils, enjoying their unexpected holiday, gave three cheers for every German they saw, and the prisoners were comforted by several days of fine warm weather.

They spent most of their time on the beach, and their favourite occupation was to watch the fisherfolk hauling their nets.

The nets were towed out to sea in a great semi-circle, and then the fisherfolk would lay hold of the end-ropes and slowly, with a small formal step, drag them ashore. Most of the haulers were old men and women and girls.

57

As the nets came in, running water from the mesh, the bare-legged, bare-armed women would kilt their skirts high above the knee. There was a girl there who reminded Angelo of Lucrezia; not by any physical resemblance, but because she stirred something of the same emotion in him. She was little and childishly plump, though she wore a wedding-ring, and when she had gathered her skirt to the waist, and was leaning far back on the rope, and the salt sea-drops fell with a tiny splash upon her smooth round thighs, then Angelo thought of Lucrezia at the washing-trough, and his lungs contracted as though a ghostly arm encircled him.

One day, observing a yard of rope unoccupied behind her, he stepped forward, took hold and helped to pull. She turned her head, and smiled.

Angelo soon discovered that it did no good to heave and strain, but when he lay upon the rope there presently came, as if the sea were lifting it, an easing of the weight, and then he must take — one-two, like dancing — a little step, and somewhere behind him a fathom of slack would be coiled upon the sand. The net came in, the circle narrowed and became a bag. Two score small fishes, wriggling silver, were gathered from it. Softly the girl asked him, 'Why do you look so unhappy?'

'I am a prisoner,' said Angelo.

'So is my husband.'

'To be separated from you must make him the unhappiest man alive.'

'Are you married too?'

'She said she would not have me until the war was over,' said Angelo.

'I think she is wise,' said the girl. 'But my husband is going to escape.'

'How?'

'Come back to-morrow, and I shall tell you.'

'What is your name?'

'Annunziata.'

The next day Angelo took his place on the rope behind Annunziata as though it were his right, and addressed her

58

so warmly that she frowned at him, pointed her glance at an old grey-bearded man, and whispered through careful lips, 'Be sensible! He is my father-in-law.'

But Angelo, with hope like a bubble in his blood, answered, 'Dear Annunziata! Tell me how your husband is going to escape, and if he fails perhaps I can succeed and take his place.'

When they began to haul he fell easily into the rhythm of it, and once or twice put an arm round Annunziata's waist, when she leaned far back, and pressed her to him. She grew offended, or made a pretence of it, and would not talk to him until they were pulling-in for the third time. Then she said, 'You must volunteer for the front line.'

'Oh, no!' said Angelo. 'I should hate to do that.'

'That is how my husband is going to escape. He was taken away and set to work as you have been, but then the Tedeschi asked for volunteers who would join their army and serve them where they are fighting. Mario, my husband, said to himself, "If they send me to some place where there is a battle, I shall be quite near to the English or the Americans, and therefore it will be much easier to escape and join the other side." So he volunteered, and by now, perhaps, he has already deserted.'

Angelo said in a subdued voice, 'Perhaps your husband is a brave man?'

'He is quite fearless,' answered Annunziata. 'He has been in prison three times for fighting, he is beautiful and strong and absolutely courageous.'

'I am not in the least like that,' said Angelo.

Annunziata let down her skirt. 'But you are very kind,' she said. 'You have helped us greatly, and I hope you will be rewarded by good fortune. — No, I must not talk any longer, for my father-in-law is watching us, and he is very stern. Good-bye!' said Annunziata.

Angelo thought very earnestly indeed about her suggestion, and the more he considered it, the more he hated the prospect of going anywhere near the firing-line. He lay awake all night and frightened himself into a fever by picturing the horrors of war. He saw himself dying in dreadful agony, unable to rise from the little icy pool in the cup of a bomb-crater, while Lucrezia in her lonely bed lay weeping three hundred miles away. His fever broke, and a cold sweat bedewed him. When morning came he felt so weak that he could hardly get up.

But during the day he thought: How else can I escape? There isn't the smallest chance of running away from here, for I am quite ignorant of this part of the country, I shouldn't in the least know where to make for, and the English and the Americans — who are still fighting along the river Volturno, they say — might as well be in the moon for all the help they can give me. This business of liberation, about which there was so much talk, is going to be a slow process, and I may grow old waiting for it. The sensible thing, if it were not so dangerous, would certainly be to go and meet it half-way. Ah, if only I had the *dono di coraggio*!

During the day some of the prisoners heard a rumour, and quickly spread it, that they were to be taken to Germany and set to work at clearing the damage in some cities which had lately been bombed by the Royal Air Force. — That will be Essen and Cologne, said some. Berlin and Stettin are more likely, said others. Or Munich, suggested a third party.

Angelo's fellow-prisoners at this time were all Italians, and whenever they heard that a German city had been bombed they were delighted, for they hated the Tedeschi and also it was worth remembering that bombs which fell in Germany could never be used against Italy. But none of them had any wish to go and see for himself what damage had been done. The idea of being sent to Germany was their greatest fear, and no one was more profoundly affected by it than Angelo.

He slept that night, for he was too tired to stay awake, but his sleep was haunted by a dreadful nightmare in which he saw himself labouring in the horrid ruin of a German street, while a monstrous armada circled in the white-striped sky above, and the roar of its engines for ever threatened the louder roar of an exploding bomb, He woke, and felt more tired than ever. The nightmare had been even worse than his waking thoughts of war.

The greater fear diminished the less, and now that the alternative, as it seemed, was to labour like a slave in Germany, he longed to be engaged upon a battlefield in Italy. He decided to take Annunziata's advice as soon as the opportunity occurred.

He had not long to wait. About a week later an elderly German major arrived, the prisoners were paraded, and the major made a speech about the honourable profession of arms, and the still enduring friendship between Germany and Italy, the crimes that were daily being committed by the Allies, and so forth. Then he asked for volunteers to serve at the front in a pioneer regiment.

Angelo was the first to step forward.

CHAPTER VI

'We do not get enough sleep,' said the Count.

'What is sleep?' demanded the Marchesa. 'Pure negation, and why you should want to enlarge a mere nothing, I cannot think. It is, moreover, so boorish. It puzzles me that you, who are otherwise courteous, should be so ready to turn your back upon a friend.'

'I have two friends,' said the Count with a gentle yawn, 'and the other is repose.'

'I think of sleep as a rehearsal for death,' replied the Marchesa, 'and as I feel sure that when the last night comes I shall wear my coffin with conviction, I see no purpose in wasting time on unnecessary practice.'

'I have a simpler mind than yours, and less vitality. I enjoy both the prospect and the process of going to sleep; and I need a great deal of it.'

'People in our position should not require very much. It is different for the poor, of course. Their life is so horrible that naturally they do not wish to endure consciousness for more than a few hours at a time. But we are different —'

'We have become like the poor in one respect: we are equally vulnerable nowadays.'

'Our life remains interesting. It is precarious, perhaps, but still furnished with beauty.'

'It is possible to over-furnish either a room on your life,' said the Count.

'That would be foolish, of course.'

'It is always surprising to see how many fools win the love, or at least the companionship, of beautiful women. — Or is it surprising? Perhaps not. Let us admit that a beautiful woman may be the desire of the noblest, and should be the reward of the bravest among us. But a woman requires to be wooed, and who make the best wooers? Fools, because they have the time for it, and the necessary frivolity of mind.'

'I dislike you when you grow introspective, dear Agesilas.'

'I am sleepy,' said the Count.

Among her many excellent qualities the Marchesa owned a single disability. She had an unusually quick digestion. She ate heartily and often during the day, and she rarely passed a night without waking for a meal in the middle of it. Sometimes she would be satisfied with a glass of milk and a biscuit or two, but generally she wanted something with more bulk and substance in it. The Count had never quite reconciled himself to this idiosyncrasy, and since his release from prison he had found it more and more trying. He had recovered his health but not all his equanimity, and he blamed his own weakness as much as hers for the annoyance he suffered. But to be fair about it did not, he found, diminish the annoyance.

A maid, who had been roused for the purpose, brought into the little drawing-room a tray that bore a large omelette well stuffed with mushrooms and ham, a loaf of bread and a dish of butter, a bottle of wine, a small decanter of brandy, a bunch of grapes, and some pastry. For friendship's sake the Count accepted a small portion of the omelette and a glass of wine. It was an excellent white wine from Orvieto, and presently he began to feel more cheerful. He drank a little brandy, and started a discussion on political life.

'Mussolini was my friend,' he said, 'and I shall never conceal or deny it. Nowadays he is being adversely criticized by people who are as devoid of gratitude as they are incapable of memory. They have, for example — these ingrates — entirely forgotten the ubiquitous, the general, the inescapable corruption that made the life of Italy shameful, and so crippled our resources before the advent of Fascism.'

'There was plenty of corruption under Fascism.'

'But how tidy it became! In the same way as he drained the Pontine marshes he drained great lakes of bribery and peculation, and canalized their flow into official channels and official pockets. You must admire the magnitude of his work.'

'He was vulgar,' said the Marchesa.

'What else would you have had him? No person of true

refinement can take a prominent part in public life, except perhaps, as an unwilling martyr; by no possible chance could such a person become a dictator. A dictator, being the product of social indigestion, is by nature as vulgar as a smell. You must not hold it against Mussolini that he made no effort to conceal his origin. No, no! The man was my friend, I tell you.'

'You are no better for his friendship now,' said the Marchesa, and helped herself to the last of the omelette.

'I am a little wiser, I think, and if others shared my perspicacity they also might be wiser. He did excellent work — this you cannot deny — in bringing the business of government into disrepute. This was desirable because popular education has been accompanied by, if it has not deliberately promoted, a growth of superstitious faith in government. The people have come to believe that government can procure for them, not merely prosperity, but happiness. Side by side with this nonsensical delusion there has marched the increasing professionalism of government. Many astute people have seen the business of government as a business indeed, and therefore, into the council chambers of the world, there has come a great deal of rascality. Now Mussolini, with real genius, perceived this tendency and pushed it to its logical extreme: he created a government that was frankly criminal, and then for universal enlightenment — or so I think, for I believe the man to have been misunderstood — he led it by a route congenial to criminals, a route congenial, that is, to certain elements in every government upon earth, to a destined and complete disaster. For that disaster, of course, we ourselves are fundamentally to blame, because our ridiculous credulity let us repose in his government all the faith a savage African has in his wooden idol, and with as much reason. Mussolini — and the world will remember him for this — exposed our folly to the depths, and like another Moses cast down the idol of total government. The corollary is obvious: We must grow up, we must cultivate ourselves. Our goal must be a world in which every man is his own republic — '

'Good God!' exclaimed the Marchesa. 'Who are you?'

A man stood in the doorway. He was tall and well built. His light brown hair was streaked with grey and in his left eye he wore a monocle of clouded tortoiseshell. He closed the door as quietly as he had opened it, and came into the room.

'I have some disturbing news for you,' he said.

The Marchesa had risen in alarm. Her breast rose and fell, her nostrils were slightly dilated, and she pulled her *saut-de-lit* more tightly round her with hands that slightly trembled. The Count remained in his chair, apparently calm, having adjusted his dressing-gown to conceal the agitation of his knees.

'Who are you?' repeated the Marchesa, while the Count declared, a little hoarsely, 'This is an extraordinary visit, sir! What do you want?'

'My name is Fest,' said the stranger. 'Some weeks ago I became acquainted with a protégé of yours, a young man called Angelo — '

'Where is he now?'

'I don't know. He was taken by the Germans, and, I believe, drafted into one of their labour battalions. But I have failed to discover what has happened to him. It was while I was seeking information about him that I heard of a new intention to arrest you.'

'Me?' exclaimed the Count. 'But that is impossible. I have already been arrested, and also set free.'

'You paid too handsomely for your release,' said Fest. 'You gave Hammerfurter five million lire to get out of prison, and now Brilling, the new chief of the Gestapo here, has heard of that and is going to have you arrested to see what he can squeeze for himself.'

'No, not again!' cried the Count. 'I have been squeezed enough. I cannot endure it again!'

'I thought as much. And so, if you will take my advice — '

'But who are you? What is your purpose in coming here? Why should you go to the trouble of warning me, and incur danger to help me?'

'I have a hobby,' said Fest, 'a simple hobby that gives me, nowadays, all the pleasure I know. It is to annoy the Tedeschi.'

The Count no longer made any attempt to conceal his perturbation. He walked up and down, wringing his hands, and glancing sideways at Fest in a grimacing alternation of anguish, appeal and suspicion. The Marchesa, who had been standing silent and still, now asked him, 'When are they coming?'

'Within a few minutes,' said Fest.

'What are we to do?'

'Find him a hiding-place.'

'My house is very small. There is nowhere a man can hide and be safe.'

'Nowhere,' exclaimed the Count. 'I know every inch of the house, and there is not room to hide a dog. My late father, in similar circumstances — a jealous husband was looking for him — once hid behind a woman's skirts, but nowadays that is quite impossible. The modern architect and the contemporary dressmaker have no sense of responsibility. Their creations are paltry, they offer neither protection nor concealment. No, no, I am already a prisoner!'

'The modern woman,' said Fest, 'is appreciably bigger than her mother. You have given me an idea. Lie down on that sofa.'

The Count was suspicious, a trifle querulous, and foolishly concerned about his dignity. Fest, however, disclosed a masterful temper, and the Count yielded. The sofa was long and broad. He lay down and was covered with cushions, of which there were many in the little drawing-room. The Marchesa took her place in the tableau with a look of restrained indignation. Fest instructed her to recline on the cushioned sofa in the attitude of Madame Récamier in the portrait by David; but he was dissatisfied by the picture she represented. She lacked repose, and the displacement of a cushion revealed one of the Count's feet and gave her the appearance of possessing three.

66

'Have patience,' he said, and went into the adjoining bedroom, from which he returned with a hairbrush and a mirror.

'I concealed some clothes belonging to the Count,' he said, 'and now we must make adjustments here. It is absolutely necessary to cover his feet, and if you will take off your dressing-gown I shall drape it carelessly over this end of the sofa.'

'My night-dress is very thin,' said the Marchesa coldly.

'You need have no fear. Even the Gestapo has admitted my self-control.'

With manifest displeasure the Marchesa put off her dressing-gown and resumed her seat. Fest gave her the mirror.

'The Germans,' he explained, 'are incurably sentimental, and take immoderate pleasure in the contemplation of domestic bliss. I propose to show them a romantic scene in a homely setting. You, with pardonable vanity, must look at your mirror while I, with a delicate and adoring hand, brush your hair.'

'In your overcoat?' asked the Marchesa.

'I was about to remove it,' said Fest, and threw it on a chair. The Marchesa loosened her hair.

'You are not without practice,' she said, as she felt the first strokes of the brush.

'But my pleasure, if I give you satisfaction, is without precedent.'

The Marchesa settled herself more comfortably. 'Poor Agesilas,' she said. 'I hope I am not stifling him.'

'Be calm now,' said Fest. 'Here they come.'

The front door of the Marchesa's house was stoutly built, but the lock yielded to the blow of a sledge-hammer, and this rude entry woke the maid, now dozing in the kitchen, and set her screaming. It woke another in an attic room, who piercingly replied. Male voices roughly exclaimed, and heavily booted feet drummed upon the stair.

'Sit still!' said Fest.

'I have not moved. It is Agesilas,' whispered the Marchesa.

Three Germans in dark uniform, an officer and two others, entered the room with unnecessary violence. With a protective hand on the Marchesa's shoulder, the brush still engaged in her dark hair, Fest turned toward them his glaring eye and a face that was apparently convulsed with rage.

All three pointed their pistols at him, and the officer brusquely inquired, 'Are you the Count Piccologrando?'

Fest answered him in German. His voice was harsh and arrogant. 'You blundering misbegotten fool!' he said. 'You ill-advised untimely ape! What in the devil's name do you mean by bringing your insanitary press-gang into a lady's house at this time of the morning?'

'I am acting under instruction. My orders are — '

'What's your name?'

'Bloch.'

'Have you no manners, Bloch? Has no one ever told you how to address a senior officer?'

Lieutenant Bloch grew unhappy and perplexed. His face, gone pale about the mouth, was patched with red over the cheek-bones. He appeared to swallow a crumb or two, then straightened to attention and saluted.

'That's better, Bloch. Now take off your hat and tell me what you want.'

'I have come here to arrest the Count Piccologrando.'

'And why do you suppose that I am interested in your miserable ratcatcher's job?'

'You are not he?'

'God in his scorching heaven, do I look like an Italian? Do I sound like an Italian?'

'I was told that I would find him here,' said Lieutenant Bloch, and looked at the Marchesa, and looked away again, embarrassed. His two policemen stared at her without shame.

'And now that you have discovered your mistake,' said Fest, 'I suggest that you leave us, Bloch, and take your dung-rakers with you.'

68

A third policeman, a stolid sergeant, appeared in the doorway and reported that he had searched the lower part of the house and found no one.

'So your flatfeet have been rummaging, have they?' demanded Fest.

'My orders were to search the house, and I cannot leave until that has been done.'

Fest confronted him with a deeper frown, but Bloch muttered, 'I cannot!'

Then the Marchesa spoke. 'Let them go where they please. They will find nothing.'

Fest raised her hand to his lips and said loudly, 'I apologize for the manners of my fellow-countrymen. — Hurry, Bloch, and get your rummaging finished.'

Lieutenant Bloch spoke in a low voice to his policemen, who, after looking behind the curtains, went into other rooms. He himself remained, awkward and uncomfortable.

'Sit down!' said Fest sharply, and to the Marchesa: 'I am inexpressibly sorry for this outrage. To-morrow, in other quarters, I shall have more to say about it, but to-night I am dumb with shame.'

'It is a lunatic world,' said the Marchesa, 'and I am no longer surprised by its oddities. You must not fret yourself. — Dear friend, you had promised to brush my hair. You have not forgotten?'

'In such gracious employment I may forget my anger,' said Fest.

Softly but strongly, with earnest but caressive strokes, he began to brush her darkly gleaming hair from brow to the curving crown of her head, from crown to the hidden nape of her neck. She held her head high, straining a little against the pull of the brush. She lifted the mirror and looked at her reflection and the youthful sharpening of her features as the muscles tautened. Then, stooping as the brush went down to her neck, she made little forward movements like a bird preening.

Lieutenant Bloch looked at her with sorrowful and hungry eyes. The blush had faded from his cheeks, he was pale as a plank of wood by now, and his short hair was the colour of a sponge. He sighed, and his lips began to whisper. He sighed again and in a soft voice recited:

> *'Nun muss ich gar*
> *Um dein aug und haar*
> *Alle tage*
> *In sehnen leben.'*

'How charming of you,' said the Marchesa.

'So you're a poet, are you?' asked Fest.

'That is not my own composition,' said Lieutenant Bloch, 'but nevertheless I am a poet. We Germans — are we not all poets?'

'Poets and policemen,' said Fest. 'My poor Bloch!'

The Lieutenant flushed again and said angrily, 'I have been doing my duty. I am not ashamed of it!'

One after another his policemen returned. 'Well?' he asked.

'There's no one else here, sir, except the servants.'

'So now you can go with a clear conscience,' said Fest.

The Lieutenant hesitated, but then said stubbornly, 'You must inform me who you are.'

'So that your ratcatchers can tell everyone where I pay my calls? I don't think so, Bloch.'

'I shall have to make my report. I cannot say there was no one here.'

Fest rubbed his chin and for a moment or two was thoughtful. Then in a friendlier voice he said, 'I am thinking of more than my own reputation. I wonder if I — if we — can rely on your discretion?'

'I am by birth a gentleman, sir!'

'A poet, a gentleman, and a policeman! — No, do not be angry, my dear Bloch, I am only making a little joke, as one does between friends. Well, come here.'

He bent and whispered closely in the Lieutenant's ear. Bloch retreated a step and gravely bowed. He ordered his policemen to go. Then, with a sudden fluency, he made an elaborate apology for his intrusion. The Marchesa gave him her hand to kiss and he bent profoundly. He found his cap, but held it under his arm and was clearly reluctant to leave. Fest took him by the arm and led him downstairs. He stood and watched him go. Then he moved a carved chest to hold the broken outer door in place, and returned to the drawing-room.

The Marchesa had lifted a couple of the cushions and was looking at the Count with some anxiety. His face was darkly coloured and he was breathing very slowly and laboriously. His eyes were half-closed. Fest raised him to a sitting position and gave him a glass of brandy.

The Count laid his hand upon the Marchesa's and said wearily, 'I was sure that you had been putting on weight, my dear.'

'I am thinner than I have been for several years,' said the Marchesa, and did on her *saut-de-lit*. Then she rang a little silver bell. 'Let us have an early breakfast,' she said.

'That will suit me very well,' said Fest, 'for I should like to stay here for an hour or two in case they are watching the house. — The Count, I suggest, should leave Rome as soon as possible. You also, for a little while at least.'

'There is a small house belonging to Agesilas in Montenero. It is easy to reach, we might go there.'

A few minutes later she asked, 'Did you tell the policeman your true name?'

'That would not have been helpful.'

'Then whose did you give?'

'You must realize that these people are quite ignorant,' said Fest, 'and it is easy to deceive them. I invented a very simple name, but gave myself a good address. I told him that I was their Military Attaché at the Vatican.'

CHAPTER VII

It was night, it was raining, and Angelo was drunk. The wind blew coldly, and he was alone on the mountainside.

In his mind, like a bird in a wood before morning, a voice was crying, 'Free, free, I'm totally free!' But he was extremely frightened, and the voice increased his fear. If the gods should hear it, swaggering like a blackbird, they might take him by the heels and haul him into captivity again. He tried to silence the voice, but it would not be quiet. Sometimes it was more like a meadow-rill chuckling deeply through summer grass: 'Happy Angelo, lucky Angelo.'

Below him in the darkness a pebbly torrent fell with a hiss and a rumble into a granite linn. The mountainside was patched with pale shapes of snow, and sagging from the southern sky hung a black and monstrous cloud. He stumbled and slipped on the rutted path, his feet gathered great overshoes of mud, and he felt upon his legs the coldness of his sodden clothes. 'Free, free!' sang the wilful voice, and he looked dreadfully over his shoulder to see if he were followed. There was a German army behind him.

For ten weeks he had served it, and for much of that time his body had felt like a scoured egg-shell. There was no substance in it. Fear had emptied it with a spoon whenever a shell burst near him, and the last month had shed all its withered days under shell-fire. He had seen five of his fellow-privates killed, and for ten days he had been lousy. He tripped again. The sole was coming off his right boot, and tears ran down his rain-wet face to comtemplate such gross injustice. The blackbird voice no longer sang, and he remembered his friend Giuseppe who, an hour ago, had also been drunk and free. But Giuseppe had been unlucky in the minefield. They had not known about the mines until Giuseppe set his foot on one.

It was Giuseppe who had found the bottle of grappa that gave them both the courage to escape. They had been rebuilding a bomb-ruined bridge not far behind the front line, and Giuseppe had discovered the bottle in a cupboard that had survived the shattered walls of a nearby cottage. When dusk descended they had privily returned to the cottage, and their company had been assembled and marched away without them.

They resolved to take their chance of deserting, and Angelo with dutch courage went out to reconnoitre. Sixty yards away, beside another shell-torn house, he heard German voices and lay discreetly behind a tumbled wall to listen. A German officer was talking to a friend who had newly returned from leave with two bottles of Spanish brandy in his haversack. They had to visit their forward positions, and then they proposed to spend a pleasant evening. The Fundador, they decided, could be left safely under their blankets.

Angelo waited until they had gone. Then, without difficulty, he found the haversack and took it back to Giuseppe, who promptly knocked the neck off one of the bottles, took a good draught, and handed it to Angelo.

Never in their lives had they tasted such brandy. It mingled with the strong grappa in their blood, and made the business of escaping seem an easy jest. They felt no need to make a plan, no need for caution. They would simply walk out. Giuseppe corked the broken bottle with a rag, and Angelo put the other in his pocket.

The rain fell in black cascades. Before they had gone a dozen yards they lost each other in the darkness, thought it comical that this should happen, and shouted till they met again. Then they fell into a panic to think that someone might have heard them, and hand-in-hand began to run.

They were lucky. They knew the way by daylight, and unthinking memory guided them. They knew where there was a thicket of barbed wire, for they had helped to lay it. The rain fell harshly from a viewless sky, and no one challenged them.

Then Giuseppe complained of a stitch, and lagged behind. Angelo forgot him and went on. When the mine exploded he threw himself flat on the mud and lay there while machine-guns hammered nervously behind and strong lights, bursting in the sky, made visible like rods of brilliant wire the slanting rain. The firing did not last long, and presently he got up and began to run again. A sensation of relief, as though he had vomited and were rid of a load of sickness, was all he felt at first, but soon it became a bubbling happiness that he could not repress, and the blackbird voice began to sing and he could not quieten it.

But now, remembering Giuseppe, he cried most bitterly for the death of his friend and for the loneliness in which it left him. He sat on a rock and tried to repair his torn boot, but a sudden consciousness of guilt swept over him like a curving wave, and left him shuddering.

He was to blame for Giuseppe's death. It was he, Angelo, who had first whispered of desertion, and how shameful that now appeared! The Germans had fed him and clothed him and trusted him, and he had deserted them. He had already deserted his own army, the men with whom he had lived and the officers to whom he owed obedience: he had taken to his heels at Reggio and never seen them again. He was twice a deserter, he had broken faith with both sides.

He felt the cold eyes of the world upon him, and he could not escape their scorn. Now, thought Angelo, my poverty is immeasurably increased, since I, who never had much to live on, have now got nothing to live for. No one will ever trust me again, or want my company, and what is life worth without friends, a little respect, and a little liking?

He sat for a long time spell-bound in grief. It was only to break the spell that at last he got up and with fumbling steps continued his journey. 'I have nothing to live on,' he said aloud, 'because I have rejected the bread of both sides. I have nothing to live for, because both sides despise me. I am a man only because I suffer.'

His loose sole caught in a root, and falling heavily he struck his knee against a sharp rock. Physical pain expelled his moral agony, and he remembered the Spanish lenitive he carried. He sat in the mud, rocking to and fro, and with a knife dug out the cork. He tilted the bottle to his lips, and after swallowing three or four times felt the pain diminish to a fiery patch. Tenderly, tentatively, he began to rub the injured bone.

'My poor little knee-cap!' he groaned. 'Oh, what a blow it was! Oh, how sore it is! Oh, my misery, miserable me!'

Little knee-cap! he thought, and with cold fingers explored its smooth round edge. It was like a pebble on a beach, a white pebble polished for a thousand years by that old craftsman the Sea. By the monstrous hands of the Sea. The Sea had carved for his own delight the Sporades and Cyclades, and drawn with a whimsical finger fantastic bays between the feet of soaring mountains, and polished in his idle hours a million multitudes of smooth white pebbles to scatter on his beaches. The gods were cruel, but God, what artists! And here, beneath his bruised and dirty skin, lay like an ocean-jewel his own dear knee-cap on a throne of ivory clothed with satin. He had seen a knee-joint stripped for inspection by a shell-splinter, and he remembered how beautiful were its smooth surfaces. Like an archaeologist in the Sila discovering a temple to Diana, a piece of metal had revealed the architecture of a soldier, and Angelo had stood amazed.

'But now, my little knee-cap,' he announced, 'I realize that I also am a masterpiece, for lovely though you are, *cara rotellina*, you are not the only marvel in my territory. I have, for instance, a pair of kidneys that perform the most remarkable tasks, and other glands that contain a family-tree which Adam planted. As a telephone-system my nerves are astonishingly good, and they also carry power to my remotest parts, with the most gratifying efficiency. I have, moreover, a brain that in time of drought can always turn on the tap for tears, and in better seasons will instruct my tongue to utter the most intricate and delightful thoughts. My tongue is a highly skilled performer, and obeys upon the instant. Listen to him now: he's doing very well, isn't he? Oh, my dear

75

rotella, I am a truly remarkable person, I do assure you. And also — note this! — I am free! And do you know what freedom means? It means that some day we shall go home to Pontefiore and be re-united with my adored Lucrezia.

'There will be many nights like this in the years to come, but you and I won't be out in them. Not a bit of it. We'll be snug indoors, and we'll listen for a minute or two to the wind howling and the rain beating on the window, and then we'll think how blessed we are to have a roof above us: and I shall turn and tuck the sheet round Lucrezia. What bliss awaits us, my *rotelletta*! To turn our back upon the darkness and the cold, and tuck a sheet round Lucrezia!'

He drank a little more brandy, put the bottle in his pocket, and got to his feet again. His colloquy with his knee-cap had greatly comforted him, and he went on his way, somewhat unsteadily, but with fresh resolution. He had a very vague and slender notion of where he was, but after some time it occurred to him that if he had been walking in a straight line he must now be very near, if not within, the Allies' outpost line. He perceived that he was walking on a road again. It would be a good thing, he thought, to warn the Allies of his approach. So he began to shout.

'Hallo, Englishmen! Hullo, Englishmen!' he shouted. 'Please do not shoot me, because I am a friend. Do not shoot me, I am a friend.'

He was answered almost immediately. From somewhere in the darkness a voice called, 'Then stop making that disgusting noise, and come and help me.'

Angelo, surprised, looked left and right but could see no one. The swollen black cloud had passed, and in the southern sky were the grey embers of dead stars. Above him was a pale hillside, a snowfield roughly combed by the rain, and below him the ground fell steeply and was dark.

'Hurry up!' said the voice.

'Where are you? I cannot see you,' said Angelo nervously.

'Don't argue. Come and get me out of this hole.'

Angelo went slowly forward. The road curved to the left, and was built like a terrace on the slope of a hill. Twenty yards on, to the right of the road and below him, Angelo discerned four wheels, and beneath them a motor-car of some small kind.

'How much longer are you going to keep me waiting?' demanded the voice. 'Don't stand up there admiring the view, come down and get busy.'

Angelo scrambled down, and lying beside the over-turned jeep peered into the hole beneath. It had fallen like a lid over a small trench, that might sometime have been a machine-gun position, and in the cavity sat a figure whose pale face was now very close to Angelo's. 'See if you can lift it,' the prisoner suggested.

Angelo, with great willingness but no effect, did his best. First from the one side and then from the other he heaved and he strained, but his feet slipped in the mud, his strength was insufficient, and when he stood to get his breath he felt his arms trembling with exhaustion. 'I am not powerful enough,' he confessed.

There was a little pause, and then the voice said, 'Well, if you can't, that's all there is to it, I suppose. It's not your fault.'

Angelo sat down where he could converse more easily. 'I am truly sorry,' he said.

'Who are you?' asked the voice.

'I am a deserter,' said Angelo with some flavour of pride in his words.

'From us or from them?'

'From the Tedeschi, of course!'

'Where did you learn to speak English?'

'At school in Siena.'

'You were educated, were you? With education a man can go anywhere. Look where it's taken me.'

'Are you wounded?' asked Angelo respectfully.

'I have a cut on the head, a fractured collar-bone, and a twisted ankle. If it hadn't been for this hole in the ground, into which I fell like a well-played red loser, I would also

77

have a broken back. So I don't complain about my injuries, which are trivial. It's the cold that's worrying me. I'm freezing from the feet up, I'm sitting on a stone that was deposited here in the Ice Age, and I shall probably be dead before morning.'

'I have a bottle of very good brandy,' said Angelo. 'If it would comfort you — '

'Brandy!' exclaimed the voice. 'Are you St. Bernard himself?'

'My name is Angelo,' said Angelo, and passed the bottle to the man in the hole.

Half a minute later his voice had become warm and friendly. 'Spanish brandy!' it said. 'I've changed my mind. I'm going to live for a hundred years. Where did you get it?'

'It formerly belonged to a German officer. I acquired it by good fortune.'

'My honest co-belligerent! I drink to you with enthusiasm.'

Angelo was deeply touched. 'Thank you very much. That is most kind of you,' he said. 'May I ask to whom I have the honour of talking?'

'My name's Telfer.'

'An officer?'

'A substantive lieutenant, a temporary captain, and an acting major: three in one, divisible yet not divided. It's a trinity of officers that you have rescued, my dear St. Bernard.'

'My name is Angelo,' Angelo repeated.

'Then you were well christened. Take a drink from your own bottle, and tell me how it all happened.'

Encouraged by the brandy, Angelo told his story at considerable length, and when at last he had finished he was disconcerted by Major Telfer's silence. He waited and repeated his concluding sentences; and still there was no comment, no reply. Nervously he thought that Telfer might have fainted, and reaching into the hole he grasped him by the shoulder and gently, then more forcibly, shook him.

Telfer was sleeping soundly, but Angelo succeeded in waking him. He apologized very handsomely for falling into a doze during what must have been a most interesting story.

A few minutes later he said, 'I'm feeling sleepy again, and I don't want to go to sleep. I don't believe it would be a good thing in the circumstances. What can you do to keep me awake?'

'Shall I talk to you about my early life?'

'No, don't do that.'

'Would you like me to sing?'

'That will depend on your voice. I don't want to be soothed.'

'I sing rather loudly,' said Angelo, 'and I have a good memory. Do you like Verdi?'

'Very much,' said Telfer.

'I also.' And after a little thought Angelo sang the duet of Manrico and Azucena from *Il Trovatore*; which inappropriately began, '*Riposa, O madre*.' Then, more suitably, he doubled the Conte di Luna and Manrico: '*Tace la notte*,' observed the Count; '*Deserto sulla terra*,' replied the other.

'And now,' said Telfer, 'let us each drink a little brandy. You have a splendid voice, it keeps me wide awake. — Drink up, and sing on.'

'*Libiamo, libiamo ne' lieti calici*,' sang Angelo, and then he sang fragments, large or small, of *Aïda*, *Otello*, and *Un Ballo in Maschera*. He sang a couple of songs from *Falstaff* and most of *Rigoletto*. His throat grew rough but his memory did not fail him. Telfer praised him judiciously and encouraged him as though he were a horse. They finished the brandy.

Dawn rose slowly with a grumbling wind, and when the sky about the eastern mountains was no darker than a grey-goose-wing, and Angelo had no more voice than a goose, they heard in the distance a rattling noise on the road, and presently a Bren-carrier came in sight. Because Angelo was stiff with cold he had difficulty in getting to his feet and raising his arms in recognizable surrender; and for a moment or two he was in some danger of being shot. Then one of the carrier's crew came forward, covered by its gun, and as soon as he heard Telfer's voice appreciated the situation correctly and signalled to his comrades.

Within a few minutes the jeep had been set on its wheels, and a tow-rope attached to the carrier. One of the soldiers took the steering-wheel and the jeep was hauled on to the road. With clay-cold limbs and a face as grey as an old sandbag Angelo sat huddled in the back seat, and as well as he could supported Major Telfer, who was colder than he and white as marble. Slowly, for the steering-gear had been damaged, they drove southward. It began to rain again.

CHAPTER VIII

MAJOR SIMON TELFER of the 2nd Carabiniers (The Duke of Rothesay's Dragoon Guards) was a healthy young man, tall of stature, with a lean face that grew a large fair moustache, who had originally joined the Army in order to play polo for his regiment. He quickly achieved his ambition, and when war broke out he had a handicap of six goals and grave anxiety about the cumulative products of concussion, from which he had suffered a good deal. Two years of arduous campaigning in the Desert, however, had done him a world of good, and he was now — save for the effects of severe exposure, a broken collar-bone, a sprained ankle, and a lacerated temple — in excellent shape and spirit.

He had lately transferred from his own regiment to a less formal body known as Force 69. There were several such irregular formations in the British Army, and all who belonged to them were regarded with greenest envy by the disciplined majority that remained in regimental employment and were subject to a constant supervision, standing orders, and regular administration. The members of Force 69 were, from time to time, required to risk their lives in strange adventure. They made perilous voyages to hostile islands in fragile craft that amateur sailors navigated; they had reconnoitred, by routes that camel-ribs signposted, the farthest Libyan oases; they dropped by parachute on mountainsides in Albania; they drove their jeeps through the enemy's lines to join Partigiani in the Apennines — and so on and so forth, but they never drilled, they avoided contact with senior officers, they grew beards if they felt inclined to, they rarely returned a parade-state, they cocked a long snook at the bureaucracy, and in a world of dour obedience congratulated themselves every morning on the freedom they enjoyed, while their friends with equal regularity complained loudly of the chicanery and favouritism by which they had won it.

To join and remain in Force 69 it was necessary that an officer should be naturally brave, uncommonly resourceful and know a great number of people by their Christian names. In common with all other civilized armies the British Army used many thousand tons of paper to promulgate its orders, instructions, plans and policies; but that was merely to conform with modern practice and provide a livelihood for elderly majors and disabled captains in areas remote from battle. Operations in the field were governed otherwise, and decisive action was taken only in consequence of something that General Oliver or Colonel Peter had said to Dicky This or Nigel That. The executive order usually wore the look of a friendly suggestion, and the officer who loosed the fury of a barrage or led his squadron to death and glory was almost certainly responding to the syllables that had dripped upon his infant face with the water of baptism, or with which he had been labelled in the Lower Fourth. Battles were fought and won by Christian names — and many privileges were granted to those who knew them.

Simon Telfer knew at least three hundred, and as in addition to that good fortune he was brave without effort, and unusually resourceful, he had been allowed to join Force 69.

The jeep that he had capsized he had taken by piracy, only a few hours before, from a German officer who had captured it in ambush from a British patrol on reckless reconnaissance. Simon had been returning from a mission to partisans in the Abruzzi, and though he had used great caution during most of his journey, the taking of a jeep had filled him with exuberance and exuberant driving had lifted him off the road. Good fortune, however, had not wholly deserted him, for he soon discovered that the carrier patrol which came to his rescue belonged to a battalion commanded by an old friend called Michael. The battalion was at present holding a slight salient not far from Alfedena, and shortly after their discovery Simon and Angelo were brought safely to its advanced headquarters.

Their appearance created no particular surprise, for

Michael, a lieutenant-colonel at twenty-seven, had long
since grown accustomed to the unheralded entrances and
sudden exits of his fellow-actors in the war. Simon's
broken collar-bone was quickly set, and he was given
what comfort could be provided in a ruined village in the
mountains. Angelo received equal hospitality because
Simon loudly proclaimed that he, with his singing and his
brandy, had saved his life. The Intelligence Officer of
Michael's battalion, moreover, regarded him as a welcome
guest, for Angelo was willing to talk at great length about
the Germans' battle-positions and life in their army.

A little after noon on the following day, in a wintry sun-
shine, they were sitting outside the house in which Michael
had established his headquarters. It was a house of two
storeys, painted salmon-pink. The front of it was splinter-
scarred, an upper window had been raggedly enlarged by
a shell, a chimney knocked off by another, and the roof
holed. It wore the dumb and sorrowful expression of a
man who had been beaten by hooligans.

While Michael and Simon were casually gossiping, and
the Intelligence Officer corrected a typewritten copy of
the information that Angelo had given him, Angelo sat
and regarded them in grave perplexity. A pause in the
conversation gave him the opportunity for which he had
been waiting.

'Excuse me, please,' he said, 'but do you no longer wear
uniform in the British Army?'

They turned and gazed at him with mild astonishment.
'Of course we wear uniform,' said Simon. 'What sort of
stories have the Germans been telling you?'

'I have heard no stories,' said Angelo. 'I have been
looking at your trousers.'

Michael and Simon wore sheepskin jackets, the Intelligence Officer a fisherman's blue jersey. Tied round their
throats were brightly coloured scarves. Michael was bare-
headed, Simon wore a bandage, the Intelligence Officer a
stocking-cap of rakish pattern. All three wore corduroy
trousers: Simon's were grey, the Intelligence Officer's
green, and Michael's a dark brown tucked into gum-boots.

With a transient curiosity they considered their own and each other's small-clothes.

'Oh, yes,' said Michael. 'I see what you mean.'

'We do dress informally at times,' said Simon, 'but comfort is the main thing, isn't it?'

'It began in the Desert,' said the Intelligence Officer.

'In Africa,' said Simon, 'one felt a resurgence of individualism.'

'I would give a great deal to be there now,' said Michael.

Simon agreed with him. 'There's a lot to be said for Libya.'

'It's ideal country for a war,' said the Intelligence Officer. 'You can't do any damage there, except to yourself and the enemy.'

'One had a lot of freedom in Libya,' said Simon, 'but the landscape needed colour to give it variety: that's where we began to wear chokers.'

'It's a pity we had to come into Europe,' said Michael. 'I enjoyed myself in the Desert.'

'One had so many friends there,' said Simon.

'Everybody knew everybody else,' said the Intelligence Officer. 'Of course it was uncomfortable from time to time, but on the whole — '

'At its best,' said Simon —

'Taking it all round,' said Michael, 'it was good.'

For a full minute they sat in silence, revolving behind reminiscent eyes nostalgic thoughts of quivering heat, engulfing dust-storms, and immensities of barren soil; till Angelo, in a voice hoarse with amazement, interrupted.

'Excuse me, please,' he said again, 'but are you truthfully saying that you enjoyed the war in Libya?'

'In a way I think we did,' said Michael. 'Didn't you?'

'It was fearful, it was horrible!' cried Angelo with passion. 'I hated every single hour of it!'

'What bad luck,' said Michael.

They looked at him curiously. They tried to be sympathetic, but they were puzzled by his attitude and disappointed in him. Simon had said he was one of the best fellows alive. 'He carries Spanish brandy and his voice doth murder sleep. He sat in the mud and sang to me all night, and saved my life.' That was what Simon had said, and now Angelo was talking about their war in Africa with embarrassingly bad taste. Foreigners were full of complexities and self-contradiction, they felt.

Then Simon's attention was taken by a pair of newcomers. 'Who,' he asked, pointing to the end of the village street, 'are your enterprising friends?'

The farthest houses had collapsed into grey mounds of rubble, and in a space between them, as if in a small ravine, stood two soldiers of savage and repellent aspect. Their faces were blackened, they wore stocking-caps like the Intelligence Officer's, their battle-dress was dark and filthy, over their shoulders were slung tommy-guns, and one had a long knife in his belt, the other a bludgeon. Each carried, dangling to the ground, a dead goose and a turkey.

'They're two of my battle-patrol,' said Michael. 'Corporal McCunn and Private O'Flaherty, I think. — Come here!' he shouted.

The two soldiers, as though overcome by a sudden shyness when they saw their Commanding Officer, had halted between the ruined houses; and now, with an assumption of careless ease, were retreating in the direction from which they had come. They stopped reluctantly when they heard the Colonel's voice, looked round, and with a philosophic acceptance of the situation marched towards him.

'Sir,' said Corporal McCunn.

'Where did you get those birds?'

With a far-away look the Corporal thought for a moment and answered, 'From an old farmer.'

'In a small farm on the hill beyond,' said Private O'Flaherty. 'He was very grateful to us, sir.'

'For liberating him and his family from the Germans,' said Corporal McCunn.

'He was that grateful,' said Private O'Flaherty, 'that he told us we could liberate as many as we needed of his geese and his turkeys, sir.'

'But we weren't wanting to be greedy,' said the Corporal, 'and we couldn't easily carry more than the two apiece.'

'So we just liberated the four of them, and that's the whole truth of it,' said Private O'Flaherty.

'I see,' said Michael. 'Well, I'm glad you weren't greedy.'

'If we'd happened to have any money with us,' said Corporal McCunn, 'we'd have been glad to pay for the birds.'

'Now don't overdo it,' said Michael. 'Your story, I mean, not your goose. A goose like that needs to be cooked for about an hour and a half.'

'Thank you, sir.'

'I am very fond of those two,' said Michael when they had gone. 'I have a good battalion, and my battle-patrol is quite excellent. In private life Corporal McCunn used to sell children's toys in a shop in Glasgow, and O'Flaherty was a steward in a passenger-ship. After earning their living by cosseting people, and persuading people to buy things, they find spiritual refreshment in their present occupation — which gives them a chance to assassinate people.'

'Excuse me,' said Angelo, 'but when I went to school in Siena, I was taught that to liberate means to set free. Is that so, please?'

'It is,' said Michael.

'And in September we were told that you and the Americans were coming to liberate Italy.'

'And now we have come,' said Michael coldly.

'But those soldiers, who said they had liberated the turkeys and the geese, had taken a most drastic way of giving them their freedom. I do not deny that turkeys and geese, especially in winter, lead a very dull and disagreeable and apprehensive life. So do many human beings, however, and if the Allies have decided that all who are unfortunate can be liberated only by wringing their necks — '

'I'm afraid I can't spend the whole day gossiping,' said Michael, and stood up. 'I have work to do.'

'So have I,' said the Intelligence Officer.

'I usually take a short drink about this time,' said Simon.

Angelo was left alone with his troubled thoughts. He got up and walked slowly down the village street, then stopped to look at a house which had been hit by a bomb. It had been a good house, with a portico and pillars and well-proportioned large windows, but now, cut diagonally in two, a half of it lay in a heap of untidy masonry as though it had been caught and melted by a draught of infernal flame, and run to waste. On the remaining fragment of an upper floor stood a carved arm-chair upholstered in wet red velvet.

A passing soldier of Michael's battalion, a burly man with a great red face, also stopped to look at the wasted house. He gave Angelo a cigarette, and said, 'It makes you think, doesn't it?'

'It does,' said Angelo.

'In the olden times, before people like you and me were educated and enlightened,' said the soldier, 'they used to go to war to capture towns, and when they had captured them, they enjoyed them. There was drink, there was loot, and there were women. The victorious army went into winter quarters and had a good time. But nowadays we're fighting for something fancier than towns. We're fighting for ideas about freedom and justice, so we despise mere stone and mortar, and consequently knock it to bits. So the wine runs down the gutters, and the women pick up their skirts and scuttle, and the conquering soldiers don't find any winter quarters. We're living in uncomfortable times, and you've got to admit it.'

'Would you say that this village had been liberated?' asked Angelo.

'Oh, properly liberated,' said the soldier. 'There isn't a roof left in it.'

'It makes me sad to look at such destruction,' said Angelo. 'I am Italian, you see.'

'You ought to have a look at Coventry,' said the soldier. 'It was a big town, as towns go in England, and they laid most of it as flat as a plate. That's where I come from: Coventry.'

'And surely it made you very sad to see your native town in ruins?'

'Sad?' said the soldier. 'Don't you believe it. I'm a bricklayer by trade, and as soon as this war's over, and I get back to Coventry, I'm going to be worth my weight in gold.'

'You Englishmen are very practical,' said Angelo in a melancholy voice.

'Yes and no,' said the soldier. 'We're more practical than many, I grant you, but we fall short of perfection, there's no denying that. Now I'm a bricklayer, as I've just told you, and consequently I'm not only valuable but important. But is my importance recognized? No. Would I myself live in one of the houses that I built before the war, or that I'm going to build after the war? No. And why not? Because they were shoddy, and they'll be shoddy again. I used to live in a house that was built in seventeen-sixty, when people built well because they thought it important to build as well as they could. — Now take my wife's eldest brother, he's a different case. He was a farmer, and he went to live in New Zealand. Why? Because he was a good farmer, and in 1930 England didn't believe that farmers were important, so England lost him. — Then there's a nephew of mine, he was never fit for honest work because of his kidneys, but he learnt to play the fiddle, and he played it well. And what's he doing now? Playing the sort of stuff that makes you sick to listen to, and earning thirty pound a week in a dance-band. — Now you see what I mean, don't you? As a people we can still hold our own, because in my opinion nobody's much good nowadays, and everybody's going down hill; but we're going slower than the rest. But I often feel we're not as good as we used to be, or as good as we ought to be, and the reason is that our feeling for what's really important is part-worn, and most of us don't know why it is important anyway. And nobody's really practical who doesn't recognize at sight that some things are valuable, and other things are trash. Here, have a cigarette.'

Angelo spent the rest of the day in solitary thought, and an hour or two before dusk was rescued from so depressing an occupation by a sudden storm of shells and mortar-bombs that fell upon the village. Ten minutes later the Germans made a small but resolute attack, which was energetically repulsed, and for some hours there was intermittent gunfire and sufficient excitement to put a stop to intellectual exercising. Shortly after midnight the noise diminished, and Angelo slept.

In the morning Simon Telfer decided that he was able to travel. His captured jeep had been repaired, and it was tacitly assumed that Angelo would go with him. Simon had not only taken a liking to him — despite his heretical views about the Libyan campaign — but acquired a possessive pride in Angelo's singing voice and his knowledge of English. With his broken collar-bone, moreover, he needed a driver. So Michael lent them a spade, and they set off soon after breakfast.

Only twice had Angelo to dig deeply, to extricate them from snowdrifts, and without untoward incident they reached a village near Piedimonte d'Alife where a detached company of Force 69 was then quartered. Simon immediately discovered that he was no longer a major. During his mission to the Abruzzi partisans a senior officer had arrived from England, and Simon in consequence had to revert to the rank of captain. But he had long since recognized that promotion in war-time was like a greasy pole, or a game of snakes-and-ladders, and was philosophical about the change; though Angelo was indignant.

Simon's reduction in rank, however, did not impair his friendship with useful Christian names, and he had no difficulty in arranging that Angelo should be attached to the Force as an interpreter. Angelo was given a suit of battle-dress, a small stipend, and a place in the sergeants' mess. His official adoption by the army of liberation pleased him immensely. A few qualms that he felt to begin with — the queasy offspring of his experience in the mountain village — he quickly put aside as unmanly and trivial, and he set himself zealously to acquire the sang-froid and practical outlook of the Englishman. Within a week or two he was putting on weight, and the sergeants' mess thought highly of him as a vocalist.

Because the detached company was enjoying one of its idle seasons, Simon was able to remain with it while his collar-bone mended, and under his patronage Angelo quickly extended his knowledge of England and the English.

Much of what he learnt surprised him. He had always heard that the English were an arrogant, wealthy, and aggressive people; and he was astonished to find that they thought of themselves as very mild and easy-going creatures, chronically hard-up, and habitually deceived or over-ridden by their continental neighbours. They did, however, take a pride in their sense of justice, and to Angelo this was quite incomprehensible; for he had often read of the many millions of Indians, Canadians, Australians, New Zealanders, Basutos, Zulus, Kikuyus, Scots, and Irish whom they held in slavery.

They were curiously heartless, he decided, for although they were far from home he never saw them weeping and sighing for their distant wives, their deserted lovers, and their half-forgotten children. They wrote, indeed, innumerable letters, but said remarkably little in them. They ate enormously, and were continually making jokes that no adult European could understand: Angelo did his best, but was forced to conclude that their sense of humour, though deceptively robust, was quite elementary. The private soldiers grumbled prodigiously and professed a fearful cynicism about the intentions, practice, and good faith of their Government; yet strangely continued to serve it with zeal and do their duty with alacrity. They appeared to become dirty very easily, for they were always washing themselves. They talked a good deal about fornication, but looked askance at the Americans for their excessive indulgence in it. They all regarded foot-ball as a more exacting and therefore more praiseworthy art than making love, and many of them preferred it.

Angelo one day persuaded Simon to speak of English politics. Did Simon, he asked, truly believe in democracy?

'Yes, I think I do,' he answered. 'It doesn't work very well, of course, but what does?'

'Would not the ideal government,' asked Angelo, 'be that of an autocratic ruler who was also a philosopher?'

'Not in England,' said Simon. 'No one would admit that it was ideal, in the first place, and in the second we regard philosophy as a rarefied sort of entertainment, like chess or the more difficult crosswords.'

'You are a Conservative, I suppose?'

'Yes,' said Simon, 'yes, I suppose I am. I have never actually voted, but then I am also a member of the Church of England, and except for an occasional wedding I haven't in fact been to church since I left school. The Conservative Party and the Church of England are rather similar in that respect: you can belong to both of them without doing much about it. — I belong to two or three very good clubs, now that I think of it, that I never use though I still pay my subscriptions. — But what I do believe in most devoutly is the party system, because when you get tired of the party in power you can always kick it out. You can kick it fairly hard, indeed, throughout its tenure of office. I should say that democracy is really represented by a party with a mind that knows how to act, a tender bottom that tells it when, and a well-shod electorate.'

'I find that very interesting,' said Angelo, 'but how are you going to ensure that your electorate can afford good shoes?'

'That's a problem, isn't it? Some people say that we shall have to work very hard and export everything we make; others maintain that we must work even harder, but buy it all ourselves; and others again declare that our real difficulty is to know what to do with our spare time. To tell you the truth, we're in something of a muddle, and that is just what you would expect if you knew us better. We have been in a muddle for so long that most of us now regard it as our normal environment. And probably it is.'

Angelo regarded him gravely. He did not like to say that he had studied at school the long course of England's history, and often heard his teachers expound and deplore the cold calculation, the Oriental persistence, the diabolic art of English statesmen through the ages. Muddle indeed! — But more recently he had discovered that the English hated to be asked about their history, for none of them remembered it. So tactfully he changed the subject and asked, 'Are English women very passionate?'

'Between their tennis-playing in girlhood and their later addiction to the card-table, there is a season during which they are not indifferent to love,' said Simon.

'But the war has affected their traditional way of life, has it not?'

'It has indeed. They have gone into the Services, they have gone into factories and offices. They have given up tennis altogether, and postponed their bridge.'

'And their season of love?'

'Love has adopted a war-time policy like that of the farmers,' said Simon. 'With equal enthusiasm it has cultivated both field and furrow; and assisted by the foreign troops now quartered in Britain it has ploughed thousands of hitherto neglected acres.'

Time passed agreeably. Thin blue skies and a hint of warmth in the morning breeze foretold the return of spring. On the southern slopes of the mountains the snow-line grudgingly retreated and exposed a wet black earth. Hail-storm and sleet-squall blew with a slattern's fury, but never lasted long. Winter was fighting a losing battle and retiring slowly to the north. Every day the sun rose a little earlier, and sometimes shone with a brief but splendid promise.

Simon one day proposed to visit some friends near Venafro, and invited Angelo to go with him. On the way there he spoke of a great air-assault that was going to be directed against the enemy's hitherto impregnable position at Cassino. All winter, in a frozen landscape like the mountains of the moon — but besmeared with blood and lashed by fire — the Allies had been fighting with a sorrowful heroism for possession of Monte Cassino, and now at last Cassino and all the Germans in it were to be blasted out of existence by the concentrated attack of a huge fleet of bombers. By noon of the next day, said Simon, Cassino would be merely a scar on the landscape. It was the fifteenth of March.

Simon's friends, whom he was visiting, were on the staff of a general whose camp was pitched on a wooded hillside. Angelo was by now on very easy terms with his English co-belligerents, for his command of their language persuaded them that he was of superior character to the majority of Italians; he had learnt to speak respectfully of the campaign in Libya; and Simon told everyone he met that Angelo had saved his life. Simon's friends invited him to have a drink, and he listened with great interest to what they were saying about the coming air-attack.

It began soon after breakfast on the following morning. They stood outside the mess-tent and watched the attacking fleet pass overhead, and listened to the rolling thunder and blunt reverberating echoes of a myriad bursting bombs. Hidden from sight by the mountains, Cassino was about twelve miles away as the bomber flew.

Presently they went in to drink another cup of coffee, and a flight-lieutenant described, with professional enthusiasm, the extraordinary accuracy of the bomb-sight by which missiles could be successfully aimed from prodigious heights at targets far below them. But a nervous member of the company made some comment on a drumming noise of aeroplanes directly overhead, and his uneasiness affected the others. They went out from the tent and again stared upwards at the sky. They were just in time to see the sunlight glinting on a shower of swiftly falling objects, and to throw themselves flat on the ground.

Only a few of the bombs exploded near them, and as soon as they had decided that the attack was not likely to be repeated most of them rose again, wiping stains of grass and mud from their battle-dress, with no graver injury than a shocked surprise. A young captain, however, an officer with a pale and intellectual cast of features, whom a large fragment of hot metal had missed by a few inches only, was so annoyed as to be openly critical of the flight-lieutenant who had spoken about the accuracy of aerial bombardment. But the flight-lieutenant explained that a good bomb-sight was still good though a navigator might bring it to bear on the wrong target.

'It is as a target that I am speaking,' said the Captain bitterly.

'You were very nearly hit,' said the Flight-lieutenant. 'You cannot deny that the bombing, as bombing, was excellent bombing.'

'Art for art's sake,' said the Captain.

'I admit,' said the Flight-lieutenant, 'that a bomb is no respecter of persons.'

'If persons are not entitled to respect,' asked the Captain, 'why are we fighting this war?'

'It is easy to criticize,' said the Flight-lieutenant.

'On the contrary,' said the Captain. 'For those who could criticize you with the authority of personal experience are too often left speechless.'

They stared at each other with some dislike, until another officer asked, 'Where are Simon and his Italian friend? Has anyone seen them?'

They were discovered, close together, on a narrow shelf of the hillside. Angelo lay unconscious, having been clouted on the head by a flying clod as big as a tea-tray; and Simon with a disconsolate expression sat holding his left thigh which had been laid open by a bomb-splinter. Angelo was bleeding from the nose, and to a hurried examination Simon's wound appeared to be co-extensive with the damage to his trousers, which were torn from the knee to the haunch. An ambulance was quickly summoned and the two casualties, roughly bandaged, were removed to a field-hospital without delay. There it was soon discovered that neither of them was seriously injured, for Simon's wound, though fifteen inches long, was little deeper than a scratch, and Angelo was merely bruised, bewildered, and very angry.

'Do I, in any way, resemble Cassino?' he asked Simon, as soon as he was allowed to visit him.

'There is no apparent similarity,' Simon answered.

'Then why was I bombed?'

'We all make mistakes from time to time.'

'We do not all carry bombs. To make a private mistake in your own house is one thing, but to make a public mistake with a bomb of two hundred and fifty kilogrammes is different altogether.'

'Year by year,' said Simon philosophically, 'science puts more power into our hands.'

'So that we may throw bombs at the wrong people?'

'Science like love,' said Simon, 'is blind.'

'I prefer love,' said Angelo. 'It makes less noise.'

He was still angry, and not to be pacified until Simon told him that in a day or two they might be going to Sorrento. Simon was on terms of friendship with the senior surgeon of the hospital — they called each other by their Christian names — and his contention that such wounds as theirs would heal most quickly in convalescence by the sea had not been seriously disputed.

Angelo was momentarily pleased. 'It is very beautiful in Sorrento,' he said. 'Many people used to go there for their honeymoon.' — And then he fetched so deep a sigh that Simon asked him what the matter was.

'For the last two days,' said Angelo, 'I have been thinking about nothing but bombs, and whenever I fell asleep I had a nightmare. And now I have begun to think about my sweetheart Lucrezia and the honeymoon we cannot have until the war is over; and that is worse than bombs, for I shall not be able to sleep at all. It is very difficult to be happy.'

CHAPTER IX

'LET us maintain our good temper,' said the Count. 'Let us keep a sense of proportion. There are seven deadly sins and only two redeeming virtues, which are faith and love — '

'I should include good manners,' said the Marchesa.

'So should I, if I had my way,' the Count agreed. 'I should include tolerance, a judicious taste in music, a preference for the baroque in architecture, a certain refinement in the apprehension of physical beauty and one's responses to it, a talent for imparting gaiety to conversation, and so forth. These would all be redeeming virtues if I were the ultimate authority and final court of appeal; but there's no use pretending that I am any such thing. It has been decided otherwise, and we have to recognize facts. The essential virtues are two, the deadly sins are seven, and therefore the virtues are in a permanent minority and we should not be surprised that sometimes they suffer a heavy defeat. We should not, that is, be so destructively surprised as to fall into a state of wrathful despair before the scene of a human battlefield from which the virtues have fled shrieking in dismay, and on which the triumphant sins for a little season strut and revel, maltreat their captives, and quarrel among themselves. It is tiresome, I admit — '

'My maid refuses to leave Rome,' said the Marchesa. 'The perfume that I have used for ten years is unobtainable in this paltry village, and to-day the hairdresser, clumsy to begin with, was finally insolent. The few clothes that I was able to bring here now seem like a vulgar admirer whom one has allowed to perform some opportune but regretted service: their excessive familiarity has become revolting. There is, moreover, no company in Montenero, and what is hardest of all to bear, you have turned philosopher.'

'No, no,' said the Count. 'That is too kind of you. I explore the fringes of thought, I contemplate human affairs with a certain interest, but that is all. I am not yet conscious of a complete and orderly system of cognition.'

'You should be glad of that,' said the Marchesa, 'for it is sheer misfortune to be much aware of any system, whether physical, political, or merely plumbing. The plumbing in this house has now finally collapsed, and no one can be unconscious of the fact. And except for a few hours in the middle of the day we live in such gloom as only good eyesight can distinguish from total darkness.'

'It was the Germans who cut off the electric light,' said the Count.

'And an English or an American bomb that cut off the water. If our old friends and our new ones both remain in Italy, we shall soon have nothing left at all.'

'And then upon the stony soil of our destitution the seven deadly sins may dwindle and faint with hunger, and by strenuous cultivation the redeeming virtues will show their heads again.'

'Do you look forward to the prospect?'

'No,' said the Count, 'I cannot bear to contemplate it. — I am going for a walk.'

'I shall not come with you,' said the Marchesa, 'for I cannot afford such an expense of shoe-leather.'

The little town of Montenero di Roma, where they had been living in seclusion for several weeks, had formerly been a popular resort of tourists. There were several good churches in it, the largest being that of Santa Maria Maggiore, which had an elaborate façade and contained four large paintings of the Holy Family by Luini. There were also a palace that had once belonged to the Orsini, in which there were frescoes by Ghirlandaio, and two restaurants well-known for their cooking. The municipality had built a new sulphur bath below the ruins of that which had been more splendidly created for Diocletian, and but for a surplus of statuary the public gardens would have been charming. The main street, a narrow thoroughfare smoothly paved, curved like a half-hoop round the hill, and in summer time the houses were decked with red geraniums that grew in little balconies of wrought iron beneath their windows. From many places there were broad views of the Campagna, far below and reaching spaciously to the north, and of St. Peter's dome, small in the distance, in the flat haze of Rome. The town was built upon a wooded hill-top in a broad bay of the mountains, and above it, on either flank and behind it, rose their wrinkled sides. But the wrinkles were hardly visible in winter, when the snow filled them.

How cold it was! thought the Count. How different from the warm seasons when tourists had filled the streets with their clamorous tongues from Birmingham and Bremen and Minneapolis! Heigh-ho for progress: what a lost beatitude that genial vulgarity now appeared!

The sun shone with a pallid glitter, and the snowy breath of the wind came shrilling down a *salita* on the right-hand side of the street. The Count turned up the collar of his coat: it was lined with Persian lambskin, tightly curled. Two plump and red-legged girls with scanty dresses ran past him, laughing loudly. An old man stood in the gutter, begging, but seemingly indifferent to the frozen air. A burly fellow with a bare head and his shirt open to the waist stood in the mouth of a lane and shouted to a friend on the other side of the street . . . There were gradations of sensibility, thought the Count, and no one should generalize on social affairs until everyone had been furnished with an equally efficient circulation of the blood.

The smoothly paved and curving street led to the Piazza Santa Maria where, in the tourist season, a fountain had risen from the triple source of three dolphins' mouths and splashed the generous forms of two nereids clinging to the knees of a benignly bearded Neptune. There was no fountain now, and the basin was half-full of dirty snow. Printed posters, signed by the German commandant, defaced the columns of Santa Maria Maggiore on the north side of the square. There was a scattering of German soldiers among the idly moving people. — 'And how superfluous and out of place they are,' murmured the Count with a sudden distaste for their strong but awkward figures. The Italians, the several score of them who loosely filled the piazza, were doing nothing in particular to justify their existence, but nothing at all to perturb it. They were talking and gesticulating, they were contemplating eternity and abusing the present, they were behaving like the digits and fronds of a great anemone that reasonably filled its own sea-cove; but the Germans were manifestly a foreign growth and stood out like proud flesh.

Their alien condition became still more obvious when a senior officer approached in company with a person in civilian clothes who walked with the self-conscious strut of someone whose importance was considerable, but not long established. His hands were clasped behind his back — though with difficulty, for his arms were so short that his fingers barely met each other — and his head had been characteristically moulded by a Teutonic pelvis. They crossed the square, and with a harsh contraction of their muscles the soldiers stiffened to attention and saluted as they passed. In the north-east corner of the square, near the church, there was a little shop whose proprietor sold silversmith's work, intaglios, and reputed relics of the Etruscans' art. The officer and his civilian friend paused for a few seconds to look through the window, then went inside.

The Count knew by sight most of Montenero's German rulers, but these were strangers, and beneath a small cloud of anxiety he was wondering who and what they might be when he caught a glimpse, in the shadowed portico of the church, of a tall and unforgettable figure. The figure had swiftly vanished, presumably into the church, but the Count had no doubt as to who it was.

It was Fest, his mysterious visitor whom he had not seen since the night when he had been nearly suffocated in the Marchesa's house above the Piazza di Spagna. — Circling a stolid group of dark-clad peasants, narrowly avoiding a running child, dodging between idle talkers, the Count hurried across the square and ran up the steps of the church. There was no one in the wide porch who looked

99

like Fest. He pushed open a creaking door and went in.

Before one of the side altars a priest in a shabby white chasuble was marrying a thin young man to a plump young woman in the presence of fourteen of their friends and relations. On the steps of another altar a kneeling girl had been so overcome by fear or grief that she crouched like a beaten child, leaning against the wall, her shoulder and her yellow head on the black stone. The Count passed her, then paused and looked discreetly back. She was a pretty girl. Poor creature, he thought, it is the pretty ones who suffer most. But then he caught sight of another woman who was by no means pretty, nor ever had been in all her fifty years of unfulfilment, and on her hatchet face, as she lifted her squinting eyes to the darkness under the roof, there was a misery so forlorn and unrelieved that the Count looked hurriedly away and muttered to himself, 'No, no, I was wrong, I was very wrong. *Dio mio*, how unhappy it always makes me to come into a church.'

He walked round again, to make sure that Fest was not there, and while re-passing the wedding-group he observed that the bride, though young, had a hard and greedy look, and the bridegroom, but little older, was nervous and ill-tempered. The walls of the chapel in which the ceremony was taking place had been painted with graceful exuberance to represent the marriage at Cana in Galilee. The principals in the picture, and all their guests, were strikingly handsome. Shrugging his shoulders, the Count bent and whispered to an astonished woman, a cousin of the bridegroom's father, 'We must be patient, we must be very patient.'

The creaking door closed behind him, and he breathed more happily the colder air outside. But he wondered, with annoyance at his failure to find him, where Fest had gone. And then he saw him.

He saw a figure come gently but swiftly into sight at the north end of the portico, and flatten itself behind the farthest column. He was about to go forward and claim acquaintance, when the figure withdrew its right hand from its overcoat pocket and swung it slowly back like a man who is about to throw, very carefully, a rubber ball to his little boy. With a sudden pulse beating in his throat the Count looked outward, in the direction of the projected throw, and saw that the German officer and his square-headed civilian friend had newly come out of the shop where intaglios and objects of reputed Etruscan art were sold, and for a moment stood in conversation.

The percussion bomb burst at their feet, and within a second another had followed it. The Germans fell with a curious violence, as if trying to leap away from or over the explosion, and the shattered windows of the shop flung upon them a wild confetti of broken glass. The Count felt a sea-sick rising of his tripes, and in a slow horror looked round again at the figure behind the left-hand column. Fest recognized him and turned so that the Count saw his monocle of clouded tortoiseshell and his smiling lips. With a courteous gesture Fest raised his hat, and then, swift as a sprinter starting his race, vanished round a corner of the church into an alley that steeply descended to the lower parts of the town.

The explosion of the bombs had first thrown the crowd into a wild confusion during which people screamed loudly, ran hither and thither, and waved their arms about in a dark fluttering of limbs and garments that looked like the frightened rising of a cloud of rooks. But soon their panic-movement was seized and held, their legs were haltered and their thoughts captured by over-mastering curiosity. With a force like gravity curiosity drew them all, their scattered circumference gathering tightly in, to the bloodstained doorway of the shop that had sold Etruscan statuettes to tourists.

The Count moved slowly at first, yielding reluctantly to a horrible attraction, but when other spectators began to push him aside and unfairly thrust themselves in front of him, he became insistent on his equal rights and struggled for a good place with the best of them. He was entirely taken by surprise when a cry of alarm went up and the crowd again began to run. The Germans had acted promptly, and, now, in a very methodical manner, were dealing roughly with the sight-seeing inhabitants of Montenero. The Count offered no resistance to arrest, but while one German soldier seized him by the arm, another hit him on the head with a rifle-barrel.

He appeared to recover consciousness fairly soon, but for some time took no interest in his surroundings. When he did he found himself, with twenty or thirty other men, in a classroom in an infants' school. A score of little desks stood on the floor, and the walls were gaily decorated with a fresco of the farmer's year. On a blackboard, in large white figures, there was a simple sum in addition. Concussion had left him with a headache, but the Count's mind was now clear, and quickly it filled with apprehension and dismay when he perceived that all his companions — or all but one — were in a state of extreme dejection. Some were quietly weeping, others noisily expostulating to friends who paid no attention, and a few sat on the floor in a silent surrender to grief that reminded him of the girl in church. The one person who retained his composure was an elderly small man with a red nose, a scanty combing of dyed hair across his half-bald head, and a well-worn but decent suit of professional black. The Count knew him slightly. His name was Toselli, and he was a retired school-teacher. The Count beckoned, and Toselli joined him in a corner of the room beside the blackboard.

'What is the explanation of all this?' asked the Count. 'What has happened, and what is going to happen?'

'Several things and one thing,' answered Toselli. 'What has already happened is a tangle of events, what is going to happen is a single event. At six o'clock to-morrow morning we are going to be shot.'

'But why?'

'To expiate the murder of two German visitors who seem to have been people of some importance. I have heard many suggestions as to who they were, but none of us really knows. From the behaviour of some German officers, however, which I observed with interest, I think the inference is justified that they were highly regarded by their own people, and I gathered that they had only recently arrived from Berlin.'

'But the man who murdered them isn't here,' said the Count.

'Oh no,' said Toselli. 'They are searching for him, of course, but if they catch him they will certainly not execute him in a hurry, like us. They will examine him, and interrogate him, for days and days. But we are people of no importance. We are no more than those chalk figures on the blackboard. We are merely integers in a German sum, and can be rubbed out as easily. One German life, they say, must be paid for by twelve Italians — so here we are.'

'There are more than twenty-four people here,' said the Count.

'They may have thrown in a few extra for good measure,' said Toselli carelessly. 'We were chosen without much consideration. There is little Ercole the boot-black, and there old Bartolomeo who is a great-grandfather. You recognize blind Roberto who begs in the streets, or used to? You, my dear Count, represent the nobility, and I the learned professions — but fortuitously, I assure you. We are a casual collection, and who cares though the sum is not exactly correct?'

'How can you speak so lightly of this appalling crime?' demanded the Count. 'You yourself are going to die; how can you sit and talk with such inhuman composure?'

'I have for long been indifferent to life,' answered Toselli. 'Why should I not be indifferent to death?'

'Surely they are not identical?'

'We may be subject to new illusions, or merely cease to be plagued by those with which we have grown familiar. I cannot suppose there is anything else to suffer or worse to fear.'

'I do not want to die,' said the Count.

'Neither do our companions here, yet who among them has had even the illusion of a happy life? They fear to die because they have been taught that life is good, and therefore they are alarmed by the thought of losing it; but if they had never heard such nonsense — '

'Their senses would have told them so, and reason convinced them.'

'The human senses are very poor guides to reality, for it is well known that one man's meat is another's poison. A Hottentot beauty would excite only derision in Rome, the table delicacies of Tibet would nauseate a French epicure, and where you shivered with the cold an Eskimo would throw off his shirt and complain of the heat. — No, my dear Count, you can repose no great trust in the senses, and as for reason, that is simply a product of time and locality. Reason can prove anything, but it does best of all at turning somersaults.'

The Count was silent for a few minutes, and then he said again, 'I do not want to die.'

'It is a word,' said Toselli, 'but is it anything more? Death may be only a name-plate on an empty house. Neither of us knows, and I do not care. My master is the philosopher Pyrrho, who was probably the wisest man who ever lived, and he knew nothing and knew that he knew nothing. A friend of his, a Greek of Byzantium, after dining with him one day went home and wrote, proleptically, his epitaph. It may be roughly translated like this:

'"And oh, dear Pyrrho! Pyrrho, are you dead?"

'"Alas, I cannot tell," dear Pyrrho said." '

But the Count was no longer listening. He was overcome by a plain and quite intolerable sorrow to think that he must die so soon. The bare and simple fact of living became unutterably dear to him, and the prospect of being shot implied so huge a deprivation that his natural fear was swallowed in a vast engulfing grief.

All the days of his life joined themselves together to make a Chinese scroll of the most rich and delectable entertainment; to tear it would be unforgivable. Yet the scroll did not lie, and many of the pictures, very clearly drawn, showed him haggard with pain. He saw himself swollen with the toothache and badgered by the ear-ache;

and he thought of those suffering days, so long ago, with wild regret. In spite of its aches and pains, life was good.

He saw in sharply drawn pictures the countless humiliations to which he had been subjected. Public snubbing and secret rebuff, a friend's forgetfulness, a girl's indifference: he had suffered them all and kindred shames beyond counting. Sleep-walking at seven, a clap at college, the piles at forty — he had fallen from his horse in the Pincio, he had choked on a fish-bone when dining with the Colonnas, he had gone to the races with his buttons undone — oh, the stabs of minor misfortune that drove so deep and left so hot a wound! And yet, though they were ten times as many, life would still be good.

He thought of graver torment. He remembered Angelo's mother, and the liquefaction of his heart when she died. He saw upon the scroll the death of later love and the dull hue of women's bodies when it was no longer possible to see them in the light of love. What arrant flesh they then became, a something that might be weighed but had no other meaning; and how lonely he used to feel, at such a time, to think he had lain with those cold strangers. But even love in its most melting warmth had never quite dissolved his knowledge of his loneliness, nor hidden totally the outlines of his immanent incommunicable singularity. Every man was alone, born in a caul of solitude that none could tear. He must live in the narrow confinement of himself, and into his cell disaster came to beat him cruelly. Yet life was good.

He wept, and as the tears ran down he remembered that other men had died. He recalled, with a sudden horror, how many and how many had lately died, and all had lost a life as dear to them as his. Chinese and Ethiopians had perished by the thousand, a multitude of Russians and Germans had gone back to clay with Englishmen and Poles, with his own fellow-countrymen, with Norwegians and Frenchmen and Jews — and never had he given a thought to the sad infinity of farewells they spoke, before the bullets parted them from their distracted lives. They had felt as he felt now, and their fate had never troubled him, never touched the hardness of his heart. That was the great vulgar sin of these dishevelled times, hardness of heart. — But he would die as he had lived, he promised himself.

'Do you believe in honour?' he asked Toselli.

'No,' said Toselli.

The Count dried his eyes. 'I have just perceived,' he said, 'that I am under a certain obligation of decency. During the last few years a vast number of men have died, and I have not pitied them. Therefore it would be indecent and wrong to pity myself. I shall go to my death unweeping.'

'I see no occasion for tears,' said Toselli.

'I do,' said the Count.

'Nor, if it comes to that, for refraining from them.'

'Again I do.'

'The great world will certainly not weep for us, because it has grown too much accustomed to what was once called tragedy. Though men are still upset by their own misfortunes, they have acquired wisdom enough to be indifferent to others.'

'That is not wisdom,' said the Count.

Toselli yawned and lay down, and appeared to sleep. He tied a handkerchief round his eyes, for the room was brightly lit. Throughout the night a dynamo throbbed, and the unshaded lights filled the room with a radiance that threw quivering shadows. The door of the classroom had been taken off its hinges, and two soldiers stood in the opening. Other soldiers in heavy boots passed and re-passed in the corridor. The Germans had commandeered the school to serve as an emergency prison and accommodate some of the additional troops they had brought into Montenero. For most of the night there was a mingled noise of harsh voices, doors slamming, ponderous feet on wooden floors, and occasionally a nightmare-scream; but in the harsher coldness before dawn there was comparative silence. Then, with a sudden clamour, the prison woke to a simmering fury and the day's business began.

New snow had covered the school playground, but so thinly that feet printed it with black. Large flakes of snow were falling from a still darkness. A dozen soldiers with rifles stood at the gate, and there were two motor-lorries on the road outside.

The Italians were marched out in single file. Soldiers were on either side and dragged forward those who hesitated, passing them on as if they were tubs of water to put out a fire. The lorries were filled, and set off slowly through the darkness. In a whisper the Count repeated again and again, 'I had no pity for others, I owe none to myself.' He was so intent on believing this that he heard nothing of what the others were saying.

About two miles from Montenero, in the hillside some eighty yards above the road, there was an opening like a long and very shallow arch. It was between five and six feet high in its middle part, and the cave behind it was extensive. There was a little space of flat ground in front of it.

The lorries halted on the road below, and the Italians were dragged or driven up the hill to the narrow level in front of the cave. There were some German soldiers already there, and an officer with a powerful torch whose beam he swung slowly from end to end of the huddled line. Within the cave, shining erratically in its darker gloom, were other lights, and men moving behind them.

'How many of them are there?' demanded the officer with the torch.

'Twenty-eight,' answered the lieutenant in command of the escort.

'That's too many.'

The lieutenant did not reply, and the officer with the torch shouted, 'That's more than I want, I tell you!'

The lieutenant approached him, and they argued in low voices. Then he with the torch exclaimed loudly, 'I must have authority, that's all. I don't care how many I take, but I won't do it without authority. If you say it's all right — '

'It is,' said the lieutenant.

'Then for God's sake let's get a move on.'

He began to make a short speech to the Italians, but was interrupted by a fit of coughing. He coughed as if his throat were being torn, and spat in the snow. Then hoarsely went on with his speech. The Germans, he said, had improved the Hebrews' law of an eye for an eye and a tooth for a tooth. They had put up the price of German eyes, and required a dozen in payment.

At this point the philosopher Toselli, who was standing beside the Count, began to scream; and when a soldier clapped a hand over his mouth he bit it, and hacked the soldier's shins. In the darkness Toselli had caught a glimpse of reality, and lost on the instant his indifference to life and contempt for death. His example upset the other prisoners, most of whom also began to struggle and scream, and for a minute or two there was wild confusion. When order was restored they all turned their heads to listen to the noise, very loud in the gloom, of a motor-cycle climbing the hill.

The motor-cycle came to a stop beside the lorries, and the officer with the torch sent a soldier to see who had come and ask what he wanted. The soldier quickly returned with a dispatch-rider. The two officers, their shoulders touching, read his message by torchlight, and then the senior fell into another paroxysm of coughing.

When he recovered he announced, as though it were a matter of no importance, 'Your execution has been postponed. The actual murderer has been captured, and you will be taken back to Montenero to await a final decision as to what is to be done with you.'

He lighted a cigarette, but his throat was sore and he could not smoke it. He threw it away, and little Ercole the boot-black picked it up.

On the way back to Montenero the Count felt that his legs were made of green cheese, but his chest was like a barrel bursting full of new wine, and he could not restrain himself from talking very volubly to all his fellow-travellers, who listened to never a word, for all were talking with an excitement no less than his.

They were taken to the school again, and into the classroom decorated with pictures of the farmer's year. Shortly after their return the Count saw Fest. With a soldier on either side, and one behind him, he walked past the open door. His head was high, and he seemed quite calm. He still wore his monocle of clouded tortoiseshell.

Later in the day a squadron of Allied bombers attacked some German transport on the road near Montenero. A few of their bombs fell in Montenero itself.

CHAPTER X

MOVING briskly on his crutches, Simon Telfer was walking along a high cliff-road in Sorrento with Angelo beside him At the entrance to a large white villa, temporarily occupied by the military, stood a tall sentry, gravely still. As Simon approached he sprang to attention, with smart and sudden action clapped his rifle on to his left shoulder, and with a hard hand resounding on the small of the butt, saluted. At every movement a small thick cloud of dust rose from his clothing as though he were an ancient carpet that someone was beating with a cane.

From the cone of Vesuvius across the bay rose thick columns, densely spiralling, of purple smoke shot with a fierce flush or melting glow of pink. High into the tall and clouded sky they rose in oily whorls, until the upper wind caught and bent them suddenly, and sent them flying over the sea in a flat brown canopy from which descended the close volcanic dust. Oozing from the crater's lip and trickling down the upper slope of the mountain came scarlet rivulets, thick and slow, of molten lava. Below them, under clouds of evil smoke, the glaciers of iron-dark cinders crawled down hill, filling the hollows, shirking heights and promontories, and crushing houses, tumbling pines and chestnut-trees in their sluggish flow.

Angelo coughed and blew his nose, and turning to shake his fist at Vesuvius exclaimed, 'This is too much! It is really too much!'

'I agree with you,' said Simon. 'Whatever else one may ask from a landscape, one does expect stability.'

Angelo smacked a puff of dust from either shoulder. 'My poor Italy,' he said. 'Now your stuffing is coming out.'

They were on their way to visit two of Simon's friends, brother-officers who were spending a few days' leave with an Italian family which, before the war, had occasionally acquired an American stepmother, sometimes an

English daughter-in-law. Their villa commanded a view of the clouded bay, and there were about twelve or fourteen people in a handsomely furnished but somewhat chilly drawing-room. A well preserved woman of fifty, with dark eyes and gleaming teeth, was loudly declaring as they went in that the eruption had been caused by a treacherous airman who had privily dropped into the crater of Vesuvius a bomb weighing two thousand kilogrammes, which had acted like a violent emetic.

A brisk debate on the weather followed, and everyone agreed that the exceptional severity of the winter, so unlike the temperate climate to which they were accustomed, was due to the air being shaken and battered by gunfire. A gentleman with a jaundiced eye said that the future of the world was dark indeed, for its atmosphere would be increasingly tormented by aeroplanes, ships in the stratosphere, and wireless; with appalling consequences.

'Everywhere the climate will deteriorate,' he said. 'On five days out of seven there will be rain or sleet, and neither corn nor fruit will ripen.'

An English daughter-in-law — pretty, plump and petulant — was describing to a lieutenant of the Royal Navy the hardships of life in Sorrento during time of war. A saturnine young man, passing with a bottle of Italian vermouth in one hand, a bottle of Plymouth gin in the other, halted and turned his head to listen. 'For many years to come,' he said, 'the world is going to be full of people competing for attention with stories of what they have suffered. And those who have suffered the least will have the most to say. It will be extremely boring.'

In a corner of the room Simon was looking at a replica, in bronze, of a whimsical piece of some ancient statuary's work that one of his friends had recently bought in Herculaneum or Pompeii. It represented a satyr making satyric love to a briskly co-operating nymph.

'Our follies,' he said, 'have such antiquity that it is almost impossible not to respect them.'

'But our virtues,' said his friend, 'are like a litter of

puppies untrained and delicate. Some are gun-shy, some will chase rabbits, and all require worming. Their noses cannot distinguish between a skylark and a grouse, their mouths are untaught, and most of them will be carried off by distemper.' — With his forefinger he drew an arabesque on a dusty table-top, and added, 'There's brimstone in the air to-day. Oh, damn Vesuvius!'

Angelo took the bronze and looked at it with eyes that swam in unshed tears. 'Does it not make you sad,' he said, 'to think of all the beautiful girls there have been, whom we never knew and could not enjoy? To have missed so much: I can hardly bear it! I imagine them turning their heads so neatly on their little white necks to look at me as I come in, and their voices when they are soft and husky, and their slim round arms — and then I remember they are dead, they are the dust that the wind blows round the corner, and I am overcome by the cruelty of life.'

'You must look forward, not back,' said Simon. 'Think about meeting and marrying Lucrezia — '

'But there again I see the unfairness that rules the world!' cried Angelo. 'Because I am in love with Lucrezia I am faithful to her; or very nearly faithful. And therefore I am deprived of a hundred enjoyable experiences that a person less sincere, or not quite so sensitive as I, could quite easily obtain! It is wrong to suppose there are principles of natural justice in life, or that life is ever peaceful. Life is war, and we who are virtuous may well lose every battle but the last one.'

'That,' said Simon's friend with noticeable stiffness, 'is the prerogative of the English.'

'Because you are good?' asked Angelo.

'It is an attractive hypothesis,' said Simon.

'There was a time when we aspired to goodness,' said his friend, 'and the world regarded us as hypocrites. Then we decided to pose as realists; and the world said we were effete.'

'But why do you win your last battles?' asked Angelo.

'We are amateurs,' said Simon's friend with a noisy

yawn, 'and the amateur lasts longer than the professional.'

At night the molten lava, creeping slowly in blunt-headed streams, shone like wet silver, and the dark air smelt more strongly of sulphur. So long as the eruption continued Angelo was melancholy and given to superstitious fear or dubious philosophy, but as soon as the volcano recovered its equilibrium he regained his good spirits, and discovered the truth of the matter. Vesuvius had felt the need to purge itself, and having purged was better. There was the symbol. Now Italy must take heed of it, and would. And oh, the content, the relaxed and satisfied euphoria that follows a deferred and large purgation! Yes, he declared, the future was bright.

Some days later Simon received an official letter which informed him that he had now, as a result of his wound, been absent from duty for three weeks, and had in consequence been reduced in rank from captain to lieutenant. This was in accordance with an old-established regulation of the War Office which saved the taxpayer money and dissuaded junior officers from staying in hospital longer than was strictly necessary. It also discouraged unruly ambition; for the British War Office has always set its face against militarism.

Simon took a balanced view of his diminished status, made a hurried calculation, and thought it might save him a few pounds of income-tax; but Angelo was deeply mortified and for several days refused to speak English, which, he said, was the language of injustice and ingratitude.

Simon was in no hurry to return to duty until he heard that some part of Force 69 was about to begin training for a new operation, when he at once presented himself for medical examination, was declared fit, and promptly set out for Benevento, whither his company had lately removed. An elaborate secrecy enclosed their training programme, and Angelo, to begin with, had no part in it. But the general preparation for large events could not wholly be concealed, and as April vanished from the calendar and May came in, expectancy grew large and taut like a balloon plumping for the ascent.

The battle began a little before midnight on May the eleventh. From the mountains beyond Cassino to the lighted water of Gaeta's gulf a thunderstorm of gunfire bellowed among the hills and over the sea, and filled dark valleys with reverberant echoes. An army mustered from the five continents of the world advanced to the attack, to destroy the opposing army of Germany and its subject peoples, and to open the gates of Rome. On the Allied side there were Poles and Englishmen, Frenchmen and Scots, Irish and Welsh: that was the European contribution. There were New Zealanders who looked like Cromwell's Ironsides and fought with pride and professional severity: that was the Antipodean levy. There were small and merry highlanders from the mountains of Nepal, tall ones from the passes of the Afghan frontier, bearded plainsmen from the Punjab, the heirs of Rajput chivalry and Shivaji's Mahrattas: they were the voluntaries of Hindustan and High Asia. There was on the coast an American army enlisted from New England and California, from Oregon and Kansas and the Carolinas, and at the mountainous end of the line a Canadian corps: that was the New World's share in the venture. From the fifth continent there came an armoured division, some of English stock and some of Boer descent, with black auxiliaries, and panting for the signal to start a wild and huge array of tribesmen from the Atlas mountains; and the latter, who were compendiously known as Goums, were the *semper aliquid novi* out of Africa.

The Eighth Army had already won fame enough to make its story live, but none of its battles had been so fierce and hard as this, and the blood of many valiant men ran with the waters of the Rapido and the Garigliano to the Great Sea. In the mountains beyond Cassino the Poles were checked, and British troops and Canadians found the entrance to the Liri Valley held strongly against them. On the coast the Americans of the Fifth Army made progress, but slowly at first. Soon they would go like a river in spate, but to begin with their advance was hardly won. It was on the high hills near the middle of the line that the German defences were most decisively broken in the early days of the battle, and the troops who went through them, farther and faster than anyone else, were the wild men from Morocco: the Goums.

Quickly they created, not merely a salient pointing like a spearhead to the north, but a legend of fear and a fabulous renown. They worked in silence and by night, and terror was their ally. They killed with long steel blades, and in lonely farmhouses the women dreaded them for another reason. Many a German sentry lay headless behind their patrols, and many a woman, it was said, looking up to see the swart and narrow face of a Goum at the window, had miscarried on the spot. In the broad pathway of their advance German outposts betrayed themselves by the chattering of their teeth, and the *contadine* fled from evening shadows screaming '*I Marocchini, i Marocchini!*'

When the battle had been raging for nearly a fortnight, Simon sent for Angelo and said to him in a casual way, 'We are going to have a little party of our own. There is a rumour that the Germans are about to do something that we take a poor view of, and I'm going to see if I can put a stop to it. It will be quite a small party, but I've got permission to take you with us. You will be very useful, knowing your way about Rome as you do, and I thought you might like to come. We start to-morrow.'

'And where is your party going to be?' asked Angelo.

'In Rome,' said Simon. 'Didn't I make that clear?'

'But Rome is still occupied by the Germans!'

'That will add to the interest of it, don't you think? — Why, what's the matter?'

Before Simon could catch him, Angelo fell to the ground in a dead faint. Simon made haste to turn him over, to loosen his belt, to pour water on his face and chafe his hands. As soon as he showed signs of recovery, Simon gave him rum in an enamel mug, and Angelo sat up, pale and shivering.

'What is the matter?' Simon repeated with anxiety in his voice. 'Are you ill?'

Angelo stared at him with wide-open, terrified eyes. Never in his life had he heard a more fearful proposal than this calm suggestion that he should join a party of desperadoes to break through the German lines, and enter by stealth the enemy's citadel! The shock of hearing it had frightened the blood from his brain — and who, he thought with a passion of returning fear, who could blame it for retreating before so monstrous a prospect? Never, never would he consent to put himself in such agonizing jeopardy, and throw his life away to crown it! And yet, when he tried to speak, he could not find the words of refusal. He looked at Simon and thought: He and his friends are going, and they have asked me to join them because they regard me as a friend. They are very brave, they do not think deeply but they laugh a great deal, and in a careless way they are very kind: it is a good thing to have such friends, but O my God, what a price to pay! If I refuse to go, if I admit that I am too frightened, I shall lose their friendship for a certainty; and if I agree, and make myself one of them, I may very well lose my life, and how much good will friendship be then? What a choice for a May morning!

'Give me some more rum,' he said, and emptied the mug.

He gasped and shuddered slightly, but soon felt a warmth inside him like a great lusty visitor coming with a laugh and a heart-stirring greeting into a cold quiet house. That was excellent. The visitor was most welcome, and when he laughed again it sounded throughout the house, and lamps were lighted in every room. But then, surprisingly, the visitor took charge of the situation, and borrowing Angelo's vocal chords, his palate and teeth and tongue, addressed Simon in quite unforgivable terms and offered an explanation of the fainting-fit that was wildly mendacious. — It was the idea of seeing Rome again, long before he had considered the possibility of such happiness, that had keeled him over, he said. An emotional type was Angelo, quite unlike the English, and his lack of self-control must be forgiven him. — So said the rum-bold swaggering visitor, and a moment later, to make things infinitely and irretrievably worse, declared: 'And I shall, of course, be delighted to come with you. We are a band of brothers and nothing shall divide us!'

An hour later Angelo lay in his tent and felt his heart beating against his ribs like a funeral bell, with a slow and melancholy stroke. He had signed away his life, he was convinced of that, and in return for the indifferent friendship of a score or so of young men as callous as they were reckless — a friendship that would be long-lived if it lived for a week — he had done no more than ensure that his last week upon earth would be spent in a torment of gathering dread. Never a thought came into his mind that he could survive the adventure. Danger had always filled him with such awe that any danger had seemed all-powerful to destroy, and this was no common danger but stark peril for a hero to gamble with. He was self-doomed, there was no doubt of it, and he listened as he lay to his heart that beat a funeral-knell.

In the morning the face in his shaving-mirror looked at him so whitely, from such dark enormous eyes, that he was at first startled and then impressed by it. His cup of warm water grew cold while he studied it. It was the reflexion, he thought, of a tragic but romantic figure. It was the face, he told himself, of a man of destiny. It had caught its pallor from the coldness of fate, and he could not avoid his allotted task however deeply his eyes might mourn the necessity. — This perception did not exactly give him courage, but lent him a kind of resignation, or hypnotized his wilder fears, and let him pass the next few days without drawing much attention to his utter unsuitability for service with Force 69.

Simon, quickly promoted to captain again, was to command the foray. His party consisted of two subalterns and a score of men. They were all heavily armed, and though Angelo knew most of them fairly well, and had seen photographs of their wives and sweethearts that made him feel very much at home with them, he was deeply impressed by their appearance in battle-array. How little, he thought, their wives and sweethearts really knew of them.

They went first to Naples, and there before nightfall embarked in a very small ship for the port of Anzio. Fortunately the sea was calm, and nothing interrupted their passage. The starlit darkness was warm as new milk, and Simon, sitting under the lee of the deckhouse in a mood of pleasant anticipation, told Angelo what they were proposing to do.

Allied sympathizers in Rome had reported that the Germans were preparing to blow-up the bridges over the Tiber. The Allies, who were looking forward to pursuing a defeated German army across the bridges, would be seriously hindered by their destruction, and Simon's task was to prevent it. The circumstances, he said, would probably favour him, because the Germans would not explode the charges until they had withdrawn all but the last rearguard of their troops, and by then there might be some confusion in the city. There would be a period favourable for attack, and if he could strike in the very bull's-eye of opportunity, they might well be successful. They would enter Rome from the north. . . .

The canopy of the sky was wearing thin. The moths had been there, and through it in prickle-points shone the brilliant vacancy beyond. Nothing was real, thought Angelo. They were ghosts on a sterile sea, and there were holes in the sky. This mad adventure was certainly unreal, for only in the fantasy of a dream could he have embarked upon it. He listened to Simon with the accompaniment of a running prayer that he might wake up.

But in the morning, at Anzio, he had to admit the reality of the scene, though it was different from his expectation of it. The sun shone brightly on a calm sea and about fifty soldiers, stark naked and as brown as chestnuts, were noisily bathing in the clear boulder-strewn water on the outer side of the breakwater. The little harbour was full of strange craft, and mean were shouting, working, hurrying to and fro, with unceasing busyness. Inland the view was screened by a wall of artificial smoke, and a rumble of gunfire came from the invisible hills beyond it. The tall painted buildings along the water front, scarred and torn by shellfire, looked calm and decorative among their companion-trees. Though vibrant with activity, the scene was unexpectedly peaceful.

Simon marched his little company up the cobbled wharf through part of the town, and into a scrubby wood. The wood was thickly populated and strewn like the floor of a gigantic customs-shed with military stores in great variety and vast abundance. Wherever they went they saw little dumps of oil and food and ammunition. Shells here, cheese and pickles over there. Elsewhere blankets and barbed wire, pick-helves and canned peaches and more ammunition, and grenades in wooden boxes. The air also was crowded, and full of odours. It smelt of a sickly vegetation, of sweat and leather, of acrid smoke and dung. There were soldiers everywhere, working or sleeping, smoking and brewing tea and eating ration beef out of the tin. Many wore nothing but khaki shorts, and the sun had burnt their shoulders to flaming red or polished brown. Their common expression was a tough indifference, and their language was shocking.

Simon was shown a small unoccupied area in which his party might bivouac, and after he had given some necessary orders he walked idly towards Angelo, who was standing deep in thought at the edge of a large hole. A German shell, falling by chance on a store of ammunition, had exploded it and opened an untidy crater; and now in the loose earth of its circumference a border of scarlet poppies bloomed.

'After the last war,' said Simon, 'they took those flaming weeds for a symbol of remembrance. But the poppy is the flower of oblivion, and the poppy did its own work in its own way.'

'There are always poppies at this time of year,' said Angelo. 'I wasn't thinking about them, but about the Emperors Nero and Caligula, who were born here. In Anzio. I mean.'

'Had they any voice in the matter? They could no more choose their landfall than the soldiers who are here to-day.'

'Of course not. But in such a time as this it is refreshing to think about the lives of wicked Emperors. They sinned for their pleasure, and in good style.'

Ambulance-jeeps, laden with wounded men, came slowly down the road from the front of battle. The troops so long confined in the narrow acres of the bridgehead had now broken their perimeter and were fighting their way through a gap in the Alban hills to the Via Casilina. American soldiers from the main front, advancing through the flooded Pontine Marshes, had joined the beleaguered garrison in Latium, and both were striking tumultuously at the Germans' seaward flank. For the next few days Simon spent most of his time observing the battle at close quarters, but Angelo put off several invitations to join him, and passed the time in wistful melancholy on the sea-shore.

North of Anzio there are low cliffs of a soft stone that breaks easily into caves. Some of the caves had been enlarged, and soldiers were living in them. They spread their washing on the rocks, and the shore had something of a domestic look. Lying on the warm sand or swimming in the mild sea there were always soldiers, free from duty for a little while, making a brief holiday of opportunity. Gunfire seemed no more than thunder in the hills, and Angelo would swim out to sea and wish that he might meet a friendly dolphin. In classical times, as he had learnt at school, it was no uncommon thing for a young man to win a dolphin's regard and be carried on its back to some delectable island. But he wished in vain, and searched to no purpose the silver-sprinkled sea. The character of dolphins, like that of Emperors, had presumably suffered a change.

The day came when they must go forward with their adventure, for now the fall of Rome was imminent. For their transport Simon had procured two half-tracked German vehicles, captured from the enemy, and a suffi-

ciency of soft, long-snouted caps, such as were worn by the
Africa Korps, to give his party a rough disguise. At sunset
they embarked with their vehicles aboard a sheer-sided
ungainly craft with a blunt bow, and put to sea and
headed to the north under the rising moon.

Their landfall was a point on the coast some twenty
miles beyond the mouth of the Tiber, and they made it
in the darkness between moonset and dawn. A pair of
partisans, with two dim lanterns in line, guided them in.
Their vessel grounded on a shelving beach, the door in the
bow was lowered, and Simon's party in their vehicles
drove ashore. The partisans led them through a minefield and a wood. A couple of miles to the south there was
much excitement on the beach, for the Germans had discovered what appeared to be an attempted landing. Two
motor-gunboats had caused the alarm to divert attention
from Simon's invasion, and after manœuvring off-shore
at high speed and firing several thousand rounds of
coloured ammunition, they drew away and set their
course for Anzio again. Simon's party, by this time, was
motoring comfortably towards the farmhouse where he
proposed to go into hiding.

The vehicles were concealed, the soldiers brewed-up
and ate a hearty meal, then most of them lay down in a
barn and went to sleep. A guard was inconspicuously
posted, and Simon with one of the subalterns set off to an
appointed rendezvous. They had not long to wait.
Within half an hour two excited Italians appeared, who at
once declared that the Germans were in full flight from
Rome, and that Allied aircraft were now bombing their
transport on the main roads north of the city.

They knew nothing about the bridges over the Tiber
except that they were strongly guarded. The rumour was
still current that they had been prepared for demolition,
but now a counter-opinion declared that the Germans
had no intention of destroying them. A story was also to
be heard that some of the bridges had already been
blown-up, and both the Italians said they had been
alarmed during the night by loud noises that must have

been demolitions of some kind. — So much they told, with great pleasure and volubility, constantly interrupting each other and repeatedly breaking their narrative to describe with animated and expressive gestures the weary, hang-dog, and shamefaced air of the retreating enemy. What a contrast, they exclaimed, to the arrogance with which the Tedeschi had entered Rome, their bands a brazen triumph, their great boots thumping the road, and their stupid faces starched with pride!

Simon put many questions without getting much more information, and after some thought he said to his subaltern, 'I think we had better start.'

'I believe you're right,' said the subaltern.

They returned to the farm and roused the soldiers. Simon said to them: 'We're going to start in half an hour. So far as I can learn, the Hun is pulling out of Rome as fast as he can, so we haven't any time to lose. I think our two half-tracks, going as fast as they can in the opposite direction, will have a good chance of getting through. You look quite ugly enough, in those caps, to be mistaken for Germans, and till we get on the main road we'll take turns in leading so that we can all get a good coating of dust. We shan't fight unless we have to. If we're held up, we'll try to bluff and run. If we get separated, we'll continue independently to our rendezvous on the outskirts of Rome. Then we'll go to ground again until we've done a further reconnaissance. Is that quite clear?'

The soldiers briskly began to wash in the green water of a long stone trough. They propped-up fragments of mirror and shaved. They were quite calm, but their language, as they discussed their prospects and their commanding officer, was shocking. They themselves, it appeared, were shocked. Not by their language, but by Simon, who asked too shocking much from them, they said. But they took pride, as it seemed, in being so deeply shocked, and no one had a word to say against Simon himself. Not a shocking word. It was just the shocking demands he made.

'Shock me,' said a tall brown fellow with long hairy

arms and a long lean jaw, screwing his mouth to tauten the skin for scraping, 'shock me if that shocker gives a shock for any shocking Jerry that ever shocked. I'll be shocked if he does.'

'What about the shocking tea?' shouted another. So they brewed-up again, and quickly ate another hearty meal, then climbing into their open vehicles sat there as primly upright as if they had indeed been Germans.

To begin with they drove along a country road where there was little chance of meeting traffic. Two of the partisans had volunteered to go with them. On the landward side the country was lightly wooded, but towards the sea it fell gradually in broad uncovered slopes. They could see where they were going, and drove with confidence. But the country road led to the main road, the Via Aurelia, and they must use that for some three or four miles. Then, if they were fortunate so far, they could turn inland on a vagrant lesser route that served a rural traffic only, where they might hope to avoid interference and circumvent such minor obstacles as they would encounter.

A little distance from the Via Aurelia they halted under cover, and Simon with a sergeant went forward to regard the scene. – A German convoy was moving northwards at high speed, with long intervals between the lorries, and a battalion of infantry, immensely elongated, was on the march. Two staff-cars came in sight, travelling fast, and in succession overtook a heavy-laden lorry. The footsoldiers made way for them. Then quite suddenly, as if they had that instant crystallized in the bright air, three white-starred aeroplanes appeared at no great height above the road, and sped along it in a swift assassin's flight, and left behind them the roaring wash of their propellers, and dead men tumbling on the verges, and burning wreckage. Both staff-cars were hit, and leaping from the road turned somersaults into a field. The marching infantry scattered like minnows in a pool, save the sluggards who lay still. And a canvas-hooded lorry slewed sideways and stopped abruptly, then toppled over and palely flowered into shimmering grey-tipped flame.

Simon and the sergeant ran back to their vehicles, beckoned the drivers to start, and mounted quickly. The heat of the burning lorry scorched them as they passed it, and two soldiers bending over a wounded comrade looked up and shouted angrily. An officer who had belatedly brought a light anti-aircraft gun into action held up his hand against them, but Simon made a sweeping and dramatic gesture that persuaded him to stand clear. Half a mile farther on they passed three lorries, halted close together, and a corporal who stood on the road and abused the drivers. He also signalled them to stop, but Simon repeated his gesture with good effect.

They crossed a bridge that engineers were preparing for demolition. Red cakes of explosive lay on the parapet. Here they excited suspicion and three men pursued them for a few yards, one of them firing his revolver. Road and railway now ran side by side, and more engineers were tying small cutting charges to the rails. An officer stood at the roadside, in argument with another, pointing furiously at his watch. These also turned and stared with suspicious curiosity at Simon's troop, but did nothing more than stare. Ahead of them, marching wearily, was another battalion of infantry, but before they reached the leading files the partisan who sat by Simon pointed to the left, and with barely moderated speed they turned into a side road. Three soldiers at the corner were laying mines in the verges.

For some distance ahead the lesser road was empty, and all of them felt in their muscles a small but pleasant relaxation. All but Angelo, that is. Angelo, sitting with his eyes tightly shut, was praying that he might die without pain. His refusal to observe the situation was due to his realization that in no other way could he endure it. He had not opened his eyes since leaving the farm, nor did he open them when, some few miles from the Via Aurelia, the two vehicles came abruptly to a halt.

They were on a curving road with a wood to the right of it and a high bank to the left. Round the corner towards them, moving faster than their custom, came a herd of thirty or forty cattle. They were the great white cattle of the Tiber valley, standing as high as a Guardsman at their tallest, and immensely horned. They filled the road, and within a few seconds the vehicles were two islands, close together, in a turbulent milky sea. The partisan beside Simon stood up and exclaimed, 'They are being driven!'

Simon also stood up. 'Germans,' he said. 'I can see eight of them, and there may be more behind.'

He gave his orders: 'Two men and the driver stay in each truck. The rest of you get into the wood, quickly, and we'll take them from the flank and rear.'

Nimbly the men leaped out, and Angelo, buffeted by their movement, but with his eyes still grimly closed, asked faintly what the matter was.

'Just a little parcel of Jerries,' said someone.

The word was too much for his resolution. He could not sit and wait for death, but while strength to run was in him, he would run. He laid his hand upon the rail, and scarcely looking where he might land, jumped out.

His descent was negligible, for he fell astride the tallest ox in the herd. He pitched forward, and to save himself grasped the loose hide over its withers. The ox in great alarm struck sideways with its mighty horns, goaded a cow into movement, and found a space ahead of it. It made a ponderous and futile attempt to buck, then broke into a lumbering trot. Angelo held tightly on.

Still driven by the Germans behind, and excited by the soldiers in its midst, all the herd was moving more quickly now. The great ox thrust its way to the front, and by example and contagion increased the general pace. The herd stampeded.

In comparison with the half-wild cattle of the South American pampas, or fighting bulls on a Spanish ranch, its speed might have been considered slow; but to Angelo it seemed a wild and furious progress. He was tossed and shaken as if he had been abroad on some wild ocean. On either side of him, like the billows of a stormy sea

125

broken to white, were galloping shoulders and tumultuous pale haunches. Long gleaming horns were the naked spars of tall ships running before a gale. The broad beast under him rolled and plunged as though it were meeting confused and contrarious waves. He began to feel slightly sick, but as he was heaved further forward on the ox's back, he took a new grip on a loose roll of skin, and grimly kept his seat.

The great ox began to outstrip the rest of the herd, and turning suddenly from the road it entered the wood by a narrow path. Low branches struck cruelly as they charged beneath, and brambles tore at Angelo's legs. He lowered his head and shut his eyes again. All his muscles were aching with the effort to maintain his seat.

How long his ride had lasted, and how far he had travelled, he had no notion when at last the pace grew slower, the gallop became a trot, and the trot a walk. Angelo sat up and opened his eyes. They were approaching a farmyard, and in a cartshed two men and a woman were watching them. Spouting its steamy breath out of distended nostrils, foam dripping from its mouth and vast flanks heaving, the ox stood still. Angelo dismounted, and on failing knees tottered to the cartshed.

One of the men there was broadly built, with a fat unshaven face and a swollen paunch. He wore a soft black hat, black trousers, a white shirt fastened at the throat with a brass stud, and red braces. He carried his coat over his left arm. His voice was an over-ripe, husky bass.

'So you have joined the cavalry?' he said. 'When you left us at Reggio I realized that we of the infantry were too slow for you. Have you had a good ride?'

Angelo wiped the sweat from his eyes and recognized him. 'Sergeant Vespucci!' he exclaimed.

CHAPTER XI

A COUPLE of hours later Angelo and Sergeant Vespucci sat facing each other across a table on which were scattered the fragments of a substantial meal. Flies buzzed and fed upon the gravy smears, on cherry-stones and bread-crumbs. An empty fiasco stood among the plates. From another, half empty, the Sergeant was pouring red wine with steady care into Angelo's glass. His own was brim-full. In the wrinkles below his eyes the sweat glistened like seed-pearls, and his leathery cheeks shone with a general moisture. Great dew-drops stood upon his fore-head, and his shirt clung damply to his chest.

He set down the flask and said, 'So that's how I became a Distributer.'

Angelo looked at him with admiration. Sergeant Vespucci was a veteran of his own regiment who had served in Africa, and it was good to meet an old comrade again and learn that he was doing well in life, not only for himself but for his country. They had told each other all their adventures, and Angelo had listened with deep respect to the Sergeant's tale. How prudent he had been, and how successful!

When the retreat began at Reggio he had rescued from the administrative chaos some two dozen pack-mules which would otherwise have fallen into the enemy's hands. He had promptly set up as a carrier, serving refugees who were anxious to save their household goods, and loading other beasts with produce of the countryside. He had led his caravan through the Sila, through the mountains of Lucania and Campania, all the way to Naples, keeping ahead of the Eighth Army and avoiding the Germans. Some of his refugees travelled only a short distance to village relatives, but there were always others who needed accommodation, and the traffic was lucrative enough. So was the sale of country produce, for the usual means of transport had vanished, and when goods were scarce people would pay fancy prices for them.

In Naples he had thought of settling down, but the

typhus epidemic frightened him, so he had sold his mules and gone to Rome. There, with the useful capital he had acquired, he purchased a motor lorry, permission to move freely, and a forged certificate that entitled him to acquire petrol from the military authorities. In favourable circumstances he developed the business he had begun by chance, and buying produce where it was abundant, carried it to some neighbourhood in which it was scarce and sold it at an agreeable profit.

'I've always been a student of affairs,' he told Angelo, 'and it's a long time since I first discovered what's really wrong with the world. The life of the world, you see, depends on three things: Production, Consumption, and Distribution. Now in our time, if you care to put it so, Science has gone to bed with Production and produced Abundance. So that's all right. As for Consumption, the world is full of Consumers, a new one is born every minute, and their nature is such that they will consume anything that is put before them. So there is no difficulty there. But Distribution is a different bottle of wine altogether. Distribution has become Politics, and Politics is something that enables people who can find no other sort of pleasure to purse their lips and say. "No, you cannot do that until I give you permission!" Oh, politics is a powder to make a man spew! And I do not like that, Angelo, I do not think it is good. So then, when I am able to do so, I decide to dissociate myself from political distribution and be a Free Distributer. And what is the result? I make a lot of money and everybody is glad to see me. I feed my fellow-men, and I feed myself. I am a benefactor and I grow rich — and all because I have been thoughtful, I made plans! I saw what was desirable. I found the means to perform it, and with an abundance of good will I set to work.'

Angelo drank a little wine, and reaching across the untidy table shook Sergeant Vespucci by the hand. 'It is admirable,' he said. 'You are a good man, Sergeant. And in Rome, I suppose, you sell most of your produce in the Black Market?'

'Naturally,' said the Sergeant, 'I have my agents in the Black Market. For a Free Distributer it is the only way.'

'Have you not found the German authorities very troublesome?'

'On the contrary,' said the Sergeant. 'No, I have had no difficulty with them. They are commercial, you see, and if a man is commercial you can deal with him. They are greedy, of course, and very suspicious, but if you flatter them and pay them lavishly you can get on very well with them. During the last few months I have been able to distribute German rations and German petrol, to the value of many thousands of lire, among Roman citizens who were greatly in need of them. — But what is going to happen now? That is what I ask myself. Will the Allies co-operate in so reasonable a manner? *Speriamo*, we say, and we can say no more.'

'And when will you return to Rome?'

'As soon as possible. I came here the day before yesterday, to avoid trouble of any sort, and when I can return without trouble I shall. And now let us have one more glass of wine, and then I should like to sleep for an hour or two.'

The farmer in whose house they were was one of Sergeant Vespucci's business acquaintances. He, while they slept, went to the wood where Simon's little column had met the white cattle — he had recognized Angelo's description of the scene — and on his return reported that a vast number of dead Germans lay upon the road and among the trees, but there was no sign of the Englishmen or their vehicles. Close questioning reduced the bodies he had seen to ten, but he still insisted that all of them were German, and Angelo was infinitely cheered by the inference that Simon and his men had survived the encounter. The farmer also brought news of the German retreat. The Tedeschi, he said, were leaving Rome that night, there was no doubt about it. The countryside was full of rumours and tense with excitement. People were going to and fro, with increasing boldness, and every one of them had some new story of the enemy's plight.

None of them went to bed, and several times during the night men came in, singly or two or three together, to ask what news they had and bring in exchange their own most recent information. At six o'clock in the morning a boy pushed open the kitchen-door and shouted, 'They're in! The Americans are in Rome!' Then he disappeared, and though they at once pursued him, clamouring for details, they saw nothing more of him than his backside and the rear wheel of his bicycle. Stooped over the handle-bars, he was racing for the city.

Sergeant Vespucci told the farmer's wife to make some coffee, and went to harness his horse and trap. 'Are you coming?' he said to Angelo.

'Do you think it is safe?'

'I shouldn't be going if I didn't.'

The coffee was excellent. 'American,' said the Sergeant, 'from Naples. The Americans have very good rations, better than anyone else. Drink up, Angelo, I am becoming impatient!'

There was a freshness in the air that made the mere acts of moving in it and breathing delightful. In the east a narrow border of clouds looked like sheeps' wool caught on a wire fence, but elsewhere the sky was a pale un-differenced blue. A pair of young jays fled noisily into a bush, the mother-bird chattering behind them. Webs of gossamer gleamed in the hedge-high sun.

Sergeant Vespucci touched his mare with the whip. 'She is a good one,' he said. 'Ten years old, but she had never done any work till I bought her. No real work; nothing but hunting. I bought her cheap, because her owner couldn't feed her. But I am able to give her some corn, thank God.'

They went at a great pace and met no soldiers on the road until they came within a mile or two of Rome. Then they encountered an American armoured car, and passed another, stationary, whose commander was watching the progress of the first. Some distance farther on they were stopped and questioned by an officer who, in the open top of his car, had been volubly conversing with someone unseen by radio-telephone. Their papers were in order, the officer accepted Angelo's story that he had fallen sick while on a mission with a detachment of Force 69, and they were allowed to proceed. Then they approached a squadron of tanks. In the shade of tall trees they looked like monsters of a new pleiocene twilight, and as dinosaurs after breakfast might smell of blood, so these stank of petrol. The long gun that projected from the leader's turret travelled slowly from side to side like the long stiff neck of a brontosaurus sniffing the breeze. On the road beside it a major was eating a doughnut. He beckoned to Angelo and the Sergeant, spoke to them with his mouth full, and after questioning let them go.

Their road returned them to the Via Aurelia, where they saw a long line of soldiers moving out from Rome. Their drab uniforms were stained and dirty, they were laden with the tools and weapons of the infantry. They were bent by the weight they carried, and as if their pot-shaped helmets were intolerably heavy, their heads were bowed. The pallor of long fatigue lay on their faces, and it was many days since they had shaved. They took little interest in where they were going, but with downcast eyes followed the heels of the man in front.

'And they have won their battle!' said the Sergeant. 'What in God's name do the losers look like?'

'What a dreadful burden victory must be!' said Angelo.

But when they entered Rome it became evident that the populace thought differently, and regarded the Allied victory as an occasion at least as splendid as the production of a new opera. Everywhere on the streets there were Romans who applauded the passing troops, held their hands high and clapped them loudly, tossed flowers into jeeps and tank-turrets, and boisterously demanded in exchange caramels, and biscuits, and cigarettes.

Angelo and the Sergeant crossed the Tiber — 'So they did not blow-up the bridges!' said Angelo thankfully — and on the other side found more numerous crowds and listened to ever more jubilant applause. In every quarter the Americans were hailed as actors in a gala performance, and for some considerable time they responded very graciously. Like artists bestowing their autographs, they threw cigarettes, caramels, and biscuits to their admirers wherever they went.

Sergeant Vespucci complained loudly against this prodigality. 'It is bad for trade,' he said. 'They are worth a lot of money, all those cigarettes and biscuits, and they should be distributed in a fair and orderly manner to those who can pay for them. The Germans gave nothing away, they were very correct.'

He stabled his mare in a little street not far from the Piazza dei Satiri and the trattoria where Angelo had once conferred with Fest and the German deserters, and then they went out to mingle with the crowd and share the common pleasure. The morning was fine, the air grew warm, and the sun shone with a genial glow on walls the colour of honey or the colour of the ripe flesh of a melon. Even Sergeant Vespucci yielded to the general infection, and taking some flowers from a pair of little girls who did not know what to do, threw them to the crew of a passing field-gun.

Presently, drifting with the crowd, they found themselves near the Campidoglio, and hearing that some ceremony was toward, climbed the steps to see what it might be. At the far end of the Piazza the double flight of Michelangelo's staircase rose over a fountain to the great stone balcony of the Palazzo del Senatore. On the balcony stood a little cluster of Generals — in dress distinguishable from the common soldiers only by the white stars painted on their helmets — who, with maps spread before them on the broad stone balustrade, were busily conferring, active with their index fingers, and seemingly unaware of the spectators who stood below and gazed intently at the scene.

'What are they looking for on their maps?' asked Angelo. 'Do they not know where they are?'

'It is always the same with Generals,' said the Sergeant. 'They and their maps, they are like a woman with her knitting. When there is nothing else to do, out it comes.'

There was a sudden commotion in the small crowd as two cars drove up, and from them, before they had stopped, sprang a dozen men so fierce of aspect, so ponderous yet quick in movement — they ran with a jungle-stoop — that Angelo caught his breath in a momentary gasp of fear. He thought, in that startled second, they were assassins and this a plot to murder the victorious Generals in their hour of triumph. But then he perceived that the newcomers wore American uniform, and the implements they carried were merely cameras.

Some of the photographers, disdaining the marble staircase, ran up the balustrade that curved like an elevated bow high above the fountain, and presented their cameras at the Generals on the balcony as if they had been highwaymen and were holding them to ransom. The Generals affected disregard of their presence but assumed a more intense interest in their maps, or a more authoritative demeanour. Then, to placate the photographers who had arrived by the normal route, they turned attractive profiles in their direction and put on expressions of sapient authority. Every new pose excited the photographers to fresh demands, and some of them now clambered to window-sills above the group, so that they could secure a picture of helmets bent in studious contemplation; while others, clinging with one great hand to the balustrade, like apes in an equatorial forest, lowered themselves to some perilous roost on a scanty foothold of baroque ornament, and tilted their cameras upward to obtain a view of military jawbones in steely outline and soldier-nostrils adequately distended.

What terrifying faces they have, and with what passion they go about their business, thought Angelo as he contemplated a photographer poised like a chamois on a little peak of carved stone — another hanging like a sailor from the yard-arm — a third press closely in like a throat-specialist with his laryngoscope — and a fourth like Death himself command his victim to be still. And how meekly, yet in what comely postures, the Generals obeyed!

Posterity, said Angelo to himself, will look at these pictures and admire them. But posterity will know nothing of what I have seen, and that is the bloodshot eyes of the photographers who took them, their maniacal expression, and long simian arms. How I wish that I could live for ever and tell my great-great-grandchildren about life!

His thoughts were interrupted by a dearly loved and well-known voice. 'Angelo!' it said. 'My dear boy, how are you, and what have you been doing all this time?'

He turned, and with a blink of astonishment recognized the Count. Astonishment, because the Count had changed so much. He was bare-headed, and his hair was white as growing cotton. He still carried himself jauntily enough, but his clothes, though they were not exactly shabby, had the look of a suit that is worn without much relief. His shirt was in its second day, and his shoes had not been cleaned that morning.

'Oh, my dear — my dear Don Agesilas!' cried Angelo. 'What has happened to you?'

'Come, come,' said the Count, 'do I look like the victim of circumstance?'

'No, not at all,' said Angelo in a hurry, 'but it is so long since we have met that something or other must have occurred. No one, in times like these, can live for more than a week or two without things happening to him.'

'That is perfectly true, and when I tell you the whole tale of my adventures you will, I have no doubt, be properly astonished. But I should not like to think that I show any sign of misfortune, or carry the visible scars of unhappiness.'

'No, indeed you do not,' said Angelo. 'You are looking very well, and white hair suits you wonderfully.'

'Not white!' exclaimed the Count. 'I admit to a touch of grey above the ears, such as you might expect in a man of my years, but surely you cannot call it white?'

'It is the way the sunlight falls upon it,' said Angelo apologetically. 'But now when I look at it more closely — oh yes, I was quite mistaken.'

'You gave me a little shock,' said the Count with a smile, 'but think no more of it. Tell me, instead, about your own affairs. What fortune have you had, and why do you wear that uniform?'

'I am now serving with the English,' said Angelo, and turned to speak to Sergeant Vespucci and bring him into the conversation. But the Sergeant had gone, and as he was about to comment on his disappearance it occurred to him that Vespucci, perhaps, was unwilling to meet his late commanding officer for reasons best known to himself. So Angelo said nothing about him, but asked the Count what news he had had from Pontefiore.

'None at all,' said the Count. 'Very little news comes to me now, for I am, in truth, little better than a ghost. Officially I died in early March. But come, let us find a quiet place in which to talk and exchange our stories in peace.'

A short distance from the excited streets they found the old Forum empty and calm and still, like the garden of a deserted house, so they sat themselves comfortably on the turf under a large tree, and the Count told Angelo about his flight to Montenero, his arrest by the Germans after Fest had killed the two strangers, and his nightmare journey to the cave. Angelo fell into an extreme agitation as he listened, and the Count, seeing what an appreciative audience he had, spared no pains to make his recital as dramatic as possible.

After their last-minute reprieve, he explained, they had been taken back to the school, and there he had seen Fest, himself a prisoner, walking between his guards. They had had an hour or so in which to contemplate with tears and wonder their good fortune, and then the bombers had come. Only a few bombs had fallen in Montenero itself, but they had caused great confusion and laid open the school as if it had been a doll's house. How many of the prisoners succeeded in escaping from that smoky chaos the Count did not know, but he thought a good many, and perhaps nearly all of them. He himself had spent most of the day in a barber's shop, wrapped in a sheet with lather on his face, and whenever the Germans came in, searching for the fugitives, the friendly barber was shaving him. But in the evening the barber had grown frightened, and refused to help him further. The Count had passed a miserable night, playing in the streets a desperate game of hide-and-seek, for the Germans were still hunting the runaways, because Fest was among them. He had heard this news in the barber's.

'And then in the early morning,' said the Count, 'when I was very nearly at the end of my tether, I found safety. To be precise I smelt it. There was a baker's shop at the end of a lane down which I was slinking like a thief. He, poor fellow, was already at work, and the scent of his labour was delicious. I was drawn to it like a starving kitten to a saucer of milk. And then, as I approached the open door of the bakehouse, I heard a woman's voice raised in anger. Cautiously I peered in, and there was the baker's wife berating and denouncing her little husband for some newly discovered fault, I know not what. He was a scrubby fellow, black-avised, with the flour showing white on his hairy arms and smearing his unshaven cheeks. But she was splendid! She had crossed the lane, from their house on the other side, on her bare feet, clad only in her night-gown, and against the light of an oil-lamp I could see the shape of her body. It was a body of the sort that one turns to for comfort. Nothing of grossness about it, I assure you of that, but rather for the winter than a warm May. So I waited until the connubial dispute was done, and when she came out I spoke to her.

'She was quick-witted and no great argument was necessary. She told me to follow her, and closed the door of the house behind us. I saw then that her face also was handsome, in the hardy way of our countrywomen, and her age about twenty-eight or thirty. She smelt of new bread and the warmth of a pillow, and I almost forgot the distress I was in. Bless her heart, she was good to me and kept me hidden all that day, and later she smuggled me out of Montenero into the country where she had a sister who had married a farmer. An older sister, a dozen years older perhaps, but in her day she had been just such another as the baker's wife, and though she had lost her looks she liked to have a man in the house to make much of. And I needed care by then, for I was suffering like one of the damned from all the fears that I had previously kept at arm's length, but now came crowding in upon me like chickens to be fed. What I needed was simple kindness, and I found it in a very simple house.'

'It was no more than common courtesy to look after you,' said Angelo.

'Is such courtesy so common? I am glad to hear it. But these people, mark you, were also tactful. For it fell to the farmer's lot to inform me that I was dead, and he did it with the utmost delicacy yet with genuine feeling, and assured me that his regard for me was undiminished. The Germans, you see, had announced the execution of all whom they had arrested for the murder of the two men killed by Fest. Many of us, perhaps most of us, had certainly escaped, but the Germans had their dignity to consider, and the inevitability of their justice had to be asserted. So they put up a notice that said we had been shot.'

'That could not hurt you very deeply,' said Angelo.

'It hurt me bitterly,' said the Count. 'True, I did not feel the hurt until a few days ago, when I came into Rome, a refugee. I entered with some forty or fifty companions, expelled from their houses because the Germans were going to blow them up or fortify them. — I do not know which, and it would make very little difference in the long run. — I came back to Rome, I tell you, and discovered that after the announcement of my death my property had been seized and my furniture sold. I am a homeless pauper, Angelo! And because I am dead, I cannot even complain!'

They discussed this lamentable predicament for some time, and then the Count, with a flyaway motion of his fingers and the politest affectation of a yawn, dismissed his own affairs as being of small interest, and commanded Angelo to tell his adventures. These he listened to with close attention, and having sympathized with Angelo for the hardships he had endured, congratulated him most warmly on the success with which he had survived them.

'And now,' he said, 'let us go to lunch.'

CHAPTER XII

LORENZO, the Count's butler, disliked having to serve a dead man. He held the dish of spaghetti at arm's length, and shook his head with timorous disapproval when the Count asked for wine.

The Germans had told him that his master had been shot, and never had he dared question anything which they said. He had discussed the tragedy long and lugubriously with his friends, and then put the Count away in a cupboard of his memory that he kept for those who had met a violent end. He had watched the removal of the furniture and the formal closure of the house, and no doubt remained in his mind — such as it was — that he had finished with the Count for ever. He himself suffered no inconvenience, for he had been left in possession of his own quarters, at the back of the house, as a caretaker.

When the Count appeared and demanded to know what had happened, Lorenzo had been frightened out of the few wits he possessed, and had it not been for Giulia his wife the Count would have fared poorly. But Giulia had welcomed him with tears of joy and a bustle of preparation for his comfort. She had put clean sheets on her bed and contrived a shakedown in a sort of cupboard for herself and her husband; on which Lorenzo used to lie and shiver to think of the ghostly visitor in the room beyond. The Count enjoyed whatever amenities could be provided in so humble an abode, and, as he told Angelo, he had no scruple about enjoying them; for Lorenzo, despite his stupidity, had robbed him right and left for years.

It was late in the afternoon, after the Count had slept for an hour or two, when Giulia came in to tell them that if they wanted to hear *il Papa* they had better hurry. It was half-past five, she said, and at six o'clock the Holy Father was going to speak to his people, who were now gathering like a swarm of bees, like twenty swarms and many of them carrying banners as well, in St. Peter's Square.

Immediately the Count was in a great hurry to go, for not only was he in a fine mood for thanksgiving, he said, but the Pope would assuredly give them his blessing, and in his present state he was in urgent need of benediction. So he and Angelo became part of the multitude that was going from every direction to St. Peter's. So vast a number of people filled the roads that it seemed as if, not Rome, but all the world was on its way, and in the din of voices there was high expectancy, and the host of faces of every sort and shape and variety all wore a look of exhilaration.

'These Romans,' said the Count complacently, 'are a very wicked people, as most people are, and extremely proud. But every now and then they reveal their faith with a simplicity that is pure as a child's. You may have noticed that although they have been applauding the Americans with great good will, there has been a certain reserve in their manner? They threw flowers in plenty, but they did not throw their hearts as well. They are Romans, and Rome has seen many conquering armies and the concluding act of many well-performed historical dramas. They recognize the Americans as accomplished actors, and they give them the plaudits due to actors. But not for a moment do they believe that either the Americans or the English wrote the play. No, indeed! And that is why they have been saving their enthusiasm, and why they are going to show it now. For now they are going to shout for the author.'

They arrived at the far end of the Square as the bells began to ring, and though they were a great distance from St. Peter's still, even far from the enfolding colonnades, they could make little more progress, for in front of them was such a host of people, tightly crammed together, as they had never seen before. They were indeed carried slowly forward before the impetus of some thirty, forty, or fifty thousand late arrivals, but their further movement was involuntary. They became a little part of the crowd, and moved with it or not at all.

Two diminished beings came out of a window high on

139

the broad face of the Church, and hung from a balcony a large crimson carpet with a Dove embroidered at the centre. With six reverberant strokes the hour was struck and the white figure of the Pope appeared on the balcony with a pair of attendant officers. Wave after wave of prodigious cheering rolled across the Square and broke upon the Church, and such was the turbulence of waving arms and shaken banners that it seemed as though a great gale had instantly burst from the sky and set all those hands to frantic motion like the leaves of a vast forest. Then, as suddenly as it had broken, the gale was stilled, the whole level of the Square subsided, and the huge crowd knelt.

Amplifiers gave the Pope's voice a more than human power, and every phrase came clear and resonant from the mouth of a trumpet. He offered thanks for the safety of the City, and commanded the Romans to show themselves worthy of the grace they had received. 'Shape your lives to the gravity of this hour,' he said. 'Cease from discord. Lift up your hearts!'

The gale of applause broke again, and roared for several minutes. The Pope returned to the balcony and waved a white-winged arm. The applause was renewed.

'What did I tell you?' demanded the Count. 'Rome has been saved, and who did it? You can't deceive the Romans!' And cupping his hands to his lips he shouted, 'Author! Author!'

The Pope returned, and lifted both his wings.

Nobody was in a hurry to leave the Square. The crowd made little effort to disperse, and no one tried to disperse it, but very gradually it melted. Parts of it, in the process, piled-up on other portions like ice-floes in a river when the thaw has begun. Among the many tens of thousands of people there were hundreds of vehicles, of all sorts from horse-drawn market-gardeners' wagons to scout-cars of the Fifth Army, and when the outward movement began these were quickly boarded by pedestrians, most of them young women. Jeeps that began the afternoon with a load of four doughboys now carried in addition half a dozen well-grown girls and a couple of little brothers belonging to one or other of them. Drivers endeavoured to steer through the crowd with a girl on either knee and a prancing young man on the bonnet waving an ensign big enough for a battleship. Old men, bewildered but happy, found snug seats on the wings of a staff-car, and stout women, squawking like delighted geese, were hauled into troop-carriers. Flagstaffs were thrust into unprotesting faces, children were rescued from a thousand deaths, everybody was shouting or singing, and not an inch of soldiers' khaki but had about it a soft foliage of printed cotton, white linen, or flowering silk.

With an arm of prodigious strength an American sergeant saved the Count from the wheels of a command-car. Angelo, tightly confined by the crowd, saw Simon's troop some twenty yards away, their two vehicles so packed with nubile girls that they looked like haywains loaded with apple-blossom. Another American handed the Count a large cigar. Angelo kissed a girl who had just been given a drink by a corporal from Minnesota, and a moment later was embraced by another whose mouth was full of chewing-gum, the gift of an ammunition-number from Rhode Island. The Count was riding on a gun-tractor with a long lad from Arizona who was inviting him to come and visit the Double L Ranch near Tucson. Nobody cared if the traffic-jam should last all night. *Il Papa* had said, 'Lift up your hearts!' and their hearts were glad.

An hour later, walking idly in a street that was but thinly peopled, the Count said, 'This is the temper in which all the world should live for ever.'

'That would be most agreeable,' said Angelo.

'Our besetting sin, as I discovered in my darkest hour, is hardness of heart. Take off, my dear Angelo, the tough and leathery jacket, like a bull's hide, that encloses your natural heart.'

'I do not think it has any such covering,' said Angelo. 'I have often wished for some protection of that nature, but all in vain.'

'You are fortunate,' said the Count. 'If your heart is

141

tender, and naked to every pinprick and every joy, then you are truly fortunate.'

'It is a new way of looking at things,' said Angelo with doubt in his voice.

A little while later the Count said, 'I should like to invite some three or four hundred of these charming Americans to my house, and give them a party.'

'All your doors are locked,' said Angelo.

'We could break them open.'

'But your rooms are unfurnished.'

'That is true, unhappily. But would it matter?'

'You have no food or wine to offer them.'

'No,' said the Count with sudden melancholy, 'I have nothing. How miserable it is to have nothing for one's friends.'

Angelo was silent, and the Count said, 'You are not very sympathetic to-night.'

'I am thinking of Lucrezia,' said Angelo. 'If she were here to share our happiness, I should be happy indeed, and I might be tolerably happy if only I could forget her. There was a girl in the crowd who pleased me very much, and I was getting on well with her till I remembered Lucrezia. And then I let her go.'

'To be in love,' said the Count, 'is to suffer a perpetual torment for the sake of relieving it, from time to time, with a dab of delicious ointment. It is a ridiculous state of affairs, and the only cure for it is to grow old. But you have to grow very old.'

On the next day Rome had returned to its normal mood, and to some approximation of its normal conditions. The shops were open, a few tramcars were running, and the Army of Liberation had become merely the latest of the many armies which, in the long course of its history, had entered the city for some purpose of their own. Those who had anything for sale, be it a fountain-pen or their person, were still attentive to the foreign soldiers, but clearly regarded them as heaven-sent customers rather than divinely inspired liberators. The solid citizens went about their business, intent upon their own affairs, and charming girls in summer frocks rode their bicycles uphill and down with never a glance for the perspiring soldiers who had come to their rescue. Only the Count was still faithful to them.

All morning he and Angelo walked in the principal streets for no other purpose than to enjoy the spectacle of the relieving soldiery in holiday temper. Nine out of ten were Americans, but here and there was a little group of English or Scots from the bridgehead in Anzio. The Count was disappointed in the British, who went to and fro without displaying any emotion at all. They looked at the Coliseum and agreed that a lot of work must have gone into the building of it. They stared dubiously at the well supplied shop-windows, and said that Rome couldn't have known there was a war on. They said that St. Peter's reminded them of St. Paul's.

The Count wasted little time on the British, but courted American society with ever-growing pleasure. Britannic phlegm and Roman indifference had no diminishing effect on the exuberance of the Americans, who paraded the streets with boisterous enthusiasm or sat upon the pavements with endearing familiarity and offered conversation to everyone who passed, but especially to young females.

'They are all so friendly,' declared the Count, as two lieutenants stopped their jeep beside a couple of girls and invited them to come for a ride. 'And what boundless hospitality they offer!'

'See how confidently they make themselves at home,' he said, a little while later, and pointed to three privates who, with their backs to a shop-window, were sitting comfortably on a pavement in the Piazza Barberini. 'Truly they are citizens of the world who can make themselves at home wherever they go. And how full of fun they are,' he added as the nearest soldier seized the ankle of a young matron who was rash enough to pass within arm's reach. 'What did he say to her, Angelo?'

'He said, "Hiya, toots".'

'Hiya, toots,' repeated the Count. 'I like that. It is the

felicitous expression of a young people who are making their own language, and making poetry of it. It is brisk as a challenge, yet genial and democratic. Yes, I like it.'

An acquaintance of his own walked by: a tall lady in black with a long grey face and heavy eyelids. 'Hiya, toots,' said the Count.

'But look at him!' he went on, pointing to a thickset doughboy with a truculent expression who stood upon the edge of the pavement. On his left breast he wore several ribbons and some brooches, and from each of his hip-pockets protruded a bottle of wine. 'Now he,' said the Count, 'is quite obviously a man of sterling character and wide experience. To carry one bottle shows forethought, to carry two indicates hospitality. One for himself and one for his friend: yes, you can say with certainty that he is both provident and generous.'

An impudent little boy approached the doughboy with outstretched hand. *'Niente sigaretti!'* shouted the doughboy. *'Niente caramelli, niente biscotti! Via!'*

'Oh, the poor fellow!' said the Count, 'he has given away everything he possessed.' And with a smile of understanding he offered a packet of cigarettes that he himself had recently acquired.

'Aw, nuts,' said the doughboy, and pushed him on to the road, where he narrowly escaped being run over by an amphibious jeep that came at great speed round the corner from the Via Vittorio Veneto. It was driven by an enormous negro who wore a pair of white-rimmed sunspectacles and was smoking a cigar. He drove his curious vehicle twice round the square, and then, still at high speed, disappeared down the Via Tritone.

'Their vitality is amazing,' said the Count. 'Quite, quite amazing.'

They walked slowly on, up the tree-lined curving street, but turned to the left before they reached the Pincio gate. Outside an hotel were some twenty military cars, of various kinds, and in the doorway stood a group of officers, talking. They were British, and Angelo, suddenly exclaiming, ran across the street and with a delighted smile saluted one of them with the characteristic high-handed gesture he had learnt in Force 69.

'And where have you been?' asked Simon. 'Did the cow give you a good ride?'

'It was an ox,' said Angelo, 'and quite uncontrollable. I had to ride it for many miles in the most horrible discomfort. I am still a mass of bruises.'

'Well,' said Simon, 'you've turned up at the proper time. We are going south again to-morrow, and you can come with me if you like. I found a jeep that had no visible owner, and I am using it.'

'I should like to introduce,' said Angelo, 'the Count Piccologrando of Pontefiore.'

For a few minutes the Count and Simon exchanged small talk and compliments, but their conversation developed no warmth, and the Count's attention visibly wandered when a large car went by filled to overflowing with American soldiers and self-assured young women of the town. In his festival mood the British were no good to him. He still desired American company, and declining Simon's invitation to lunch he walked briskly down the Via Francesco Crispi towards more populous streets where he would be certain of meeting, in large numbers, the New World's uninhibited defenders.

Angelo came running after him. 'You understand,' he said, 'that I am bound to go with Captain Telfer? I am in British service now.'

'Have no qualms,' said the Count. 'You can leave me here in the assurance that I shall fare well and find a sufficiency of friends.'

'I dare say the Marchesa Dolce will soon be returning.'

'She is in Rome now. She came back a month ago, but she is indisposed. In her rustic exile she put on a little weight, and until her masseuse has restored her to her customary proportions she does not care to be seen.'

Standing in front of a jeweller's shop two khaki-clad girls were seriously inspecting the display in the window. 'Look!' said the Count in sudden excitement. 'They are Americans! American women!'

'I think they are nurses,' said Angelo.

One of them walked slowly on, the other lingered. With a quick handclasp the Count said good-bye to Angelo, and approached her. He bowed with the grace of an older world. 'Hiya, toots,' he said.

Angelo sighed and went to look for a sergeant of Simon's troop whom he had been told to find. He tried to console his loneliness by thinking of Lucrezia, but with indifferent success.

In the morning he and Simon drove out of Rome by the Via Appia and they soon began to overtake the slow traffic of returning refugees. Nearly all carried heavy loads and were bent beneath their burdens; but some were remarkably cheerful. They were going home, and few of them yet knew what had happened to their homes.

The pleasant little towns along the Appian Way had suffered, quite suddenly, such a change in their appearance as could only have been effected — without the help of science — by long eras of disaster. Our age of steel and explosives had shown itself very like the Ice Age in its ability to alter the face of a landscape, create lacunae, and remove excrescences. Wedding-chamber and warm kitchen, the smithy and the grocer's shop and the notary's office had been reduced to rags and dusty rubble by a stick of bombs that caught the sunlight as they fell. With a huff and a puff the metallurgist and the chemist had blown away the long toil of many simple masons, and whole families who had spent their arduous and patient years in the growing of corn and wine had vanished in a little acrid smoke. A bridge that had served a thousand needs, and many thousand brisk and busy people, and filled its valley with arcs of beauty and proud columns, had been demolished with boisterous success by a cartload of guncotton . . . Of all the triumphs that had marched the Appian Way none had so spaciously shown the enormity of human power as this great spectacle of destruction; and the pity was that the refugees could not appreciate it as it deserved. The refugees were unimpressed by the march and the majesty of science. They were thinking only about their homes. Tired as they were, and stumbling under their burdens, they hurried on towards their abandoned villages with hope in their straining muscles, hope in their bright eyes. And when they came to their villages they sat down and wept.

Some of them, bracing their arms against the backboard of an overloaded cart or heaving at the spokes of a wheel, laboured to keep their cargo moving while the rack-ribbed horse between the shafts trembled with exhaustion and pecked uncertainly on the uphill road. On top of the corded pile of feather-beds and chairs and cooking-pots might be a shrivelled grandmother in dusty black and a couple of astonished children.

'If there is any creature in the world more miserable than a refugee,' said Simon, 'it is a refugee's horse.'

'There is no liberation for horses,' said Angelo.

'None,' said Simon.

Angelo sighed. 'They have at least been spared that.'

They passed a very old man who was pulling a handcart loaded with a chest of drawers, a mattress, the frame of an iron bed, two saucepans and a variety of articles tied in a red blanket, and a goose in a basket.

'All these people,' said Angelo, 'have been liberated and now they have nowhere to live. And before the war is over you will have to liberate northern Italy and France, and Greece and Yugoslavia, and Holland and Belgium, and Denmark and Poland and Czechoslovakia.'

'It may take us rather a long time,' said Simon.

'And when you have finished no one in Europe will have anywhere to live.'

'You mustn't exaggerate. It won't be as bad as that.'

'*Speriamo*,' said Angelo.

The lately reclaimed fields of the Pontine Marshes lay drowned under great lakes of gleaming water, and the roofs of many little houses showed above the surface like tiny red islands. Of trees that had been planted for summer shade there remained in sight only tufts of branches like currant-bushes. A man in a boat tied his craft to a chimney and began to fish.

'I was very glad,' said Angelo, 'to see that the bridges over the Tiber had not been blown up.'

'Apparently the Germans made no attempt to blow them,' said Simon. 'Our journey wasn't necessary, as things turned out, but we had a very interesting time. After you mounted your cow — '

'It was an ox,' said Angelo.

'We fought a very successful little battle, and we had another skirmish, almost as good, at a cross-roads five or six miles further on. But when we came into Rome we had nothing to do except buy a few souvenirs. I got a dozen pairs of silk stockings and some very good perfume, and that was a great piece of luck, because by now, with all those Americans there, every shop will be stripped to the boards.'

'But surely looting is forbidden — at least in Rome?'

'Oh, they don't loot, you mustn't say that about them. The Americans aren't like that at all. They just go shopping. They have so much money there is no need for them to loot.'

'From where do they get so much money?'

'It is the same as we use,' said Simon. 'It is printed in the United States and it comes over by the ship-load.'

'And when the war is finished, and you and the Americans have all gone home, and there is nothing left in Italy but the money you have spent — will it be any good to us?'

'That is an interesting question.'

'Would it not be simpler to let your soldiers loot?'

'Angelo,' said Simon, 'there are occasions when you become tiresome.'

'I am not being unfriendly,' said Angelo in his most earnest voice. 'You must not think that, please. We are very grateful to you for coming to liberate us, but I hope you will not find it necessary to liberate us out of existence. When I think about the future — '

'Your future,' said Simon, 'is bound to be complicated by the fact that Italy came into the war quite wilfully, and then was quite decisively beaten.'

They were approaching the coast and Angelo pointed

to the promontory ahead of them. 'There is Gaeta,' he said, 'which was so named by Aeneas after his nurse. I think people were more affectionate in those days. And there' — he pointed across the glinting sea — 'there to the westward is Monte Circeo, where Circe the Great Enchantress turned twenty-two of the companions of Ulysses into swine. But when Ulysses came to their rescue, and persuaded Circe to give them back their proper shape, he did not punish them very much for the disgusting things they did when they ran about on four feet. He was magnanimous.'

'Ulysses,' said Simon, 'had advantages that we have lost. In his time no one had heard of economics, and a popular leader was not responsible to a hungry electorate, but only to the gods. It was relatively easy to be magnanimous.'

CHAPTER XIII

WHEN news of the Count's death came by devious routes to Pontefiore, his English Countess had been sustained in sorrow by her sturdy conviction that a person in her position, in time of general loss, could not afford much indulgence in private grief. She also admitted her native belief — Yorkshire was her birthplace — that foreigners met a violent end far more often, and more naturally, than the English; and a little while later she remembered, with appreciable comfort, the mourning she had been obliged to buy, a couple of years before, for an old uncle of Don Agesilas, a gentleman known as the Noble Signor of Rocca Pipirozzi. She had grudged the expense of it, for wealth had never obscured in her memory the narrow circumstances of her girlhood and youth in Bradford, and to spend more than five pounds or so, on anything that could not be regarded as an investment, always gave her a feeling of guilt. She found, therefore, in her great bereavement, a little quiet satisfaction in thinking that the extravagance with which she had mourned the Noble Signor would now be redeemed when those dreary and expensive garments became her widow's weeds.

She continued to go about her business of looking after Pontefiore with an apparent composure and real strength of mind that the villagers and the peasants thought most unnatural; but upon which they more and more came to rely as the front of battle was pushed northward into Tuscany. From the earliest days of her marriage she had busied herself among the people and with the affairs of her husband's estate, and now, when she had become the sole guardian of their interests, and life and property were equally menaced, she set about the problem of securing them, as far as possible, with great vigour and a constant anxiety.

For nearly three years her greatest solace had been the presence in her house, or in its vicinity, of the young man whom Angelo had seen and recognized as a stranger in Pontefiore, when in the previous autumn he had come home with the Count's pictures and two truck-loads of flour. This young man was an English soldier, a corporal in the Royal Engineers, Tom Trivet by name, who had been taken prisoner in Libya in the summer of 1941, and made his escape very soon after from a transit camp for prisoners of war near Bari. He had the advantage of knowing where he wanted to go, for his father had married a Miss Goodge, whose elder sister, a teacher in Bradford, had married Don Agesilas. So Tom Trivet, with the help of innumerable people on the way, had walked from Bari to Pontefiore and remained there ever since. But now, to his aunt's distress, he was about to leave.

Very soon after the surrender of Italy partisans had begun to appear who, in some parts of the country, declared for the Allies in a bold and forthright manner, but in other parts in a rather shy and tentative way. In the neighbourhood of Pontefiore they were neither numerous nor reckless, but a little company had gradually come into being under the leadership of Tom Trivet and a former member of the Guardia Civile called Pasquale; and some slight contact had been established with the Allied armies. Quite recently a signal had been received that included certain instructions for Corporal Trivet.

A few hours before he was due to leave he was sitting with the Countess in the small drawing-room that she always used in summer, for it was cool and overlooked a formal garden in which she took continual pleasure. The room itself was full of flowers, two canaries made small noises in a cage, and pale behind the mullioned glass of a bookcase showed the white and gold bindings of her favourite edition of Ouida.

A stranger, overhearing their conversation, might well have denied the Countess's affection for her nephew; for with her northern sense of duty she was taking advantage of her last opportunity to lecture him for his ill behaviour, and her disapproval was enriched and fortified by a Yorkshire accent that seemed to accuse, not Corporal

Trivet only, but all the Italian landscape of sins and follies unknown to Bradford.

'That my own sister's boy should act like that,' she was saying, 'and in a foreign country too, where it's our duty to set an example to people less fortunate than ourselves — no, Tom, no. I shall never forgive you. Though they may be the last words you'll ever hear from me, I can never forgive you.'

'You've forgiven me half a dozen times already, Aunt Edith.'

'And what's been the result? You just get worse and worse, and now you're completely shameless. And it's a falsehood to say that I forgave you. I may have agreed to overlook what happened, for the sake of peace, but that was the farthest I ever went. And it isn't as though it was one occasion only, as you know well. And you a married man!'

'I was married for five days, and I've had four years to think about it. If I'd taken four years to think about it first, I wouldn't have been married even for five minutes.'

'You never thought about the meaning of marriage, that was the mistake you made. There's nothing in life more serious than marriage, but you weren't serious at all. You were only thinking about a few days' pleasure, and how to guard against interruptions to it.'

A soldier in the Territorial Army, Tom Trivet had gone to France in the winter of 1939 and returned to England, in a motor-boat from Dunkirk, in the following May. In the peculiar circumstances of the time he had thought it reasonable to marry a girl of his own age — which was then twenty — whom he had known for some years, but who had never excited his emotions until war, and escape from battle, and the prospect of returning to battle had so heated them that any girl's breath could have blown them to flame. So they married and had their honeymoon in five days of leave, and six weeks later Tom had embarked for Egypt. Several months went by before her letters began to reach him, and when the first ones came, a whole parcel of them, he was dismayed. He had waited for them in a torment of emotional hunger, and when he sat down to read them, in a stony landscape dyed with the setting sun, he had found them as empty of nourishment as the sand that lay in crevices of the rock. There was a great deal in them, but nothing sweet or sound or satisfying.

In the weeks and months to come he read more and more of her letters, and as he thought of the well-turned limbs, the sleek yellow hair, and the innocent round face he had married, he grew increasingly puzzled and more and more depressed by the cloud of dust she created whenever she bent her head and shook out her brain over the writing-table. When Tom Trivet was captured, and his captors searched him, they found her last two letters in his pocket, unopened.

Now, to his aunt the Countess, he said sadly, 'We've had all this talk before, and it doesn't do any good, does it?'

'If it doesn't,' she answered, 'that's your fault and not mine. All you young people believe that because you want a thing, you're entitled to get it. But when I was young we were made to recognize our obligations. My generation was taught responsibility.'

'Not very well.'

'No, not very well. Human beings are full of imperfections, and you can't cure them overnight. But we tried.'

'And we're trying to do something quite different. You tried to make out that your way of life was worth preserving for ever, and we're trying to understand what it's all about.'

'By making love to half a dozen girls in Pontefiore!'

'They've taught me quite a lot,' said Tom.

'Nothing but self-indulgence.'

'And that's something too. I never had much chance to indulge myself in Bradford, and it wasn't till I came here that I realized how enjoyable life could be. I've been happier in Pontefiore than I ever was in my life before. It's an odd thing to say in the circumstances, but it's true enough and I feel all the better in consequence.'

'And the poor girls — do they feel better?'

'From time to time I've been led to believe so. — No, don't look at me like that, Aunt Edith. I didn't invent human nature.'

'You would have done, if you'd had the chance. You're brazen enough.'

Their arguments always followed the same pattern. The Countess would open the attack, and Tom defend himself with energy enough to make her deploy some early principles, a little moral indignation, and the zest that comes with berating a member of one's own family. Then when her eyes were sparkling and her lips compressed, he would begin his retreat — throwing out a few excuses to impede the pursuit — and when he saw the time was ripe for it, would offer his surrender. An acknowledgment that she was right, and he wrong, was all she ever asked for. She would assume that the past was dead and the future a clean page on which, with better fortune, no blot would ever fall. He, with a proper embarrassment, would accept her conclusion, and then for half an hour they would exchange kindly reminiscences of their native place. That was his only penance.

But now, when he had made his peace, discomfort remained in the atmosphere and with a renewed emotion, that neither would dream of mentioning, they remembered their impending separation. The Countess covered her feelings by inquiry about his socks and shirts, and Tom disguised his reluctance to leave by assuring her that he would soon return.

'I've got to go and meet this Captain Telfer,' he said, 'and there's only two things he can expect me to do for him. One is to show him the way about this part of the country, and the other is to help him with the partisans. I dare say I'll bring him straight back to Pontefiore.'

'But you won't stay here. The war has caught you up again and your holiday's over. But we mustn't grumble, I suppose. You've had nearly three years of it, and that's a longer holiday than anyone gets in Bradford. And I've enjoyed having you here, in spite of your behaviour.'

'Now don't start that again, Aunt Edith.'

She shook her head, and pursed her lips, and said, 'You'd better go now and say good-bye to her. And I wouldn't be in your shoes for a hundred pounds.'

A girl called Bianca was waiting for him on the bridge. She was tall and pretty, with an oval face and enormous eyes, one of which squinted a little. Her nature was warmly affectionate and her figure suggested that prudence had been no match for the ardours of her temperament. Tom Trivet had been in love with her for several months, and if his feelings were no longer so completely engaged as they had been, the diminishment was more than made good by the increase of her devotion. She held out her hands to him. Her lips were tremulous, her eyes brim-full of tears. Tom led her into the little wood beyond the bridge, and in the humid heat of her embrace remembered the dry impersonal kiss with which his aunt had bade him good-bye. Her kiss had embarrassed him almost as much as Bianca's. More, perhaps, for he had not cared to return it with any warmth — though he wanted to — and while to begin with he was reluctant to give Bianca measure for measure, he soon perceived what decency required, and then found it easy enough. There was a great deal of protestation, argument, tears, and renewal of promises before he was allowed to leave, but eventually Bianca appeared to find some comfort in his assurances, and he set off for his rendezvous with Captain Telfer.

At night, however, Bianca became hysterical and wept noisily for more than an hour, after which she fell asleep and dreamed that she was walking, blind and naked, in a strange land where dreadful voices made unending lamentation; but because she was blind she could not see who the mourners were, and her hands could not find them, for their bodies had no substance. A dozen miles from Pontefiore Tom Trivet lay in the darkness and tried to guess how far away were the two German soldiers whom, from time to time, he could hear talking. He felt quite as lonely and friendless as Bianca.

The Countess spent most of that evening with her housekeeper and an elderly steward. So that they might avoid conscription by the Germans, she had given orders that all the younger people of the village should take to the woods, which as they reached the higher parts of the hills concealed the entrances to many caves; and to preserve the proprieties the young women had been directed to the woods east of Pontefiore, the young men to those west of it. She listened to reports of the exodus, and came at last to the conclusion that she had done everything possible for the safety of her tenants. 'Except, perhaps, for the Donati girls,' she said. 'For Lucia and Lucrezia, whom I sent some time ago to the Noble Lady of Rocca Pipirozzi. Do you think they will be safe?'

'*Speriamo*,' said the housekeeper.

'The house of the Noble Lady is some distance from the nearest road,' said the steward. 'It is a house that may well be disregarded by the Tedeschi.'

'It is, in any case, too late to make other arrangements for them,' said the Countess, 'and so they must trust in Providence. I should be happier if they were in a cave, but as that is impossible Providence will have to take the responsibility.'

The steward and the housekeeper agreed, and presently the Countess went to bed and slept as well as could be expected. The next day passed quietly, but on the morning after, as the Countess in her summer drawing-room was busy with her household accounts, she heard an unfamiliar voice, and going to the window saw a German soldier climbing over the garden wall. He was followed by two others, and then the three of them, who all carried ungainly automatic pistols and had bombs hung at their belts, stood in a group and were manifestly uncertain what to do next. The Countess was also in a state of strong incertitude, and until she could make up her mind remained in tactful concealment behind a curtain. The soldiers in the garden continued to argue, and the Countess felt her heart beating with, as it were, a disagreeable importunity. Then she heard other voices, the crash of breaking glass, and the housekeeper came in, agitated in voice and manner, to tell her that three German officers were in the hall, who demanded to see the owner of the house at once.

The senior of the three, a Captain Schlemmer, was in appearance by far the most interesting. Of medium size, of good and powerful build, the cast of his features was so handsome as to suggest the emulous work of a new Praxiteles; but some equally strong agent had ruined the tone of his facial muscles and the texture of his skin so that his beauty, though he was still young, showed itself only in the decay of what had been. An extreme, a fervent debauchery might conceivably have been the cause, but the Countess, who in her old-fashioned way had been brought up to believe not only in Good but in Evil, was convinced as soon as she saw him that he had sold his soul to the Devil. She regarded him in consequence with horror, but also with a respect that his companions failed to inspire. Lieutenant Peiss was a short strong man, dark of eye and chin, in no way remarkable; and Lieutenant Hofmeister was a tall youth with a foolish expression, a loose mouth, and flaxen hair that had not recently been cut. All three wore the blue overalls of a Parachute Regiment.

'You are the proprietor?' asked Schlemmer in easy Italian. 'Good! We have taken over your house, and you will do what I tell you. I want for myself a large room with a comfortable bed and a good view. Where is one that would please me?'

'My housekeeper will show you the way,' said the Countess.

'You will show me the way,' said Schlemmer.

'I can do it no better than she,' said the Countess, but led him upstairs.

All three officers followed her and in silence looked into several rooms as she, silent also, opened their doors. Then Schlemmer said, 'These do not satisfy me. Where is your own room?'

The Countess, who realized that her only policy was acquiescence, turned back across the upper hall that was

157

flanked by the broad stone balustrade of the main staircase.

'A minute, please,' said Schlemmer, and stopped to examine one of a pair of large black and red Etruscan vases that stood upon the balustrade. 'A poor barbaric design,' he said. 'I do not like it at all.' And with a dismissive gesture he pushed it away. It fell with a loud crash into the hall below.

'You are quite right,' said the Countess calmly. 'They are just a bad imitation of the real thing, made for tourists only, and so I told my husband when he bought them.'

'That is a lie!' cried Schlemmer angrily. 'Do you think that I could be deceived by any modern fraud? I who have always been a lover of the arts? They are genuine Etruscan pottery, I tell you. Push the other one over, Hofmeister.'

Hofmeister with a snigger obeyed, and there was a second crash. 'I told my husband he was wasting money on them,' observed the Countess.

'You speak a very curious Italian,' said Schlemmer. 'Where do you come from?'

'I was born in Yorkshire.'

'In England? Oh no, it is too good to be true! We have an Englishwoman for our hostess, gentlemen. A lady, I beg her pardon. And so we shall be well looked after, for now I shall certainly insist upon that. Show me your room!'

He walked round it, lifted a few toilet articles, glanced out of the window, and said, 'It is not bad. I may use it, or if not Lieutenant Peiss can sleep here. What sort of rooms are over there?'

'Quite small,' said the Countess. 'That is the old part of the castle.'

Schlemmer was turning away when Hofmeister, at the entrance to a narrow corridor, exclaimed, 'This door is locked.'

'Open it,' said Schlemmer.

'It leads to some rooms that are never used,' said the Countess.

'Open the door,' said Schlemmer.

The Countess returned to her bedroom for the key, and when the door was opened a room hardly bigger than a closet was discovered. But beyond it was a larger chamber, and on one of its walls hung the Adoration of the Shepherds by Piero della Francesca. Schlemmer went close to examine it.

'That is genuine,' said the Countess.

'That is unlikely,' said Schlemmer. 'It is well done, but I am not inclined to think it is an original.'

'It was painted by Piero della Francesca.'

'Or by a skilful copyist. — Has the bed been aired?'

'Not for a long time.'

'Then have the sheets changed before night. I shall sleep here. Hofmeister and Peiss, you can go and choose rooms for yourselves. I recommend the Countess's for one of you. No, Countess, do not go. I want to order breakfast first.'

'It's long past breakfast-time,' said the Countess.

'It is breakfast-time when I want breakfast,' said Schlemmer, and throwing himself on the bed he dug his dusty heels into its blue silk covering, and doubled the pillows under his left arm for greater comfort. 'Since you are English,' he said, 'it will give you pleasure, of course, to serve me with an English breakfast. You have bacon? And eggs? That is good. I shall have three or four slices, well fried, and three or four boiled eggs. Some toasted bread and cherry jam. All that is very English, is it not? But I do not want your English tea. Bring me instead a bottle of your best white wine, and a bottle of brandy. But not Italian brandy, which I do not like. In a house such as this you must have plenty of cognac. And send a girl to take off my boots.'

He lay alone, staring at the picture of the Adoration. It was, he admitted, a masterly piece of work. The quality of the paint was right. There was none of that fulsomeness with which a copyist, striving to do his subject justice, so often betrays himself; but all the tones had the gentleness of old colour that has lost its ostentation to the centuries. The gentleness of an aged champagne found in a forgotten bin that has outlived its effervescence. The gentleness of dawn and sunset in the older countries of the world where civilization has long since given docility and form to the reflecting earth. Yes, it was good. But the Englishwoman had said it was genuine, and she of course was lying. She was lying to deceive him for some purpose of her own; and therefore the picture was no better than a copy could be.

His breakfast came. He ate quickly, drank half the bottle of wine, and filled a claret glass with brandy.

It could be an old copy, even a contemporary copy. But the drawing of the mother's head had the firmness that suggests the originality of genius. Something is made, by genius, and nothing before it was ever quite the same, and nothing after will be. The novelty of genius is so strong that straightway it seems inevitable, it could have been done no other way; but it cannot be done again. If the Englishwoman had not said it was by Piero della Francesca it would have given him great pleasure to recognize the master's work. But she, there was no reason to doubt it, had been lying. Why should she tell the truth to him, her enemy? He finished his glass of brandy, and went out.

Under the supervision of Peiss and Hofmeister his company — it was much depleted — was hard at work. Preparations were being made for the demolition of the bridge, and packages of a red explosive lay on an abutment wall. 'We've got none too much,' said Peiss. 'This old masonry was built to last.'

'Make a proper job of it,' said Schlemmer.

Some of the houses at the far end of the village offered a wide field of fire, and German soldiers were reinforcing the ceilings of their outer rooms with timber. Schlemmer walked away from the village, down a slope that would be hidden from the approaching enemy, and chose positions for his mortars. He returned to the castle, sent for the Countess, and said to her, 'There is no one in the village but old men and women, and small children. Where are the young people hiding?'

'There are no young people here,' she said. 'They have all been taken for work of some kind or another.'

'By us?'

'By you or the Republicans.'

'Is that true?'

'If I swore it was true a hundred times you wouldn't believe me.'

Schlemmer stared at her for a few seconds without speaking, then turned abruptly and went back to his men. He gave orders that no one was to leave the village, but all its inhabitants must stay indoors, and continued his direction of the preparations for defence till it began to grow dark.

At dinner he was taciturn, and Hofmeister and Peiss, following his example, also ate silently. But despite the lack of conversation the meal was slow and deliberate, for Schlemmer from time to time would push away his plate, and leaning on his forearms stare unspeaking into a web of thought. They drank between them five bottles of red wine and half a bottle of brandy. 'The same cognac as you gave me for breakfast,' Schlemmer had ordered.

Then, rousing himself, he repeated with clarity and exactitude his instructions for battle, if the battle should come before morning, and saying good night, went to his room in the old part of the castle.

The electric light was still working, and because the shutters had been closed for several hours the air was stuffy. He undressed, poured himself another glass of brandy, and sat gazing at Piero's Adoration. 'If it is genuine it is good in the highest degree,' he muttered. 'But if it is a copy, it cannot be so good. I should know which it is, but I do not know. Why do I not know? Why cannot I say with certainty *This is good*, or *This is not so good*?'

The difficulty of answering this question induced a little self-pity, and he thought querulously of the Countess. 'It is her fault,' he said to himself. 'If she had not told me a lie. I should know what to think. They tell lies too cleverly, the English. They have no scruples, they are unfair.'

Quietly, and without pain, he began to cry, and remembered how in his childhood he had often wakened crying at night. But in spite of that he had been happy as a boy, and now his early years seemed all to have been lived in sunlight or among green trees. There were gleams of yellow and gold in his memory, of oranges and honey and the dining-room curtains on a morning of summer wind. He thought of his mother's large white arms, and his father's stubble hair. His father had been a professor at Freiburg, and he one of five children. He remembered the ridiculous family procession to church, every week, all in stiff clothes, and his father's cigar on the homeward walk. One Sunday there had been a strange preacher, a distinguished visitor to the university, who had slowly climbed the pulpit stair and before beginning his sermon had stood, for a long time as it seemed, looking from one to another of his congregation. Then quietly, as if disclosing a secret, he had said, '*Seid stille, und erkennt, dass ich Gott bin.*' 'Be still,' the strange pastor had repeated, 'and know that I am God.' Believing the words to be a statement of fact, he, still a child, had been badly frightened.

When he grew up he had quarrelled with his father, and later his father had been imprisoned because he held dangerous political views, and called himself a Liberal. His father had been a talkative man, given to expounding with great energy his views on every subject conceivable to man, but readily silenced by his wife's voice. 'Now Heinrich,' she would say, 'you are becoming tiresome. It may be so, and it may not be so. You should not go too far. Let us talk now of something else.'

'How do I know,' cried Schlemmer, starting from his chair, 'if it is good or not? How do I know, how do I know?'

He heard his own voice, and became cautious. 'Quiet now,' he murmured, 'be quiet. Take a sleeping draught, that's the thing. You've been out in the sun too long, your

162

eyebrows are white as bleaching clothes. Take a sleeping draught.'

He filled the claret glass with brandy and drank it too quickly. He filled it again, took a little more, and hiccuped. Then, turning out the light, lay down and with hoarse breathing fell asleep.

In the last darkness before dawn he woke in fear. A nightmare that he could not remember had evicted him from sleep, and for a little while he lay in a panic, not knowing where he was. Then he found the switch, and light fell on Piero's Madonna, on the confident Child and the adoring Shepherds.

Schlemmer sat up frowning, biting his nails, and began to study the picture as though he had been wakened for the single purpose of learning its meaning. Though the child is confident, he thought, it is the mother who really knows its purpose. The shepherds, who are the base of the triangle, are eager to believe; but the mother, whose head is the apex, knows. That is quite clear. Nor is there any suggestion that she has been at pains to acquire her knowledge. It has come to her naturally, or she has heard a voice saying *Seid stille, und erkennt, dass ich Gott bin.* She is very grave, but she is happy.

'She is happy,' he said aloud, and a moment later, with a violent shudder, he screamed, 'It is a myth, the whole story is only a myth, and in any case the Englishwoman lied! It is not even the original, it is merely a copy!'

His breast heaved, he sat gazing at the picture. 'It is not true,' he whispered. 'It cannot be true. For if it is true — no, no! It must not be true!'

In the shuttered room the air was hot and still. The walls enclosed a little space in which all the light fell on Piero's Madonna, and she with a mild sublimity looked under white eyelids at the innocent assurance of her Son.

'It is not true, it is not true!' screamed Schlemmer, and stretching a shaking hand to the bedside table took from it a clumsy Schmeisser pistol and opened fire on the adoring shepherds.

The stuttering bullets raced up and down the picture,

163

and before the last echo was dead there were voices at the door. Lieutenant Hofmeister was shouting, asking what had happened, and the Countess in a breathless voice as hoarse as a grasshopper was making the same inquiry of the Lieutenant.

Schlemmer opened the door and coldly inquired, 'What do you want here?'

'You are safe?' exclaimed Hofmeister. 'Who is in there? What has been happening?'

'I wished to see if you were alert. Is Peiss also at his post?'

'Yes, sir.'

'That is good. You can go now.'

'If you are going to behave in that way again,' said the Countess, 'will you give me warning?'

'Do not refer to my behaviour!' shouted Schlemmer. 'It is you: your lies — but no! You are of no importance now. Your day is over. You also can go.'

He locked his door again, turned out the light, and opened the window. He smelt the acrid pistol fumes as they drifted out, and breathed deeply of the morning air. Ten minutes later he lay down and slept soundly till his servant wakened him.

A little before noon a dispatch-rider appeared and gave Schlemmer a written order to withdraw his company from Pontefiore before midnight, and prepare for defence another position some three or four miles to the north of it. He read his instructions moodily, and sent for Peiss. 'Get ready to move,' he said.

'Already? What for?'

Schlemmer showed him the order.

'It's always the same,' said Peiss. 'They don't know their own minds, that's the trouble. You sweat your soul out, digging and working, and then all your effort's wasted.'

'We should get bombed in the morning, if we stayed,' said Schlemmer.

'I don't think they saw us.'

'They always see us.'

164

An aeroplane on reconnaissance, high in the blue sky, had flown to and fro above Pontefiore early that morning. The Germans had made no movement while they were under observation, and all their defensive works had been well concealed; but the appearance of a second aeroplane, an hour later, had made Schlemmer complain that the camouflage was still insufficient.

Now he said, 'There are some good draught-oxen in this village. We shall take them with us.'

'There's plenty of pigs too.'

'Have some of the oxen harnessed and put what pigs you want in the carts. We shall move as soon as it is dark. Now I shall go and look at this other village, and see what work we must do there. And Peiss — '

'Yes, sir?'

'You can tell the soldiers that I am not fond of Pontefiore, and if in the process of withdrawing there should be some damage to property, I shall have no time to listen to complaints.'

When he returned in the early evening, he walked for some little while in the castle grounds and found much to admire in the gentle formality with which they had been planned and planted. He admired the ingenuity of the topiarist, and thought the art a pleasing one. In front of him two living peacocks strutted nervously down a path between a pair of enormous peacock-images cut from the dense foliage of yew-trees. The path was lined with other trees that had been clipped to the likeness of double candle-shades, and led to a stone balcony that overlooked a pool where among water-lilies goldfish swam, and a Triton in hoary stone blew his shell upon the bank. The lower terrace, patterned with a doubled design of dwarf hedges, was enclosed by a semi-circle of tall cypresses, all of equal stature, and beyond them the great slopes of Tuscany were clothed with the mellow evening light.

It has taken a long time, he thought, to make this beauty. From the beginning the hills were there, and the valleys divided them, but they were bare and meaningless before man came, with his art and purpose, to give them significance and define their form. The Etruscans did so much, the Romans more, and at the Renaissance they began again. They were good husbandmen who lived here. They desired beauty and they created it. It is a country I also could live in, if we possessed it. I am sorry to leave it.

His hands were swollen with the heat. He knelt and cooled them in the goldfish pond, then rising, shook the water from his fingers and squaring his shoulders walked briskly back to the castle.

In the small garden below the Countess's drawing-room he stopped, hearing above him voices raised in anger or distress. From the open window, fluttering in its descent, a book flew out, and with it an angry scream. Another book came tumbling through the air, and Schlemmer perceived that both were bound handsomely in white leather. He listened for a moment or two, and then with a pleased smile went in.

Lieutenant Hofmeister rose from his chair, and the Countess, who had entirely lost her usual composure and was struggling in the grasp of two German soldiers, greeted Schlemmer with the strangest demand. 'My Ouidas, my Ouidas!' she exclaimed. 'For God's sake, save my Ouidas!'

'I should explain,' said Hofmeister, 'that I came in to choose a few books to take with me, and as I read a little English and wanted something light —'

'Light!' said the Countess. 'She is a great writer!'

'— I chose these novels by the woman who called herself Ouida. They are very prettily bound.'

'They are my dearest possession,' said the Countess.

'That interests me very much,' said Schlemmer. 'But why,' he asked Hofmeister, 'why did you throw some of them out of the window?'

'That was after she had refused to make me a present of them,' said Hofmeister. 'She had the impertinence to snatch one from my hands —'

'I slapped your face!' said the Countess.

'— so I had her put under restraint, and informed her

that as a German officer I had the right to dispose of her property in any way I chose.'

'But naturally,' said Schlemmer. 'If, for example, you decided they were subversive, and should be destroyed —'

'Like this,' said Hofmeister, and grasping one of the volumes by its elegant boards, he tore out the pages.

The Countess whimpered like a child, and tears ran down her cheeks to her quivering mouth. Schlemmer laughed softly and said, 'I disapprove of female writers. They are an evil influence in the world, they set a bad example, for women should bear children, not books. You had better destroy them all.'

'Let me keep one,' said Hofmeister, and put *Moths* in his pocket.

The small drawing-room was in a state of extreme dishevelment when they left it, but the village piazza, to which they walked together, presented an even stranger appearance; for it was littered with bedclothes, mattresses, and furniture that the soldiers had gathered from the houses of Pontefiore, and were now throwing into a large untidy heap. At nightfall they set fire to the heap, and many of the villagers, beside themselves with rage and despair, came rushing out of their houses in a vain attempt to save their precious goods from the flames. They were quickly driven back, however, when the Germans opened fire on them.

After the main body had marched away, Lieutenant Peiss remained with a rearguard to blow up the bridge. This he did an hour before sunrise, and was very well pleased with the demolition.

On the outskirts of the village he noticed, in a small orchard, half a dozen straw beehives. 'Why should they have honey to eat, when we are going into battle?' he asked.

A sergeant grinned, and took from his pocket a box of matches and some old letters. The straw was dry, and the beehives burnt fiercely.

CHAPTER XIV

'*Com'è triste la vita!*' sighed Lucia, and lifted and stretched her plump brown arms, and opened her wide red mouth in a desolate yawn. The day was hot, and little yellow feathers clung to her fingers and stuck to her wrists. 'Nothing ever happens,' she said. 'Life goes by and leaves us here, alone and idle, without our men and therefore without pleasure or purpose in our existence. Oh, I am so dissatisfied, Lucrezia!'

She and Lucrezia, her younger sister, had been plucking a pair of hens in the green shade of a great vine that half-covered the wall and overhung the back door of a farmhouse. Beyond the farmyard the ground fell steeply to a narrow glen, and rose again to a round hill like a pudding-basin, but patched with trees and circled by a climbing path that here and there showed white among them. On the other side of the farmhouse was the large, squarely-built mansion of the Noble Lady of Rocca Pipirozzi.

The Noble Lady had been obliged to give hospitality, some weeks before, to a prolific niece and her seven children who had fled from their own house near Chiusi when the Germans entrenched in its grounds. As the Noble Lady lived in straitened circumstances, the Countess of Pontefiore had come to her help, and to augment her small domestic staff had sent her Lucia and Lucrezia Donati. They had come willingly enough, pleased by the offer of a change of scene, but soon had grown weary of a house duller than they had been accustomed to, and dominated now by a woman with a grievance and her numerous unattractive family. In memory, even so short a memory, Pontefiore and their own overcrowded home acquired a charm and a gaiety they had never, or never fully, appreciated till now. They longed to return, and with a desire sharpened by ennui they yearned for the company of their lovers.

'It is no life at all,' Lucrezia agreed, and holding up a naked hen she plucked from its loose skin a few remaining pin-feathers. Lucia clasped the other bird in her hands, and leaning forward, stared with mournful eyes at a daydream of her lost husband.

'It is more than a year since Enrico was taken,' she said, 'and who knows now whether he is alive or dead?'

'It is ten months since Angelo came home and went away again,' said Lucrezia, 'and I do not know whether he — he, my Angelo — is alive or dead.'

'You were not married,' said Lucia. 'It is not so bad for you.'

'It is worse for me,' said Lucrezia, 'because my nature is more affectionate than yours.'

'You have not so much self-control: that is what you mean, and we know that already.'

'I have so much self-control that often I am astonished at myself.'

'I remember one occasion when you astonished everybody.'

'That is the sort of occasion you would remember. But there are other occasions, which may be very numerous indeed, to which no one pays any attention; and they are the very important occasions on which a person conducts herself with virtue and restraint. All that goes quite unnoticed, but if for a moment or two a person is ill-advised in her behaviour, then everybody stares.'

'Enrico's absence has made no difference at all in my behaviour. I have been strictly faithful to him.'

'Your nature is comparatively cold, Lucia.'

'Well, that is a new discovery! Nobody ever said that before. Enrico never said so, and if anyone should know, it was Enrico.'

'Enrico, it may be, was easily contented.'

'Enrico was a husband that any woman might be proud of. Enrico was a true man —'

'Oh, do not tell me about Enrico! Be quiet, Lucia. I want to think about my Angelo, and how can I do that while you are shouting *Enrico, Enrico, Enrico*?'

'If I thought he could hear me, I would shout till my throat split in two!'

They were silent for a little while, and then Lucia cried, 'I must talk about him to someone! You are so selfish, Lucrezia, that a conversation with you is no pleasure at all. I shall go and talk to Emilia Bigi. She will listen to me, and be glad to listen.'

'Emilia Bigi has never had the chance to learn about men for herself, but only from women who have been deserted or betrayed, and go to her to confide their troubles.'

'She is truly sympathetic!' Lucia shouted, and without waiting for an answer threw down the hen she had plucked and set off with indignant speed, her short skirt in a flurry above her bare legs and her arms swinging to and fro like a soldier's. Quickly she disappeared from sight in the narrow glen, then reappeared a few minutes later on the path that girdled the round hill beyond it. Lucrezia watched her — intermittently in view among the farther trees — without much interest, and listened with no interest at all to the distant sounds of battle. Somewhere to the east and somewhere to the west the foreign armies were fighting each other. Field-guns were firing, but the explosion of their shells was muffled by intervening hills. Sometimes a machine-gun fired and was answered, as it seemed, by a boy rattling his stick along iron railings. Lucrezia sat in the very midst of war, but the war was not near enough to be frightening, and presently, with her hands folded in her lap and her head drooping, she fell into a light and pleasant sleep.

She began to dream about a harvest field, and herself cutting with a steady sickle the dry varnished stems of the wheat. Then, quite suddenly, panic took her, for another reaper had seized her hair in mistake for a handful of corn, and was pulling it towards him, ready to cut. She woke with a gasp of fear, and felt indeed the tug of a strong hand. Her head was jerked back, her eyes that were still half-full of the dream saw a familiar face come swiftly down, and her lips that were opening to scream were closed by an imperative warm kiss. The back of the wooden chair on which she was sitting broke with a crack, she tumbled to the pavement, and Angelo came down with her. Brown feathers that had been gathered tidily on a sheet of newspaper were scattered here and there as they lay for a minute in a commotion of mutual embraces. But then they sat up, and Lucrezia stared at Angelo, and cried, 'No, be still! I want to look at you, I want to be sure it is you. Dear Angelo, in my dream you were going to cut my head off!'

'I like it very well where it is,' said Angelo. 'Even in your dreams you should be aware of that. You must be getting morbid, darling Lucrezia, and the only cure for that is to be married. When shall we be married?'

'Oh, soon, quite soon, I think. But first of all tell me how you are, and what you have been doing, and how you came here. Listen! The guns are firing again. Oh, my dear, it must have been dangerous for you to come. Where did you sleep last night?'

'In a cave in the woods not far from Pontefiore. Some men I knew were also sleeping there, and it was from them that I learnt you were here. But if you want to know everything I have done since I last saw you, you will have to listen for a long time, because I have had many adventures.'

'Do not tell me about the adventures, tell me about yourself. Do you still love me, Angelo?'

Several minutes passed before he was allowed to explain his presence. He had come through the German lines, he said, on a perilous and important mission. No, he had not been alone. An English officer, a Captain Telfer, had come with him, and the manner in which he had first met Captain Telfer, many months before, was extremely interesting. To make his story comprehensible, he suggested, he should really begin at the very beginning —

'There will be time in plenty for that,' said Lucrezia. 'We have all our lives before us.'

'Indeed, I hope so,' said Angelo, 'though in times like these a long life is by no means certain.'

'Oh, do not be so gloomy when I am full of happiness to see you again. Was it not wonderful, Angelo, that I should be dreaming of you at the very moment when you arrived? Tell me about yourself, tell me everything!'

'That is what I am trying to do, dear Lucrezia.'

'Did you ever dream about me when you were away?'

'Yes, often.'

Lucrezia moved nearer to him, sighed, and leaned her head against his shoulder. 'Tell me more,' she whispered.

'Certainly,' said Angelo. 'As I was saying, Captain Telfer and I broke through the German lines in what was undoubtedly a very hazardous enterprise; though I do not wish to boast about it, for we' — Angelo cleared his throat — 'we of the Eighth Army do not find it either necessary or seemly to boast about ourselves.'

Lucrezia disappointingly made no comment, and Angelo continued: 'I was chosen for this duty because, of course, I know all the country here quite intimately. But I did not know the German dispositions, so we were met by a young Englishman called Corporal Trivet, who escaped from the Germans a long time ago and has been living in Pontefiore. I saw him when I went there last year.'

'Yes,' said Lucrezia.

'Did you know him?'

'Everybody knew him.'

'Was he well liked?'

'By some, yes. There are always certain people who will make much of a stranger.'

'I found him very friendly and agreeable,' said Angelo.

'By those who came to know him quite well, however, it was agreed that he was shallow and deceitful and incapable of true feeling; as all the English are.'

'Did you, then, meet a lot of Englishmen while I was away?' asked Angelo.

But Lucrezia was no longer listening. She was sitting upright and staring with dilated eyes at two figures that had appeared, in a gap among the trees, on the basin-shaped hill in front of them. They were a considerable distance away, but the light fell sharply on them and their costume was distinctive. They wore long hooded cloaks of grey wool.

'*Marocchini!*' she exclaimed.

'They are Goums,' said Angelo. 'They advance very quickly, and often they arrive in parts of the country where nobody expects them. But you need not be alarmed, they are on our side.'

'Not if you are a woman,' said Lucrezia; and in fierce words related the legend that these wild irregulars from the Atlas had created for themselves in their swift advance from Ausonia to the bare downs of Siena. They were devils incarnate, she said. Even the Tedeschi dreaded them, and to women they were the personification of all the terrors that walk by night. Her own cheeks grew pale as she spoke, and Angelo was infected by her fear. But he tried to reassure her, and himself as well, by calling attention to the deep shade in which they sat, that would make it difficult if not impossible for the Goums to see them. 'And look!' he said, 'they are moving now, they are going in the opposite direction.'

'Towards the house of Emilia Bigi,' exclaimed Lucrezia, 'where Lucia went an hour ago to talk about Enrico her husband.'

'That will do her no harm.'

'It will do her harm enough if she encounters two *Marocchini* on the way back. Angelo, you must go and warn her!'

'I see no necessity for that.'

'It is my own sister of whom we are talking! Lucia, my sister, is about to be raped, and you do not see the necessity to warn her!'

'You are becoming excited, Lucrezia.'

'In the circumstances that is not unnatural. Would you remain calm and unperturbed if your sister were in immediate danger of being assaulted, outraged, and assassinated?'

'I should first of all ask myself if the danger were real or imaginary.'

173

'And while you were arguing on this side and that, and never reaching any conclusion, your sister would have been waylaid and maltreated, undone and destroyed!'

'The situation is unlikely to occur,' said Angelo stiffly, 'because, as you are well aware, I have no sister.'

'But I have, and already she may be in the clutches of the *Marocchini*. You must go and rescue her, Angelo!'

She rose and dragged him to his feet, and as he felt in the strength of her grasp the intensity of her emotion, Angelo's heart began to beat with uncomfortable speed. Nervously he exclaimed, 'But you do not understand! The Goums are, it is true, our allies, and they have many good qualities. But they are sensitive people, they are easily offended. If I were to interfere with two men who are merely taking a quiet walk in the country, they would of course feel insulted.'

'You are afraid of them,' said Lucrezia.

'That is not the point.'

'You who belong to the *Ottava Armata*, who boast about your Eighth Army, are afraid of two poor ignorant *Marocchini*.'

'They are very redoubtable, everybody knows that.'

'You carry a revolver at your belt, and yet you are afraid. You are no use to me, Angelo.'

'If it were possible to gather a party, a fairly large party — '

'There is no one here but old women and children. The men have all gone.'

With a pitiable expression and a stammer beyond control, Angelo said, 'You know that I have a certain weakness. I have never tried to conceal or deny it, and all my friends are well aware of it. Many people possess the *dono di coraggio* in great measure, and never pause to think how fortunate they are. But I, who was born without it, know that life can be very miserable to those who lack it.'

'I am not thinking about your misery, but about Lucia's,' cried Lucrezia. 'If you want to stay here and pity yourself while Lucia is being ravished and strangled, you can do so. But do not ask me to stay beside you, and never ask me again to listen to your adventures, which I should not have believed in any case. — I give you a last chance: will you go and rescue her?'

Angelo hung his head and whispered, 'What you said is quite true. I am afraid.'

'Then give me your revolver,' said Lucrezia, and beating down his protesting hands she seized him by the belt, unfastened the holster, and took out the pistol. 'If you will not go, I must,' she exclaimed, and ran across the farmyard and down into the narrow glen.

Angelo followed her, crying breathlessly, 'No, no, you must not! You must not, Lucrezia. Those men are dangerous, you do not realize how dangerous they are!'

Lucrezia made no reply, but roughly pushed him away when he tried to hold her, and with swift steps climbed out of the glen and strode resolutely over the rising ground beyond it. They passed through a belt of woodland, Angelo at her heels still begging her to return, and came out on the path that ran upward round the side of the basin-shaped hill.

Now Lucrezia's pace grew a little slower, and when Angelo pleaded with her yet again to think of the danger she was inviting, she answered not unkindly, 'It may be dangerous for you also. I thought you were too much afraid to come.'

'What do I matter? I am thinking about you, Lucrezia. Oh, come back! Come back before it is too late.'

'I am thinking about Lucia,' she said, but walked closer to him and took him tightly by the hand.

Slower and slower became their pace, but both were breathing as deeply as if they had been climbing a mountain at utmost speed. Nervously they peered ahead, and furtively from side to side. Where the path ran bare beneath the sun they felt as though a thousand eyes were watching them, and when they walked beneath over-arching trees they dreaded instant capture. But still, with faltering steps, they went on.

The guns were no longer firing, and the silence of a

summer afternoon lay heavy on the little hill. Then suddenly, as if the silence were a curtain caught in a madman's hand, it was torn again and again by frightened screams.

'Oh, Lucia!' cried Lucrezia.

'But that was a man's voice,' said Angelo.

White and trembling, they stood and stared at each other. 'Take this,' said Lucrezia, and gave him the pistol.

'It is not loaded,' said Angelo.

'Then load it, for God's sake load it!'

With nerveless fingers he fumbled at the stiff button of nis cartridge-pouch, but before he could unfasten it Lucrezia uttered a shuddering cry and fell in a dead faint at his feet. Two yards away a man rose from behind a bush, a man who wore a grey woollen cloak striped thinly with bearish brown. His black eyes glittered like a hawk's, his nose had a hawkish curve. His cheeks were rather grey than brown, and the downward crescent of his narrow moustache was like a dreadful grin.

'Good afternoon,' stammered Angelo, and let his empty pistol fall. He bent to retrieve it, and with the speed of a stooping hawk the Goum leapt forward and struck him on the back of his head with a heavy cudgel.

The pain of the blow was so momentary that Angelo hardly felt it until he began to recover consciousness, and when that returned he grew aware of a further unhappiness that divided his mind evenly between it and his aching skull. The sun was now at tree-top height, and the guns were firing again. The explosions struck his sore head like little blows, and every movement he made brought a gyre of giddiness. He longed to lie still, to remain quiet and undiscovered in the cool shadow, but his fearful anxiety for Lucrezia gave him the resolution and the strength to get up.

He found her a few yards away, and the sight of her distress came near to banishing his own. Kneeling beside her, he undid the strips of her dress with which her hands had been tied and her mouth gagged, and taking her into his arms he held her for a long time until her sobbing stopped, and she lay so quietly that he thought she must be sleeping. But presently, without raising her head, she spoke to him. 'And now,' she said, 'you will never marry me.'

He held her more tightly, but did not answer, and a little while later she said again, 'You will not want to marry me now. You could not, Angelo, could you?'

'Darling Lucrezia,' he said, 'in the hope that you may find comfort in another's misfortune, I think I should tell you that I am in somewhat the same plight as yourself. For I also have been humiliated. But there is nothing to be gained by going into mourning for misfortunes that come to us through no fault of our own. True, I forgot to load my revolver, and that was negligence, but even had it been loaded in all chambers my hand was so tremulous that I could not have fired to any purpose; so I do not think my negligence mattered very much. No, Lucrezia, we are not to blame, so the best we can do is to let by-gones be bygones, and thank God we are still alive.'

CHAPTER XV

EMILIA BIGI'S house was not very far away, and Emilia and Lucia, who was still there, did everything that was possible to solace and comfort them. Emilia, an angular woman of nearly fifty, was indeed somewhat tiresomely complacent about her own escape from calamity, and perplexed them by her frequent exclamations in praise of boiling water. It was boiling water that had saved her and Lucia from the attentions of the other Goum, for there happened to be a pan of it on the stove when he came in, and Emilia had promptly thrown it in his face, scalding him so severely that he ran away making a noise, she boasted, of great lamentation.

When Angelo and Lucrezia congratulated her on her enterprise, she told them, with a mingling in her voice of pride and bashfulness, that it was not the first time she had preserved her virtue in such a way, for when she was sixteen a friend of her eldest brother had made her both frightened and angry, and without a moment's reflection — for luckily she was in her mother's kitchen at the time — she had rebuked him with a saucepan from the fire. 'And ever since then,' she continued, 'I've kept a pot boiling, and more than once, while I was still young and tender, I just grabbed it in time! Oh, I wouldn't be without boiling water for anything! I don't often leave home nowadays, just for that reason, because it's difficult to carry with you. But so long as I stay within a few yards of the stove, I'm as happy as a woman can be.'

Both Lucrezia and Lucia were unwilling to return to the house of the Noble Lady of Rocca Pipirozzi while the countryside was so unsettled, but in the evening of the following day Lucrezia decided that she must return immediately to Pontefiore. She would give no explanation of this strange resolve, and though the others all tried to dissuade her from so rash a project, they did not care to oppose her too roughly, for she was still in a condition of some nervousness, and prone to tears. Pontefiore, indeed, was little more than ten miles away, but who might be moving in the space between?

'I think,' said Angelo, 'that we are on the right flank of the French troops, with whom the Goums are serving, and on the left flank of the British, and perhaps there is a little space between them. But we cannot be sure of that. The nearest British troops, it may be, are Indians.'

'O God!' cried Lucrezia, 'they will be as bad as the *Marocchini!*'

'Not at all,' said Angelo. 'In battle the Indians fight with the greatest bravery you can imagine, but out of battle they are extremely gentle. Many of them are vegetarians, and their religion forbids them to kill any living creature except their fellow-men; and that they only do when commanded to by the English. There are no soldiers in the world who have better manners.'

'It is good treatment that begets good manners,' said Emilia Bigi. 'India must be a happy country.'

'I have heard different opinions about that,' Angelo replied, 'and I cannot tell you the truth of it. But I promise you that if we meet any Indian soldiers, they will behave with perfect courtesy.'

'Then let us go at once!' cried Lucrezia. 'I cannot bear to stay here any longer. I want to be in Pontefiore.'

'It would be wiser,' said Angelo, 'to wait and see whether Pontefiore is going to be liberated, or lucky enough to be ignored.'

'Are you not eager for it to be liberated?' asked Lucia.

'It is sometimes necessary to go to the dentist,' said Angelo, 'but I have never seen anyone eager to go; and this is a more serious operation than the pulling of a tooth. In the first place, before a town or village can be liberated it must be occupied by the Germans, and the Germans will rob it of everything they can find; but that is of no importance, that is merely the Overture. Liberation really begins when the Allied Air Forces bomb the town: that is the First Movement, *Allegro*, so to speak. The Second Movement is often quite leisurely but full of caprice: it occurs when the Allied artillery opens fire to knock down what the bombers have missed, and may be called *Andante Capriccioso*. After that has gone on for some time the liberating infantry will rush in, that is the Third Movement, the *Scherzo*, and though the Allied soldiers do not loot, of course, they will find a number of things, such as geese and hens and wine, that apparently belong to no one — for the local inhabitants have taken to the hills or are hiding in their cellars — and to prevent the wine and the geese from being wasted, the soldiers will naturally take care of them. Then comes the Last Movement, when the officials of the Allied Military Government arrive and say to the inhabitants, "No, you cannot do that, you must not go there, you are not allowed to sell this, and you are forbidden to buy that. If you want to live here you must apply for our permission, and it is against the law for you to be domiciled anywhere else." Yes, that is the *Finale*, and then you may say that the process of liberation is complete.'

None of them believed a word he was saying, but Lucia and Emilia Bigi listened indulgently, as they would have listened to any young man of good appearance who chose to exercise his wit on great affairs. Lucrezia, however, grew more and more impatient, and he had scarcely finished before she said again, with great vehemence, 'I must go to Pontefiore! Will you take me, Angelo, or shall I go alone?'

Angelo sighed deeply and tried to explain the peril of moving in what might already be, or quickly become, a battle-field. He did not know how far the Allied soldiers had advanced in the last few days, nor in what parts of the country the Germans were retreating. The line of battle curved and recurved across the country, here reaching forward like a long nose, there leaning back like a receding chin. They were, perhaps, in some no-man's-land between the armies into which both sides would presently charge with the most savage intention. Or, he admitted, because the roads in their immediate neighbourhood were neither good in themselves nor led anywhere in particular, it was just possible that neither army would come that way at all.

'Why, then, do we not go at once?' asked Lucrezia.

'There will, of course, be patrols moving here and there, and if we encounter the Goums again — '

'Bullets never strike the same place twice,' said Lucrezia.

'That may be the rule,' said Angelo, 'but can we be sure that the Goums will obey it?'

'Do you wish to drive me mad?' she inquired; whereupon Angelo, forsaking all other argument, pointed to the time and said, 'It will be quite dark in an hour, and though I know the way to Pontefiore, by an unfrequented path, it will be difficult to follow it at night. But if we wait till about three o'clock in the morning the last of the moon will be in the sky, giving a little light, and if we start then we should arrive, with good fortune, about sunrise or not long after. Go to bed now, Lucrezia, and rest yourself; and I shall wake you at three.'

The others agreed that this was the best plan, and Lucrezia allowed herself to be persuaded. She and Lucia slept in one bed, Angelo in an adjoining room; but Emilia Bigi stayed in the kitchen, and from time to time replenished the pan of water that bubbled all night upon the fire.

The air of early morning was cold, and the moon no brighter than a candle when they went out. But innumerable stars shone from a clear dark sky, and soon, when they could more easily distinguish substance from the shade, they walked with a firmer step. But in the sombre stillness they felt lonely, and clung together, and made slower progress than they had expected. A dozen times they threw themselves down, quivering with excitement, and hid behind a rock or a bush until the soldiers they had seen turned out to be merely another rock, or the stump of a tree. It began to grow light when they were still three or four miles from Pontefiore, and then they walked more quickly. They met no one on the way and heard nothing but occasionally the distant rattle of a machine-gun firing, and before sunrise, during the morning chorus of the birds, a loud explosion that rumbled and re-echoed through the quailing air.

They halted on a wooded slope from which they could look across a valley at the road leading to Pontefiore, and at Pontefiore on its cleft hill. Lucrezia was impatient to go on, but Angelo said they must wait for a little while to see if there was any movement of troops on the road, and if so, whether they were friendly or hostile troops. They lay for five minutes and saw no one stirring. Lucrezia said again, 'There is no purpose in waiting here,' but Angelo caught her by the wrist as she was going to rise, and said, 'I think it is safe enough, but let us stay a little longer and make sure.' They could not see the bridge from where they lay.

Then they heard — faintly at first, but quickly it grew louder — a noise that was more like a sensation of feeling than of hearing; for it rubbed upon their ears. Gleaming like beads of ice, with the morning sun upon them, the bombers looked very pretty under the tall arch of the sky.

It was unfortunate that the pilots' information was not up to date. They knew that the Germans had occupied Pontefiore, but no one had told them that the Germans had left it. Their bombs, that fell with great accuracy on the chosen targets, were in fact wasted; and so indeed was Pontefiore. A thunderstorm seemed to break upon the little town, and from it rose fountains of rubble that smeared the pale blue sky with grey dust. In the lower darkness of the storm red flames began to leap, and here and there a wooden beam or a large piece of masonry was thrown far above the general upheaval. The roar of the bombers, fretting eardrums, persisted through the thunder.

Shocked and dismayed by the spectacle, Angelo and Lucrezia rose and stood speechless for a little while, hand clasped in hand. Then Lucrezia began to moan, very quietly, and went slowly down the hill towards her home. Angelo seemed scarcely to notice that she had left him.

But of a sudden he uttered a little cry of pain, and followed her.

Both were unsteady in their gait, stumbling from time to time as if they were drunk or very tired, and neither seemed aware of the other's presence. The storm was nearly over when they reached the floor of the valley, and between the last few claps of thunder there were long intervals. A solitary dark spout of smoke and ruin burst from the castle, and spread against the sky, and slowly subsided as the noise of the bombers diminished. They were returning to their base, their mission completed.

When they had climbed the opposite slope and were on the road to Pontefiore, Angelo and Lucrezia began to run, but quickly were stopped by the destruction of the bridge. Between broken parapets the road crumbled into the gulf below, and at the bottom of the ravine lay a mass of shattered masonry. The bridge, their beautiful and famous bridge, had fallen down! The discovery appalled them, for the bridge had been so old that it had seemed as much a part of nature as the hill itself, and in their lives it had been something so important that neither, for a moment, could think of anything more important. Here on the bridge they had met with quickening hearts in the dusk of evening, and the bridge was their way to the world, and the way home again. And now it was gone, it lay broken before them, and the ravine — though in fact it was not very deep — seemed an impassable gulf between them and everything with which they were familiar.

But smoke was rising from a dozen places in the ruins beyond, and when they had recovered sufficiently to notice it, they remembered their separate purposes and saw that it was easy enough to climb down into the ravine and up again on the other side. Lucrezia never gave a thought to Angelo as she reached the farther edge, but with the smell of burning rafters in her nostrils ran desperately, crying 'Tommaso! Tommaso! Where are you?'

Angelo, for a moment only, wondered if he should

follow her, but then, with tightened lips and fear in his eyes, began to climb the nearest pile of rubble, that blocked the main street of Pontefiore, and ran faster still towards the castle. He was sickened by the sour stink of the crumbled houses, and once he stopped to help a woman who was crawling out of a cellar, and again he had to scramble across a rampart of crumbled stone; but with a single thought in his mind he hurried on.

The main door of the castle hung aslant from broken hinges, so that was no obstacle. A small fire was burning in a corner of the hall, but he hardly noticed it. A passage on the storey above was blocked by a room that seemed to have burst over it, but he clambered across the wreckage and made his way on yielding boards to a door that opened into a narrow corridor.

In the inner room he found the Adoration of Piero della Francesca lying face down upon the floor, and when he lifted it the near end broke off with a crack along a line of bullet-holes. More carefully he raised the larger fragment, and turned it over. Bullet-holes ran across it too, and the shepherds had suffered irreparable damage from some blunter assault; perhaps of a boot. But the head of the Madonna was unhurt and unsullied. The bullets had drawn a triangle on the panel, and the punctured lines enclosed her head.

Angelo sat on the floor, and his mind fell captive again to the pale brow and the gravity of the eyes. The coif about her head was white with starch, and through its transparency — what a miracle of painting was there! — the different whiteness of the forehead was stretched upon the bone that shaped it. The stillness of the face was something caught in the midst of movement, but the movement had never been swift or ungainly. Her peace was native to her, and the composure of her beauty was the reward of perfection. How strong were the cheekbones, how delicate the nostrils!

To Angelo's nose came faintly the smell of burning, but rapt in his admiration he thought nothing of it. He had found what he had run so far to look for, he was satisfied, and being satisfied had no attention to spare for anything else. The ruin of the picture as a whole, the excoriation of the shepherds, meant little to him, for his relief at finding the Madonna's head unspoilt had been so great that he had instantly accepted their loss as the reasonable price of her preservation. It was she whom he adored: she who was the product of Piero's paint and Piero's genius at work on some forgotten but immortal model. Angelo had fallen in love with her when he was sixteen, within a few days of his falling in love with Lucrezia, who was then a plump and vivacious child of twelve. Which had been the first to rouse his emotion he could not remember, but they had shared his thoughts and his fidelity — the ideal and the real — in the happiest division. He had never analysed his feelings for them, but had given to each the sort of devotion to which she was entitled, and for this simplicity had been repaid by complementary emotions. His twin attachment had contented him, and sooner or later the one side of it always reminded him of the other, because Piero had given to his Madonna lips that were remarkably the same shape as Lucrezia's; though Lucrezia's were the redder.

What depths of affection there were in Lucrezia's heart! Not many girls, he thought, would have shown so desperate an anxiety as hers for the safety of her old father and mother and her many brothers and sisters. He remembered the intensity of her fear, that had quite separated her from him as they ran together into Pontefiore, and he marvelled at the richness of her nature that could give so generously to those she loved. But how had she fared among the smoke and falling ruins of the town? It occurred to him that he had been neglectful of her, in his solicitude for the Madonna, and that now he had better go quickly and see what help Lucrezia needed.

He had no hesitation about taking the Madonna with him. Violence had very nearly released her from her context, and it was easy enough to complete the separation with a jack-knife. Like so many others, she was a victim of war, and though Angelo was well aware of his good fortune in discovering her, like a lost mistress on the road with refugees, he told himself that he was giving her protection and a home when he cut the panel along the line of bullet-holes, and wrapped the severed triangle in a pillowslip from the bed. The Countess, he admitted, might not have understood the propriety of his action, but she, by happy chance, was not there to see and dispute it. The Countess . . .

Among the rubble in the corridor Angelo halted with a new question in his mind. Where was the Countess? He had assumed, so far as he had given her a thought, that she had long since fled from the castle; but what reason had he for thinking that, except the natural but possibly misleading hope that it was so? She could still be there, lying wounded in a corner, unconscious probably, or imprisoned by a wall's collapse. Sorely though Lucrezia might need him, he could not leave the castle until he had made sure of the Countess's escape. With the Madonna's head under his arm he returned down the quaking corridor to the summer drawing-room that overlooked the garden.

The floor was covered with torn paper, and the Countess lay upon a couch. She was breathing hoarsely, snoring a little indeed, but though her face was unnaturally pale she did not appear to have been hurt.

Angelo knelt beside her and gently shook her arm. She groaned, but her eyes did not open, and he was puzzled by an unusual odour in the room. He took her by the shoulder and shook her more roughly.

'Oh dear,' she said at last. 'Oh dear, oh dear! Do go away and leave me.'

'Madam,' said Angelo, 'the castle is on fire.'

'I'm not surprised,' she said. 'I feel as if all the world was coming to an end, and a good thing too.'

'You must get up,' said Angelo. 'We really shouldn't waste time.'

'There's too much time,' said the Countess. 'That's the trouble with life. Oh dear,' she repeated as she sat up and looked at the enormous litter of torn paper. 'Oh dear, I do feel ill.'

'Are you wounded?'

'No, not now. I was, but that was a long time ago. They tore up my books, all my lovely Ouidas, and I didn't know how I could live without them. But then I remembered something. In time of sorrow, I remembered, people often take to drink. So I thought I'd try it too. And it works. Oh dear, it works! You drink a bottle of brandy, and when you wake up you don't feel anything at all except your stomach rising and your head going round. Do go away, Angelo, I want to go to sleep.'

'But the castle is on fire, madam!'

'Why should you worry about that? It isn't your castle.'

'But you, madam —'

The Countess groaned and lay down again. Then she whispered, 'There's a bottle of champagne in the little cupboard in the corner. Open it, Angelo, and look for a glass.'

The cork hit the ceiling and Angelo held to her lips a gently foaming goblet. She emptied it as though it had held a doctor's draught, and he poured another dose.

'It's certainly surprising,' said the Countess, 'how quickly you learn vicious ways, once you start them. They seem quite practical too, and that's a thing I never realized before. Have a glass yourself, Angelo.'

'Madam,' said Angelo, 'we must hurry. We really must!'

'And so we shall, as soon as we've drunk some champagne and my head's a little clearer. It's getting clear already. Very clear indeed. Oh, I'm not deluding myself, Angelo. I know that self-indulgence ought to be followed by repentance, but the fact of the matter is that champagne suits me better. Give me a little more, and help yourself when you're at it.'

'Do try to realize what a serious situation we are in,' said Angelo in a voice of distress. 'The castle is burning, you can smell the smoke.'

'It reminds me of home,' said the Countess. 'The

drawing-room chimney always used to smoke. We only used it on a Sunday, and whenever the wind was in the north or the east, or if it was raining, the chimney smoked. We were well brought up, in Bradford, and a happy family too.'

Angelo made a gesture of despair. 'I also have happy memories,' he said, 'and because of them I do not want to stay here and be burnt to a cinder. I want to go and look for Lucrezia. Half the houses in Pontefiore are in flames —'

'Good God!' exclaimed the Countess, rising from the sofa and swaying slightly. 'Have the Germans set it on fire?'

'Not the Germans,' said Angelo, 'but the Allies. They came over this morning and bombed it.'

'Don't talk nonsense,' said the Countess.

'But it is true! They made a mistake, I dare say, but a bomb has no political opinions and will explode in the wrong place quite as loudly as in the right place. Pontefiore, I give you my word, is now in ruins.'

'Then why do you let me sit here drinking and gossiping when there's work to be done? You've no sense of responsibility, Angelo, that's the trouble with you. Now give me your arm, and stop talking.'

The Countess quickly recovered herself, and when they found that the fire in the hall had burnt itself out, she accused Angelo of wilfully exaggerating the damage in order to frighten her.

'I assure you,' said Angelo, 'that a little while ago the smoke was most alarming.'

'It took more than a little smoke to alarm us in Bradford,' said the Countess, and with only an occasional stumble set off at a good pace for the village. There, having quickly perceived the extent of the damage, she wasted neither time nor breath on exclamations of astonishment or grief, but organized as many people as she could find — they had now emerged from their hiding-places to gaze with impotent sorrow on the wreckage of their homes — and set them to work to search the ruins for other survivors, to save whatever could be saved, and knock down such walls as would otherwise tumble of themselves and might claim more victims in their fall. With the deepest gratification she remembered her decision to send the young people of the village into the woods. There would have been many more casualties had they remained.

Angelo took the earliest opportunity of escaping from her benign conscription, and still carrying the Madonna's head in its pillowslip, went feverishly in search of Lucrezia. But nowhere in the village could he find her, and no one he met had lately seen her. The Donatis' house was unhurt, but the door stood open and none of the family was in. He grew almost frantic with fearful imaginings of her fate, and returned again and again to streets he had already traversed and to houses he had searched twice or three times in vain. Then, wandering haphazardly on the outskirts of the village, he came to a little garden where small pear-trees grew among beds of homely vegetables, onions and the like, and frogs were croaking in a brick-sided pond till someone, splashing the water with a stick, frightened them to silence. He looked over the wall and saw Lucrezia sitting on stone steps that descended from the house, and near her, by the waterside, a sturdy child some two years old whom she watched with a doting joy. Angelo's delight in finding her knew no bounds, but she, apparently, took little pleasure in being discovered. She answered all his questions in the shortest way, and made no response whatever to his many protestations of love and gratification. He sat down beside her, but she refused his embrace and presently there was silence between them. The child continued to beat the water with a stick.

'Who is that little boy?' asked Angelo.

'His name is Tommaso.'

'Whose child is he?'

'How should I know? There are many children in the village.'

'But everyone in Pontefiore knows everyone else.'

'Not now. Things are different now. People come and

189

go, and one does not inquire too closely who they are, or what they leave behind them.'

'I see,' said Angelo, and sighed. 'It is a pity when things like that happen. He is a fine-looking child, however, much fairer than most of the children here. Has his mother also gone away?'

'That would have been the wisest thing for her to do.'

'Tommaso,' said Angelo, frowning now. 'His name is Tommaso? Lucrezia, when you left me this morning, and ran off on your own, that was the name you were shouting. You were calling *Tommaso, Tommaso!*'

'Somebody has to look after these poor children who have no fathers.'

'But you were very agitated.'

'Naturally.'

'I don't understand.'

'Is it not natural to worry about an orphan child who is being bombed and murdered and possibly burnt to death before your very eyes?'

'Oh. Well, yes, I suppose it is.'

'Well, then.'

Lucrezia, expressionless, stared straight in front of her, and Angelo could not think what to say next. In his mind a monstrous suspicion had come suddenly to life, and though he was very properly ashamed of it, he could not quell it, and Lucrezia's words had done nothing to dispel it. She had merely made it difficult for him to ask more questions, unless he made a very blunt unmannerly inquiry; which he dared not do.

The orphan Tommaso continued to beat the water with his stick, but otherwise an embarrassed silence lay upon the garden. Then came a louder splash, a childish cry, abruptly muffled, and for a moment Tommaso's legs appeared like sunburnt branches among a foliage of silver leaves. Briefly he vanished below the greenish surface of the water, and Lucrezia with a hoarse scream leapt to her feet and a moment later was groping in the wavy pool. Quickly she found and hauled ashore the choking boy, and clasped him dripping-wet to her bosom, and passionately kissed his distorted features. He yelled for half a minute, then recovered from his fright, and asked what had become of his stick. In a loving voice Lucrezia scolded him, took off his soaking clothes, and roughly dried him with her skirt. He escaped her grasp and ran naked to the other side of the pool. There he caught sight of a small green lizard panting on a warm stone, and stood stock-still to gaze at it. Lucrezia, sitting on her heels, watched him with adoring eyes.

Angelo's voice, when he spoke to her, was so tremulous that he could hardly shape his words. His lips were dry, and the blood receding from his brain had left his cheeks a little pale, and made him feel weak and ill. 'Lucrezia,' he stammered, 'that child —'

'He is mine,' she said.

He knelt beside her, speechless now. 'You were away for three years,' said Lucrezia.

'You cannot blame me for that. It was not by my own choice but by force of circumstance that I became a soldier.'

'Was it not more unnatural for you to become a soldier than for me to become a mother?'

'So you are going to defend yourself?' cried Angelo. 'You are shameless, are you?'

'I must speak for myself, because no one else will. Women are less fortunate than soldiers. The poets and historians of the world are always at hand to argue that soldiers are justified in their horrid trade of destroying life, but if a woman is guilty of creating life she can find no advocate but herself.'

'This is not a proper occasion to become philosophical!' said Angelo indignantly. 'Philosophy is all very well in its way, but when a woman betrays the man who loves her, philosophy is merely an impertinence.'

'I have done worse than that,' said Lucrezia sadly. 'I have betrayed the man whom I love.'

'You have the hardihood to say that? You have the audacity to say that you still love me?'

'I do,' said Lucrezia.

'You have chosen a strange way to prove it.'

'I had other ways in mind. I had hoped that one of my sisters would look after Tommaso —'

'To conceal your fault? You meant to go on deceiving me?'

'You might have been happier if I had.'

Angelo hid his face in his hands, and in a muffled voice asked, 'Who is the father?'

'Why should I tell you that?'

'I insist on your telling me!'

'You have no right to know, unless you mean to forgive me.'

'How can I forgive you unless I know all the circumstances?'

Lucrezia said slowly, 'He is nothing to me now. Indeed, he is less than nothing, for we quarrelled long ago when he showed himself to be quite an untrustworthy person with whom, when I discovered his true character, I had no wish to associate.' Her manner grew warmer, her voice more rapid. 'Imagine my feelings,' she said, 'when I found that he was making love to other girls! Even before Tommaso was born he was having an affair with Vittoria Carpaccio, and then another with Francesca Cori, and quite lately he has got Bianca Miretti into trouble, who suffered already from a squint in one eye, about which she was extremely sensitive, and very soon she will have a great deal more to be ashamed of. That is the sort of man he turned out to be, after he had taken advantage of the little friendship that in decency I could not refuse him, and the sympathy that his plight demanded. No, Angelo, you need have no fear. He means nothing to me now, except as a type of selfish inconstancy that I heartily despise.'

'But who is he?' asked Angelo.

'Do you remember the Englishman whom you saw in the castle when you came here last year?'

'You mean Corporal Trivet?'

'Does my conduct seem worse to you because he is a foreigner? But Angelo, that in fact was the reason for my weakness. He was so far from home, he was so lonely and terribly unhappy that I, being ignorant then of his true character, was sorry for him. It was pity that moved me, nothing else.'

'You became his lover,' said Angelo, 'purely out of charity?'

'I am sure that is the correct way to think of it,' said Lucrezia.

'He has a very pleasant way with him,' said Angelo.

'Until you know him really well,' Lucrezia admitted, 'he is an agreeable companion.'

'And he is quite good-looking?'

'Most certainly!' said Lucrezia. 'Do you think I would have misbehaved with anyone whose appearance was repulsive? I am not so wicked as that, I hope. Trivet has good features, white teeth, and truly handsome eyes. Tommaso has inherited his father's eyes.'

'You liked him, did you?'

'But of course!'

'So you let him make love to you,' said Angelo, 'not merely because you were sorry for him, but because that was what you wanted.'

'How can you make such a dreadful suggestion!' exclaimed Lucrezia. 'No, Angelo, it is one thing to like a person, but quite another thing to want him to become the father of your orphan child. That I never desired. But I was sorry for Trivet in his loneliness, I felt for him in his unhappiness, and to comfort him I gave him my sympathy. There is the truth of the matter, whether you believe it or not.'

'All over Italy,' said Angelo, 'there are girls who have become the mothers of orphan-children whose fathers, for whom they felt no love but were infinitely sorry, were homeless Germans, disconsolate Englishmen, yearning Americans, melancholy Poles, miserable negroes, afflicted Greeks, desolate Scotchmen, woebegone Japs — yes, there are Japanese fighting on our side in the American army — and weeping Brazilians and suffering Goums.'

'No, no!' cried Lucrezia. 'It is impossible to be sorry for a Goum.'

'Perhaps you are right,' said Angelo. 'But all the others can inspire sympathy, I suppose, and because of that and the nature of women, there are orphans of every kind and colour in all the towns and villages of Italy, and their mothers have but the one excuse: it was charity that did it. They were kind to strangers, they were sympathetic beyond all care for themselves, and that is why their cradles are full and babies are crawling on every doorstep in the country. And this is happening, not only in Italy, but throughout the world. In England there are English girls who have been sorry for nice young men from New York and San Francisco, from Amsterdam and Bergen and Paris and Lyons, from Brussels and Warsaw and Montreal. In France they were sorry for the soldiers who first of all came from Birmingham and Leeds and Edinburgh, and then from Hamburg and Munich and Dresden, and now are arriving from Chicago and Pittsburgh and Philadelphia. All over the world it is the same, and everywhere young women, with their orphan children in their arms or clinging to their skirts, cry to their startled sweethearts and bewildered husbands, "But we did it out of charity!" — And what are the men to say? Are they to remove their hats and lower their eyes, look humbly to the ground and say, "You are nobler creatures than we ever realized. Thank God and you for this lesson you have taught us!" Or are they to say, "You were wantons from the beginning, and now you are liars in addition, so out of my house with you and never return!" '

'It will be better for everyone,' said Lucrezia, 'if they believe.'

'That charity was the motive?'

'Yes,' said Lucrezia. 'For charity is the Christian virtue. On charity our faith must stand or fall.'

'But if their plea is false?' demanded Angelo. 'Suppose there was no charity in the act, and nothing but simple lust? What shall a man do then?'

'If a woman pleads that charity was the motive,' said Lucrezia, 'it shows that she is aware of the high place that charity should have in life. It is an aspiration to virtue on her part that she should lay claim to charity. She has the seeds of virtue in her, if not virtue itself, because she knows the poor world's need of charity. Give her credit for that, and believe her if you can.'

'I must think it over,' said Angelo.

'I have been thinking it over for a long time,' said Lucrezia.

Silence again fell upon the garden, and silence again was broken by a loud splash. Tommaso for the second time had fallen into the pond. Now it was Angelo who pulled him out, and dried him on the pillowslip in which he had been carrying the head of Piero della Francesca's Madonna.

CHAPTER XVI

SOME days later Angelo was sitting by the side of an empty road that climbed on the one hand to the pinewoods of Vallombrosa, and on the other descended to the Arno. He was waiting, with considerable trepidation, to play his part in a small but daring assault upon the enemy. About sixty yards away, on the other side of the road where trees grew closely, Captain Telfer and Corporal Trivet lay hidden; and a little farther to the east the partisan Pasquale, who had once been a Guardia Civile, played shepherd to a flock of brown-skinned docile sheep. Also in the vicinity were half a dozen local partisans whom Telfer did not wholly trust. His hopeful intention, and the purpose of the ambush, was to capture two senior German officers, one of them a General.

On the day of the bombing of Pontefiore, Simon and the Corporal had reconnoitred the road, and twenty-four hours later had returned to the village to wait for an Allied agent who for some time had been living in Florence, which the Germans still occupied. They waited a day longer than they had intended, but the agent did not come. He sent a message, however, to confirm the information they already had. The General, he said, drove every evening from Florence to his headquarters in Vallombrosa, and he was usually accompanied by a Colonel of the Schutzstaffel who was organizing Republican resistance in Florence. If they set the ambush for such-and-such a time, he, the agent, would meet them at the appointed place on the road. Simon, though illpleased with this new arrangement, and well aware of its danger, had decided to accept the added risk and proceed with his plan.

Angelo, most unusually, had welcomed the prospect and the menace of action. Now that he was on the verge of it he was, indeed, acutely frightened, and wished with all his heart that he was elsewhere, and thought with regret how easily he could have twisted an ankle, or even broken it, in their swift and secret march across the Tuscan mountains. In Pontefiore, however, the idea of a skirmish in enemy country had been a timely comfort. It had rescued him, like a sailor pulled from a stormy sea, from a raging conflict of emotions.

A dozen times a day, for several days, he had fallen violently out of love with Lucrezia, and as often and as violently fallen in again. He had told himself, with a persistent hope of believing it, that her conduct had been as natural as the warmth of summer, even laudable if one could believe her defence of it, and reprehensible only to the most intemperate of moralists; but a little while later he would be sure to see it in another light, in which the betrayal of their love became intolerable, and her unchastity a barrier between them that he could never cross. Her character, he could then perceive, had been vitiated beyond redemption; and a great pity it was that he must also admit she had grown more beautiful than ever.

But what of that, he would cry in quick despair, for what is beauty but a little paint on a rotten house, and paint does not last a lifetime, but withers in the sun and cracks upon the wall and time strips it. Beauty is no argument.

To which another voice would answer, Beauty is everything, and everything is forgiven it.

But how unfair! he would protest. Justice should be a constant thing, and beauty has no right to look for leniency and special terms.

You will find it very pleasant to be lenient, said the voice. It is a fine thing to be magnanimous, and to be magnanimous to a lovely creature like Lucrezia is really quite a luxury. Try it and see.

Then he would remember the child, and see clearly that little Tommaso, yearly growing taller, would forever cast a shadow on his marriage and perpetually remind him that once upon a time — oh, not once, but often, he supposed — Lucrezia had surrendered herself to Corporal Trivet, as now to him. And how could happiness ever live with so noisy a reminder of her infidelity and the rival who had preceded him?

To which the voice would reply: That is nonsense indeed. You have no concern with what is past and over, you are concerned with the present. A man who broods upon past injustice, early hardship, and the youthful vagaries of his wife, is like a nation that cannot forget its history: he has not the slightest chance of happiness. As for the boy, he is Lucrezia's child, well built and friendly, and you may become very fond of him. When you have three or four children of your own he will be no more than one of the family, and you will never trouble yourself to think how he came there. Confess now, that when you dried him with the pillowslip in which you had been carrying the head of Piero's Madonna, you felt your heart already warming to him?

It is true, Angelo would then admit, that I have no animosity against the child, but that is a different thing from forgiving his mother. And if, as you say, beauty is everything, the pillowslip contained a paradigm of perfect beauty, that is now in my possession. One, moreover, that cannot change and grow old, put on grey hairs and fat, and wear wrinkles for its winter fashion. I have Piero's masterpiece, and with her upon the wall of my room I can live happily enough.

Try it and see, said the voice. You will need something more than perfection hanging on a wall to keep you happy. . . .

On and on went the passionate argument, till Angelo was exhausted by its double vehemence; and the order to march, the invitation to a brush with the enemy, had come like the blissful ease of holiday. They had crossed the tall ridges of Tuscany, waist-high in bracken, upon which the wind blew gale-strong, though in the dark valleys the air was warm and still, and every mile had strengthened the illusion of release and fortified his frail desire to bid Lucrezia good-bye and forget her for ever. She had failed him, she had no claim upon him, he was a free man and henceforth he would enjoy his freedom.

So he thought in the fine soldierly spirit of a soldier who is not yet in touch with the enemy.

Though to begin with he had been gloomy in the presence of Corporal Trivet, his embarrassment had been lessened by the discovery that Trivet himself was much perturbed by the claims of Bianca Miretti. She was a stupid girl, as Angelo well knew, but stupidity has never prevented a good-looking young woman from engaging a man's interest, and thereafter lying on his conscience; and having perceived that Trivet, like himself, was the victim of unruly love, Angelo began to regard him as a fellow-sufferer. He did, at first, feel an occasional wild impulse to assault the Corporal, but because his good sense told him that the sequel might be uncommonly painful, he always managed to suppress this foolish inclination; and when Trivet showed himself to be friendly — he was very generous with his cigarettes — Angelo soon became sympathetic, and from time to time he was convinced that they had both been deeply wronged.

For a whole day, indeed, he had been almost persuaded that he was done with Lucrezia, and would never see her again; but his resolution had weakened in the half-hour he had been waiting at the roadside, and now she returned to his mind very vividly as an image of comfort. Now again he desired her, and admitted his desire. The minutes passed and the time approached when he must boldly break cover, and expose himself to flying bullets, and keep his hand steady to shoot in reply; and in this horrible situation he longed for the shelter of Lucrezia's arms, the concealment of her hair, and the warmth of her body that would enclose him like the walls of a house. He was just about to take off his hat, to make a solemn declaration that he had forgiven her infidelity, and would go back to her as soon as this dreadful adventure was done with, when he saw that Pasquale the partisan was already driving his flock of sheep down the road towards him.

Angelo, sitting by a bend in the road, had a long view

of it in both directions, but Pasquale could see it only as far as the corner, and travellers coming from the opposite direction would not see Pasquale and his sheep until they turned the corner. Angelo's task was to hold Pasquale in conversation, or give the appearance of doing so, and by clumsy shepherding of the flock help him to block the road about twenty yards west of the corner. The General for whom they were waiting was a person of regular habit, and they knew, within a few minutes, when to expect him. As soon as he saw the car coming from the west, Angelo was to walk down the road to meet Pasquale.

Now, with a sudden feeling of guilt — for he had been sitting with his eyes tight-closed to think more clearly about Lucrezia — he looked westward and saw, not the car, but a peasant riding a donkey and leading another that carried a great load of firewood. Angelo for a moment was puzzled by this unexpected appearance, for he could see two hundred yards down the road, and the last time he had looked that way it had been empty; but now the peasant was barely a stone's throw from him. He must, he realized, have been daydreaming of Lucrezia for a couple of minutes, and by his neglect might well have ruined Telfer's plan. Conscience pinched him hard, and in deep remorse he determined to make amends by playing his part in it with high courage.

Before time and the working of imagination could weaken his resolution he saw the car coming, and with a quickly-beating heart and a dry mouth went to meet Pasquale. He turned for a moment to look at the peasant on his donkey, and saw that he was a tall, sturdily-built man, roughly dressed, with an old black hat pulled far down over his eyes.

'They're coming!' shouted Angelo to Pasquale, but his voice cracked and the words were no louder than the breaking of a dry twig in a wood. Pasquale with a long staff was keeping his flock in the middle of the road, and because there had been a thunderstorm in the early afternoon, and their fleeces were still wet, the strong smell of the sheep was like an invisible cloud carried by the downhill wind. They stood stock-still when Angelo was five yards from them. He said again, hoarsely, 'They're coming!' He could hear the increasing noise of the car, and now Pasquale was watching, not only his flock, but the bend in the road twenty yards away. Quite suddenly he made a little jump, all his muscles twitched, his eyes dilated and his hands flew out, like a man who has had an electric shock; and Angelo turned swiftly to see what was happening.

The peasant on the donkey had reached the corner a moment before the car overtook him. As it approached he bent towards the other donkey, and from a funnel in the load of wood on its back swiftly drew a tommy-gun, with which, very calmly and accurately, he opened fire on the car as it passed him.

The shriek of skidding tyres covered the staccato of gunfire, and the heavy car, after rocking this way and that, fell with a deafening bang into the ditch beside Angelo, on the north side of the road, crushing beneath it a couple of small brown sheep. The engine stopped, and the silence that followed was startling in its intensity. The tall peasant, who had dismounted, came running up and, before anyone could stop him, carefully fired three more shots into the wrecked car. 'That will save trouble,' he said, and with a smile asked Angelo, 'How is my friend Don Agesilas?'

Angelo, gaping and tremulous, perceived that the peasant was blind of one eye; but before he could speak, Simon Telfer and Corporal Trivet were beside them, and Simon was asking questions in a loud angry voice.

'Who the devil are you?' he demanded. 'What are you doing here? Who gave you permission to shoot on my ground? You damned poacher!'

The peasant took from an inner pocket a monocle of clouded tortoise shell, which he adjusted over his blind eye, and said urbanely, 'You are Captain Telfer, I presume? My name is Fest.'

'You're Fest, are you? Well, you're an unmitigated nuisance! You've spoiled the whole plan. First of all you leave me in the lurch, you don't turn up when I expect you, and now when you do come, you get in my way!'

Angelo had never seen Telfer so angry, but Fest was unperturbed. He made a small deprecatory gesture and said in a soothing voice, 'There is no need to be upset. Our mission has been accomplished and both the officers are dead. So, indeed, is their driver.'

Simon walked to the overturned car and looked into it. 'I wanted them alive,' he said. 'My orders were to take them prisoner.'

'That would have been too cruel,' said Fest. 'I could not, without straining my conscience, have assisted you in that.'

'Crueller to take them prisoner than to kill them?'

'Much crueller,' said Fest. 'I have been a prisoner myself, and I know.'

Simon, still angry, demanded, 'Why did you interfere in this affair? I can't understand you. It seems to me that you have shown a complete lack of responsibility.'

'I am self-indulgent,' said Fest. 'I have nothing in the world but my hobbies.'

'I admit,' said Simon, 'that you did your job very efficiently, though it wasn't done in the way I intended.'

'Thank you.'

'But we can't stay here gossiping. — Get in and search them, Trivet. See what papers they're carrying.'

'I shall help,' said Fest. 'I intend to take this officer's uniform, though it will require cleaning before I can wear it. I have long wanted to dress myself up as a colonel of the Schutzstaffel.'

Angelo, in the meantime, had been staring with a horrified fascination at the other dead officer. He had recognized his old pupil, General Hammerfurter, to whom he had once taught Italian, and though he had detested him when he was alive, he could not help feeling sorry for him now that he was dead. He thought Fest was talking utter nonsense when he said that it was crueller to take a man prisoner than to kill him; for Angelo had such a healthy appetite for life that he could imagine nothing worse than to be deprived of it. In the simplicity of his heart, moreover, he thought it strange and marvellous, an occasion for wonderment and awe, that so great a person as a general could be removed from the grandeur to which he was accustomed by a little piece of lead no bigger than an acorn. A bullet, he had supposed, was a private's ration. It was monstrous that a general should die of it.

While Angelo was musing in this unprofitable manner, and Fest was busily undressing the dead colonel, and Tom Trivet was searching for documents, they were interrupted by a little squall of bullets from the north, and then by another from the east. Some of the bullets struck and penetrated the car, others flew off it with a wicked whine, and a few scarred the surface of the road within a foot or two of where Simon was standing with Pasquale the partisan. Simon and Pasquale immediately leapt into the cover of some trees on the south side of the road, and were quickly followed by Fest and Tom Trivet; the former carrying the German colonel's uniform, and the latter a small packet of letters. But Angelo took shelter under the car.

A German patrol, on a periodic tour of the hills, had been attracted by the noise of the smash, and when the non-commissioned officer in charge of it saw three or four men gathered about the car, and a scattered flock of sheep and two donkeys in the vicinity, he immediately assumed that some local peasants had perceived an opportunity for looting. Dividing his patrol into two, and ordering both parties on to nearby hillocks that overlooked the road, he had given the signal to fire as soon as they were in position. When he saw Simon and the others make a dash for cover, he and half his patrol got up and ran towards the car.

'Angelo, Angelo!' shouted Simon. 'Oh, damn him, why didn't he come with us? Angelo! Get a move on, you fool!'

But Angelo, huddled in the ditch with his head between his hands, stayed where he was.

'I can't wait for him,' said Simon. 'He knows the orders, he knows we can't stay and fight it out. We're not equipped for fighting.'

'I'll go and get him,' said Corporal Trivet, and before Simon could answer he was running across the road, firing as he went. Simon and Pasquale at once gave him covering fire, and the Germans, one of whom was hit, quickly went to ground. Fest had disappeared, and there was no sign of the partisans who should have been supporting them.

Trivet knelt and looked under the car. 'Come on,' he said, 'you can't stay here.'

'What else can I do?' asked Angelo.

'Get up and run. I'll take care of you.'

'Oh my God!' said Angelo. 'The road is very broad.'

'Hurry,' said Trivet.

Angelo, crouching, ran nervously towards the trees, and Trivet, after firing a burst in the direction of the Germans, followed him. He was hit and fell as he reached the other side. Simon pulled him into cover, and found a flesh wound in his left thigh. 'It's only a scratch,' he said, and began to unfasten a field-dressing. A German appeared thirty yards away, and Pasquale shot him through the head.

'You can walk all right, can't you?' asked Simon.

'I'm all right,' said Trivet.

'But your arm's bleeding, too — '

'They hit me twice. I'll tie that up later. It's nothing to worry about.'

'Angelo and Pasquale will go with you. I'll follow in a few minutes.'

The Germans were now moving with more caution, and Simon waited for more than a minute before one showed himself. He was the non-commissioned officer in charge of the patrol, and Simon shot him in the chest. He fell, and another man came to his assistance. Simon hit him also, and running behind some bushes about thirty yards to the right, fired several shots at random, and repeated the manœuvre from another position still farther away.

Keeping under cover, he then followed the others.

The site of the ambush had been largely determined by the useful line of retreat which it offered. Here a little wood concealed him as he ran, and there the slope of a terraced hill and a grove of olive trees whose green and silver leaves were now straining in the evening wind. He soon overtook Pasquale, who told him that he would find Angelo and the Corporal a little farther on.

Pasquale, broadly grinning, was enjoying himself. 'That was good, that was fine,' he said. 'You saw him that I shot in the noggin? *Bic-boc!* like that, and he's bottom-up. A big Tedesco, six feet high. Oh, I'm good, but I was better still when I was a young man. We are all right now?'

'Yes, I think so. Will you do rearguard while I go on and see how Corporal Trivet is?'

'Have no fear,' said Pasquale. 'I will protect you.'

Tom Trivet, with one arm round Angelo's neck and the other hand tucked into his shirt, was keeping a good pace, but his cheeks were as white as a bone, his nose waxen, and his right sleeve drenched with blood. He was unwilling to stop, but when they came to a small stream Simon washed and examined the wound, and discovered that the tip of his shoulder-blade had been broken. He dressed and bandaged the wound as well as he could, and they continued their march to the south. Before it was dark they had reached a friendly farmhouse on the east bank of the Arno, where they waited for Pasquale and the cover of night.

Pasquale arrived about two hours later, still in high spirits, and said that the German patrol, now reinforced, had apparently picked up a false trail; the Tedeschi, he said, were watching the road and the river-bank in the neighbourhood of Rignano, well to the north of where they were. He himself had had no trouble.

Simon was a little worried and considerably annoyed by the disappearance of Fest. It was ridiculous, he told himself, to suppose that Fest would betray them; he had a long record of hostile acts against the Germans, and his assassination of a General, a Colonel, and their driver seemed to indicate, if not sympathy with the Allies, at least a genuine antipathy to their enemies. But from the military point of view his behaviour was most unorthodox, and his loyalty — well, loyalty was a difficult word to define, but even were it given its broadest definition, Fest would still appear to be deficient in it. He was fundamentally selfish, Simon decided. It was a vice that foreigners, and foreign countries, were much addicted to. They were selfish and irresponsible, and there were far too many of them in the world. — So thought Simon, brooding over Fest's unloyalty, and his mind discoloured by it.

His mood softened, however, when he turned to Pasquale, for Pasquale, his leathern face creased with delight and his broad hands filling the air with gestures, was describing for the tenth time how he had hit a giant Tedesco in the noggin, and laid him like a dead ox on the grass; and their hosts, a sturdy black-browed farmer and his broad-built wife, who were known for the help they had given to many British and American airmen who had been shot down and gone into hiding, were encouraging him with great exclamations of pleasure; and the farmer was filling, brim-full and spilling over, everyone's glass from a new flask of wine; and four children in the doorway, wide of eye and sucking their thumbs, were listening as though it were the first fairy-tale they were hearing; and the farmer's wife, without a thought for the morrow, was cutting for her guests' entertainment her last loaf of bread and the knuckle-end of her last smoked ham.

Suddenly regretting the ungenerosity of his thoughts, Simon raised his glass to Pasquale and said, 'You're a good fellow, Pasquale, and you've done well.'

'Right in the noggin,' said Pasquale happily. 'A Tedesco six and a half feet high, the biggest I ever saw, but *bic-boc!* and down he goes, arse over tip.'

'When the war is finished,' said Simon to the farmer, 'I shall come back to Italy.'

'Why not?' said the farmer. 'Before the war, all you English used to come to Italy. Italy is very beautiful.

Naturally you will return, and perhaps quite soon.'

'*Speriamo*,' said Pasquale.

'But the war's not over yet,' said the farmer's wife.

'*Pazienza*,' said the farmer. 'Even wars come to an end.'

A few minutes later Simon left them to reconnoitre the river-crossing, and when he came back, with the news that all was quiet, Angelo went to wake Tom Trivet, who had been sleeping in the farmer's bed. Trivet woke in a fright and began to talk with rambling excitement; but a glass of brandy seemed to calm him, and presently they set out with Simon in the lead, Angelo and Trivet a hundred yards behind him, and Pasquale in the rear. The night was dark but clear, with clouds like black continents dividing a grapeskin sky, and the Arno running noisily, flushed with the day's rain. They had no great difficulty in fording it, however, and two hours later they were in the upland country to the west. Then Trivet collapsed, and they found that the wound in his leg was bleeding again.

They carried him into the shelter of a nearby copse, and Pasquale went in search of a neighbouring friend of his, another farmer who had, from time to time, succoured Allied soldiers who had escaped from their captors. He returned before dawn with a short ladder, half a dozen eggs, and a disconcerting account of the increased number of German troops in the neighbourhood. The farm where they had hoped to leave Trivet, in comfort and reasonable security, was occupied by the enemy.

All day they lay hidden, listening to the not-far-distant noises of an intermittent battle, and fed thinly on biscuits, chocolate, and raw eggs. For most of the time Tom Trivet slept, and when evening came he seemed better, though he was still too weak to walk. Both Angelo and Pasquale knew the country they were in, and after long discussion over a map Simon had come to the conclusion that by keeping to the higher slopes of the Chianti mountains they might break through the German lines and reach the nearest troops of the Eighth Army before another dawn.

'I don't think they're much more than ten miles away,' he said, 'and if we can average a mile and a half an hour, carrying Trivet, we can do it in seven hours, and that gives us a little margin of darkness for safety. What do you think, Pasquale?'

'By myself I could go through quite easily,' said Pasquale. 'Carrying the Corporal, it will be more difficult, and hard work. But not impossible.'

'Angelo?'

'We must do everything we can for him,' said Angelo very earnestly. 'He should be in hospital now, and delay may be dangerous.'

Angelo had spent the day keeping flies off the Corporal while he slept. His heart was full of gratitude, and devotion, and self-reproach. Not only had Tom Trivet saved his life, or saved him from captivity, and suffered grievous wounds in consequence; but he had set Angelo an example in generosity which he now saw as a great and humiliating lesson. He, Angelo, had committed a fault unpardonable in a soldier: he had sought safety in a ditch when his plain duty was to stand up — for the short time it would take to cross a narrow road — and thereafter fight or run as he might be ordered. He had failed in his duty, he had sinned against discipline. But Tom had forgiven him and proved his forgiveness by risking his own life to rescue him. How much more, then, should Angelo forgive his dear Lucrezia, whose fault he could pardon at no cost to his skin, but only a little wound to his pride? Yes, Tom had taught him a lesson. A man should be generous always — and the mere thought of his coming magnanimity filled his mind with the anticipation of its pleasure.

'Yes,' he went on, 'Corporal Trivet needs medical attention, and though it may be difficult to carry him through the German lines, I do not think we should be deterred by that.'

'Good for you,' said Simon.

'And afterwards, I very much hope that you will allow me to return to Pontefiore.'

'For any particular purpose?' asked Simon.

'I have set my heart on being married at the earliest possible moment,' said Angelo.

CHAPTER XVII

When they had tied Tom Trivet firmly to the ladder which Pasquale had found, Angelo and Pasquale lifted it to their shoulders, inserting their heads between convenient rungs at either extremity, and began their night-march, led by Simon some forty yards in front of them. Good fortune and their choice of the most arduous route enabled them to avoid the Germans, but nothing could mitigate the burden of Tom Trivet. They had to carry him up steep hill-paths to lofty starlit ridges, where a boisterous wind assaulted them, and down again by tortuous rocky trails. They followed sheep-tracks across ground so perilously aslant that Angelo often feared they would lose their footing and go tumbling and rolling into unseen depths; and they forced their way through thickets of tall bracken. The poles of the ladder pressed deeper and deeper into their aching shoulders, or leaned horribly against their necks when they walked upon a slope. Whenever they were climbing, Tom Trivet's weight hung backward so that they were in danger of being garrotted, and when they went downhill their heads were bowed in agonizing obeisance. Long before midnight Angelo began to suspect that a wounded giant lay on the ladder. By two o'clock in the morning the giant had acquired some uncommonly heavy luggage: his tombstone, perhaps, the field-gun that he used for a fowling-piece, two thousand demijohns of the local wine, and so forth. A couple of hours later, pain had created a fantasy more malignant still, and the giant was an ogre whose monstrous thumbs were pressing Angelo and Pasquale, like drawing-pins into a board, deep into the resistant earth. Angelo wept and prayed, Pasquale groaned and swore. Tom Trivet was silent, for he was unconscious again. And Simon, with no mercy for himself or them, still sought improbable paths and compelled them to follow.

When daylight came they were some three hundred feet below the crest of a great green hill, at the upper corner of a straggling wood that climbed its southern slope, and there was nothing to be seen of the enemy, nothing of the English army. Simon at last gave the order to halt and rest, and Angelo, so weary that he could no longer bear even the sight of other men, staggered a little farther downhill, a hundred yards or more, and falling into a clump of ferns at the edge of the wood was sound asleep within the instant.

He was awakened, when the sun stood overhead, by the iron growl and screech of approaching tanks, and immediately was seized with a fear of their crushing him where he lay hidden among the ferns; but as he did not know whether they were British or German he dared not get up and run away, lest he expose himself to the enemy. The leading tank halted not far from him, and a little while later Angelo heard men's voices. He held his breath to listen, and then had to bite his fingers to keep his teeth from chattering. It was not English they were speaking.

'*En wat is daar nou te doen noudat ons hier aangeland het?*' said one of the invisible soldiers.

'*Ons kan die natuurskoon bewonder,*' replied another. '*Daar is, goddank, niks anders om te doen nie.*'

There was a pleasant tune in their voices that was certainly not German, but the words were more like German than anything else, and Angelo was well aware that the enemy had recruited foreign legions who spoke in many tongues. He lay still for three minutes more, tormented by doubt as well as fear, and then, with relief that merged quickly into gratitude and pure happiness, heard other voices and words — familiar English words — that now seemed inexpressibly kind and comforting.

'Shock me,' exclaimed a hoarse and breathless Cockney, 'if ever I want to see a shocking mountain again! It's like that shocking old nursery rhyme, this shocking war is:

> The good old Duke of York,
> He had a thousand men,
> He marched 'em up to the shocking top of a shocking
> hill,
> And shocking well marched 'em down again.

I'm browned off, I am, and my shocking feet are on fire.'

How sweetly they fell upon his ears, the homely English syllables! He was free, he must be free, in the company of these good fellows who spoke the tongue that Shakespeare spake; and crawling softly through the fern he saw presently some half a dozen tall soldiers, wiping their sweaty brows, of the Grenadier Guards, and with them the crews of two tanks of the South African Division. They appeared to be on terms of the warmest friendship, and the voices that had lately been speaking Afrikaans now joined with Cockney in genial debate. Angelo, not yet revealing himself, watched them and listened with the greatest pleasure until a Guardsman, coming into the fern on business of his own, tripped and fell on him. This caused some confusion, and Angelo for a moment or two was in near danger of his life, but saved it by his own command of English.

'I am not a shocking spy!' he exclaimed indignantly. 'I am a shocking co-belligerent!'

They listened to him then, both Englishmen and South Africans, with a proper respect, and readily went with him to look for Simon and Pasquale and Corporal Trivet.

Simon, they discovered, had already met the Grenadiers and was talking to one of their officers who happened to be an old friend of his. Tom Trivet had been carried away and put in the doctor's care, and Pasquale, who had never before seen tanks on a mountain-top, was patting their steel flanks with admiring hands, as though they had been fat cattle.

For a little while, in this small segment of it, the war had the innocent look of some old pastoral foray. The day was fine, and the great shoulders of the green Chianti hills showed firm and muscular beneath a tall blue sky. A gentle wind rustled the bracken and whispered in the branches of some lonely trees. Two officers with field-glasses, patient and quiet as deerstalkers in a Highland forest, searched the opposing mountainside for a possible head; and the Guardsmen and the South Africans — the sons of Queen Victoria's infantry and of Kruger's ɪong-sighted riflemen — lay gossiping together and drinking tea.

A tank moved slowly forward, and its gun was depressed till its barrel lay on a downward slant like the slope of the hill. Three shots were fired, and from the wall of a farmhouse in the valley below floated small clouds of dust. A man, crouching, ran from the farm into a copse behind it, and in the flat fields to the east little khaki figures could be seen advancing. Three aeroplanes, circling their target, stooped like hawks upon it, and as they climbed again tall plumes of smoke rose behind them. The sound of distant machine-gun fire mingled with the stridulation of grasshoppers.

Angelo and Pasquale ate some bread and bully, and went to sleep again. Then Simon sent for them, and they found him, half a mile downhill, sitting with a Guardsman in a borrowed jeep. They had no difficulty in returning to Pontefiore, for the curving front of battle was now several miles to the north of it, and peace, with a look of stunned surprise, lay upon the ruined village. In the castle they found Fest drinking white wine with the Countess.

Simon's manner, when they met, was cold and constrained, but Fest was bland and smiling, and the Countess took such obvious pleasure in his company that Simon had to master his feelings and assume a friendlier air than he had any mind to. What would otherwise have been an acrimonious discussion became in fact, at the Countess's table, a protracted dinner-party with Fest, on her right, playing the part of the distinguished guest, accomplished in conversation, until they retired to her drawing-room, where the Countess herself kept the talk going with anecdotes of her early life.

Angelo, in the meantime, had found Lucrezia, proposed immediate marriage to her, and been accepted. Lucrezia's objections to a wedding in war-time had seemingly vanished, and though Angelo warned her that he would certainly have to leave her again, she made no reference to the sad plight and many difficulties of a young wife, married one week and left alone the next, which had been the mainstay of her argument the year before. She had responded, indeed, with such a melting warmth as Angelo had never seen in her. She had hung upon his neck as though in utter abandonment to his will or care, and lying in his arms had looked up at him with eyes so lovely in their trust and gratitude that Angelo, at one moment ravished with delight, was at the next intoxicated with the pride of his triumphant manhood.

He was, however, somewhat taken aback by the coolness with which she listened to the tale of Tom Trivet's heroism and the wounds he had received. She made no concealment of her agitation when Angelo spoke of the danger that he himself had been in, when he found himself on the wrong side of the road; but the news of Tom Trivet's wounding did not affect her in the least.

'He is all right now?' she asked, with plain indifference in her voice.

'By no means!' said Angelo indignantly. 'He was hit in two places and it will be a long time before he is all right again. He will recover, certainly, but at this moment I suppose, he is lying in great pain; while I, who owe everything to him, am alive and well and supremely happy.'

'Oh darling, how glad I am that you are alive, and very, very glad that you are happy!'

'But we must also think about Corporal Trivet — '

'Let us think about him some other time. Just now it is enough to think only about ourselves.'

On subsequent reflection he admitted that her loss of interest in Tom Trivet would be a decided advantage to their married state; but he was surprised, and dubiously hurt, and even alarmed a little by the completeness of her unconcern. That Tom had jilted her could not be denied, and to get a girl with child and then desert her was something, of course, quite unforgivable. But even so, the spectacle of unforgiveness was a trifle shocking; or so it appeared to Angelo.

He was, however, far too happy in his possession of Lucrezia to waste time in fault-finding, and early the next

213

morning he sought the village priest and told him that he wanted to be married as soon as possible.

The village church and the village priest had both suffered badly in the bombing of Pontefiore. The church, with its west wall blown down and most of the roof gone, stood wide open to the sun and the rain, and the priest, having lost the placid view of life that had protected him for half a century, now seemed equally exposed to the elements. He shivered in the noonday heat, he was frightened of the dark, and when Angelo said firmly that the day after to-morrow would be most suitable for a wedding, he at once agreed. The sacraments, he said, were always available for those who needed them, and marriage was a sacrament like baptism and penance. 'Though indeed,' he said, 'I should not be happy if you had to be carried to it, as you were to your baptism, or returned for it again and again, as undoubtedly you will in penitence. Oh no! One marriage is enough for anyone, and you'll come to it on your own legs or not at all. — Bless you, my child. Our poor church is draughty now, but I dare say it will serve.'

All the villagers were delighted by the prospect of a wedding, for they saw in it a brave assertion that life must continue in its ordinary way, despite the outrages of war; and Lucrezia's mother laughed and wept alternately for the better part of a whole day, while the Countess with a stern and furrowed brow went to and fro to see what could be provided for a marriage feast. She found little enough, for the Germans had taken with them everything they could carry, and the general feeling of elation was quickly followed by a widespread gloom when it became apparent that the celebrations would be dulled by hunger.

Angelo was further depressed by a conversation he had with Simon. 'I have been thinking about your future,' said Simon.

'I am going to be very happy,' said Angelo.

'Yes, I hope you will be. But I think you should know that I've recommended you and Pasquale for transfer to one of the new Italian Brigades that are being formed.

I'm going to one of them myself, as a liaison officer.

'And what shall I have to do there?' asked Angelo.

'Training, to begin with. We're starting to train and equip a large number of Italian troops, so that by next year they'll be able to take their place in the line along with us and the Americans.'

'By next year? Is the war going to last as long as that?'

'Nobody knows how long it's going to last, but obviously we must be prepared for the worst.'

'I don't think I could live,' said Angelo, 'if I were truly prepared for the worst. Why should I, indeed? Why should anyone?'

'Now you're being obstructive. You are talking for the sake of talking, and that won't do you any good at all. What I mean is that we must face facts.'

'In an infantry regiment?' asked Angelo sadly.

'Yes, you're pretty certain to be posted to the infantry.'

'But why, why! Why must I go and spend month after month being drilled, and running to and fro carrying very heavy weights, and firing rifles and mortars and machine-guns, and throwing bombs of which I am extremely frightened, and lying out all night in the cold, and marching hundreds of miles without going anywhere in particular — and all to be killed in the most unpleasant manner by a total stranger in some part of the country that I have no wish to visit?'

'I think it is the proper thing for you to do,' said Simon stiffly.

'Oh my God,' said Angelo, 'now I am doomed indeed!' — For he knew that when the English say *It is the proper thing to do*, the inexorable laws of nature are supplemented by another that they discovered, and only they can understand. Oh, their wild notions of propriety! They are like sunspots, he thought, for they cannot be explained or foretold, and their effects are incalculable. Whether they have indeed certain absolute standards of behaviour, or merely a tribal instinct, or perhaps an hereditary taint — a sort of itch — it is impossible to say. But you can no more argue with them than you can dispute the law of gravity. — Yes, he admitted, I am doomed, and there is no escape.

'Lucrezia,' he said, 'will not be pleased when she hears that I am to become a soldier in the infantry again. It will be very difficult to say good-bye to her.'

'Well,' said Simon, 'that sort of thing is always difficult. But it has to be done, of course.'

Always difficult! thought Angelo in a sudden wordless rage. *Always* difficult indeed! He wanted to ask Simon — but dared not, for he knew it would be improper — he wanted to ask him how often he had bidden good-bye to a woman who loved him, and broken her heart, and comforted himself with the cold reflection that *it had to be done, of course*. Oh, they were insufferable, these Englishmen! They made life impossible — and the expectation of it highly improbable.

But he knew that he must hide his feelings, for though he had come near to losing his temper, he retained his manners; and the English, as he had learnt, disliked above all things a display of feeling. So with a stiffness like Simon's own he said, 'I shall do whatever you think it befits me to do. You can be sure of that.'

'That's good,' said Simon warmly. 'You're a good fellow, Angelo, though you talk a lot of nonsense, and I knew I could rely on you.'

Walking by himself, with desolated spirit. Angelo pondered this last remark and could not decide whether he had been flattered or insulted by it. Simon relied on him to do something which was quite unnatural for a man to do; something to which he was wholly disinclined; something that could only be justified by Simon's ridiculous notions of propriety. And Simon was clearly wrong in some of his ideas, for it was absurd to pretend that people should always be prepared for the worst. Shadowed by such a future, the present would be intolerable. To make the most of the present one should be prepared for the best, and risk a little disappointment. Yes, Simon was wrong in that, and so he might also be wrong in his expectation of a long war. The war might be over to-morrow, or next week, or at any rate before he had to return to the penal servitude of infantry training.

Hope crept into his mind, rosy-fingered as the dawn, and like the quick-rising sun swelled in imagination's sky to golden confidence. He was going to be married: that was the main thing, and nothing could prevent it now. As for the future, it was unpredictable. There might be fair weather or foul, but no one knew which till it began to blow. 'And if it is the former,' said Angelo, 'I shall enjoy it; if the latter, I must endure it. But what folly to start shivering now!'

On his wedding-morning he dressed himself carefully in a borrowed blue suit, that was somewhat tight over the chest and a little short in the leg, but looked smart enough with a clean shirt and a white tie and a flower in the buttonhole. Pasquale accompanied him to the church, where they arrived an hour and a half before anyone else appeared, and spent the time in trying to re-assemble the pieces of a ruined fresco, of the Flight into Egypt, that lay scattered on the floor of the north aisle.

In the midst of destruction the painted walls of the church were incongruously gay. The frescoes that covered them were cracked and torn, but their faded colours were brightened by the sun, and Saints and Martyrs, Shepherds and Madonnas and Patriarchs, all seemed to be in festival attire for their first sight of the outer world.

Angelo found the ears of the Ass, and said, 'It was Gozzoli who painted this.'

'They were good little animals that that fellow had on the road over by Vallombrosa the other day,' said Pasquale. 'It was a pity we had to leave them behind.'

'Gozzoli was an extraordinarily industrious painter,' said Angelo.

'It's a disease,' said Pasquale, 'Now what do you make of this? Will it be the Ass's tail or the half of St. Joseph's beard?'

'It fits this piece here. — Do you really think that to be industrious is a disease?'

'I never caught it myself, but my poor wife died of it. — Put all these blue bits together.'

'I hope Lucrezia will be a good worker,' said Angelo.

'It's useful,' said Pasquale, 'but they're apt to be shrewish, those who are. And those who won't work are sluts, and that's worse.'

'Here's part of the halo,' said Angelo. 'I suppose you never get perfection in a woman?'

'I never heard of it. But you're sure to get surprises, so you might be lucky.'

'This, I think, is the Ass's tail.'

'Some of them change their character over night,' said Pasquale. 'You take what you think is the mildest and softest little creature you ever saw, and you give her a house of her own and a husband of her own, and as like as not she turns into a regular tyrant.'

'I think I'll go and sit in the shade,' said Angelo. 'The sun is hot this morning.'

Pasquale followed him and they sat on the pavement under a badly scarred representation of Sheba's visit to King Solomon.

'There are things that go on in the mind of a woman,' said Pasquale, 'that no man can ever guess at. And because of that there are things that happen in married life that you've got to experience before you can believe in them.'

'What sort of things?' asked Angelo nervously.

'Injustice,' said Pasquale in a graveyard voice, 'is one of the worst. They've got a longer memory than we have, and your own words will be used against you.'

'But surely, with a little patience and common sense, you can easily put right small misunderstandings of that kind?'

'No,' said Pasquale. 'There's something in women that can't ever be put right. You can't do anything about it. You've just got to suffer.'

'What, what is the time?' stammered Angelo.

'They ought to be here in about ten minutes now.'

'I think I'll go for a little walk first.'

'Don't go too far,' said Pasquale. 'It won't help you if you make a bad start by being late. That's the sort of thing they never forget.'

'O God!' said Angelo, walking very rapidly. 'Please give me courage! I mustn't run away now. I really mustn't. But oh, how I wish I hadn't been so impulsive! There was no need for me to get married — not yet — and though I do love Lucrezia, it may not suit either of us to be tied together for ever and ever. And she has such a strong character. I'm sure she can never be cured of that. Oh, I do wish I could have another chance.'

He was walking quite aimlessly, and only recognized the lane he was in when he was startled by a furious female voice, and, looking up, saw a figure in white running towards him, her dress furled high to the knees, and fifty yards in front of her a small child making what haste it could in the tumbling gait of a two-year old. The child ran into a garden, and Angelo perceived that it was the garden where, so short a time before, he had heard Lucrezia's confession of infidelity. He also perceived that the figure in white was Lucrezia herself, and the child was Tommaso.

The need for action drove out fear. He too began to run and entered the garden side by side with Lucrezia, who in a voice breathless with anger and exertion told him how Tommaso, freshly clad in new clothes for the church, had at the last moment escaped her vigilance, and disappeared on some purpose of his own. A moment or two later his purpose became apparent: it was to look for the frog that croaked so loudly in the garden pool. They heard him smacking the water with a stick, and then they heard a louder splash. Tommaso had fallen in again.

Angelo pulled him out, and Lucrezia boxed his ears. Gasping and whimpering, he promptly attacked her, and Lucrezia pushed him away, fearful lest her white dress be soiled. Tommaso then began to cry in earnest, and went on crying with the implacable resolution of which only a simple child is capable. Two or three of Lucrezia's sisters arrived. They too were dressed in wedding finery, and

Tommaso in a berserk rage assaulted them in turn. They screamed, and pulled their frocks away from his wet hands. Angelo picked him up and held him, dripping, at arm's length. Tommaso's anger subsided a little and his cries diminished to a small braying noise.

'What are we going to do with him?' asked one of the sisters.

'Do with him?' demanded Lucrezia. 'We must take him with us, naturally. There is no one else to look after him, and if we leave him alone he will drown himself. But he is going to be a good boy now. Put him down, Angelo, and he will walk with me.'

As soon as Tommaso's feet touched the ground he began to cry again with alarming vigour. He would have nothing to do with Lucrezia or her sisters, but clung passionately to Angelo's leg.

'Angelo knows how to manage him,' said one of the sisters.

'He would be quite good if Angelo carried him,' said another.

'He is going to spoil everything,' cried Lucrezia, on the verge of tears. 'It is my wedding day, and everything is going wrong. Look at my shoes. They are quite dirty already, and it is getting late. Oh, Angelo, what shall we do?'

'If you want me to,' said Angelo unhappily, 'I suppose I can carry him.'

Lucrezia with a radiant smile whispered in his ear and called him a darling. The sisters clapped their hands, and Angelo lifted the soaking Tommaso to his shoulder. Tommaso sat there with a look of grave satisfaction, and they set off for the church.

The whole village was assembled, either within the gaping building or among the adjacent ruins, and a murmur of sympathetic pleasure rose from the spectators when they saw that the wedding had already become a family occasion. Angelo tried again to set Tommaso down, but a piercing howl was the immediate response, and Lucrezia once more showed signs of the most painful agitation.

Angelo by now was nearly as wet as the child. He shivered a little, straightened his tie, and hoisted Tommaso to the other shoulder. They walked up the open nave to a little chapel that had not suffered greatly, where the priest was waiting with the Countess and Simon Telfer and Lucrezia's parents.

The poor bomb-shocked priest was quite bewildered by the appearance of the dripping child, and to everyone's surprise he began to recite the service for public baptism. When the Countess informed him of his mistake, however, he showed no ill-will but proceeded to marry Angelo and Lucrezia with the utmost kindliness, and manifestly in a great hurry lest he go wrong again.

Tommaso sat solemnly on the bridegroom's left shoulder, little runlets of water trickled down the bridegroom's neck, and Lucrezia, gravely beautiful, put her hand in his. The cloudless sun lighted the ancient frescoes, and the Madonnas and the Saints, the Patriarchs and Angels that the industrious Gozzoli, and Pinturicchio, and Lippo Memmi had painted long centuries before, looked down in mild benignity. On the one side of them Saint Sebastian endured his martyrdom with astonishing equanimity, and on the other Noah discovered the secret of making wine with pious gratitude. Rubble from the broken walls was crumbled by restless feet, and as soon as the ceremony was over the villagers surrounded Angelo and Lucrezia in warm congratulation. Tommaso allowed himself to be transferred to the shoulders of Pasquale.

After that nobody quite knew what to do, and all stood talking in little groups among the shattered masonry, under the heat of the bright sky, hoping to hear some good suggestion for enjoyment of the day, but what they chiefly heard was the hunger rumbling in their bellies. The Countess's intention to offer a wedding-feast to the whole village had come to nothing, for the simple reason that there was nothing to eat. Or very little. Far too little to feed the assembled men, women, and children of Pontefiore. They were all aware of this, but still they waited with a lingering hope in their minds, their ears alert for better news, and their eyes turning wistfully in the direction of the Countess and her foreign guest.

She, for the third or fourth time, was telling Angelo of her failure and her disappointment, and her reluctance to sit down with a small party to the small meal that was all she had been able to provide, when the great majority must remain unfed.

'But what else can I do?' she asked. 'I can't work miracles and I don't know anyone who can, more's the pity. I could give them something to drink, for there's wine in plenty, but when you pour wine into empty stomachs you don't know what may happen, though you can make a good guess. And we've had trouble enough in Pontefiore without that. No, I'll just have to tell them all to go home, if they've got homes to go to, and wait for better times. It's cold comfort and I don't like the sound of it; but I can think of nothing else.'

Twice while she was talking Angelo heard the noise of a motor-horn some distance away, and now it sounded insistently. Some of the villagers were already moving in idle curiosity towards the ruined bridge, with children running ahead of them. The harsh irregular voice of the horn seemed increasingly to demand attention. The drifting movement of the crowd became a purposive current as more and more people joined it. The horn grew louder: a rasping noise with occasionally a fierce warbling note to break its monotony. Angelo and Lucrezia, Pasquale and the Countess and Simon Telfer and Lucrezia's parents, all followed the crowd. Everyone hurried towards the bridge.

The children who had led the way came running back, chattering excitedly. Their words were repeated, incredulously at first, and then in triumph, and became a noisy chorus. '*Il Padrone!*' shouted the crowd. '*Il nostro caro Padrone!*'

On the road, on the far side of the broken bridge, stood a six-wheeled canvas-roofed military lorry with an American star painted on the bonnet. An American soldier sat in the cab and another, a huge fat man, stood beside it. As the crowd gathered about the near abutment a slim and handsome figure, slightly flushed by exertion, came climbing out of the ravine. It was Don Agesilas.

'*Ben arrivato!*' shouted the villagers. '*Ben arrivato!*'

The Countess pushed her way through the excited people and Don Agesilas, kissing first her hand and then her cheek, exclaimed, 'My dear! How long since we have met! Far, far too long. But how well you look, and younger than ever. I am devoted to you.'

'What's in that lorry?' she asked.

'It is what is called, I believe, a mixed cargo.'

'Is there any food?'

'It is full of food.'

'You've come just in time,' said the Countess. 'We're going to have a feast.'

CHAPTER XVIII

'ONE of the advantages of living in a castle,' said the Count, looking up at the fallen ceiling, 'is that one recognizes a periodic destruction as part of its natural existence. In a town flat or a suburban villa a bomb or two, a little flight of shells, are catastrophic. But this small castle of mine, of no importance to anyone but myself, has survived all manner of disasters, and I cannot feel seriously perturbed by the present damage. The walls remain and the holes can be patched.'

He and Simon Telfer were sitting at the end of a long dinner table, empty now but for a bowl or two of fruit, the decanters, and their glasses. The villagers, abundantly fed, had long since returned to their ruined homes, and Angelo and Lucrezia had retired to the housekeeper's room, happily undamaged, which had been chosen as the nuptial chamber. The Countess had left the table early and nothing had been seen of Fest since the afternoon. He had attended neither the wedding nor the wedding feast.

'You were going to tell me something about the two American soldiers who came with you,' said Simon.

'Indeed I was,' said the Count. 'My attention was distracted for a moment by the fall of plaster — the cornice over there is also loose — but the case of the American soldiers is deeply interesting. They are, in fact, not Americans, but deserters from my old regiment who, by nefarious means of which I remain happily ignorant, acquired American uniform for a criminal purpose which, by pure chance, I was able to defeat. The senior of the two, the fat man, is Sergeant Vespucci, of whom you may have heard. Our dear Angelo knows him well. He and Angelo entered Rome together on the morning of its liberation.'

'Vespucci?' said Simon. 'Yes, I think I've heard Angelo speak of him.'

'What a scoundrel the man is,' said the Count complacently, 'and yet how much we could learn from him! For your true rascal is to-day your only true citizen of the world. He plunders all nations without pride in one or prejudice against another. He despises frontiers — and what an unmitigated nuisance a frontier is! We should all learn to hold them in contempt. In bygone times any educated man was free to live or travel where he chose, but now it is only your rascals who claim such a privilege; and there is nothing international in the world but villainy. Sergeant Vespucci, who certainly deserves to be shot, might serve a better purpose if he were given the chair of philosophy in one of our universities.'

'He stole the lorry as well as the uniform, I suppose?'

'Let me tell the story in my own way,' said the Count. 'I have in Rome a very dear friend, to whom I have been devoted for a number of years, called the Marchesa Dolce; whose circle of acquaintances is always large and some-times influential. One of the latest to enter it is an Ameri-can Colonel, now stationed in Rome. He is a man of great charm and his knowledge of the world has made him both wise and humane. He realizes that the war, almost certainly, will come to an end some day, and we shall then have to deal with the as yet unsolved problem of how to live together in peace. He is already doing what he can to ease the situation — into which we may be plunged without warning — by meeting some of our more liberal industrialists and discussing, quite informally, of course, the possiblity of their resuming trade with his own firm. A prudent and far-sighted man is the Colonel. He, as an American, has access to many commodities, such as petrol and food and blankets, of which we are sadly in need; and we in our poverty have still an abundance of little pictures, *objets d'art*, and so forth, that he, being a man of culture, can appreciate. We have already made, through his agency, a number of transactions that, I like to think, have been beneficial to both sides.'

The Count paused to replenish his glass and Simon's, and continued: 'You can imagine how upset I was when the Colonel told me, only the other day, that the generosity and good-nature of his fellow-countrymen were being abused, and that some of our people, with a quite shocking impatience, were not waiting to be given such stores of food and clothing as the Americans could afford to exchange for little pictures and so on, but were actually stealing and exposing them for sale in the Black Market. The American Army, said the Colonel, was in fact being plundered by those whom it had come to liberate; and in consequence of its very grave losses the authorities had decided that in future they would have to take care of their stores. They had, in fact, adopted such a serious attitude that the Colonel himself was unable to bring the Marchesa Dolce a side of bacon, a sack of flour, and some cases of fruit that he had promised for her birthday.

'Only a day or two later,' the Count went on, 'I made a discovery that seriously perturbed me. I had recently given Sergeant Vespucci permission to keep a lorry or two, that he used in business, in the courtyard of my house in Rome; of which I had been dispossessed but where, by the kindness of my butler, I still slept. I had met Vespucci some time before, and he had apologized so handsomely for deserting my regiment that I was persuaded to forgive him; more readily, I must confess, because I myself, at that particular time, had had very little control over it. Vespucci told me that he had set up, in a modest way, as what he called a *Free Distributer*, and naturally I was pleased to help him, as I would be to help any old soldier whom I found striving, with the small means at his command, to make a humble place for himself in a world that is too prone to neglect old soldiers. I was more than a little worried, however, after my conversation with the Colonel, to see one night Sergeant Vespucci driving into my courtyard, not one of the shabby vehicles that he had formerly used, but a brand-new American lorry.'

Don Agesilas was interrupted in his story by the return of the Countess, who came in and took the empty chair beside him. 'I thought I'd come back and drink a glass of port wine with you,' she said.

'Nothing could give me more pleasure,' said the Count, rising to receive her with surprise in his voice and wonder in his eye. He reached for the decanter.

'I'm getting quite a taste for port wine,' said the Countess. 'I think it's better for you than brandy.'

'If drunk in the same quantity,' said the Count, 'brandy may produce unfortunate effects.'

'That's what I mean. And you can drink port wine without wincing: that's another advantage. — But go on with what you were talking about; I didn't intend to stop you.'

Don Agesilas found it difficult to conceal his astonishment at this unexpected development in his wife's character, who in all their life together had been abstemious to a degree that he thought dangerous to her health. He watched her, fascinated, while she sipped her port, and with a growing admiration refilled her glass.

'Go on,' she repeated. 'What were you talking about?'

'I really cannot remember,' said the Count.

'Sergeant Vespucci,' said Simon.

'Ah, yes. Yes, Sergeant Vespucci. Well, to put it as briefly as possible, he and a friend of his — another deserter from my regiment, I am sorry to say — had procured American uniform, stolen a six-wheeled lorry and with the aid of accomplices of whom I know nothing, filled it with American goods from the nearest American dump. Then he had the gross impertinence to conceal his booty in the courtyard of my house, and I found myself in a very painful dilemma. It went against the grain to return such a treasury of viands to the military authorities who, from my own observation, were by no means undernourished; but if I let Vespucci sell his loot on the Black Market — and, to give him his due, he offered me a very generous share of the profit — I should be unable to meet my friend the Colonel without embarrassment and a little sensation of guilt. What was I to do? A few minutes' reflection decided me, and I said to Vespucci: "Sergeant, you are a man of good feeling, and at the moment you are completely in my power. You call yourself a Free Distributer, and that is precisely what you are going to be. I am deeply concerned for the welfare of my people in Pontefiore. They have, as I hear, been plundered by the Germans and liberated by our Allies. They are in a sad plight and need comforting. We have here the wherewithal to comfort them. Your cargo, Vespucci, will go to Pontefiore!" — He protested, but ineffectually. I reminded him that I was still his Commanding Officer, and that though he had deserted with the rank of sergeant, I had the authority to reduce him to private. He has his pride, has Vespucci, and eventually he accepted my ruling. So northward we drove, that very night, and I am deeply happy to think that our arrival was so timely.'

'I never thought, when I lived in Bradford, that one day I'd eat stolen meat and be glad of it,' said the Countess.

'Our troops,' said Simon, 'occasionally help themselves to the produce of your country. A few weeks ago, west of Lake Trasimene, they were living very well on roast goose. Then there was a slight epidemic of jaundice, and the rumour got about that it was due to eating Christmas dinners in the height of summer. It was only jaundice that saved the geese from total extinction.'

'You can't expect people to have much respect for property when they're taught to have no respect for each other's life,' said the Countess. 'Whenever there's a war the first casualties are the Ten Commandments.'

'Another glass of port?' Don Agesilas suggested tactfully.

'I don't mind if I do,' said the Countess. 'And now tell me about Rome. What's happened to all the Fascists?'

'Many of them have become Communists,' said the Count. 'And really, can you blame them? After wearing a black shirt for twenty years, what a pleasure it must be to go out in a red muffler!'

'That hardly seems a sufficient explanation,' said Simon.

'It would be sufficient for me,' said the Count, 'but then I am a frivolous person. Many of my Roman neighbours,

I admit, are extremely serious — serious and simple — and some are not so simple. There are those who say to themselves, "There is always someone who cooks the joint, and others who dip their bread in the gravy. Yesterday the chef wore a black shirt, and so did we. But now, if red is to be the fashion, let us go out quickly and buy a new handkerchief".'

Presently they retired to the small drawing-room above the garden. The windows had been blown out and the shutters broken, but the night was calm and the heavy curtains hung without motion to the floor.

The Countess halted on the threshold with an exclamation of surprise, and the others, looking over her shoulder, were momentarily startled to see, at ease in a tall chair, a man dressed in the sable uniform of the Schutzstaffel. They recognized him almost immediately, though he had contrived some alteration in his appearance, and slowly approaching regarded him with a puzzled and rather unfriendly curiosity. He had dyed his hair a dull yellow, and in place of his tortoise shell monocle wore one of frosted glass.

'The sleeves are a little short,' said Fest, 'but otherwise the tunic fits very well. There were one or two small holes in it which needed repair, but I am quite skilful with a needle; you hardly notice them, do you?'

'Why are you wearing those clothes?' asked Simon.

'You may call it a dress rehearsal,' said Fest. 'To-morrow I am going to Florence, and from there, at the first opportunity, to Bologna.'

'But Florence and Bologna are full of Germans,' said the Countess.

'That is why I am going.'

'It's madness,' said Simon. 'You'll be caught immediately and shot out of hand. If you work with us, in a proper and orderly manner, you can do a great deal of good — '

'But I have no desire to do good. I want to amuse myself, that is all. My hobby, my only pleasure in life nowadays, is to annoy the Germans, and since working with your organization I have often been handicapped by its narrowly utilitarian aims. My hobby demands freedom of choice and freedom of movement.'

'The Germans,' said the Count, failed to find a small cellar in which I keep a few wines of some interest to myself, and so I can offer you this tolerable cognac, or this armagnac that I have often found uncommonly agreeable to one of my occasionally robust and youthful moods.'

'The armagnac, without a doubt,' said Fest.

'I am inclined to praise your decision,' said the Count. No, I do not mean your choice of the armagnac — though I shall follow your example there — but your resolve to play a lone hand against the enemy. I am bored by the spectacle of people moving hither and thither in great masses. One cannot even be sorry for a horde of people. It is only the individual who rouses either interest or compassion. But the lone fighter, the solitary genius, the inconversable artist; the outlaw, the eccentric, and the anchorite; the craftsman with his single-handed skill, the wandering gipsy with his fiddle, the neighbourless shepherd proudly sufficient in his wilderness — all these are being crushed, as if beneath a landslide, by the regimented multitudes of to-day. It is a day of Great Powers, great causes, great events — and how dull they are! I want to go and watch a lapidary at work in his lonely room, cutting a solitary gem. I want to read, not some great overstuffed history of the world's calamities, but the brief and well-told tale of one embittered man, moved by a single hatred, who cut his sweetheart's throat in a deserted house. I want to turn my back upon mankind in order to see, against the great horizon on the other side, a man alone. Yes, my dear Fest, your proposal pleases me; though it is most unwise.'

'I have had my fill of wisdom,' said Fest, 'and I want no more of it. For twenty years I was a serious person. I was a good man. I knew what was true and what was false, and I revered the truth. I saw where virtue pointed, where wisdom led, and I went that way. And at the end of the road the Gestapo was waiting for me. So now I am entitled to a holiday. A little holiday of unwisdom.'

'I understand you perfectly,' said the Count.

'No!' said Fest. 'You do not understand. You cannot. Nobody can understand what we are like, we who have been tortured. We are different from you.'

'I also,' said the Count stiffly, 'have been in a German prison.'

'So?'

'I was arrested in Rome. I was arrested again in Montenero, where I was very nearly shot in reprisal for one of your exploits.'

'I remember, of course. And what did you think about when you were in prison?'

'Generally about hot baths and food.'

'You cannot have been very long in your prison. When a man has been hungry for a long time — but really hungry, very near starvation — he is no longer worried by the thought of food. He becomes proud and indifferent. You cannot bribe him. That is an important difference, is it not? But it occurs. And torture, if he can survive it long enough, makes him indifferent to fear and pain. He does not even scream when they hit him. When he is back in his cell he may scream, but not at the time. No, no. Then he can be impudent. He can say mischievous things to his torturers, and defy them. He gives them cheek. And when he goes back to his cell he does not think about hot baths and a big dinner, he thinks of one thing only: am I still sane?'

Fest removed his monocle and with a handkerchief wiped his eyes. 'The blind one still weeps,' he said. 'May I have a little more of that good armagnac?'

No one spoke for a minute or two, and then Simon said, 'You can take your revenge far more effectively by working with us.'

'But then it would become your revenge,' said Fest, 'and I want my own, you see. I am quite selfish. No, you can do no good by argument, because we do not think alike. We are quite different people. — And now, if you will excuse me, I think I shall go to bed; for I must leave early to-morrow morning.'

'Look here,' said Simon —

'No,' said Fest. 'I am looking in another direction.' He bent and gravely kissed the Countess's hand. 'Good night,' he said.

Again there was silence, till the Count murmured, 'Poor fellow! I hadn't realized till this evening that he himself is a German.'

'Oh yes,' said Simon, 'he's a German. We know all about him.'

'He's going too far with that hobby of his,' said the Countess. 'But that's just like them. They always overdo things.'

'He was in a concentration camp for two years before the war,' said Simon. 'When he was released he went to Switzerland, where his wife was waiting for him. They lived together for a few months, and then she left him. That upset him badly, and when the war began he went back to Germany with the simple purpose, apparently, of making trouble. He was arrested again, but escaped from a camp in East Prussia. The Polish Underground took care of him, and then he disappeared in the Balkans. He was a steward in a Danube river-steamer for a little while, and for some time he lived in Bucharest. But we first met him in Syria.'

'He told me about his wife before you came here,' said the Countess. 'I'm sorry for him, but she had a lot to put up with too. He used to get up at night and play with the bedroom door. Just opening it and shutting it again. For a man who'd been locked up for years, he said, that was a very pleasant thing to do. But it got on his wife's nerves, and I don't wonder.'

'I ought to stop him,' said Simon. He rose and stood, irresolute, midway between his chair and the door. 'It's his own life, of course, and I suppose he has earned the right to do as he pleases with it. But he's throwing it away.'

'Socrates in his last hour,' said the Count, 'told his

judges: "This is the time to say good-bye, and now we must part: you to live, and I to die. Which is the better, God only knows".'

'If Socrates said that, he was talking nonsense,' declared the Countess. 'Go and stop him.'

Simon followed Fest to his room, but when he got there he found it empty.

CHAPTER XIX

'How extraordinary!' said Angelo, speaking to himself, as he pulled a wallet from the pocket of a dead German and began to count the notes it contained. 'Three thousand, four thousand, five thousand — he must have robbed somebody — six thousand, seven thousand — oh, but here is a fortune! And how truly astonishing to think that I have killed one of them at last, and I myself am still alive!'

He sat down beside his late enemy, in the comfortable knowledge that the flood-dyke behind him was an adequate protection against most of the missiles of war, and with a feeling of grateful wonder contemplated the scene of battle. It was horrible, of course, and he disliked the cold flat fields of the river-plain; but because he had endured so much in the company of this earth, and helped in the winning of it, he now regarded the drab untidy landscape almost with complacency. To some degree, and after a fashion, it was his.

Another winter had gone, and though every afternoon the *bora* blew from pale skies like a fluency of melting ice, the ground was dry and the sun rose clear in the morning. The winter had been harsh and wearisome, and the soldiers of the Allied Armies had spent it, in sad persistence and complaining valour, under mountain-snow and mountain-rain. The Germans had entrenched themselves from sea to sea across the Etruscan Apennines, and against their ramparts of concrete and steel and cloud-swept hill there had striven, week by week for the advantage of another mile, the polyglot forces of democracy, born of many lands and bred to divers habits, but all alike in that all could shiver and bleed. On the left of the line, by the western sea, there had been Brazilians and American negroes, and on the right, on the Adriatic shore, Greeks and Poles. In the mountains north of Florence men had given their orders to advance, and others had cursed them, in the accents of New England and the

Middle West, in voices from the cornfields of Kansas and the cold plains of Nebraska, from the black soil of the deep South and the arrogant immensity of Texas. Voices from the Transvaal and the Cape had answered them, and to the eastward came a clamour of tongues from Hindustan. Soldiers had died with a sentence, half-spoken, of Urdu on their lips. They had called gently to each other in the night in Gurkhali and Mahratti, and heard the debate of comrades in the broad accent of Yorkshire, the lazy flow of Cotswold villages, the quick traffic of a London borough, and here and there the softness of Gaelic. Christchurch and Dunedin had spoken to Glasgow and Liverpool, Manitoba and Quebec to Warsaw and Athens. Pietermaritzburg had conversed with Little Rock, the Grampians with the Punjab, and tied each other's wounds. Hardly since the confounding of the people at Babel had such a diversity of tongues been heard, and month by month their hopeful or their weary speech had sounded a little farther to the north, till now, in the cold bright air of spring, the languages and lingos, the argots and parley and paronyms of half the world, to the orchestration of their innumerable artillery, were shouting for the kill.

Since the autumn Angelo had been serving in the Cremona Brigade of the new Italian army. He had been toughened and bored and drilled in the use of strange weapons during long weeks of training in the Marches, and in January his Brigade had gone into the line near Ravenna. Slowly the darkness of winter had grown lighter, April had come at last, and now, in what was to be the Eighth Army's triumphant last battle, Angelo, a troubled particle of its fame, was fighting among the stiff-sided streams of the valley of the Po. Somewhere not far away, invisible between its tall banks, flowed the Santerno. To his right was the highway that runs from Ravenna through Alfonsine to Ferrara. And beyond the dyke that sheltered him, about two hundred yards away, was a German machine-gunner watchful in his muddy embrasure.

But Angelo, for the present, hardly gave him a thought. He had not become indifferent to danger, nor acquired any surprising degree of courage, but the irritable mysticism of discipline, in this new army, had so deeply infected him that often he did not feel afraid for several hours at a stretch; and now his mind, after travelling a little in space and briefly in time, was occupied with one person only, and she was far away.

Pasquale, stooping cautiously, came to join him and offer a crust of bread and a piece of sausage. Pasquale had done well in the Cremona Brigade and was now a sergeant.

'I was thinking about Lucrezia,' said Angelo with his mouth full.

'She must be getting near her time,' said Pasquale.

'Very near. It may be to-day, it may be to-morrow, or perhaps it was yesterday. I should be with her.'

'There's nothing a man can do at such a time but look miserable and get in other people's way. If it's the first one he goes about snivelling with fear, and if it's the fourth he grumbles because there's no one to cook his dinner. That's all a man can do.'

'I could comfort her,' said Angelo.

'Don't you believe it. When his wife's lying-in his home's no good to any man, and he's no good to his home.'

'She is all alone,' said Angelo.

'Except for her mother, and three or four of her sisters, and every woman in the village who can think of an excuse to go along and see what's happening,' said Pasquale.

A few hours later they attacked again. The air was full of the wild whistling of passing shells, the earth shook and rose in black fountains. Angelo waited, and because he was no longer alone, but one of many inspired by firm intention and welded by discipline, his fear no longer entered and destroyed him, but only hovered above him like a carrion bird that dares not strike a living man. Then Pasquale spoke. '*Andiamo!*' he said.

236

'*Andiamo!*' Angelo repeated, a trifle shrilly, and got up.

He climbed the flood-bank and bullets spat in his ear as they passed him. He splashed across the stream and clambered up the farther bank. *Piou, piou!* cried the bullets, and shells burst like lions roaring under a cliff.

Angelo ran with his elbows out and his head down. He was dimly aware of the men on either side of him — men who had become his friends — and their presence comforted him. But what he chiefly desired was to reach, as quickly as possible, some place of shelter. The smallest hillock, any meagre protuberance of mud behind which he could lie concealed, would serve his purpose. There, over there, was a little weal of earth and greenery. What bliss to reach it!

Then like a drowning man he gasped in the squall of a near explosion and something hit his left hand so hard that he spun round, facing the other way, and after a wild stumble fell flat upon his face. Fear and indignation, mingled together, poured into his mind. He had been wounded. Oh, what injustice, and ah, what misery! He looked at his hand, and was seized by an overwhelming sorrow for his poor body that had been so mutilated.

It was not long before someone came to help him, and as he returned unsteadily to the flood-banks from which the attack had started, he was surprised to find how near they were. He had been running, he thought, for a long time, but now he perceived that he had gone no more than forty yards before being hit.

He fainted when his wound was dressed, and his first anxiety when he recovered consciousness was for the safety of his wallet. He felt for it, with his good hand, and found it still in his pocket. He took great care of it on his way to hospital, and put it under his pillow as soon as he got to bed.

When he was told that his left hand would have to be amputated, he fell into a profound melancholy that was curiously charged with a feeling of guilt, and for some time he was convinced that the loss of his hand was a deliberate punishment. He could never decide, however, for what he was being punished, because the more deeply he searched his conscience the more sins he discovered, many of them grave indeed, and the innumerable little ones were so wanton that it was difficult to imagine how they had escaped correction for so long. But though justice had been tardy its penalty was severe, and night after night he wept for his cunning fingers and the finger-nails that were the shape of almonds, the brown skin and the blanched knuckles, the strong palm calloused by work and scored with inscrutable lines, the sturdy thumb on its plump throne of muscle, and the adept strength by which he could hang from the branch of a tree or gently enclose a girl's soft arm. A marvellous thing was a hand, and a fearful calamity to lose it. His sin must have been grievous indeed, but still, out of so many that lay upon his conscience, he could not see which was the blackest nor decide for which he had been condemned.

And then, after days of anguished inquiry, it occurred to him one morning that he had been lucky beyond all hope or expectation. There he was, with all the sins in the calendar growing out of him, a vast crop of them every year, like figs fattening in August on an ancient tree, and by some great stroke of mercy he had been punished for only one of them, while hundreds had been ignored, perhaps even forgiven. What a marvellous clemency! He was still alive, and upon the stump of his wrist he could wear a smooth steel hook. A hook flashing in the sun, with which he could hold an ox by the bridle and with a gesture frighten small boys. A hook would be a fine appendage to his arm.

He sat up in bed and declared, 'Now I am going to get well!'

Almost immediately his health began to improve, and after a few weeks he was sent to a convalescent hospital in a village on the Adriatic coast south of Rimini. He was, he discovered, not very far from Pesaro, where in the service of the Germans, more than a year and a half before, he had helped to demolish a lot of houses. He remembered the officer who had commanded his company, the pale and earnest young man like a student, who had despised the Allies for their inefficiency; and wondered what had become of him. For by now the German army in Italy had surrendered, after its total defeat on the Po and beyond it; and the war was over and the Allies were the victors.

He was returning to hospital one evening, after walking on the pale bright beach, when he observed in the village street a girl with a baby in her arms who was trying to attract the interest of a group of soldiers. Though the soldiers wanted nothing to do with her, she was insistent. She took one of them by the sleeve, but he made an impatient movement and would not look at her. '*Niente mangiare!*' she was saying.

Angelo, who had stepped off the pavement to avoid them, paused to glance in her direction. '*Niente mangiare,*' she said again in a piteous voice, and suddenly he realized that he had heard her voice before.

In great confusion he spoke to her. 'Do you remember me?' he asked.

She was thinner than she had been, and the childish roundness of her cheeks had become a small sad oval. But her eyes were the larger by contrast, and the new fragility of her wrists was even prettier than the smooth sturdiness of her forearms when, a year and a half before, he had watched her hauling on the sea-wet rope.

She shook her head when he asked again if she remembered, and holding out her hand repeated dully, '*Niente mangiare.*'

'Oh dear,' said Angelo, 'this is a dreadful state of affairs. Well, you had better come with me, for it happens that I know of a place where we can get something to eat, and I have plenty of money at present. But I wish you remembered me.'

For a little way she walked beside him in silence, and then she said, 'You used to come and help us haul the nets. Your name is Angelo.'

'Of course it is! And you are Annunziata, I recognized you immediately.'

'You have been wounded?' she asked.

'At the battle of the Santerno. We of the Cremona Brigade suffered very heavily,' said Angelo proudly.

'Was that where the Poles were fighting?'

'No, they took Bologna, I think — But is it true, really quite true, that you and your baby have nothing to eat?'

'Somebody gave us a meal yesterday, but it was only a little one.'

'And where is your husband?'

'He was killed. He was serving with the Tedeschi, and when he tried to escape from them, they shot him.'

'He was with the Tedeschi when I first met you. Did you never see him again?'

'No, not after that.'

'I am very sorry,' said Angelo, and looked at her and her baby, and deeply sighed. They said no more until they came to a small inn that Angelo sometimes visited when the meals at the hospital were not to his liking. The innkeeper served only those whom he knew, for he never had very much to offer, and what he had had usually been obtained in some clandestine manner. But Angelo, who was very well off with the money he had taken from the dead German, had become a favourite customer, and when he told the innkeeper and his wife that Annunziata was his sister, and the victim of evil circumstance, whom he had encountered in the nick of time, for she was starving — but before he could finish his explanation the innkeeper's wife had taken charge of the poor girl and her baby, and was bustling to and fro to prepare a meal, while the innkeeper stood watching her, shaking his head, and commenting profoundly on the sad state to which the world had fallen.

They would give her a bed, said the innkeeper, and Angelo could be sure that she would be well looked after. Annunziata said little, for she was too tired even to be surprised by what had happened. Her baby lay in her lap and sucked a thumb. It was a large child, fatter than she, and appeared to be about three or four months old. When the meal was ready the innkeeper's wife took the baby and Annunziata pulled her chair to the table. She had been wearing a cotton shawl round her head, and when she took it off Angelo saw that her hair had been cut short. It was no longer than that of a young man who had neglected to go to the barber, and very ragged and untidy. Angelo did not stay much longer, but said he would return in the morning.

In his dreams that night he remembered his first meeting with Annunziata when she and the old fishermen, and their wives and their grand-daughters, had been hauling their nets, and Annunziata with her skirts kilted high had leaned on the greenish rope, and little salt-water drops had fallen from it on her plump brown thighs. How pretty she had been! — And how pretty she is! he thought when he saw her in the morning.

Her eyes were bright again, and she had washed her hair and brushed it tidily. The innkeeper's wife had lent her a clean blouse and a skirt that was too big for her, and her legs were also well washed. She had recovered something of her spirit, and she began to thank Angelo so warmly for his kindness that he had to caution her, when the innkeeper and his wife were out of hearing, against showing too much gratitude. 'For you are supposed to be my sister,' he said, 'and a sister takes a great deal for granted.'

He gave her some money to buy new clothes, and two or three days later they went for a walk together. She tied a kerchief round her head, and said, 'You will not be ashamed to be seen with me now.'

'I shall be very proud,' said Angelo, 'for though I searched from Rimini to Ancona I do not think I could find a lovelier companion.'

'If I look well,' she said, 'it is due to your kindness. I have never had such nice clothes before.'

She took his wounded arm and said, 'Oh, your poor hand! It makes me sad to think how you have suffered.'

'Very soon,' said Angelo, 'I shall be wearing a fine steel hook. That will be very distinguished.'

241

They sat on the beach and looked in silence at the placid sea. Presently Annunziata said, 'When I asked you if there were any Polish soldiers fighting beside you, in the battle where you were wounded, I was hoping that you might be able to tell me about someone of whom I am very fond. I thought you might have met him. His first name is Stanislas, but I cannot tell you his other name. It was too difficult to say. He is very good-looking, with grey eyes and a dimple in his chin.'

'No,' said Angelo, a little sadly. 'I have never met him.'

'It is a long time since I have heard from him,' said Annunziata, 'and perhaps he has been shot. Then my poor baby will be an orphan.'

'It is Stanislas who is the father of your baby?'

'Oh yes, he is already very like Stanislas. If you knew him you would have no doubt about it. And I am not a bad girl, you must not think that. I have never gone with any other man. But when I heard that my husband had been killed my heart was quite broken for a long time, and I became very lonely. And then I met Stanislas, and he also was lonely.'

'And you were sorry for him,' said Angelo.

'Very, very sorry. But how did you know?'

'It is nearly always so. Women are constantly being sorry for foreign soldiers.'

'But no one could help being sorry for Stanislas, because he had no home to go to. He came from a city called Lwow — it is very hard to pronounce it — but Lwow is no longer in Poland, for the Russians have taken it, and Stanislas did not want to become a Russian. And I cannot understand why Russia should behave in such a way, for I thought that Poland and Russia were both fighting against Germany.'

'They were indeed.'

'And therefore they were on the same side, and surely it is very wicked to rob one's neighbours.'

'Hush, hush! You must not say such a thing, Annunziata, not even as a joke. Russia is a very dignified and important nation. She is, moreover, extremely sensitive about her reputation in the world, and any Russian who heard you suggesting that she was capable of robbery would be extremely hurt. You do not understand these things.'

'Do you?'

'It is quite certain that the Russians had some good reason for taking Lwow, though it is possible that no one in our position could fully comprehend it. Perhaps they thought they could look after it better than the Poles, and took it away from them, not because they wanted it, but because they felt it to be their duty.'

'And Stanislas, in consequence, has no home to go to.'

'We ordinary people always suffer when a great nation develops a sense of duty,' said Angelo.

'Even though he may be dead by now,' said Annunziata, 'I continue to be sorry for Stanislas. We were so happy together for a little time. He had a very deep voice and a way of saying things, even the most ordinary things, that made you quite sure he had some strong emotion about them. Everything he said sounded impressive, and it was most moving to listen to him. But often, of course, he was extremely unhappy, and then I also had to weep. I suffered in other ways because of my friendship with him. That was why they cut off my hair.'

'Because of Stanislas?'

'There were some young men at home who had been Fascists, as everybody knew, but when the situation changed they became Patriots. So naturally they wanted to do something to show that they were now Patriots, and prove their enthusiasm. They told me that it was wrong for an Italian girl to go out with a foreigner, and I must stop it. But by then I knew that I was going to have a baby, so it was too late to stop. And because I was in love with Stanislas I told them to mind their own business. So then they cut off my hair.'

Angelo took her hands and pressed them fiercely. 'What cruelty! I do not want to think about it.'

243

'They were rough with me,' said Annunziata. 'We are not all so good-humoured, we Italians, as we pretend to be.'

'I am certainly not good-humoured when I think of such hooligans! But how anyone could ever fail to treat you well, I do not understand. Everybody, it seems to me, should want to be kind and tender to you.'

'Life has by no means been like that,' said Annunziata.

'But it should be!' cried Angelo. 'I know it should. And why is it not so?'

'It would be very pleasant if it were,' said Annunziata, 'but I do not think we should expect too much from life. — And now we must go back. My baby is very good and sleeps well, but I have left him alone for a long time.'

As they walked towards the inn she asked him, 'Are you married now? Your sweetheart, I remember, said that she would not marry you until the war was over. But perhaps she changed her mind?'

'Yes,' said Angelo, 'I have now been married for nearly a year, and when I go home again I shall find more people in the house than when I left it. Our son is already two months old.'

'You must be very happy. It is a good thing to have a home.'

Every evening they walked together, or sat among the little fruit-trees that grew behind the inn, and with good food to nourish her body and Angelo's flattering attention to please her mind, Annunziata became prettier and more cheerful day by day. The innkeeper's wife said that never in her life before had she seen a brother and a sister so devoted, but the innkeeper himself was increasingly suspicious and took to asking Annunziata certain questions that she found difficult to answer; and of which she made no mention to Angelo.

His suspicions grew darker as their evening walks became longer, and one night when their return was late indeed he told his wife that he was going to get the truth out of Angelo if he had to squeeze it out of his gullet.

That evening, as it happened, Angelo had accepted a

great responsibility and asserted himself in a very proud and singular manner. He and Annunziata were sitting in a secluded hollow on the shoreward side of the dunes which, along that part of the coast, rise in tufted hillocks above a narrow beach. The night was starless and the sky so dark that the sea was invisible, and the earth no more than a palpable obscurity. There was no wind nor any sound to be heard except the lapse of little waves and the crumbling of the sand beneath their touch; until the silence was broken by Angelo's inquiring voice.

'Are you, by any chance,' he asked, 'behaving like this because you are sorry for me?'

'Dear Angelo,' she said, 'of course I am sorry for you. How could I be hard-hearted when you have suffered so, and lost your poor hand —'

'That is enough,' he said. 'I refuse to be an object of pity! If, like so many others, you regard your love as the bread of charity, I do not want it.'

'But Angelo —'

'You can do no good by argument. My mind is made up. There is, I am well aware, a widespread belief that because of the war a woman is entitled to be sorry for anyone who takes her fancy. But I do not share that belief. If it became the accepted rule, we should never have peace at all. — No, I am not going to listen. And I am not going to join the bread-line for love, either yours or anyone else's.'

Annunziata began to cry. 'I don't know what you are talking about.'

'The gift of understanding is very rare,' said Angelo coldly.

'I love you because you have been so kind to me. You found me starving, and you helped me. You have been more generous to me than anyone I have ever known. I do not think that anyone has been generous to me before.'

'You are now admitting,' said Angelo, 'that our friendship began, not because you were sorry for me, but because I was sorry for you.'

'I know that! Do you not think I am grateful? But because you have been sorry for me, I do not see why you should not love me.'

'But this is a very different state of affairs,' said Angelo. 'This alters the situation entirely. — No, wait a minute. I must see to it that the difference is quite clear in your mind. — Do you realize that if we become lovers, it will not be the result of your being sorry for me?'

'That is what you have been saying.'

'But it may well be the result of my being sorry for you?'

'How glad I am that you were!'

'Dear Annunziata! I knew that you could understand if you tried.'

It was not until they had returned to the inn that Annunziata asked, 'Will it make you angry if I admit that I still do not see why you had to decide which of us was sorry for the other? What difference did it make?'

'It was a matter of principle,' said Angelo.

Before the innkeeper could make up his mind to speak openly of his suspicions, and demand from Angelo the true account of his relations with Annunziata, the military authorities announced that his wound was now healed and he must go and be fitted with a hook, as he desired, and receive his discharge from the army.

'And what will happen to me?' asked Annunziata with misery in her eyes.

'It is going to be difficult,' said Angelo, 'but I dare say I can make her see reason.'

'Whom do you mean?'

'Lucrezia, of course. I shall tell her that as many young women have given hospitality, during the last few years, to lonely soldiers, I feel entitled to give similar hospitality to you, who are certainly as lonely as any soldier I have ever known.'

'I am entirely alone, except for my baby,' said Annunziata.

'Another baby or two will make very little difference

in the house; if, indeed, I have a house to go to, about which I am still in doubt.'

'You are going to take me with you?'

'Had I allowed you to be sorry for me,' said Angelo, 'I might have deserted you without compunction. But when I insisted on being sorry for you, I accepted the responsibility for what has passed between us. I can do nothing else. Nor indeed — dear Annunziata! — do I wish to.'

CHAPTER XX

STOOPING to look into the cradle, Angelo gave a gasp of horror, and turned to Lucrezia a face of consternation and dismay. 'But he is black!' he exclaimed. 'You never told me he was black!'

'Black indeed! Oh, how unfair! He is nothing of the sort. A little dark, I admit — '

'He is a Moor, there is no doubt of it.'

'He is my baby! I suffered a misfortune, you know that as well as I do, and such a thing often leaves an effect. But to say that he is a Moor is too much.'

'Why did you not tell me?'

'Until he was born, how should I know what his complexion was going to be? And after he was born, what could I do to change it?'

'I thought it was my child that you were carrying,' said Angelo.

'You do not think he resembles you, even a little?'

'No.'

'I am sorry,' said Lucrezia. 'I should be very happy if he looked like you. But during the war there were very few of us who had the chance to order our lives as we would have liked them to be. We were little better than sheep, and it was only by good fortune that we escaped the butcher. If my baby is too dark for your liking — '

'He is.'

'That is a vexation, of course, but only one of many that we have suffered. He is one of an infinity of vexations, and it is very sad for him as well as for us.'

'This is not the home-coming that I had looked forward to,' said Angelo.

'It is not precisely the home-coming that I had expected,' said Lucrezia, staring with no friendliness in her eyes at Annunziata and her baby.

'His name is Stanislas,' said Annunziata. 'His father came from Poland. He had no longer any home to go to, and he was very lonely.'

'So she took pity on him,' said Angelo.

Little Tommaso fell off the kitchen table and began to cry; but no one paid much attention except little Stanislas who made it a duet.

'Oh, I cannot bear it!' shouted Angelo. 'What am I but a poor Italian soldier, who has done nothing wrong, unless under orders, and now I am expected to settle down as a married man with three children to care for, one of whom is an Englishman, another a Pole, and the third a Moor! It is too much, I say, and I cannot bear it!'

He ran out of the house and through the nearby fields in a kind of panic, and did not stop until he had climbed nearly to the crest of the hill opposite Pontefiore, where for about half an hour he lay exhausted, flat on the ground and staring at the sky. High clouds in the tideless blue were sailing slowly to the east. He watched them until he grew slightly giddy with a sensation that the earth was spinning westward, and then sat up, and with his right hand violently rubbed his face and head, and spoke aloud: 'But one does not run away. There was a time when I thought that I could always improve my position by leaving it; but that is not so. Even when we are outnumbered it is necessary to stay and return the enemy's fire. As a man grows older, moreover, the world appears to become smaller, so that every year there are fewer places available for refuge. No, I cannot run away.'

He let his mind accustom itself to this decision, and then he began to think: I have served in three armies, the Italian, the British, and the German, without wishing to serve in any, and now I have three children, none of which I desired. That is only a coincidence, of course, but coincidences are very interesting and should be useful. They should help to remind us that there are patterns in life, and design in the world, and a purpose in the universe; though God only knows if it is the sort of purpose we should be glad to know about. Even accidents, it may be, are not wholly accidental. — But how I wish that the youngest of my family had not been black! I shall have to call him Otello.

He looked about him and was enraptured, as so often before, by the rich and mannerly beauty of his country. — Oh, those Englishmen! he thought, remembering a conversation with Simon and two young officers in a wintry village near Alfedena. They loved the desert because it was empty! How incomprehensible they are. For I who adore this land of mine, this Tuscany of the green candles and the terraced hills that are crowned with men's houses, adore because it is complete. As the little grapes in the valley are sweet already and coloured with their ripeness, so Tuscany wears its bloom and is plump as a young grape with sweetness.

He said aloud: 'The land is very ancient, yet summer comes to it with the colour of a new invention. When Rome was but an angry thought, we were civilized and had our arts, and when the world was in its dark despair we woke it with our painting and our poetry and quarrelling. And still our olive-trees are silver and green, and the olives grow fat. All the countries have come to us, either to conquer or to learn, in love or envy, and we are still Tuscany, and the grapes are ripening again, and in a little while from now my family — the Englishman, the *Marocchino*, and the Pole — will drink the vintage and be the better of it.'

He stood up, and walked to and fro, and declared: 'It is possible, it even seems probable, that I have a mission. I must demonstrate that all the peoples of the world — or four of them, at least — can make their home together in civilization. I shall bring up these children in such a way that they will have no obsession about their nationality, and that will be a very good thing indeed. For even the best of nations may have a bad influence on its subjects, and human nature being what it is, the majority of its subjects are likely to prefer that to anything else it can offer. But my family will merely retain a sentimental regard for the places where their fathers were born, and sentimentality, which can relieve itself in a song or two and an occasional tear, is an excellent thing.'

He stopped, and looking towards Pontefiore with a

frown, thought: But I must not say anything of this to Lucrezia. If she were to suspect that I have discovered a mission in life, or a theory, let us call it, she would never let me forget it. She would refer to it at the most inconvenient times, and taunt me with it whenever the children happened to spill a bowl of soup on the dinner-table. For women do not approve of theories, but are jealous of them because they take up a man's attention. Nor do I blame them for that, because when a man's theory goes wrong it is a woman, of course, who must dry the table and wipe up the soup. — But that does not alter the facts of the case, and so I must remember to be discreet. I must also be firm.

He sat down again, a little worried by the thought, and exclaimed: 'This is a time — though the war is over — when I should be very glad of the *dono di coraggio*. I know exactly what I am going to say to Lucrezia, in the matter of Annunziata, but I do not relish the prospect of saying it. I have a good logical argument, but she has great strength of character and a formidable tongue: can logic prevail against such a combination? Not without courage, I fear. Or shall I use the little blackamoor to support my case? It will be unfair to Lucrezia, poor girl, but the whole situation is unfair to me and we must come to terms in some way. I had better consider our little Otello as part of the bargain.'

He contemplated his task with some reluctance still, and when a fly stung him on the ankle slapped thoughtlessly at it with his hook and deeply pricked himself. 'Well, that is a lesson,' he said. 'What strength I possess, when a mere gesture can draw blood! I had forgotten how much I have changed since going to the war again. Why should I be frightened of words — even a woman's words — when I have learnt to endure the screaming of shells and the extraordinary repetition of machine-guns? A moment in which to muster my arguments — and then, *andiamo!*'

He rose once more, and shaking his hook at another buzzing fly, set off at a steady pace for the ruined farm where Lucrezia had set up house. The previous tenants, an elderly man and his wife, had both been killed in the bombing of Pontefiore, their sons were either dead or prisoners of war, and their daughters had been carried off by various misfortune. The Countess had given Lucrezia permission to use what remained of the house — the kitchen and one other room were habitable — and promised the farm to Angelo if, on his return, he should want it. It was small and the ground was thin, but it was pleasantly situated.

When he arrived he found the kitchen full of women. Two of Lucrezia's sisters were living with her — Lucia, who still had no news of her husband, and a plump noisy girl of sixteen called Simonetta — and several neighbours had already come to make the acquaintance of Annunziata. She and the infant Stanislas were, indeed, the centre of the group.

Angelo from the doorway spoke coldly. 'Lucrezia! I have something to say to you.'

'In a little while,' Lucrezia answered. 'I am busy at present.'

'No,' said Angelo, 'I want to speak to you now.'

She looked at him again, surprised by the tone of his voice, and for a moment appeared to be on the point of making a brusque refusal. But then she thought better of it, and with tightened lips and an added colour in her cheeks came to the door. The other women, all silent now, watched her with a lively interest.

'Let us go for a little walk,' said Angelo. 'Gentle exercise calms the mind, and what I have to say must be considered without prejudice or heat. The fact is, my dear Lucrezia —'

'The fact is,' interrupted Lucrezia, 'that you have come home in very strange circumstances, and now are making matters worse by treating me without respect in the presence of my sisters and several of my friends. The fact is that I want to know, immediately and without beating about the bush, what your relations are with Annunziata.'

'Annunziata,' said Angelo, annoyed that he had been

forced into explanation so early, 'is the daughter of a fisherman, and her husband was killed by the Germans —'

'All that I know. She has already told me her entire history, including her compassion for a Polish soldier named Stanislas, so far as her meeting with you when you were in hospital.'

'That was quite a remarkable coincidence,' said Angelo.

'Are you her lover?' demanded Lucrezia.

'I will not be questioned in this way —'

'My God!' said Lucrezia, 'if I have not the right to question you on such a matter, I who am your wife, then who has? Here is this woman whom you bring home with you, who has already had a baby by a Polish soldier on whom she took pity, and what I ask is whether you have succeeded the Pole. Has she been sorry for you also?'

'No!' shouted Angelo. 'There you are wrong indeed. There you show how little you understand me. It was I who was sorry for her!'

'What!' said Lucrezia.

'Sauce for the goose,' said Angelo, 'is sauce for the gander. You, some time ago, were sorry for Corporal Trivet, with a result that is likely to be with us for a long time —'

'So you would reproach me, now when we are married, with something that happened when I was a mere girl! I do not call that generous, or even kind of you.'

'I am not reproaching you,' said Angelo. 'I am simply stating a fact. And if you were sorry for Corporal Trivet, surely I have an equal right to be sorry for Annunziata?'

'No, no!' cried Lucrezia. 'A man cannot be trusted to be reasonable in these matters. A man has no sense of proportion, he is too self-indulgent. But a woman, because of her nature, has a proper responsibility, and I who have once been sorry for a man shall take good care never to be sorry for another.'

'And yet,' said Angelo, 'I come home and find that you are the mother, not merely of little Tommaso, but also of a little blackamoor —'

253

'Was it my fault? Am I to be blamed for that? Oh, but that is truly unfair!'

'It is very unfair indeed,' said Angelo, 'but the whole world is grossly unfair and we have to put up with it. Many husbands, perhaps a majority of husbands, would deeply resent the appearance of two little foreigners in their home, whatever might have been the manner of their arrival, and if I take a lenient view of the situation it is not because I like it, but because, whether I like it or not, I love you.'

'That I can well believe!' said Lucrezia bitterly. 'To browbeat a woman, to bully and humiliate her, is a well-known sign of love.'

'It may well be,' said Angelo sadly. 'For I have loved you so long that my love has become very stubborn, and neither of us, I think, will ever escape from it.'

'But now your love also includes Annunziata.'

'I have already explained my position with regard to her.'

'And if you expect me to be satisfied with that, you are going to be very much disappointed!'

'No, do not go!' cried Angelo as Lucrezia turned to leave him, and reaching with his left arm, took her by the shoulder. She uttered a gasp of pain and he, with a responsive cry, enfolded her in his arms — but now with extreme care — and babbled a little stream of endearments mixed with apology for his clumsiness. 'I am not,' he said, 'quite used to my new finger. I forget that it is harder than my old ones.'

'Give me your handkerchief.'

First with his right hand, then with his hook, Angelo felt in pockets and sleeves, clumsily but without appearing to care that he was clumsy, and then admitted, 'It does not seem that I have one to-day.'

Lucrezia watched him, his patience and his fumbling, then covered her eyes and turned away.

'Is it so painful?' asked Angelo. 'I am very sorry.'

'No, it is not that.'

'Then I think, perhaps, we should be going home. We

254

have talked enough for to-night, and it is nearly dark.'

She turned again and flung her arms round his neck. 'Oh, your poor hand!' she cried. 'Oh, Angelo! I have not been kind to you. I meant to be kind, I was going to ask you to forgive me, I was determined not to say a word that would anger you. But when you said the baby was black, and when I looked at that woman —'

'She is only a girl,' said Angelo.

'That makes it no better! But do not let us talk about her. — Angelo, do you swear to me that you love me still?'

'There is no doubt about it.'

She hung more heavily about his neck, and cried a little, and kissed him with a sort of desperation. 'His skin is going to be rather brown,' she said, 'but you cannot call him black.'

When at last they went home, walking slowly in the darkness, Angelo wondered if he had behaved as firmly as he intended. It cannot be denied, he thought, that to some extent it was Lucrezia who took the initiative, and whereas I was going to make it quite plain that I, on certain conditions, was ready to forgive her, she now believes that she has forgiven me. I have, I think, achieved what I set out to achieve, and that clearly proves that Lucrezia has a certain respect for me. But if we do succeed in living together on friendly terms, she will undoubtedly take the credit for it, and I really think the credit should be mine. — But what does it matter? Let her have the credit; it is a small price to pay for peace.

He was tempted to speak once more about Annunziata and make sure that her position had been properly recognized; but discretion intervened, and it occurred to him that Lucrezia might tolerate Annunziata's presence the more easily if she were not required to make a formal acceptance of it. I shall say no more, he decided, but await developments.

Despite his wisdom he was surprised, within the next week or two, by the quick growth of friendship between Lucrezia and her guest. They had discovered, it appeared, some common cause with which Lucrezia's sisters were associated in a less degree, but to which Angelo was certainly not a party. If, for example, Lucrezia made some small reference to his behaviour, his appearance, or an opinion recently uttered, Annunziata and Lucia and Simonetta would all laugh together, and it was evident that to them her words had a peculiar illumination and a special significance, though to Angelo they often sounded quite irrelevant.

All four women paid much attention to the infant members of the household, and not only were such practical matters as feeding and cleaning them taken seriously, but what, to any man, would have seemed the imperceptible vagaries of their inexistent characters were very gravely discussed. Into these activities Angelo had no wish to intrude, but he observed with interest that the four young women appeared to regard the three small children as their common responsibility — if not their common property — and that Tommaso, the young Stanislas, and the little blackamoor could equally depend on the service and interest of Lucrezia, Simonetta, Annunziata, and Lucia; whoever happened to be nearest responded to the cry.

When he proposed that the little blackamoor should be called Otello, they combined against him in open resistance and for several days the division in the house was manifest, and courtesy was strained. But Angelo saw clearly that if his wishes were flouted now, his authority would be denied before long, and with a firmness that gravely offended the others and deeply astonished himself he insisted on having his own way. Lucrezia's second child was called Otello.

The major factor, however, in maintaining peace in the family, or in restoring it after this and some other disputes, was not so much Angelo's authority as the abundance of work that had to be done. Though the farm had been neglected, the grapes and the olives had ripened, the fields had to be tilled with what primitive tools they could find, and the greatest need of all was to patch and fortify their ruined house against the winter rains and Christmas cold. Because the Germans had driven off so many draught oxen, the whole village had suffered during the past year from a grievous lack of beasts for the plough, and had it not been for the pictures that Angelo had once brought from Rome in a cargo of flour its plight would have been far worse.

When the Count — more than a year ago now — had returned in time for Angelo's wedding feast, he had found all but two of his pictures safe and in good condition. The Adoration of the Shepherds had been destroyed, and one of the small Bronzinos had been discovered by the Germans and removed, by a major who appreciated art, as a souvenir of the war; but the others remained, whole and intact, and on his return to Rome the Count took them with him in the six-wheeled lorry that Sergeant Vespucci had so opportunely stolen. Little had been heard of him since, but it was understood that he was very busily engaged in several schemes for the welfare of his tenants and the promotion of good relations between Italy and the United States of America. That he had sold one, two, or three of his pictures was easily inferred when two pairs of matched plough-oxen arrived in Pontefiore; for the Countess let it be known that Don Agesilas had had to pay the monstrous price of 900,000 lire for each pair.

The oxen worked hard but the villagers worked harder, and day after day laboured with their mattocks to open the fields for seed. Two of them were killed when their mattocks struck mines that the Germans had left in exchange for the beasts they stole.

Now winter came again, and everyone was cold, and often wet, and not seldom hungry. But all except some of the youngest and a few of the oldest survived, and went on toiling, and Angelo was widely envied because he had four women to work for him. He himself, however, sometimes thought with regret of the easy times he had had when the world was still at war, and he had nothing to worry about except his recurrent fear of being killed, or wounded, or taken prisoner, or punished for some breach of discipline. — The rain came through the roof, the fire smoked, the children cried in concert, and life was hard indeed. But there was consolation, he admitted, in the warmth of Lucrezia's love, though there was warmth in her anger too; but Annunziata had the sweetest of tempers. And hanging on the kitchen wall, mounted on a square of pale wood, was the head of Piero's Madonna that he had salvaged from the wrath of the German officer.

Angelo was by now quite sure that this was the perfect expression of all beauty, and to possess it, and be able to look at it every day, often seemed to him the very height and culmination of good fortune. For nothing in life either was or could be more agreeable to the senses than beauty to the eye, and to the understanding — or so he thought — there was no such justification of life, or much need of any other. 'What a blessing have I won from the wreckage!' he would say, and looking from Piero's Madonna to Lucrezia or Annunziata he would perceive in their comeliness the living tutor of Piero's art, and very often, in his delight at this relationship, embrace them one after the other in the heartiest manner. Sometimes, if he had been staring too long at the Madonna, so that his eyes were a little dazzled by her, he would turn and see her reflection against Lucia's wistful face or Simonetta's hoydenish red cheeks; and embrace them also. On such an occasion Lucrezia would be sure to utter one of her veiled remarks, that he could not see through, but which always made the others laugh.

Spring at last returned, and then the fact that they lived in a ruin became of no importance, for they hardly used it except as a place of darkness in which to sleep. All day they worked in a golden light or a green shade, and their thoughts, like the thoughts of everyone in Pontefiore, were flushed with an approaching triumph. Their famous bridge had been built again, and in a little while, when the road had been levelled across it, it would be opened to traffic.

All the young people thought the new bridge a vast improvement on the old, and their parents and their grandparents were hard pressed to find a single fault in it. The masons had worked with the cunning and craft of their forefathers. The stone had been nobly hewn and trimly dressed, the abutments ran sweetly into either bank, over the ravine the arch soared serene as a rainbow.

The day came when the road was finished, and while a few workmen sprinkled gravel on it — as though powdering its face for a party — the villagers stood at the near end and debated with loud good humour as to who should have the honour of being the first to cross. They were still arguing, and pushing and resisting, when some of them caught sight of an approaching motor-car. It was a very small car, black as a beetle and remarkably like a beetle in shape; and quickly recognizing the driver, they greeted him vociferously.

'My dear friends!' exclaimed the Count, emerging with difficulty from the tiny vehicle. 'What a beautiful bridge! What a magnificent achievement! Our national and domestic difficulties are still enormous, but now I am convinced that we shall overcome them. Indeed, I never doubted it. I have lost my fortune, but not my faith. Nations totter, empires crumble, crowns go tumbling down the abyss of time, tyrant states are blown out like candles, but man is invincible, man is the true phoenix, and our dear Italy is the native home of the *risorgimento*, the renaissance, the indefeasible and recurrent spring of beauty. Primavera shall walk across this noble bridge with a pledge of richer years, and I myself, preceding her like a herald, have brought you something that will give you pleasure, profitable employment, and the promise of security in your old age. Will someone fetch me, as speedily as possible, a table and a chair?'

While the furniture was being sought, the Count gossiped with his acquaintances — shook hands, clapped shoulders, patted cheeks, inquired for brothers, sisters, fathers, cousins — all in the liveliest manner; and when a chair and a table had been fetched, and set conveniently in the middle of the road, he raised his arms in the sort of gesture that the conductor of an orchestra makes to gather attention for the opening chords of a Beethoven symphony, and returning to his diminutive motor-car, dived into it like a rabbit entering a rudimentary burrow. For a moment or two his hinder parts were curiously agitated, and then he reappeared with a burden in his arms that was shrouded with a coverlet of green baize. He carried it to the table, set it down, and removing the cloth displayed the bright enamel and shining steel of a sewing-machine.

'My dear friends!' repeated the Count. 'After Noah had been afloat for forty-seven days — in great discomfort, one may assume — he sent out a dove from the Ark, and in the evening the dove returned with an olive-leaf in its beak. Now what was the significance of that? — It meant that normal conditions were returning, and the time was ripe for reconstruction!

'My friends, history repeats itself, and I am Noah's dove! We, like that sturdy patriarch, have seen the devastation of our world, and now I, like the dove, come to you with a promise of better times. Not an olive leaf — of which you have plenty — but a brand new model of America's finest sewing-machine, for the sale and distribution of which I have lately been appointed Principal Supervising Agent in Umbria, Tuscany, the Abruzzi, and the Marches. This sewing-machine is the favourite instrument of many of the most intelligent, cultured, and virtuous women in the Western Hemisphere. It is at once the ornament and the assurance of well-being in a million high-class, happy, and essentially modern homes in Canada and the United States. When it has been introduced into Italy in large numbers — as I hope and intend to introduce it — it will be a potent factor in the reconstruction of our country, which, no matter what political system we may enjoy or endure, must begin in the home and cannot be well founded unless it is founded on the prosperity and happiness of the home. With a sewing-machine in the house you can never be bored, you can never be listless; and with a sewing-machine like this in your house, your house will quickly become the envy and example of all your neighbours!'

Sitting down, the Count put a square of white linen in position and speedily stitched a broad hem in it with scarlet thread. This he handed to the nearest villagers for their admiration, and to others distributed leaflets that explained how a sewing-machine could be bought outright for so much, or by a series of fractional payments for a somewhat larger sum.

'I want you to realize,' he said very seriously, 'your good fortune in being offered this machine, on such reasonable terms, in times that are still gravely perplexed by the evil legacies of war. Had it not been for my close friendship with an American officer, and our realization in the midst of war that we must prepare for the sterner tasks of peace, you could not possibly have been given such a marvellous opportunity. With all the force of which I am capable, I advise you not to neglect it.'

Having instructed an elderly man named Dino to look after the machine, and told him to let customers make a fair trial of it, the Count re-entered his motor-car and was about to drive to the castle when he caught sight of Angelo, who, somewhat embarrassed by his patron's latest activity, had till now remained on the outskirts of the crowd. The Count greeted him in the most amiable fashion and proposed that he should ride a little way with him.

'What times we live in!' he observed as they drove slowly through the ruined village. 'With what triumphant invention has science filled our lives — those of them, that is, which it has not destroyed. Inventions of all kinds, racing to perfection. Sewing-machines, aeroplanes, radio, rockets and bombs, and drugs that cure unmentionable diseases almost before one has time to mention them. Progress has become a race — and only man has not entered for it. Our sewing-machines are better than they used to be, our aeroplanes fly faster and have a greater expectation of arriving, our medicines are more deadly year by year; but man, dear whimsical man, shows no improvement whatsoever. And on the whole,' said the Count, 'I dare say that is a good thing. Try to imagine a human being, emulous of the machines, who had become perfect in all his parts and scientifically efficient. How horrible he would be!'

'Wait for me if you have nothing better to do,' he said when they had reached the castle. 'I must speak to my wife, but I shall not be long. I must let her know that I shall be dining with her.'

He returned in a few minutes wearing a look of worry and perplexity. 'She is asleep,' he said. 'She never used to sleep at this time of day, but she is actually snoring.'

'The Countess is no longer quite young,' Angelo suggested.

'Nonsense,' said the Count. 'She's younger than I. — Well, it does not matter greatly. Let us walk in the garden, and you will tell me how marriage suits you, and how you are prospering as a farmer. Let me walk on your other side, dear boy. Your hook alarms me.'

He listened with the closest attention to Angelo's description of his household, and often exclaiming in admiration, made him repeat it twice so that he could memorize it in detail.

'It is magnificent, your menage!' he declared. 'I must come and visit you to-morrow.'

'Lucrezia is not looking her best at the moment,' said Angelo.

'You mean —?'

'Yes,' said Angelo, 'in about six weeks from now. We hope for a daughter this time.'

'What excellent news! I congratulate you most warmly. — But you will permit me to meet the other lady: Annunziata, is it?'

'It so happens that she is in a similar condition,' said Angelo.

'My dear fellow,' exclaimed the Count, 'let me embrace you! You are a credit to our old regiment. What a pity the war is over, for otherwise I should certainly have recommended you for a decoration. But have you any money?'

'A little,' said Angelo, who still had four or five thousand lire from the dead German's pocket.

'With a family so rapidly increasing as yours,' said the Count, 'you certainly need a sewing-machine. I had better put you down for one. I shall let you have it at a special price. — No!' he exclaimed, 'I shall do more than that. I shall make you a present of it. Though you did not win a medal, you have decidedly earned a sewing-machine!'

ANOTHER year went by, and it could no longer be denied that the Countess had taken to drink. Her appearance suggested it — little veins whose presence had never been suspected showed themselves in a rosy reticulation upon her nose and cheeks — and her manner completely betrayed it. She was happier than she had been since the first few years of her marriage, and the villagers who had often quailed under her reprobation now found that their silly ways and venial sins were condoned with a chuckle of sympathy; while the elder servants of the castle were often invited to share a flask or two and exchange their native legends and the local gossip for tales of her idyllic youth in Bradford. Such comfort and such kindliness, such moral goodness and worldly prosperity, such jollity, such benignity of climate and handsome scenery were now ascribed by the Countess to her Yorkshire home that presently there became popular in Pontefiore — almost proverbial indeed — a mode of approval which ran: 'That's good, that's very good. That's good enough for Bradford.' No one thought worse of the Countess because occasionally she lost her way, and sometimes her balance, for everyone knew that she had had a great deal to put up with.

The Count came more frequently to Pontefiore, and though his affairs did not prosper as he had hoped, he kept his head above water. More and more he made Angelo his confidant.

'My old friend the Marchesa Dolce, whom you know very well,' he said once, 'is beginning to show her age, and for that I blame the Americans. Since they left Rome she has become careless about her figure. She had always a tendency to put on weight, and now she does little to control it. Her mind is still brisk and youthful, but the mind is not everything; especially in women. A nimbleness, indeed, of thought and speech sometimes draws attention to the relaxation of the body. I wish they had remained in Rome: the Americans, I mean.'

With the Countess's weakness he was most sympathetic, when he had recovered from the surprise it caused him, and he told Angelo: 'I must confess that I have not been the ideal husband. There are men, a few of them, designed by nature for the married state, and they make women happy and destroy their souls. But I am not one of them. We had two or three years of mutual delight, and then a progressive disappointment in each other that was mollified by charity and good manners. Love and wine have much in common — though the former is apt to be exclusive, and the latter inclined to invite others to share its happiness — and if she can find pleasure in the bottle, I call it just compensation for the failure of bed and board. I have given her good advice. I have told her that she should drink nothing before lunch, and not much at lunch; for to drink in the morning obscures the outline and destroys the individuality of a day. And a day is something that dawn and sunset enclose, and should not be demeaned.'

At another time he asked: 'Do you remember a young man called Trivet? I knew nothing of him till recently, but my wife tells me that he spent several years here during the war, and that you shared an adventure with him. — It appears that he is not happy. After being wounded and discharged from the army he made some attempt to resume a domestic life, but without success, and volunteered for service in the Far East. Then the war against Japan came abruptly to an end, the unfortunate Trivet was again discharged, and now he is desperately anxious to escape from a wife whom he finds intolerable, but with whom circumstances compel him to live; for both families are thoroughly respectable in the peculiar fashion of the north of England. So he wants to come back to Pontefiore. Do you think that would be a good thing?'

'Yes,' said Angelo, 'I should like to see him again. — But no, it would not be a good thing. He was very popular with the girls here, especially with Bianca

Miretti, Vittoria Carpaccio, and some others. Bianca is now married to Vittoria's brother Roberto, and Roberto has recently discovered that Bianca is still somewhat in love with Corporal Trivet. No, it would not be a good thing if he came back.'

'I shall tell my wife what you say,' said the Count.

About this time Angelo's labour on the farm was much lightened by a sturdy young man from the mountains north of Udine who, in the last days of the war, had had a series of unfortunate experiences in that part of the country which had persuaded him to leave it for ever. He had joined a group of Italian partisans and fought in some small actions against the Germans. Then, for no reason that he could understand, his group had been attacked and he had been taken prisoner by Slovene partisans, who had used him with some brutality, and from whom he had escaped by the timely but inexplicable action of a band of Independent Croats who treated the Slovenes, so the Slovenes said, with great cruelty. Losing his head completely, the young man had fled to the north and fallen into the hands of a regiment of renegade Cossacks who were running away from the Bulgarians who were endeavouring to rescue them from the pluto-democratic forces of the Americans and bring them back into the arms of Soviet Russia. The Cossacks, when they had robbed him of everything he possessed, showed no further interest in him, and he succeeded in joining a company of Free Austrians who, because neither the British nor the Americans would recognize them, grew very morose and handed him over to a ridiculous little party of people who called themselves Werewolves. They, by mere chance, fell foul of a lost company of Ukrainian Separatists, who were also on the run but could not decide whither, and the young man presently found himself alone on a road between Judenburg and Graz. He was desperately anxious to escape — not from anyone in particular but from danger in general — but he found it difficult to decide which way to go; for on one side of the road there were many refugees trudging to the east, and on the other an equal number limping to the west. He finally decided to go west because a female Brazilian war-correspondent, having halted to ask him his political views, offered him a ride in her jeep as far as Klagenfurt.

After re-entering Italy he had managed to make a living for a year or two in the provinces of Lombardy and Emilia, but a persistent impulse to escape kept him moving south until he came into Tuscany and eventually to Pontefiore. There he had met Lucrezia's young sister Simonetta, by now a very handsome and lively girl, and having fallen wildly in love with her he had agreed to work for Angelo for a merely nominal wage.

One hot day when they were all busy in a field of barley, cutting with steady sickles, Angelo said he would go home to fetch a flask of wine, and Annunziata decided to walk with him to see if the children were safe and happy. There were by now five of them in the house. Annunziata's baby, a charming little girl just a year old, was a few weeks older than Lucrezia's, which was also a girl. Tommaso had been left to look after them. Tommaso, a well-grown boy of five, had developed a sense of responsibility and a serious manner, but the young Otello, though an extremely handsome child, was difficult to control, and the little Stanislas had moods of wild exuberance. Otello, now rather more than two years old, had sometimes shown a fondness for killing chickens, and Annunziata was always a little anxious about her infant daughter when he was in the vicinity. On this occasion, however, her fears were groundless, and under Tommaso's supervision the children were all peacefully occupied.

'Let us have a glass of wine before we return to the field,' said Angelo. 'Simonetta's young man is doing twice his share to show her how strong he is, so we shall not be missed.'

'He is nice,' said Annunziata, rubbing her wrists that the rough beard of the barley had scored with red. 'Oh, what a happy life we lead here!'

'Well,' said Angelo, 'it is far from perfect, but in comparison with many others we are fortunate. Pontefiore is a small place, of no great importance to the world, so we miss a lot of excitement, but miss a lot of trouble too.'

'That day when you saw me begging from the soldiers with my baby — look at him now! — was the luckiest day of my life.'

'Dear Annunziata! You have repaid that little kindness a thousand times.'

'I am very happy,' she repeated.

'Do you never regret your home by the sea? Are you truly contented in this landward place?'

'I should like some fish for dinner. Fresh fish. I cannot think of anything else I want.'

'Some day,' said Angelo, 'I shall go to Livorno and bring you some fish from there.'

'Then Pontefiore will be quite perfect.'

He kissed her and said, 'The wine here is better than anything you grew on the other side. Let us have another glass.'

When she returned to the field, Angelo made an excuse to remain and decided, a little later, that he was disinclined for more work. After thoughtfully drinking a third glass of wine he strolled into the farmyard, and where a broken wall threw a triangle of dark blue shadow lay down, and yawned a little, and presently fell fast asleep.

Voices, some time later, invaded his sleep, but not so strongly as to drive him out of it. He lay between waking and slumber, and listened to the words that were spoken without, at first, hearing anything strange in them or anything very relevant. There were two speakers.

One of them said, 'Well, there's no one here except those children. I suppose they're all at work.'

'They work hard,' said the other.

'What they've done,' said the first voice, 'is really remarkable. When you think of the state their country was in, and look at it now with the fields decently tended, and the crops growing, and bridges built again, you've got to give them credit. Credit for courage as well as hard work. It looked such a hopeless task. Here in

Pontefiore, for example, and all down the Liri valley. Quite hopeless. But they tackled it and they did it. They've got courage.'

Angelo by now was sufficiently wide awake to realize what was strange about the voices. They were talking English! And one of the voices was well known to him, though he found it very hard to believe that the owner of it had returned to Pontefiore and now stood no more than a few feet away. While he considered this charming improbability, the other voice continued.

'I think I agree with you,' it said. 'You remember all those wretched little towns and villages that we bombed and shelled till you wouldn't think a human being could live in them? But when we went in there were always some people waiting to cheer us, and throw flowers and give us wine, though we'd smashed their houses and scattered them on the road. I couldn't do that, and I wouldn't if I could. Yes, we may have been wrong about them. We laughed at them in Africa, because they ran like rabbits from time to time, but we may have been wrong. They've got something. It's their own sort of courage, but they've got it.'

Angelo leapt to his feet, and clutching the flask of wine — which he had thoughtfully taken out with him — stepped round the ruined corner of the house and exclaimed, 'Oh, Captain Telfer, Major Telfer, or is it Colonel Telfer now? I am transported into bliss to see you again! And do you really and truly believe that I have the *dono di coraggio*?'

'Angelo, my dear fellow,' said Simon, 'how are you? We went to the castle and saw the Countess — she's beginning to feel her age, isn't she? — and she told us where you lived. This is a friend of mine: Major Crowther.'

'How do you do?' said Angelo. 'But is it true that I have the *dono di coraggio*?'

'You were listening, were you?'

'I was sleeping, but not quite asleep after you began to talk. — Let us have some wine: hold the flask and I shall get some glasses. But no! I have a house of my own

269

now, you must come inside and we shall drink in comfort.'

He ushered them into the kitchen and then inquired, with a little anxiety, 'You do not dislike children, I hope? We have rather a lot here.'

'Are they all yours?' asked Major Crowther.

'In one way, yes. In another, no,' said Angelo, and briefly explained the ancestry of his family. 'The babies, however, are truly mine.'

'Angelo,' said Simon, raising his glass, 'have no doubt about it. You possess the *dono di coraggio*.'

His face beaming with pleasure, Angelo replied, 'That is something I never expected to hear you say. It makes me very happy to hear it. — But tell me, what are you doing here?'

'We are on leave,' said Simon. 'We are on holiday, we are revisiting familiar scenes and reviving old acquaintance.'

'Then clearly,' said Angelo, 'we must have another drink. This is a day of celebration. And when you have refreshed yourselves we shall go and talk to Lucrezia and Annunziata, who are working in the fields.'

It was nearly an hour later when they set out for the barley-field, and as they left the house Angelo said, 'I must warn you that Annunziata, who in ordinary circumstances is quite uncommonly pretty, is at the moment not looking her best.'

'I am sorry to hear that,' said Simon.

'No,' said Angelo, 'there is nothing to worry about. It is quite natural.'

'Oh, I see.'

'I hear that your wife is extremely handsome,' said Major Crowther.

'Yes, I am very fortunate,' said Angelo. 'But Lucrezia too, just at present, is at some disadvantage so far as looks are concerned.'

Simon Telfer and Major Crowther stopped, and stood, and stared at him in astonishment.

'It is a remarkable coincidence,' said Angelo modestly.

'It is a good thing,' said Simon, 'that your fields are also bearing well.'

'Our country is very fertile,' said Angelo, and leading his guests through the barley, introduced them to Lucrezia, Annunziata, Lucia, Simonetta, and the young man from the mountains north of Udine. 'Lucrezia,' he said, 'there can be no more work to-day. We have honoured guests. You must go home at once and prepare a meal for them.'

'There is not very much to eat in the house,' she whispered.

'There is *prosciutto*,' said Angelo, 'there are hens in the yard. Carve the one and kill the others. We must eat well to-night.'

'We are sleeping at the castle,' said Simon.

'But you will dine with me!'

It was late in the evening before they had had their fill of food and wine and talk, and not until his guests were about to leave did Angelo remember to ask if Simon had any news of a former companion, the strange adventurer who had worn a tortoiseshell monocle.

'You mean Fest,' said Simon. 'Poor Fest went to look for trouble, and found it. He was killed in Bologna. When the Poles went in they met a person in the uniform of a German colonel. He was eager to be friendly with them, so they shot him immediately. It was Fest.'

'I remember him clearly in that affair on the road to Vallombrosa,' said Angelo. 'He was very brave but rather selfish.'

He and Lucrezia walked a little way towards the castle with Simon and his friend, and when they had arranged to meet again in the morning, said good night.

'What a day it has been!' exclaimed Angelo as he turned homeward with Lucrezia. 'I was sleeping when they arrived, and when I woke I lay for some time and listened to them talking before I got up to greet them. There was one thing they said that pleased me greatly, whether it was true or not. They said I had the *dono di coraggio*.'

'Is that really important?' asked Lucrezia.

'It is highly important when one has had to do without

it for most of one's life. It gave me so much pleasure to hear what they said that all day, whenever I have thought of it, I have wanted to sing. Shall I sing now?'

'No,' said Lucrezia.

'Just a little song? It would be appropriate, I think.'

'Courage is a common quality in men of little sense,' said Lucrezia. 'I think you over-rate it. A good understanding is much rarer and more important.'

'I have always had a good understanding of things,' said Angelo, 'and I assure you that it does not always make for happiness.'

'You did not show much understanding when you insisted on inviting your friends to dinner. I told you there was hardly any food in the house, and now there is none at all. We ate the last of the ham and there is no more *pasta*.'

'But when one meets an old friend,' said Angelo, 'one does not count the cost of entertainment. That would be base indeed.'

'It is not your way. I know that.'

'Darling Lucrezia! My way is to be so deeply in love with you that I am in great danger of drowning.'

'You are a little drunk, aren't you?'

'Perhaps — but only a little — and what does it matter? We are going to live for a long, long time, and to be always sober would be most ungrateful.'

'I hope life will become a little easier if we are to live so long.'

'It will. I am sure it will.'

'And some day, perhaps, we shall have enough to eat as well as enough to drink.'

'We shall have everything we need!'

'*Speriamo*,' said Lucrezia with a sigh.

'*Pazienza!*' cried Angelo. 'We have stood up to a great deal, we can stand what is still to come, whether it's poverty or plenty. For we have learnt the most useful of all accomplishments, which is to survive!'

Rome, August 1944 — Orkney, August 1945